PAGING LYNCH MADISON

CHAPTER ONE

I know you're going to like this.

This is the kind of story where you know the guilty secrets of our hero (or black-hearted villain) right from the start. A sort of who-dun-it where you'll know who-dun-it and why.

The point is, was what he dun - did, sorry - so dreadful?

It certainly made a lot of people unhappy for a long time and it certainly took inordinately long to put it straight.

Examine, members of the story-jury, one or two of the salient facts.

Until he disappeared a couple of weeks before Christmas (that might be a significant date; make a note of that,) Leslie Merrett used to be the name of this guilty party whom we see in front of us right now.

PAGING LYNCH MADISON

Watch how he is making a painful-looking scene struggling to get out of a cab, paying the driver, limping himself strangely up the awkwardly shallow steps of a property in Harley Street, ringing a bell and (good lord, whatever is he up to now) announcing himself as Lynch Madison, the liar.

Leslie Merrett just disappeared, that's what happened.

Don't sit there saying 'oh dear is that all' like it's nothing. Think about it. It's dreadful. If someone in your life decided to vanish and never said why, you too, like his wife and daughter, would spend most of your life wondering why, blaming yourself, wouldn't you?

You'll be hearing quite a few legless, unwheeled explanations from him. But ask yourself, is there really any proper excuse for such unnecessary cruelty?

To put you further in the picture so that you'll be quite clear who did what to whom (though you may never know why) come and take a look at the facts.

Leslie Merrett, a hitherto unremarkable man, disappeared for good one day, leaving no trace. His large local bank account lay dormant. His bike (you'll hear about his bike later) was never found. He never contacted his good wife who mercifully never knew she had never been loved by him, nor did he contact his lovely little daughter who loved him as lovely little daughters will.

PAGING LYNCH MADISON

The police say that quaintly enough, despite initialled handkerchiefs having gone out with laundry-baskets and lavender-bags, disappearing folk, (two thousand a year real disappearances, you can check that yourself) still use their old initials for their new names.

Sure enough, Leslie Merrett turns up as Len Matthews in the transition period of fear and some painful regret, and as many other names briefly. Later as Laurence Miller and as Lynch Madison, as you've heard.

He finds he is happiest, most natural, most 'himself', dressed like this, being Lynch Madison from the inside out.

He must always be holding most of himself back in a tight scared little parcel inside. The depth of deception and fear of discovery must be harming him psychologically. Yet looking at this poised poser, looking at the man who represents himself as Lynch Madison, easily a stone lighter than Leslie Merrett had been, he seems carefree enough - or is he a great actor?

Yes, he is a bit of an actor, actually.

To explain, there now follows a brief history of Leslie Merrett's past but you are warned - it doesn't explain much; the very ordinariness of his life ---

Leslie and Jan Merrett had a nice detached house with a super little garden, a colour coordinated living-room and a sweet little school uniform for Charlotte which hung neatly in her sweet little wardrobe.

PAGING LYNCH MADISON

Leslie left very early every morning to get on the Inter-City to London, kissing Jan and Charlotte goodbye. When he used to use the car he always gave a tiny toot at the end of the road that she and Charlotte waited for and smiled about. When he took up cycling to the station for exercise and to beat the appalling traffic, he rang his bicycle bell instead.

Once the noise of the bell had faded away, Jan, who was nervy, unpredictable, who went to pieces easily, felt the familiar shiver of panic. She now had to get Charlotte ready, pick up Timmy Dee and Philippa and get them all to school by eight-fifty. Even worse pressure, the heaviness of being responsible at 3.30 to be back at school and parked to pick them up on her school-run rota week,

Her 'nerves' became her way of life, her friendships usually crippled by them. The three school-run-children, especially her own Charlotte, also hated it to be Jan's rota week. She was always late and flustered and still hung around the longest of anyone, telling sweet little Charlotte-anecdotes to the teachers, talking endlessly about nothing to those other mothers who would bear with her.

It had been slightly better since Leslie had found her that little morning job at the art shop, when she was up to it; aerobics when she wasn't too exhausted; the swimming for the handicapped that she helped with, when she remembered it was her turn, and everything else she tried and gave up.

Leslie Merrett, however, though he didn't say much, showed an understanding of her nature. By his allowances for her, everyone said, he calmed her

PAGING LYNCH MADISON

down, made her feel better, got them back on lists she nearly got them off.

Leslie Merrett had been born and brought up in the town in the unhappy sort of poverty you don't brag about even when you're better off.

He worked hard to educate himself away from it all - then worked long hours to pay for his tuition fees and sit his exams successfully.

Cyril Graygrove, Jan's father, was pleased to employ such an ambitious young grafter on his architectural team. Graygroves was the biggest builder in the county at that time (very well thought-of, was Cyril) and it made sense to have in-house architects. Easier to get your own way.
For Cyril Graygrove, getting his own way was a priority. Lily Graygrove, his wife, and his two daughters Madeleine and Janet had all found it best to see he got it.

He brought the tall, good-looking deep young Leslie Merrett home for supper to meet his family and it wasn't long before he was marrying into Jan's big money. Maybe he had really seen something in Jan that night. Apart, that is, from the junior partnership he was slyly offered with the coffee and chocolate mints.

No one ever said he wasn't a loyal husband or a conscientious father. And he acted himself into the part of a real local's local. He was, everyone said, a good sort. This, as usual, meant that the guy was generous enough with his money to be neither noticeably flash nor in any way stingy, didn't grate, wasn't coarse, got promotion on his own proved

PAGING LYNCH MADISON

merits, pulled his weight, would give free design advice to his friends without hesitation and if a little deep and silent like snow, always, if called upon, would be reliably helpful, discreet, safe to confide in and sure not to talk about himself.

There was theatre somewhere in his background (no one could quite remember what) but it wasn't only that, or his tall attractiveness, that made him first choice for every leading role in any amateur production the town set up.

He could become anyone you asked him to be. He could sing and dance if it were needed for the show; his good memory for his and everyone else's lines also made him a safe choice for worried, inexperienced directors.

"Funny he's so restrained off the stage," everyone would say, after marvelling at the way his personality overcame any amount of amateurish back-up, bad make-up and dreadful acoustics in whatever church-hall had been hired.

"He's a very private person," they said, the fashionable phrase that covered both those too deep and those too shallow to understand. "I suppose Jan talks enough for both of them," they'd add, in case they had been caught being too kind.

Leslie was everyone's choice for chairman of the Rotary club, that year. Everyone agreed that he was the most innovative, the most proficient organiser, the most reliable. But, afterwards, everyone would remember the obstinate stand he'd made about the small embarrassment of having, as chairman, to dress up as Father Christmas on the float

PAGING LYNCH MADISON

in town. "Only another bit of acting, for goodness sake," the outgoing chairman said, infuriated, red-faced, impotent. "You can't be chairman if you don't, Leslie. Not because we're so hide-bound by rules --" not much --"but because it's Crossbridge town tradition and we can't over-ride tradition for you or ---"

Quietly, unmoved by all this, Leslie Merrett wouldn't do it and that was that. Aha. You see where the clues are leading, do you?

So Johnny Fletcher became the most amazed Father Christmas and chairman of the decade. (It is not part of the story that Johnny's boy, a first-year at the comprehensive, got beaten up for bragging about this unexpected family rise to the top.)

Jan had a tantrum about the silly Rotary hiccup, living her life, as she did, solely through his excitements and successes. Despite the temper, she could get nothing out of her husband about his reasons for the sudden defection. Jan was often quite notably proud and supportive of Leslie and the few of his hopes that he had shared with her. Sometimes tempering her big ambitions for him with tolerance, often, especially when upset, wildly aggressive about his mildness.

His marriage-long rather noble and surprising independence of her parents' amazing fortune, after they had set the house up for them mortgage free and excepting the bloated salary he took because he could repay that with utter hard work, was the source of a long-running argument of some bitterness with Jan.

PAGING LYNCH MADISON

But as he had done so financially well anyway, especially the share-dealing he had begun as an idle little hobby, which had paid off so amazingly, their life was super-comfortable enough anyway for her not to snipe too much about the amazing perks and luxuries he had refused to grab, citing Madeleine and her husband, the grabby but infinitely noticeable Robby Darlington.

If she fantasised a bit about Robby Darlington, who skied and sailed more than he worked, who carried his bronzed sexy glamour around with him in his swanky car like a trophy, so did all the other wives and she swore, like all the other wives, that she'd run a mile if Robby 'tried' anything. As, in any case, Robby was all talk and not much do, Jan's mile-running ability remained unchallenged and her fantasies untested.

It was about two and a half weeks before Christmas, (ah - you remembered - good) after Leslie had supported Johnny Fletcher's preparations for the last big charity push of the year, after he had personally seen to it that the float was decorated the best it had ever been, after he had bought Charlotte the doll's pram of every girlie's dream, written a sweet little card for her, locked it in the spare-room, after he had, Jan remembered clearly, told Jan and her parents that he wished he could see Charlotte's face on Christmas morning.

It was after all that that Leslie Merrett had vanished.

Leslie's whim of a bike had at first been a great little idea for exercise and was used exclusively for the ride to the station, and a few slow rides round

PAGING LYNCH MADISON

the block with Charlotte on her little bike with stabilisers.

Then he had, at the weekends and light evenings, found a new hobby in cycling longer and longer distances as he built up his stamina. Unusually for him, he showed a great enthusiasm for it. Even chatting a bit about the growing number of miles he could manage.

He went off cycling that end-of-the-year Sunday, the moment he and Charlotte had finished 'clearing the lunch-table and the gravy-stained cloth for Mummy.' "I'd like to catch as much light as I can," he had said. (Was that significant too?)

Then he'd phoned. Around four, it must have been, the carpet a mass of dressing-up clothes and cassettes as Charlotte and Philippa continued to rehearse an all-dancing, all-singing 'show' they were making up for Leslie's return.

"It's getting dark. I went mad today," he had said. (That seems a blatantly deliberate clue.) "I'm so much further than I meant to be. I'm completely puffed out. Sorry, but I'll never make it back. Shall I stay over? What do you think, darling? There's a lovely little inn, here. I know you hate driving in the dark, but do you want to get a babysitter and come for me? We could strap the bike on the back. Or both stay overnight. What do you think?"

Jan hesitates, thinking of the narrow dark lanes, the blinding lights of the on-coming cars, the high hedges and the shadows. "No. No, go on, you stay," she says, biting her lip, thinking of the alternative.

PAGING LYNCH MADISON

She'll ask Philippa if she'd like to stay over and phone Philippa's mother to confirm it.

Then Jan would have one of her rare and favourite treats: share some silly television with the two little girls, they would all choose their favourite snack and she would bring it in for them to have on their laps - something Leslie didn't approve of and wouldn't allow. An all-girls'-together treat. She could see Charlotte's face shining with the fun of it.

"We'll be OK," she said happily, feeling OK.

She remembers clearly that she had asked him exactly where he was but he didn't seem to know and he went on discussing the surprising menu at this completely off-the-track 'Red Lion.'

He said he'd cycle back early in the morning and go into work late; he joked about taking a little barmaid to bed with him instead of a hot water-bottle as Jan had refused him; he said don't worry he had his Barclaycard with him; he said 'bye, darling.'

And he rang off while she was still saying "ring me in the morning ----" and before she had asked for the telephone number at the pub.

By lunchtime the next day she had tried every 'Red Lion' in the phone book, and every other one that directory enquiries would give her in adjoining counties.

She tries to remember, for ever, was it goodbye darling he really said. Or did he say

PAGING LYNCH MADISON

goodnight, or cheerio, or sleep well, or what. He definitely had not said 'see you soon.' Or had he?

The police, she was overwhelmed to find out, wouldn't do much. Leslie Merrett was not vulnerable.

Wasn't he? Aren't we all?

In police-searching terms he was not old nor young, nor ill nor strange nor criminal. He must therefore have perfectly good reasons to push off and it was nobody's business but his own.

The questionnaire they wanted her to fill in made her so upset the doctor had to be called again and it was weeks before she could face it.

Jan's father, furious with the British police that he had always chauvinistically bragged about before, hired B. Carfax, the only private detective in Crossbridge's yellow pages, to do all the silly searches it was possible to do, Cyril trying hard to overlook the man's unpolished shoes and his unmilitary bearing.

And Jimmy and Christine, people Jan had regarded as not so terribly specially friends, practically moved in to help the family, taking their new and exciting role as protectors and police substitute very seriously indeed.

By request, B. Carfax started a 'Red Lion' search all over again, Jimmy and Christine sharing the work, if not the fee, even in the face of B. Carfax's extreme reluctance. Leslie Merrett could have been

PAGING LYNCH MADISON

anywhere when he rang. Why would he tell the truth about the pub?

In fact, the detective had other quite harsh and frightening questions to ask.

Was Leslie a habitual liar?

Was he? Are you? Who can answer such a question?

Had Leslie seemed hurried or worried or tense or threatened. Had his voice seemed strained? Might he have been under duress? Had he said anything that seemed odd then or now? Did he have strange friends or strange meetings lately? Had he started to come home at inexplicably late hours? Had women phoned the house? Had she answered the phone to find nobody there lately? Had he changed his habits lately? Ah the cycling was recent, was it? Carfax had to agree that that wasn't, actually, very odd.

Had he said he loved her, had he asked after Charlotte, had she been sure he had been in England at the time?

(Had he indeed, Jan looked fearfully back over the years, ever said he loved her?)

And what was this with England? In England? How would she know? Why wouldn't he be? How far can you go in two hours? A waiting helicopter. What did Leslie know about helicopters?

All the ends couples leave untied during the close-distance of marriage were to tie her up for

PAGING LYNCH MADISON

years and haunt her for ever. She had needed his prop rather badly but once struggled-up from this devastating crash she found the pride never to use another crutch.

Most of all, of course, she cursed herself. If she had not been so selfish, if she had not been so feeble, if she had just taken out the car that night and gone to the Red Lion to meet him -----

They never found his bike - or the key to the spare-room.

The locksmith broke into that room for them a few days later. There, beside the doll's pram with the big red bow, was a carefully packed mound of thoughtful presents for Jan with normally kind but otherwise insignificant notes, a present with normal greetings for every member of their family and friends, (the job Jan and Leslie would normally have done together the following week), and no hint of trouble ever found amongst his neatly-kept papers or belongings.

Everyone had theories. A road accident early in the morning and the body and the bike buried by the frantic driver. Too fanciful and unlikely.

Terminal cancer and a cleverly organised suicide, was the next most popular. (But Jeff, their good friend was their doctor, and Leslie had only just had his new big insurance check-up with pleasing results.).

'Another woman' and a faked disappearance to save the family name? (Cyril Bryant's out-of-date suggestion. These days, husbands simply say the

PAGING LYNCH MADISON

new woman's better in bed and save the arguments for the money-money-money angle and who keeps the cat.)

Financial ruin? (With Leslie unable to fill all the commissions he already had and Jan's family, in any case, in the background dying to help?)

A motiveless murder like you read about? (Where, like the road accident, in that case, was the body and the bike? B. Carfax said in his experience that only happened in bad fiction.)

A mugging and memory loss? (The local hospitals had no tall thin tiny-scar-on-the-knee unknowns in stock and who ever got mugged in Crossbridge?)

They searched, they agonised for days, for weeks, for months, B. Carfax, Jimmy and Christine – and Victor, of course. Victor was a bit of Jan's past that also got itself discussed ad nauseam for a while as he "stepped in" to comfort her. Many other friends and family at first made contacts and suggestions both likely and unlikely for an uncharacteristically persistent Jan.

These people drove her, less and less willingly, to pester airlines and airports and train stations and sea-ports. They accompanied her on a silly and very upsetting search-party of the forests at the right distance away just for something positive to do, though even Carfax hadn't liked to take his money for that fruitless time-wasting. They checked second-hand bike places, though it hadn't been Leslie's bike long enough to get any distinguishing feature on its ordinary silveryness - B. Carfax

PAGING LYNCH MADISON

wouldn't contemplate such a pointless check-up, even for money.

For a long and patient while, friends and family continued to call to comfort her until inevitably they all got just a tiny bit sick of it.

Not long after her parents had dismissed the unsuccessful but wealthier B. Carfax, her friends started to agree righteously with each other that Jan couldn't go on like that or she'd crack up and the dreaded words 'Jan should snap out of it' were heard in the land. Even from Christine.

Jan went double-headed, not unnaturally. She acted both as though she were just waiting for his return and as if she were completely convinced that Leslie had been pointlessly murdered and horribly mutilated to boot.

She obsessively watched every television news, shushing everyone so she could concentrate, scanning every face on every documentary, sure that she would suddenly see Leslie, unaccountably there at some event or place, unaware of the filming, easily contacted, everything forgiven.

Despite her certainty that he was dead, she knew that he was positively alive and it was probably her fault. On the other hand, if he wasn't dead or mutilated and had just gone off, she hoped he would get dead or mutilated.

Which is where we leave Jan, her supportive family and friends now a little weary of their kindness, and Jan forced to re-think the life she'd

PAGING LYNCH MADISON

taken on casually at twenty and that she thought was for ever.

"It's the not-knowing," they all say. "It's the not-knowing that hurts."

But we are not amongst those feeble not-knowers. We know where Leslie Merrett is.

He looks very different, he's obviously got shocking back trouble, but that's him all right.

One more tiny mystery. Aside from the sameness of the initials, which makes some sort of sense, if he's trying to disappear so hard, why ever did he choose such an unforgettable name as Lynch Madison?

PAGING LYNCH MADISON

CHAPTER TWO

Quietly please.

Lynch Madison, the marriage-crusher, the disappearing trick, the puff-of-smoke, the flag-of-all-nations must never find out how closely and crossly he is being watched, never find out how many of us are tiptoeing round corners and holding glasses to thin walls to hear his secret lying words. Follow him now, with your hat pulled firmly over your face, follow his bad-back-walk into the bad-back specialist in Harley Street which draws him to our attentive interest in this first instance.

The bad-back specialist's mistress, (absolutely not just his receptionist with such tasteful clothes and subtle perfume,) is emphatically desirable and safely sexy, in this room that welcomes men patently unable to lie down in a hurry. She is positively flaunting her straight vertebrae and her un-slipped intervertebral discs right in front of Lynch as he lurches in dangling himself as neatly as he could.

"Ah, yes, Mr Madison, you're a little early, would you like to ---"

Surely, surely, this waiting-room was the place where it would be understood that not being able to 'take a seat' with normal dignity was half the reason for being here and that such a specialist could afford and would know to provide some lean-over

PAGING LYNCH MADISON

rests, some especially designed seating or at least something more tactful than low easy chairs.

But they hadn't, so Lynch Madison did his strange version of a demi-plie to reach the creased Punch Summer number of 1986, unbent his knees, leaned against the wall and tried to look like a man too impatient to sit.

A lady weighing nothing, the sort who has retired from head-teaching, had smiled kindly at his lean and lovely face which showed its pain. She'd been quite sympathetically matey until she spotted his neat ponytail tied back with black ribbon. Jumping to her hidebound conclusions, she instantly re-assessed his class (downwards) and concentrated her attention on her neat brown brogues.

Soon, this woman, horribly bent into a question, was scooped out of one of these chairs and half-carried into the specialist, coming out quite a long time later, Lynch noticed, unanswered but very cheerfully booking another appointment as his own waiting continued, a young man in a wheelchair going next.

If the specialist says 'what seems to be the trouble' or 'man wasn't meant to be an upright animal' or any of that doctor-doctor crap, Lynch thought, impatiently dropping the Punch magazine back on to the table, the only way to do it without bending, it might be enough to pull him to his full height and thus cured, he would give yet another false address and never pay his bill.

Twelve minutes later, he had been in and was out booking another appointment himself. "Come

PAGING LYNCH MADISON

and see me in a month but as suddenly as it came, Mr Madison, it will surely go, and I look forward to hearing that you've no need to come back to me."

"And if I do?"

"We'll think again. If all else fails, we can certainly operate. Success is fifty-fifty. You've let your BUPA lapse, you say? Cash? Yes, of course. Fine. Pay it to me, I think, Mr Madison. Save troubling my assistant ---" Oh yeah. Still, the great man had kept his mouth quiet in the face of no medical records and no referral from any doctor.

'It might cure itself,' was all the great man had said, which isn't much for the hundreds he had paid to private medical insurance in his healthy years.

Lynch used their old polished come-round-to-trendiness-again mahogany toilet before he left, defiantly opting to save further pain by not bending to lift the seat, so that he had the energy to face the awful journey down the steps.

His hand theatrically but necessarily on his back to hold it in place, he limped to the main road, groaned his way into a sympathetic cab, whose driver had 'a back' himself and had himself dropped at his own special cafe, in the Earl's Court Road, a hundred yards from his rooms.

Lowering himself into the mercifully hard chair at Amoretti's, and ordering a late breakfast cappuccino from Signora Amoretti herself, he demanded hot thickly buttered toast and honey and damn the expense, though the specialist, the taxi and

PAGING LYNCH MADISON

this gastronomic extravagance about cleaned him out and no certainty that he could ever work again.

Though he had learned a lot about hand-to-mouth management and payments under-the-counter all the time that he had been Lynch, he would still never take something for nothing. (Make a note of that, too. Even if it doesn't prove to be significant, it is a point in his favour, is it not?)

Signora Amoretti sent her third daughter, Annetta, with the coffee. Lynch winced at the swiftness of her exhausting movements whilst all Annetta did was to imitate his agony with a hand on her own lovely stuck-out hip and give him a swift smile of somewhere between pity and que sera sera on her way back behind the counter.

Lechery came more easily to Lynch than it had to Leslie, but he was too worried about himself today to do more than lift his chin a little to Annetta. This gesture clearly promised that he would insult her in the usual ways next visit when her parents weren't looking and when he was well and when he wasn't worried sick about money.

Disappearing is never easy. As in most aspects of life, it is the money that is the big problem.

But he had done his homework well, moving large amounts of money around, sending the benefits of his secret and overwhelmingly successful investments consistently and carefully to Luxembourg, rented himself these rooms in London over a year ago both for an address and as a bolt-hole, grown long hair and a neat moustache, applied for a passport for Lynch Madison which had amazingly

PAGING LYNCH MADISON

come through without questions and kept himself to himself.

In the past, he had planned a dozen different types of exit from Crossbridge, but suddenly he had been simply unable to face another Christmas and, worse, another new year of pretence, and had in the end left in a great hurry, rather more than a year earlier than his original original plan, leaving some things rough and unready; especially, he had had no ready cash. Almost nothing.

Right from the start, on the run had been curtailed to a crawl as he had been held up from his greater and wilder plans by his every day necessities. He had had to get himself jobs that paid cash quietly, no questions, no forms.

Just enough, he kept saying to himself, for a bit in the pocket and enough to get him to Luxembourg with a suitcase, some unexceptionable clothes and enough money to put on a front at the bank and get his funds back. Just enough earnings to eat, keep himself in toilet rolls and pay the rent on time, normal living that would attract no notice. Just enough.

(Let us not divert ourselves even for a moment with discourses on what the concept of 'enough' really is.)

Lynch, also known briefly as Lenny or Lionel in the interim, had settled for very small beer indeed in his blackest fears at the beginning of his disappearance. Very small stuff.

PAGING LYNCH MADISON

Washing-up. Car-cleaning. Small painting jobs. Always moving on.

Often tempted and befriended briefly by kind, lone women who fed and cared for him along the way, Lynch never dug in for long. They understood his impermanence; partings were only what they were used to. Some wondered, briefly, if they might dissuade him from his set plans of which he gave daily reminders. "One day I'll simply be gone," he would keep saying to them. And one day he was and each of them thanked him in retrospect for the fair warning.

So. Another little fact in his favour you should note. This apparent reluctance ever to inflict anyone with his unexpected disappearance again.

Also, there is his own pain to take into consideration; a father doesn't lightly shrug off a child, whatever women tell you. And please remember the everyday terror he faced. In his roles and guises maybe he would be recognized, found out, dragged back.

He had never lived in London before. Business trips had given the place a clever and purposeful gloss; a cohesion it did not, any more than any other big city, possess.

He couldn't tell and no longer cared about the status of an address and just moved into barely furnished dives and hovels as they became vacant, knowing the bliss of having not a shred of responsibility towards a single tile on the roof. He went around humming 'I got plenty of nothin"

PAGING LYNCH MADISON

painting other rooms and flats for those with only very slightly more.

The condemning of the house he had been rooming in and his desperately homeless two weeks living with and off Dawn before he was paid for the last job was the bottom-line for him. He bought her the first warm clean new duvet she had ever owned with some money as a thank-you and paid back what he had owed her and he honestly thought he saw tears in her hard eyes as he left.

Finally settling on long hair, settling on Lynch Madison, settling in Earl's Court with the Amoretti's.

They let him have a room upstairs at first for nothing more than a bit of table-clearing at night when they were busy. "Just till your money from the last job it come," Papa Amoretti said mildly, an expert on casual staff for whom money sometimes came and sometimes didn't come.

A family. Lynch took notes, watching their easy laughter and their loud fights. Nice being with them, so whilst he built up his jobs, he insisted on paying something every week, though they insisted on feeding him whenever he was hungry.

At Amoretti's, under the sunshine of their kindness, he made the breakthrough that would take him to Luxembourg to collect the money and his wits and go on to live the life he had planned. Somewhere by the sea. Somewhere hot. No strings. No. Only the strings he chose.

PAGING LYNCH MADISON

On his blackest day, the Amorettis, as he sat warming his hands round one of their expensive cappuccinos, told him of a room nearby he might like now he'd been paid up although no 'next job' was yet in view. When he came back to rave about how cheap it had been and how comfortable the bed was, he impulsively offered to paint out the cafe, really 'do it over' cheaply, in gratitude for their help.

The Amoretti's said yes.

And that's how they became his first business customers, maybe the first real friends of his life and practically his new family.

That was how the Amoretti's ran their business, in the old continental way; regulars and cronies; most of them doing some kind of business with the Amorettis in turn. As soon as they first hired the chef, for example, he had demanded and was allowed to go out with their oldest daughter, till seeing how serious it was with them, they took him quick out of the kitchen and put him through catering college. Now they had a small cafe of their own down a side-street nearby, a wedding everyone still talked about, and a baby on the way.

Ah, parents. Even attentive parents. While all this was going on with Maria, their attention was off Francesca, the next daughter down, for a while. Fatal. Immediately, everyone tried to go out, get off, get away with anything with the beautiful Francesca until her less memorable but very sudden wedding and her pregnant reappearance at the cash-desk.

All the Amoretti's had loved the bright lightness Lynch had made of their cafe when they

PAGING LYNCH MADISON

had 'just left everything' to him. A completely modernistic but friendly overhaul. They still spoke about the cane-furniture he had made them buy and the lowered ceiling and the air of spaciousness he had achieved.

So they had recommended him to an absentee Arab landlord who had a small block of flats he needed to get ready exceptionally quickly. Lynch did it with flair and speed. A good move. The grateful Arab had plenty of friends to recommend him to after that.

Voila.... Raise the prices a little. Lynch Madison, Interior Design.

The second Arab had been ecstatic about his blocks of flats and Lynch was on target with the finishing of the second block when his back went. They brought someone else in right away, of course. They paid him off and finish - nothing. When the money ran out this time - how long before he could get away and start that new life he had planned for so long and still couldn't reach.

Worry, pain and tiredness, maybe, that made him hallucinate as he sat there at the old marble table, dry in here out of the rain, playing with the packs of sugar, not at ease, not comfortable, yet as certain as if suddenly uncharacteristically visionary, that something was just about to happen. Trouble, maybe. So long as it was lucrative trouble, under his current circumstances and allowing for the fear of being found out he had been living under for - however long it was - don't bother to rule out anything illegal, immoral or disgusting.

PAGING LYNCH MADISON

Notwithstanding the lack of beautiful, dangerous spies called Olga in WC2, there certainly was some interest being shown in him over at the counter there. Annetta, the current Amoretti daughter in the business, was taking the wet coat of a bright, chirpy, flat-stomached happy little number in white jeans, a flimsy but heavily patterned blouse over happy breasts, hanging it up, turning to look at him and obviously discussing him in some detail.

She was coming over. She really was. With a leaflet in her hand.

The paper would depict shocking atrocities in the third world and she would say "Mr Madison, Annetta tells me you are the man we need. As is natural the world over, my people fight only for their rights and their freedom. Will you fight at our side? The meeting is by torchlight at midnight. We sail at dawn."

Glorious poached egg-white of the eye. Truffle-dark eyes. Touchable golden-coffee skin which must be of foreign origin because it had not at all a tanned way with it. An indoor girl.

First she looked over her shoulder as if to check with Annetta that she was speaking to the right person, then getting the nod, she held out the leaflet very confidently and stood waiting for him to open it.

Lynch smiled and picked it up. "After reading this I eat it, right? I don't usually buy at the door but I'll look just this once."

PAGING LYNCH MADISON

Difficult to describe what happened to her face, then. She didn't flush, and you can't pale when you have that sort of skin, but she sort of disappeared down her own large eye-sockets.

"It's OK," she said, leaning over to take it from him. "I'm used to it. In the street they never even take the leaflet unless you practically force it on them. They just ignore you and your hand and the leaflet like it might, you know, give them a disease? When it rains very hard, like now, Annetta and her parents often let me -" she pointed around with her left ear, "give out a few at the tables, stay dry, take five, you know, it's very good of them. So when Annetta said - never mind."

Lynch drew the leaflet to his chest. "If Annetta recommended you, let's see."

Cheap paper. Amateur computer graphics and printing. He'd tried it all himself. And he was wrong. Not third-world atrocities. Hypno-therapy.

"Ah yes, phobias. No, I'm afraid I don't have any of those. Or- no, no sale, I'm afraid. All I've got is a back I'd like to exchange for a new one. He doesn't hypnotise backs, does he, this 'Stan'?"

"That is what Annetta asked. Maybe he does. I don't know. I don't think so but you could try, why don't you?"

So she didn't want him to be a terrorist in a good cause or even want him for his body. She wanted him, or anyone else, to hurry for a place at Stan's Self-Help College at a very reasonable price

PAGING LYNCH MADISON

and lucky-lucky, just for this one month, oh yeah, at a vastly reduced price.

Back to the leaflet. He read it thoroughly, now. Lynch could, the leaflet promised, kick smoking, (too late, he'd done that,) control his drinking (he was already the only clarinet-player, maybe the only musician in the entire world who hated the taste of booze and was for ever apologizing about it,) enhance his sex-life, (pass,) lose weight, (heaven forbid, with his instantly noticeable hungry bonyness) and control pain. Interesting.

"Have you been working for Stan long?"

"Too long," she said, suddenly smiling as if she were deeply happy. "This is until I get a proper job. Here, take another leaflet - that one's a bit wet. Annetta says you are usually in here with a friend. You could give it to her, maybe?"

That would have been a good idea, but a bit late. Maybe Stan could have cured Jo's materialism?

He nodded, took the fresh leaflet and creased it into six more pieces. thinking as he tried not to think lately that Annetta, amongst others, needed bringing up to date with his news.

When he had stopped living with Jo and she had started living with a computer-king in dockland, after the weeping had stopped and the dreadful letters, he hadn't gone shouting their parting around.

Jo and he had not only divided up their belongings but Jo, always thinking ahead, had insisted that they shared out the places that had been

PAGING LYNCH MADISON

'theirs' so that all accidental meetings would be spared. He was granted the freedom of Amoretti's and the pub. She had been given the parting gifts of the Covent Garden place, The Donmar Warehouse from him and now she had everything including a stereo-microwave, probably and certainly an in-house telephone in the blue BMW at her beck and call.

But he hadn't missed Jo - not even the first day. Only the company, honestly. Jo had brought him to a nasty conclusion. She had accused him of never having been in love. Not with Jo - not ever. Something in his childhood? Something in himself? "You'll die alone," Jo had screamed. Funny how effective cheap phrases can be.

As the girl with the leaflets started to walk away, humming a little, he called to her, not quite wanting her to go. "Do - do you have anything brewing in the way of something else - some other job?" Just something to say.

"I wish," she said. "Is that an offer? Do you have something in mind?"

Lynch looked at her. His thoughts were hazy. Was he thinking she might decorate some places for him while he was incapacitated? Could she? He shook his head.

"Ah," she said, disappointment clearly defined, shifting the big bag up and back a little. "No, frankly this is just better than nothing. There isn't that much that I can do. But I can sing. I sing here at the weekends," she said, nodding to the corner by the emergency exit, "that's what I love to do. But

PAGING LYNCH MADISON

I can't live on singing. I need money. Everybody has to earn a living," she said. "But why don't you and your friend come and hear me."

"That's funny." Lynch was all attention. "I'm never in here at weekends. You know why? I play clarinet. In any group that will have me. I'd love my own band but ----

But even if he ever got the time to practise enough to front his own band, it might be just ever so slightly too conspicuous. He cursed his Jan and Charlotte life, when he had been too busy and conscientious about the wrong things; right back to the days of school and college, in fact. Life had been one foot in front of the other to get out of his gutter and none of the mad crazy running on the green grass that he had heard and seen and coveted.

"I hated most of the groups I played with," he confessed suddenly. No need to mention how they patronised him and called anyone else but him if they had a good gig.

"But I've got this regular gig, now. Bud and Chi - he's from Guyana and she's Japanese - they make these beautiful sounds but they've got a drummer and a bass who don't like me, still - our gig's a bit of a grotty noisy pub where they don't listen anyway."

"Don't listen?" the girl said, shaking her hand. "Hey, I'd hate that."

"I don't kid myself. I'm not all that worth listening to yet. Bud says it takes years to play and listen too. I haven't had -- I'm still hearing the new

PAGING LYNCH MADISON

way I want to do it but not daring. And it's not my outfit, I suppose. Still, anyway, this guy who happened to be in the pub came and said I was really not that bad and I ought to go solo with a singer, maybe, you know, ballads and he said 'find a pretty girl singer and the audience will be so busy looking at her, you can concentrate on' ---"

"That's disgusting," she said, gravely but quite pleasantly. "No real singer would allow ----"

"No, but I mean -----"

"Singing should be a real duet. The voice and the strings or the reed, like, two voices, you know? I would only sing with such beautiful music. Feeling music. Feeling musicians. Not someone - practising behind me."

Lynch took up the leaflet again crossly and tried to remember how to make it into a paper boat. Two voices. Bloody hell.

"My Mario is that kind of a musician. When you hear Mario you hear angel's music. When you hear me with him it is like two angels."

He was beginning to pick up an accent and a foreignness to her speech. And her Mario didn't sound terribly British either.

"Your husband? He plays clarinet?"

"Somebody else's husband. Guitar. But I tell you, when Mario plays and I sing, it's like going to bed with him. You know?"

PAGING LYNCH MADISON

Lynch nodded in a very sophisticated manner, hoping this conveyed his close acquaintance with such high musical feelings and wishing at the same time that he had ever experienced any.

"Music does that. You make music with someone - you love them a little."

Lynch nodded again. Bud and Chi, though. Yes. They were certainly the second real friends he had made; maybe it was the music; or maybe he had left home in order to study how love worked. He'd like to discuss that with someone.

"Anyway," she said, brisk and still smiling so hard Lynch began to wonder if it was a kind of a tic, "you'll try Stan? You don't have to --- look. I'm not supposed to tell you this until you've resisted all the other sales talk," she said, "but you can go to Stan's for a free trial session, if you like. See if it helps - whatever you need help with. Maybe, for example, you might just be imagining the pain in your back to hide something else from yourself?"

Lynch looked up swiftly. Hiding. The Big Fear hit him again. He listened for a moment to his back. Surely a pain as enveloping as that could not be imagined.

"Do you get commission?" he asked, suddenly very aware of her tensions through his own.

"Yes," she said, in an ashamed proud voice. "Yes, I do. And I need the money. But I'm not selling anything bad. I mean it's sort of useful what I'm doing. I mean people do need to diet; smoking and drinking are killers and ---"

PAGING LYNCH MADISON

"Sit," he said, nodding at the other place at the table. She glanced at her watch and looked behind her to Annetta. "I'm inviting you," he said, nodding for her to sit down. "Are you hungry? Thirsty, then?"

"Annetta? Due cappuccinos, subito, per favore."

"Subito," Annetta called, pulling at the lever that pulled the milk to a froth. "Where did you learn to speak Italian like that? Madrid? Uno cappuccino, due cappuccini, Signor Madison."

"Madison?" the girl said, putting her big bag over the other chair, and sitting down, somehow conveying her gratitude together with the certainty that she wouldn't be sitting for long.

"Lynch Madison."

"Really," she said, looking ready to laugh at any instant. "It sounds like you made it up."

For the second time in one conversation Lynch halted fearfully, looking for crystal-balls.

"Mine too," she said. "Vanda Raimunda Neocita Baptista Vasconcelos, in full. It sounds so stupid in London. Nobody can even say it, here. So when I sing I call myself just 'Vanda.' It's enough."

"They are Spanish names, aren't they?"

"Portuguese," Vanda said, raising her eyes to the ceiling, bored with the same old conversation.

33

PAGING LYNCH MADISON

"Oh, you're from Portugal. Ah -"

"Brazil," she smiled. "And in England everyone says 'oh, like the nuts, yes?"

Lynch felt his face was trying to smile back at her, but it could only just about clear for take-off. He thought he liked her but his back hurt. He wasn't sure if he could be bothered. Was that how it would be when you got old?

She was very attractive but Jo, he had decided, was to be the last of his living-in women. It had been tiring being with the others: watching every word, scared of talking in his sleep.

"What is this Lynch? A family name?"

"I don't have a family," he said, in the way he had said it over and over again. It usually stopped dead all further questions.

"Lucky you," she said. "With the family I come from, I should know. What happened to yours?"

He picked out the one of his three stories that he always used at Amoretti's. "Car-crash," he said briefly. "I lost everyone. Worse than that, my memory of the whole thing's gone -trauma, you know what that means? Look, I don't --like to talk about it."

Vanda looked a bit stricken but not nearly so stricken as was usual. "Jeez, everyone's got a story, right?"

PAGING LYNCH MADISON

Lynch sighed. He'd just wiped out a whole family, demonstrated the horror of memory loss and all it made was a story. He'd have to think up something more startling for the next girl.

He wondered if he should ask about her family out of politeness. No. Don't get involved.

"So - Mr Madison, I can sign you up for this free session - initial consultation, I mean."

Wildly incompetently looking for a pen in a bag where pens must, by the nature of the bag's design and according to the immutable laws of gravity, sink to the bottom, Vanda first took out a double sheet of self-carboned paper that was also very creased, triumphed over the escaping Bic and handed him the one to fill in the other.

"How does it work? Your commission?" Lynch said, writing his name in big letters and wondering what to put this time for occupation. He was up to 'L' wasn't he?

"A pittance for every leaflet with my stamped name on it that anyone brings in, a little bit more for one of these free sessions, and a percentage on every real 'sale' I manage to make for one of the courses. And by the way, if you come across Millie in there, and Stan tries to pass you over to her, run. And don't sign anything. But it would be nice if he really could cure you. I'd really like that. You've been – interested in talking. Nobody here in England is very kind, you know? Very interested, I mean. Except the Amorettis. But they aren't English. I mean

PAGING LYNCH MADISON

people, like, don't care, I mean." She drifted to an awkward stop.

Lynch shifted his legs back into the only position in which he could bear the pain.

"Hey," she said. putting her golden hand on his arm, sympathetically. "Are you OK?"

She had noticed. And no. They don't. Like, care, I mean, usually.

He grimaced a thanks and watched her more closely.

Nodding nicely to the new young waitress Annetta had sent over and to Lynch for the cappuccino in front of her, still smiling, she was wholly at ease now. She took a small spoonful of the white froth with the grated chocolate, openly enjoying it, took another one, tore open and added two whole packets of brown sugar, stirring, tasting, mmming, drinking, as if she were on the third day of her holidays with Lynch and in no hurry to wear out all the things they might have to talk about.

Licking her spoon in anticipation of the first hot swallow to come, she looked properly at him, made some decision and pulled round the half-finished form to read it.

"Occupation?" she said, pointing to the blank spot with a bitten nail that could be put right by a bit of therapy, according to Stan.

A terrible thing was happening. He wanted to tell her everything. How had she done that? When

PAGING LYNCH MADISON

he wasn't looking, she'd punctured his secrets-pouch and the truth bubbled at the edges.

"I've done a bit of everything," he said, sticking a big plaster over the leak for now. "But by training, I'm a local historian," he said, writing that down, trying to remember what he'd told the Amorettis when he'd first met them.

"That's lucky," Vanda said. "At least your back trouble won't affect your job. I mean you don't need to run about to be a historian."

"Wrong," Lynch said, remembering a really good London guide book he'd read at the bookshop and meant to buy one day. "Are you aware of the fact that near the teeming rush of Liverpool Street, no, Leicester Square Underground, lie two of the most interesting alleys of London? One a thing of beauty, the other, maybe only 15 inches wide and as dark as the inside of a shark's mouth. Come this way, ladies and gentlemen, keep close to the walls please so as not to jostle the people of London as we go."

"Oh, a guide. How interesting."

"Not quite a guide," he said, ad-libbing smoothly, enjoying his own plausibility. (Certainly not a guide, he'd done 'graduate' for 'g'.) "I run a very large agency for the guides and I also run the courses and the examinations they must pass before receiving their official status." Yes, that was a nice occupation. He'd quite like to do that.

"Very large? Good money huh?" She spoke conspiratorially.

PAGING LYNCH MADISON

"Of course. I couldn't live where I do in London and run the car I do without money."

"Jeez," she said. "So you can afford a course of treatments from Stan. You don't need a freebie?"

"Things aren't just very busy at the moment," Lynch said, flushing, furious.

"Listen if things get better, keep me in mind, right? I know London and - I learn quickly. I'm really broken at the moment, too."

Lynch opened his mouth to correct her English but she had a last hasty swallow of cappuccino-froth and stood up.

"I don't mean to push myself - it's just I hate to work with the leaflets, you know? But better than nothing, yes? Sure. I have to go. Thanks again. For the coffee and for signing up. And. See you around."

"I'll see you tomorrow after I've seen Stan, won't I? You're there most of the time, presumably?"

"No," Vanda laughed. "I only go into the office for leaflets or for my money. Why don't you come and listen to me singing real music here tomorrow night? Maybe we can find somewhere to go afterwards? Talk about the job? Yes?"

Caddish and weak to ask whether Mario was included in the outing. Or maybe caddish not to ask.

"Maybe," he said, thus leaving himself a skeleton key, a passport down his socks and three easily-accessible exits, which had been his minimum

PAGING LYNCH MADISON

and understandable preference since leaving Crossbridge.

"Not maybe," she said. "Come. I'll be singing one song especially for you," she laughed, her face full of as much loving laughter as if he were her most intimate confidant.

A trick, Lynch warned himself. A trick she has used successfully for so long she didn't even know she was doing it any more. So long as he stayed aware of it.

"Thanks for what you did," she said, putting the big bag on her shoulder and walking away. "Ciaou, Annetta and thanks," she called. Annetta looked up, raised her hand and stood watching her.

"I'll be looking for you tomorrow night," Vanda called bossily to Lynch, as if this wasn't the best way to make someone like him determined to stay away. "Come early so you'll get a good table," and she was gone after a quick sentence and a wave to another table near the door.

Sod. Bastard. Prick. Lynch tried out a few names on himself. They all fitted. Putting that girl's hopes up for a totally fictitious job. Sod. Bastard. Prick.

"So?" Annetta said, not waiting half a second before coming over to bring him a fresh free cappuccino. "Are you going to try that man, Vanda's man, to make your back better?"

Lynch shrugged then nodded.

PAGING LYNCH MADISON

"Nothing to lose," he said, miserably.

"Did you like her?" Annetta wiped the table thoughtfully. "Yes, everybody does. She's sympatica, yes?" she said, clearing the memory of Vanda's visit to the table with another few brisk wipes. "Did she tell you ---?"

"That she sings here? Yes. I'll bet she tells everyone." Lynch added two extra sugar packets to his coffee in a moody way.

"Yes, she does. She's very good for business. All my family, everyone who comes here thinks that she is wonderful," Annetta said. "You noticed always she seems happy? Me, I'd be always looking over my shoulder, scared. She didn't tell you?"

"Tell me what, Annetta?" Lynch said impatiently. "She told me she's a great singer, she told me she's broke, she's told me she's crazy about Mario the great musician who is somebody else's husband. Is that why she's scared?"

"It's Mario's music she's crazy about, not Mario," Annetta laughed. "At least I hope so. Mario's my cousin's husband. My cousin, you have seen her, she is always here. She is her husband's best audience when he plays and they have, maybe, a hundred children. I am surprised," she said, deliberately coming back to the conversation that really interested her, "that Vanda didn't tell you about herself." Annetta was wiping the pattern of the table off. Lynch said nothing.

Talk about 'how daft these mortals are' as Puck didn't quite put it. Annetta has a great story to

40

PAGING LYNCH MADISON

gossip and Lynch is keen to hear it. She's bound to be telling the well-embroidered story any minute and he's going to be all ears but before they can settle down for this revelatory binge, they must observe the proprieties of polite disinterest.

"Annetta, Vanda and I had a coffee together; she was rude about my sort of music, she's got me to go to this 'Stan' quack, who will be conning me one way or another, and other than mild curiosity, I'm not too interested in her life-history," he lied.

"Of course. A one-woman man," Annetta teased. "Soon you will marry your Jo and all the Amoretti's will dance at your wedding. Maybe I will be your bridesmaid? But does that stop you from listening about Vanda? She ---"

"I have finished with Jo," Lynch said, anxious to get that said out loud for the first time to see how it sounded. It sounded like the last slipping fingernail of a handhold lost on the last ledge of Beachy Head. No more women.

"Nonsense. A lover's quarrel."

"Absolutely finito, Annetta, if that's how you say it in Italian."

"Oh." Annetta wiped the table for the twelfth time. "Oh. I'm sorry." Her eyes looked sorry but also as if she were half-glad to receive a current story to share with other regulars. Cafe clientele is like that.

"You must feel very sad. So. I will cheer you up. I will tell you the story of Vanda. After you hear

PAGING LYNCH MADISON

such a story, you will feel that even your terrible sadness is not so sad as hers. Maybe."

Lynch thought about the false car-crash he'd said had wiped out his whole family. That wasn't bad? And what about the real wiping out of his whole family?

Lynch thought about Jo's suitcase which had bumped briefly against the door of his room as she left and that dull tiny remembered sound still came back every few hours, jerking more hollows in him. You'll die alone ---

So he prepared himself to listen to Vanda's trivial setbacks like a man who had seen and felt it all.

"Vanda comes," Annetta said, with the cool warmth of the practised raconteur, "from a big family with two fathers, you know? Some brothers and sisters belong to one father and the others, you know? Yes. And always there are arguments and fighting in the family, because they are all clever and want their own way in the family business ----"

"What business?" Lynch said, pushing one of the toothpicks through the little band of crisp white paper that contained it and idly clearing his first lower bicuspid with it for something to do.

"Big," she said. "Motor-cars," she said. "So three of them, they become unhappy and they persuade Vanda, who is the only girl from the other father, the one who dies, yes? - to leave and come with them to England and start on their own."

PAGING LYNCH MADISON

"Why come to England?"

"Why? They come from - oh from --"

"Brazil."

"Brazil, sure. She tell you? Why England I don't know. My father too. I ask him, why England and he say 'why not England?'"

Annetta's laugh was as tasty as just the right amount of garlic.

"So - anyway the four come here with plenty, plenty money and when it's all gone, this I also don't know how, they go back to - where did you say?"

"Brazil."

"Sure, Brazil and leave her here not one penny she have in her pocket. So, she write to her family in North America? South America? One of them."

"South."

"Si, South America, and they say the others have come back and said it was Vanda's fault that the money was lost and goodbye. So, this rich girl, with now not any money, and not any big family, she cries and she never have a job before but never does she seem unhappy. Except," Annetta said rounding out the significance with her eyes, "when she sings those sad songs of Portugal with Mario. In Brazil they sing the Portuguese songs," she adds, in case Lynch didn't know.

PAGING LYNCH MADISON

"That is terrible," Lynch said, now cleaning his nails with the toothpick, whilst trying to place Vanda's and his own crashingly shattering pasts, real and imaginery, in order of nastiness.

"And the friends she makes!" Annetta adds, having obviously saved this until last. Lynch asked no questions. Annetta shook her head with drama. "A shame. Such men! Mama, she threw one of them out and then gave Vanda a talk like she give to me and to Maria and Silvia and Francesca. And not like us she listened," Annetta laughed. "Vanda is so sympatica. You like her? You will fall in love with her when she sings. Everyone does."

Lynch, knowing that every member of even the lousiest gig found that their playing, no matter how pedestrian, attracted a certain looseness in susceptible women, supposed this was universally true and, therefore, must be guarded against and resisted. Such foolishness was only for the foolish.

"Basta, I have work to do," Annetta said, as if Lynch were holding her against her will. "My Papa is frowning. Hey, you don't have to go, too. Do you ---" she watched him, "need help to stand up?"

Shaking off the small hands kindly held out to him by Annetta, her bracelets jangling, Lynch manoeuvred, winced and rose gradually, unable not to make elderly noises from the strain.

"I hope this man Vanda works for will help you," Annetta said. "All right, I'm coming Papa. Ciaou, Lynch."

PAGING LYNCH MADISON

Waiting casually at the door of the cafe, but actually gathering the pluck to walk painfully on, Lynch considered his options. Home. It wasn't far. Then up the stairs to use the first-floor payphone to make an appointment with this Stan. Down the stairs to his basement, up them again when he got hungry, round the shelves at Food Galore, down them again to eat, to wash, up them again for the appointment --
---

"Signor Amoretti? May I use your telephone? Grazie," Lynch said as the proprietor waved away his proffered ten pee. He demanded and easily got an immediate consultation with Stan himself.

Inside the cab he laboured into, the driver made only a little fuss to hear he'd have to take a cheque. Lynch sat back, never comfortable, and sighed, dispirited already. Any quack who can fit you in right away can't, it follows, be any good. (This Lynch theory can be proved any Saturday night; if the restaurant you fancy going to on the spur of the moment can fit you in easily, you don't rejoice, do you. You no longer want to go.)

The cab had dropped him at an imposing if dirty building. But Stan's Self-Help College turned out, of course, to be only one aluminium label in a steep double row of them at the bottom of a dark concrete stairway.

Five flights up. He couldn't make it.

Someone holding a greasy paper bag and a packet of crisps they'd already started to crunch rushed past him two-at-a-time up the stairs.

45

PAGING LYNCH MADISON

"Is there a lift?" Lynch called.

"Only service, mate. Down the corridor, turn right, left, right."

Miles and miles of corridors, through half a dozen heavy doors, he should have added. Finally, the lift. FIVE, it read eventually on the wall through the glass panel. Painfully jerking the pleated gate of the lift open and pushing on the scratched plate of the outside door, Lynch limped out to a narrow corridor, darkness and a choice of three doors, two marked private.

Cautiously opening the other one, he found a girl, eating a sandwich from a greasy bag with pink lettering, a sister to the one he'd seen on the stairs. Her paper mug of hot drink stood steaming on the flat piece of her typewriter and her shoes were off, the heels badly in need of repair.

"Stan's Self-Help College?" Lynch said.

The girl looked at her watch then looked at him to see for sure that he had received her message that it was her lunch break and by her statutory rights she was not obliged to put her shoes back on, wipe her mouth or answer. However, gifted as she was with a heart of gold, she licked the crumbs off her lower lip, sucked some tomato pips off her fingers and pointed with them behind her to a scratched half-open door which announced the college on a grey plastic sign the size of a lapel badge. It was going to be a complete waste of time. Good story for the boys in the band, though, if he ever played again, Lynch

PAGING LYNCH MADISON

sighed to himself, pushing the door wide open after a quick arrogant knock.

Stan had finished his lunch. The top of the greasy crushed-up pink-lettered bag stuck out of the white polystyrene cup in the over-flowing waste-bin with a chocolate-bar wrapper for company. Stan himself was lying beside the desk, his knees hugged up to his chest.

Though Lynch was by now in enough pain to be eager to meet Stan, keen to believe in him, he felt any last smears of hope vanish, only staying to speak at all rather than face the long journey out of the building until he had rested.

"Relaxation. I find this the most calming position of all," Stan said, in such a camp voice that it might or might not be put on for effect. "Are you into Yoga at all?"

"My name is Lynch Madison. I rang and spoke to you from a coffee place after being persuaded by - by Vanda, is it? Yes, Vanda. She said that you might help me with my problem. Yoga? I couldn't even get down on the floor, let alone --"

"Oh Vanda. Yes, of course. You said." Sitting up awfully slowly, Stan stayed on the floor, placid as a plaice fillet, breathing in deeply and counting the breaths out.

Standing now, as thin as Lynch himself but exaggeratedly short and angular in his thin black tracksuit, Stan smiled "art thou troubled?" his face speaking fluently.

PAGING LYNCH MADISON

"Vanda is a treasure," Stan said. "She shouldn't be working for me you know. Now, your problem. Which of my courses were you attracted to, Mr Madison," he said, more to the point.

Lynch fished out the signed paper now and watched Stan's face concertina.

"You will find," he said, not even glancing again at the 'trial session' paper in Vanda's little writing, "that one session, being complimentary, will not, psychologically, cause you to believe in the cure I'm sure I can bring to you."

Had Stan gone to the filing cabinet behind him and reached in it for a bank statement to prove his current insolvency, he could not have revealed more clearly exactly how his financial matters stood.

"I gave deep thought to what you said to me since we spoke on the phone, and I will, of course, need your own complete cooperation, if it is to be resolved. And that cooperation is more easily given if - if you have a real investment in the endeavour, sir."

"One only values what is expensive, you're saying," Lynch smiled, shifting defensively, aware that he would be getting no respite nor his one trial miracle from Stan. He should, in fact, gird himself for an almost immediate journey down in the bumpy lift. And tonight, at bedtime, he would be high on pain again.

"I've heard the theory. I used to subscribe to it. Nowadays, without the money to prove it, I will

PAGING LYNCH MADISON

have to take your word for it," Lynch said, not very interested any more, now that he knew the whole exercise had been pointless. He gazed down at his left trainer, anxious to tighten the lace but unable to screw up the courage it took to bend.

Stan stood implacably, but whether consulting his inner strength or calculating the odds on Lynch being a rich eccentric in disguise it is hard to tell.

"May I ask," he said, "a few questions?"

Even nodding was beginning to hurt, Lynch realised and suddenly wanted to be out of here and comfortable in a nice safe operating theatre with a fifty-fifty chance.

"May I ask what work you do, for example and in what way you first hurt your neck."

"Back," Lynch said, holding it, angry that Stan hadn't even bothered to remember which part of him to be interested in.

"The spine," Stan said impatiently, "begins at the neck. It is the neck that rules the body. I sometimes call it the seat of all pain."

Or a bloody good cover-up for slips of the tongue.

"I'm- a local historian. An official London guide. Not just at the moment, though," he half explained. "It's a bit slack just at the moment." Just a bit.

PAGING LYNCH MADISON

"Ah it's so easy to damage yourself in such circumstances. Even something like reaching up to point to something of interest - or maybe bending to help someone with their ----- well anything could bring on your condition. How exactly do you think it happened?"

"It was so stupid," Lynch said quietly.

"It usually is," Stan said, sitting cross-legged on the chaise-longue, revealing so much of himself in the thin track-suit that Lynch had to look him in the eye.

"I was playing a gig at The Robin Hood. We'd done the first half when Jo - I lived with her - came in. I'd just made up my mind to leave her."

He hesitated. What the hell was he doing telling the truth to this quack?

"I suppose I was showing off to her before the row I knew we'd have later. I took Jim's sticks - he's the drummer - he was using his brushes and I played her our own silly dah-dah-dee-dah-dah on a music stand with them and I was just going to do it again when one stick fell into a very awkward place so I bent down and I still couldn't reach it, so I took another reach for it and wallop. Me finished.

And then there had been trouble. The manager trying to get out of paying us and Bud being so calm ----

"Clarinet. Professional? I had a friend in the LSO once."

PAGING LYNCH MADISON

"No. Very amateur. I just love playing. The Robin Hood every weekend. We get some college bars, sometimes, because of Bud. Bud, my friend. He's - . Bud wants us to do a college gig tomorrow."

Enough music talk. Something difficult had to be said, so Lynch said it.

"Look, er --Stan, I only came here to get the commission for Vanda because she seems a bit desperate," Lynch said, ready to leave. "Nearly as desperate as me. I mean I'm desperate about my back. Like I said on the phone it's you or surgery and I haven't got a bean, at the moment, so it's no use you talking me into a course. I shouldn't have come. I've lost my steady job when I was just -- now I can't even lift my arms to play the damn clarinet and I need to work. I'm going to lose my rooms within the fortnight if I can't pay - "

"In that case I had better at least try to sort you out." Stan had a prissy look on his face. "When did you last eat? Hmm," he said.

Stan made Lynch wait for these charitable sandwiches to come from the shop with the pink bags, explaining a lot of things in the meanwhile. He added that he would, after all, give Lynch a free session, just one, it being a quiet afternoon, but warned that certain personalities were not suitable subjects for self-hypnotism.

Stan gave him the reasons and the facts. Lynch sat very still, frowning and arguing with himself.

PAGING LYNCH MADISON

Would he prefer to be one of the macho superior sods too strong-willed to let themselves be cured that Stan had just described. Or would he prefer the other option; to be a wimp of easy virtue ending up with a normal back.

And if by some chance Stan cured him, shouldn't he go treat this disabling accident as a dreadful warning, pack up and go home to Jan.

No, he couldn't do that. Two reasons. Jan was dead to him. And secondly, weak as it was, he was afraid he wanted to see Vanda again. Didn't he? He pictured her. Maybe just to swap stories.

Listen to the attention and time Stan was giving him to talk about himself. So he told Stan that he'd lied about being a guide. He told him he needed to work again as an interior decorator to get the money to go on with his 'real career' and Stan didn't press him for more.

This newest world he was limping into seemed to contain plenty of people who could care without wanting something back and Lynch began to feel an unfamiliar hopefulness.

If you didn't know what we know, you could really like Lynch unconditionally.

Lynch ashamedly realised as he wiped his hand to free his mouth from the remains of the free-range salad sandwich and horribly healthy yoghourt drink, that he hadn't even said thanks for the free food, let alone the agreement to do the free session.

So he thanked him now. Twice.

PAGING LYNCH MADISON

"De rien, if it works I can add back-pain to our leaflets, and my fortune," Stan said, watching him, "is made. Need a pee?"

Finding, as always, that if asked you needed one, Lynch went out to the cramped little lavatory, coming back with nice clean hands to find Stan sitting very grimly on duty in a chair set opposite another.

"Do you wish," Stan said, "to be cured --"

Holding himself back from laughing at Stan's new 'trying to reach the dead' voice, he simply shrugged, half annoyed.

Stan shook his head and gestured to Lynch to listen.

"Stop and think. I mean you must be sure that you want to be cured and do not secretly prefer to be pitied, sympathised with and pampered by those who can easily notice your pain. Recent research points to it," Stan nodded, seeing Lynch, frown, consider, check the logic and nod back.

"I need to be cured horribly badly," Lynch said, looking hard at Stan, and looking again, surprised to find Stan had lost his air of a weak cup of tea in a draught.

Would Stan swing an amulet in front of his nose now? Open his tiny eyes to big piercing ones and tell him he was under his power? Ask him to empty his mind completely? A hopeless idea, that.

PAGING LYNCH MADISON

It always made him think of every dangerous and worrying thing.

But it was, amazingly, a 'next thing he knew' situation.

***

There he was, in the same chair, goodness knows how long later, feeling confused and tireder than tired, feeling thirstier than he could ever remember, Stan standing, a picture of non-committal, by the window.

He checked; damn it, he had the same, rather sorer pain, maybe starting, now, an inch or two higher.

In the new unnatural way he had developed of standing that caused the least distress, Lynch got up and tried not to show how much he minded.

"Thanks for trying, anyway," he said, feeling quite silly to have expected anything from this clowning and also, considering his complicity, illogically angry at Stan for playing this game with him.

"Need a drink?" Stan said, gesturing at a fruit juice carton on the table behind him. "Everyone feels thirsty afterwards. I don't know why," he smiled.

PAGING LYNCH MADISON

"No thanks, I couldn't drink a thing, thanks," Lynch lied, his tongue all but out and panting. "I must go. I've - got things to do." Like what? "Thanks," Lynch said, eyes firmly elsewhere, heading for the door, taking a deep breath for the pain to come in the pulling of the lift doors, the stubborn doors, the passages, the journey to his room. "Well, thanks."

"Want me to call the lift for you? Is someone waiting for you outside?"

"I can manage. Thanks."

"Look, if you ever want me to try again ----" Stan said, from the door as Lynch limped towards the lift.

"And my best wishes to Vanda. Don't get there too late tomorrow. She'll feel dreadful if you don't turn up."

Once painfully and thankfully inside his own sparse neat room, limping first desperately to the tap, Lynch drank two cups of water straight down before putting the kettle on, then just half of one cup more, wishing above all, he could get the old comfort he used to have, just throwing himself across the bed eyes shut to refresh himself. He took three painkillers not one, something he had made himself not do before, and held his back reproachfully, counting his miseries and misfortunes which multiplied drearily as he moaned out loud until at last the pills began to take effect.

Almost carefree and optimistic the second the pain began to ease off, he began to cook what he

PAGING LYNCH MADISON

could salvage from the few raw materials he'd brought in with him. He'd snatched half of them up and eaten them as he walked, but now, with time to ponder, his forehead was soon furrowed again with new larger fears.

Stan. His words came echoing back. Stan could only have known that Lynch had decided to go to hear Vanda sing tomorrow from things he had blurted out under hypnosis. Obviously. And quite unimportant. But what else had he said?

Too damned much, he'd bet.

Looking on the bright side, Lynch thought, it was impossible for Stan to blackmail him, as he was skint here in London, and with a bit of luck he'd die under the surgeon's knife and all his troubles, back and front, would be over. And surely even a back-street pseudo-guru had some sort of code of confidentiality. Yes. Lynch now set his mind to thinking beautiful thoughts (Vanda singing, Vanda singing undressed, Vanda undressed not singing), pushed himself to take a long wonderful bath in the ugly old tub two floors down and hoped to get to sleep before the pain could start again.

PAGING LYNCH MADISON
CHAPTER THREE

The pills flattened him until lunchtime and then half-waking, white, dead and clueless he slept in and out of snatches of cold dreaming again until three.

Properly awake now and frantic, he was convinced that his memory had gone again like the time when he had fallen from his bike, only this time it had gone for good. No. Here it came. Piece by uneasy piece. Fear. Worry. Never mind that, up and survive. Cold wash. Clean teeth twice. Eat.

It was only when he reached to the only shelf tall enough to hold the Twinkle-Choco-Pops that he realised.

He was totally out of pain.

Cured by Stan? Cured by natural causes? Cured anyway. He checked everything recklessly. He bent, he stretched, he crouched, he windmilled his arms. He nipped quickly up the steps with the bag-full for the laundrette and rushed back. Lynch Madison was the owner of a beautifully useful body that he would for ever cherish and adore (and would like to have cherished and adored for him.)

Glorifying in his healthy energy, savouring every simple movement, he played a chorus of 'Tenderly' tenderly, he shaved, spick and spanned all

PAGING LYNCH MADISON

the harder as he listened to the item on Radio Four about the murderer who had been apprehended at last and detained for questioning just because he had been spotted hitchhiking on the road 'looking unkempt and weak.' The Big Fear was never that far from him.

Lynch put the clean sheets on, sorted and tidied the mess that had been left to lie during his incapacity, housewifed and fussed, back up to collect the perfumed nearly-dry washing, folded it neatly into the airing cupboard as the radio said "Kaleidoscope today takes a look at the neglected poets of Roumania ---" Four-thirty, sod it. He'd miss Bud if he didn't rush.

Fast past the ticket office waving his wrongly named pass vaguely in the right direction, shoved and pushed into the crowds and forced his way on to the tube, still aware and proud of the way his legs were once more attached to his body. Hanging on to the strap, he swayed happily to the soporific high-toned andante of the rails, jumped off at High Street Ken, up the steps two at a time, catching a busy number nine at a traffic-light and swinging off it again at Holland Park, alive with energy, sick with freedom, striding long and hard, prideful pleasure in every normal step, but with plans to send a donation to someone now he was cured.

Who would he send it to? To Stan? to God? He swore he would never forget the miracle of easy movement ever again (though of course it will only be until the next snag on the barbed-wire fence of life) finding he is able to run across the road and up the side entrance to Bud's place, panting healthily in

PAGING LYNCH MADISON

the normally unhurried tiny space of the Commonwealth Institute's lobby.

The security guard agreed to call his office but no reply. He's out 'researching' but should have been back an hour before.

Lynch fidgets and waits and paces, unwilling to sit down. Finally here comes Bud, raincoat over his arm, looking very worried. That's Bud for you.

To the complete indifference of the waiting guard, Lynch throws up his hands and does a wild toe-touching routine, showing off how cured he is.

You can tell how pleased Bud is to see him out of pain only if you look very closely into his eyes where all his smiling is done. The rest of his face is a Guyanian-of-Chinese-descent marvel of the inscrutable.

"I will be five minutes," Bud says and is, exactly.

"I know it's late to expect you and Chi to get the boys for that college gig tonight," Lynch said, trying to keep from walking ahead of Bud's small feet, trying not to bend down when he spoke to him. "What do you think? Could we do it?"

"It's very late," Bud frowned, seeming to check the stock market index, the weather in Wales, then the time on his complicated watch - the innumerable gadgets he had sent to him the only outward sign of his family fortune.

PAGING LYNCH MADISON

"They want us to start at nine. Say, setup at eight? Hm. We'll ask Chi what she thinks," Bud said precisely. " I know that they hadn't managed to book another band. They were ---"

"Peed off, I'll bet. So can we?"

"It's all right with me. So, it will depend on the arrangements of Gerry, John and Andy if ---"

"If she lets him," they laughed. Andy, the one with the wife and kids. Poor Andy.

Nothing was said about rehearsing or the lack of preparation time. They hadn't got where they were in the musical world by worrying about the little things.

"Come home with me and we'll phone round."

Bud was the Chinese-Guyanian child of many Guyana dollars. His people had sent him to the LSE to study international economy and expected him home to run his Honourable Daddy's considerable enterprises as soon as he finished his education.

Having done as brilliantly academically as was expected, instead of catching his flight home, he told his family that he had fallen in love with London, which was only sketchily true and failed to tell them that he had mostly fallen in love with a Japanese girl he had studied with and now lived with, herself the child of billions of yen.

PAGING LYNCH MADISON

Chi was expected home with her newly acquired skills to marry her betrothed, and impart her wisdom to her many children.

Despite calls from their respective families to come home at once, they were so contented in their two high-salaried jobs at the Commonwealth Institute, (Bud's recommendation got her in) each earning a great deal of their own money for the first time in their privileged lives.

They had, not unnaturally, also fallen in love with the freedom that gave them.

To clinch things, they played music together, the best glue of all. Chi was only good enough to play for close friends but when Bud formed his own group, light years from her sort of music, she became the group manager, their arranger and loved this role best of all.

They now played music together very rarely but had stayed close, hiding out, safe together, each painfully trying to work out some inoffensive way to stay together without losing their families.

Chi's smiles were all open for viewing and she spent quite a few of them just preceding them now into the predominantly white, bright comfortable flat she and Bud lived in, overlooking the park, the balcony full of tubs of healthy flowers, the kitchen full of Bud's acquired gadgets, the whole well-used, the living area free and welcoming.

John and his drums were available; they could call for him any time, Chi said and he would call Gerry while she called Andy.

PAGING LYNCH MADISON

Gerry could make it too, John reported ten minutes later and would arrive at the Union Bar at eight sharp or a bit after. John had laughed when Chi told him why Andy couldn't play at such short notice. Good. They had a quartet and who needs a trumpet, anyway.

Chi had 'wokked' them a good meal after the telephoning was done. Watching Bud with Chi in their natural habitat of friendly-lovingness made Lynch ache.

If he could make only one excuse for his inexcusable disappearing act from his marriage, Bud and Chi's relationship, or his own seen version of it, was what he had run away to look for. Dawn and the women before her on his journeyings had been just adolescent swipes at lust. Jo had been, sorry, a mistake.

Watching Bud and Chi's easy love was tortuous to him and Lynch was glad when they were stop-go-ing through the traffic in Bud's quite old but big estate car and up and down the steps of John's place for several journeys packing the drum-kit into the back and Bud was getting his usual steam-up about being late, impatient with Chi as if it were her fault. (It doesn't do to have friends who are perfect.)

Slowly through the late-night shopping crowds of Thursday night, Bud called off their not very large repertoire as he drove. They agreed easily with each other, they chose the programme. Lynch wrote the list on a piece of card, for something to do, but it was pretty routine: a noisy start, a well-known ballad, a dodgy bebop with awkward bits and a blues.

PAGING LYNCH MADISON

Then it would be the break, the band following a carefully ordered technique for the avoidance of awkward requests at this time, a dazzling enthusiasm at the choice (no matter what) then an earnest wish that they might find time to play it.

A few drinks at the bar and as much admiration as they could hold, a quick pee and back to thank everyone for their enthusiasm and interest, even if imaginary, and now, to open their second half, a 'request' they had just had for "Lullaby of Birdland." Usually this easy choice received enough approving applause however they played it, a ballad or two more and a very noisy finish with something well-known and finally the slow packing up to give any likely groupies their chance.

And it had turned out to be a good gig, more or less, except for the blues. But tonight, for a wonder, Lynch was able to extend his last phrase until Gerry, Bud and John blended with him, so they went out together on a storm of polite indifference from the main bulk of the noisy bar and an earnest bit of attention at the front.

Bud, the front-man, called them all for their spatter of acknowledgement - clarinet, bass, drums and me on the piano, he said, thank you and good night.

"Your back is still good?" Bud called, playing over and over a middle section and some runs that would have been lovely in the first ballad if he had thought of it then.

PAGING LYNCH MADISON

"Totally better," Lynch said, breaking his clarinet apart and squinting down its body.

"Before you play that blues again someone had better tell you exactly -precisely - how the middle goes, and Gerry – well - " Chi said quietly, helping John pack his cymbals, never favouring Gerry's sometimes off-target improvisation.

It was a long half hour before they were seeing Gerry off with his bass, packing John's drum kit back into Bud's vehicle and arranging a practice next week at Bud's for some new stuff.

Shining with the shine they got from playing music together, never mind the traffic, they sung bits they had played, bits they wished they had played. Time. Eleven-twenty-five. Why not?

"Hey," Lynch said, yawning, as if it had just occurred to him. "Will you all come somewhere with me? To hear a girl sing?"

"Where?"

"What for?"

"Near here. It's quite near my place. Amoretti's. An Italian place. She's really something."

"She's Italian?"

"She's South American, like you."

"Guyana?"

PAGING LYNCH MADISON

"Brazil."

"OK. Left here?" Bud frowned round to him. "You're thinking she may suit the band? I don't like singers. They make trouble. Don't you think?"

Probably.

Bud would rather get home to be with Chi, naturally, but he shrugged reasonably, Chi agreed, John had little choice as he had to stay with his drums.

"You'll see," Lynch said. "If she's as good as she says she is you'll beg her to sing with us. She might make you change your mind."

"OK. Where now?" said Bud. "I don't want to be too long."

"Here," said Lynch, pointing to the place and a space to park simultaneously. (This is fiction, remember.)

"She sings our sort of music?" Bud said, checking that both the boot and the doors were locked in his carefully patient way.

"Any sort of music!" Lynch said rashly, not knowing.

They could hear the applause from the road. It was undeniably enthusiastic. They found, however, that it was applause for the end of the performance and most of the crowd were turning back to their companions, their coffee, their

PAGING LYNCH MADISON

cigarettes, their propositioning and their worries, the pleasures of the music quickly forgotten.

But for the performers and the people who love them and their music, the pulse races a little longer.

Lynch watched the guitarist, (Mario presumably,) still plucking the faintest little tweets and rifts, all of it, now, for the sole admiration of himself and a short squat adoring woman who had to be Annetta's cousin with the hundred children. She spoke quietly to him and he nodded, still playing trills and decorations, shocked by the advance of any outside enthusiast, barely nodding at their praise, back over his quiet strings again in an instant.

Vanda, on the other hand, was on the move, called for from table to table, milking the adoration, queen, empress, goddess of song. "Thank you, I'm so glad you enjoyed it, I enjoyed it myself," she said everywhere, ingenuously, the bland universality of her charmingness diminishing any pleasure Lynch wanted to feel was exclusively his. Now she had spotted him and was showing crude joy at his arrival. Insincere and embarrassing.

"Too late. Hey listen, I'm real glad you came. Is your friend here? Oh, hi," she said vaguely to Bud and Chi and John, still gazing only into Lynch's face, as if trying to conquer his cynicism again.

"I sang your special song already, thinking you might be here. No more singing tonight." She looked around her as she said this, expecting and getting the right response.

PAGING LYNCH MADISON

Everything she was saying was actually said rather loud and aimed not at him directly but to the part of the audience that had not yet finished her ovation and were hanging on to the hem of her gown.

She asked Lynch to introduce her properly now to John and Chi and Bud. He explained them blandly, briefly, impatiently. Wanting her on her own or not at all as he watched her start her tricky winning, winning them easily too, Lynch noticed, irritated at himself for coming back here and humiliating himself for nothing.

"A shame you haven't got a piano here, Annetta," she sparkled loudly, "we've a great pianist here tonight. I could sing while Bud played. Still nobody wants to hear me squawking anymore tonight, anyway," she said.

The sycophant knows a cue when he hears one and here came the roaring for more, the calling for encores exhaustively, until, caught up in the enthusiasm, even the tables who would have been as happy with silence had joined in the clamour.

"I see what you mean," Chi said, watching Vanda with serious admiration as she whispered into Mario's ear and he nodded and checked his tuning to roars of anticipatory applause. "She's special."

Lynch could see Vanda turn up the volume of her public happiness even louder and was furious.

"She hasn't even sung yet," Lynch said. "It's just free entertainment. The crowd here aren't much better than our pub. They just want a bit of noise to shout over, that's all. Don't expect too much."

PAGING LYNCH MADISON

"You said she was good, Lynch. What are you talking about?"

Lynch, having lied himself into a corner, made himself busy getting a few chairs, forcing a bit of room at a reluctant table, calling coffees over and a large plate of sandwiches he could afford again now that the gig had paid them.

He felt half-amused, half-jealous to see the Amoretti's hurriedly using the milk-frother now so as not to intrude the crude sound of it on to their musical public. Who would care like that at their gigs?

Tucking her clean cream Dr Zhivago top into her brown drill jeans, as if only to draw attention to the flatness of her stomach and the slimness of her legs, her eyes flicked alert and everywhere as she began humming and la-la-ing as if simply unable to wait for Mario to finish his fine tuning.

And Mario responded immediately to her, without glancing towards her, (certainly no vulgar 'two, three, four,') and listen, all of you out there. Just listen to this.

Vanda's voice was singing out, clearly without her help, and though the song was in a foreign language Lynch didn't even recognize, no question but that it was about heartbreaking unrequited love with a sad end, and he wanted to take it to bed, like she'd said.

"Thank you," Vanda said professionally, over the clapping and cheering, Bud nodding his head with delight at Chi. "That was a Portuguese ballad

PAGING LYNCH MADISON

called 'Two Doves' that Mario wrote himself. I hope one day to be able to translate the words and sing it to you in English, if Mario won't mind," she wiffled at him. He showed none of her type of enthusiasm in his polite half-bow towards her - English, he seemed to be thinking, was a poor language and a poor substitute for music.

Finally," Vanda said holding out her hand to Bud and Chi and John and Lynch , "we have some jazz enthusiasts here tonight, so we're going to sing ----" She bent forward and Mario whispered something to her. What could anyone ever say to make anyone else look that happy? If all this joy of hers was just an act, it was a good one. "Yes, we'll sing ----"

And she did it again. A kind of humming and the stillness that she stirred into the tune, singing it slowly with control, she just sang, the simplicity of this highly individualised arrangement changing 'Georgia' from a good standard to something new and devastating.

Lynch watched with jealousy as Bud started the standing clapping for them - for her, he was sure - followed by silly sheep everywhere.

"She is something," Chi said, looking into the inside pocket of Bud's neat jacket and taking out his leather notepad. "She would never sing with us, Lynch, she's in a different class. She shouldn't. But I could make a start on the business I always wanted to start with her. You know. Management. I spend a lot of time almost pleading for our gigs. If Bud and I could just launch her right, they'll be begging for

PAGING LYNCH MADISON

her. The guitar is terrific but she doesn't really need him. Anyone would do."

Lynch was awash with feelings. Mostly of jealousy.

"She could make trouble," Lynch said stubbornly.

"How?" Chi asked, surprised.

Lynch shrugged sulkily.

"When did you find her? Bud go and talk to her. Tell her ---- I'll come with you. I must go and speak to her. Or someone else will."

Chi and Bud and John hurried over to queue up for an audience with Vanda the mouth. Lynch stood by and watched, dully.

He had thought of Vanda as his personal light-in-the- darkness all day. Stupid. A female that bright needs no ordinary male socket to plug into her.

Lynch reached for his jacket, hooked it over his shoulder with one finger, took his clarinet case in the other hand and pushed his way through, nodding goodnight to the Amorettis. Conscious of Vanda's headlights dazzling all indiscriminately behind him, he walked out, walked home and went to bed.

***

PAGING LYNCH MADISON

"Bud and Chi are really something, you know," Vanda said, in her what he realised was a sort of picked-it-up-from-the-Hollywood-movies style of speech that she had, when he had finally woken, grabbed his robe and opened up to her chirpy persistent knocking and banging at the door of his flat.

"It's the most wonderful morning," she said. "I couldn't sleep another moment. So ----"

She lifted a corner of his rotting curtains open a crack and then pulled them fully back with difficulty on their rusting hooks, the bright light jeering at the shoddy bareness.

She didn't seem to feel the need to explain why she had come, uninvited, to his place, and Lynch resented the way she was taking in every corner of his (thank-the-lord-he'd-cleaned-it-up) room like it was an abandoned suitcase and she was Customs and Excise.

"I wish you'd stayed, last night," she said, ripping out another false lining or two with one eye, feeling for false bottoms with the other. "We talked for ever after you'd gone, me and Mario and his wife and Annetta and her brother Marco and your friends. John didn't say much but, oh, isn't it sad how he - Bud I mean - can't just go back home with Chi and marry her? It's what I said to you, isn't it? Everybody's got a story?"

PAGING LYNCH MADISON

Vanda's lovely eyes were everywhere, as if she would be expected to be deadly accurate when she described his room to her superior officers.

"I see you lied about your place," she smiled. "As if I'd mind! It's really grim, isn't it?" If she had been talking to a third party about it, she couldn't have been less embarrassed. "My place is cheap but at least it's cheerful. They told me you were an interior designer or something? Jeez. Still I suppose it's like cobblers and their own shoes, sort of thing.

"You know what, I wouldn't mind bringing my paint-roller over. Just a can of light paint, even white, maybe, two rollers, you give the directions - one evening would do it. Fancy some breakfast yet? Can I make toast for both of us? Do you mind?"

She was on her way over to the toaster, frowning at a little patch of matted crumbs at the front of it and wiping it away fussily with a tiny tissue from her sleeve.

"Your friends weren't gossiping or anything, so don't blame them for telling me where you live and everything. I don't know why you told me so many lies and please don't feel you need to explain," she said, pausing nonetheless, to give Lynch the time to apologize and explain.

Lynch stood, still unspeaking, one naked foot on the other and consciously tried to unclench his teeth.

"It's just that I was so interested about you, Lynch.

PAGING LYNCH MADISON

"I mean, naturally I wanted to know more about you. I mean if we're going to be friends. I mean, anyway, I think it's awful to lie about -- everything. I mean, saying you live a grand flat and run a big car and that stuff is - childish, isn't it?"

Could she really be still smiling while she suffocated him with this muck?

"Yes, that reminds me. You haven't even got a guide agency. I said to Bud I was going to ask you for a job. I felt so *estupido*. Painting and decorating's all right. No one cares what you do. You don't have to lie about it. Whatever you are, you're a real mystery man, aren't you? Maybe you're lying to Bud and Chi and John and everyone too. I don't understand. Still, I'll make you tell me everything, one day. I've got a lot of secrets to tell you, too," she said, smiling sympathetically, conspiratorially.

"Do you like your toast dark or medium?"

Lynch rolled his hand experimentally over his deep stubble, pulled his luxurious, deep-dyed, thick towelling monogrammed robe (that had been Jo's first gift to him) around himself more firmly, coughed his first cough of the day and politely failed to spit. He even went to the dresser and took out a rubber band that he could remember having left amongst the cutlery and bunched his black ponytail with it before walking his rather nice legs over to Vanda.

He pulled her firmly into his body with both hands, looked her coldly in the eyes and said, "Vanda, you are making a nuisance of yourself. You are intruding. If I want you to come and criticise me

PAGING LYNCH MADISON

early in the morning or if I want you to - to do my cooking or paint my room or wash my pants - or take over my friends and their lives, I'll certainly let you know. OK."

"OK," she said, not moving away. "Bud and Chi got a booking out of Amoretti's for you to play there, by the way. I said I'd tell you. They want to play badminton with us today but I said I didn't know if your back was up to it, yet. I said we'd phone them later. OK?"

Badminton? Foursomes? Had she not heard? No tears? No fury? No angry stiffening? No accusations after his intentional rudeness? Just more interference? Lynch was used to a better response to the direct and deliberately callous coolness he had found universally effective since he left Crossbridge.

It had proved a nice simple way to preserve the safe distance he now preferred. He dropped his hands hastily, beginning to feel and respond to her nice body-shape and warmth.

Of course. The trap. He remembered, now. Her gimmick. Kindness. Laughter. Willingness. All sticky honeyed vacuous webs to get what she wanted. Then, like all that type of female spider, she would eat him, spit out the bits and move on.

He now made that most aggressive of all moves: the thrown-back-cuff look at the watch. This gesture, even though spoiled rotten by the fact that he was cuffless and that his digital was over on the floor by the unmade bed, had a sort of effect.

PAGING LYNCH MADISON

"I can see the trouble," Vanda said, her eyes softening even more. "You're the type that needs a little while to recover when you wake in the morning. I'll pop back in, what, half an hour? You decide where we'll all go today and we can phone Chi then --"

Lynch had never ravished a woman before. He did it in complete silence, in absolute revenge, as a punishment for her possessiveness, with care not to be rough but with a greedy insistence. He found a sort of experienced festina lente he would have died for when he was eighteen, with not too much regard for the preferences of who was lying beneath him.

Triumphant and finished, he lay heavily, unwilling to look at his victim. A bit guilty, but you could rationalise that it was entirely her own fault for coming here, just worried that he might feel more than guilty about it tomorrow.

She was crying of course.

He waited for the gulps to become sniffles. He waited for the screaming to start. He remembered again Jo's case banging against that door-post. He'd sign on in the merchant navy and never see another woman. (If he didn't get sea-sick, he would.)

He began to move away from Vanda cautiously. He hated violence and she could be the type to hit out when she finally got around to retaliation.

"Oh Lynch, the moment I met you I knew. When did you know? I knew when you signed that form for Stan's session that you only did it to see me

PAGING LYNCH MADISON

again. Stan told me you couldn't stop saying my name under hypnosis. Oh Lynch."

Christ, she was kissing his shoulder with little gentle kisses. She was the nymphomaniac he and the guys had been trying to meet since acne.

"Lynch, Lynch." Gentle kisses, down from the top, stopping at all floors. Lynch flashed himself a danger signal and made himself not respond to it.

She was going to be a real pain to get rid of.

"Look, get out, will you. I've got things to do," he said.

He pulled his towelling wrap round himself and sat with his back to her as she put herself together, refusing to answer anything, saying nothing at all.

She was surprisingly silent, just humming happily as she straightened herself in the freckled mirror, kissed him lightly on his head, put that heavy bag over her shoulder and turned to call out "Ciao," softly from the door.

"Let's skip today," she said thoughtfully. "I'll wait for you at Amoretti's tonight, OK? You never did ask me what that special song I sang for you was. I'll sing it for you tonight and you'll understand."

She smiled warmly as if he were nodding and charming, kissed his head tenderly, breathed "a bientot" like something she'd seen in a movie and always wanted to say and was finally gone.

PAGING LYNCH MADISON

Moments later, even before Lynch had collected his shaving gear and gone down to the bathroom, remorse and self-disgust popped in for a long chat, followed by their more palatable friends, anger and self-justification.

No sign of him at Amoretti's that Sunday night. No answer at the door of the flat all week and by Friday the new occupants were doing the painting Vanda had volunteered for and, no, they told her, uninterested, mind the loose floorboards, will yer, they didn't have a clue where the guy with the long hair had gone.

PAGING LYNCH MADISON

CHAPTER FOUR

"Lynch?"

Laurence Miller dropped some of the change the programme seller was giving him, picked it up and gave the programme to the groomed girl beside him, who smiled her thanks.

"Lynch?" Chi said again, touching his shoulder lightly, looking into his face, waiting to buy her programme behind him. "Is it you?"

"Are you speaking to me?" Laurence Miller said, pushing his glasses up a little, checking his bow-tie for straightness and speaking in a particularly up-market English voice.

Chi blushed. "I'm sorry. I thought -- I'm sorry."

Laurence Miller smiled understandingly and walked on, finding their row and their seats, courteously helping Geraldine off with her jacket and putting it across his well-cut trousers, checking the bow-tie again.

He agreed with Geraldine that it was a beautiful theatre and agreed with beautiful Geraldine, as she twisted and turned her head, that it was an extra bonus to have parked so easily and been

PAGING LYNCH MADISON

able to come early and watch the sparkly, dressed-up glittery charity preview audience arrive.

For himself, he only watched tiny Chi, in a tiny white beaded jacket, walk to her seat and watched until he saw Bud's face over his shoulder, looking round to where Chi pointed him out.

Lynch turned his face half down, then, and when he looked up again he could watch Bud shake his head and tease Chi, perhaps for making such a stupid mistake and he watched her shrug, watched them laugh and chatter. Maybe they would discuss Lynch kindly for a moment or two. How much had they missed him the last two years. Not as achingly as he had missed them. He couldn't take his eyes off them for too long; Chi had sounded so warm, so hopeful - he dreaded walking away from them again.

And it was more than that, of course. What was he constantly twisting and turning himself for? Watching every entrance? For Vanda. She might be here. No seats empty next to Bud and Chi but she might be sitting somewhere else. She might be sitting with someone else.

When, anyway, wasn't he watching for Vanda?

Bud and Chi might know where she was. Bud and Chi had been the second friends after the Amorettis he had, well, loved, since Mark at grammar-school.

Mark and he had been unlikely, unalike, perfect companions with enough irritating gritty annoyances to keep them from anything peculiarly

PAGING LYNCH MADISON

close. When Mark had died on the motor-bike he had been specifically forbidden by his parents to ride, Leslie Merrett, 16, had crossed close friendship off his list of possibilities for the future.

A disastrous decision? Not right away. For the time being this resolve had made him into a fine student, a success in business, and a reliable, responsible, conscientious father and husband.

A disastrous decision? In the end, yes. This cheated the innocent Jan and small Charlotte out of any of the wild loving, silly fun, mild bickering and carelessness of real family life. Jan had been unwittingly hitched to a potentially attractive frozen corpse. A frog no one had thought to kiss into a prince.

Leaving them had been his best gift to them yet.

Geraldine, regrettably, also did not possess the right spell to undo his frogness. Time to leave her, too. He saw that as clearly as if it had been written on the proscenium arch. Funny he should see Bud and Chi tonight because he had planned tonight for so long. He was walking out on Geraldine in the interval.

He squeezed her hand as a sort of goodbye she could think about afterwards and smiled into her eyes. The warmth she looked back with nearly thawed one of his flippers.

But honestly he hadn't used Geraldine DuBois. He wouldn't have that on his already bulging conscience. Her father had almost begged

PAGING LYNCH MADISON

him to run the business, no questions asked, no paperwork. (Mr DuBois's own paperwork especially centred around some contracts in Addis Ababa that would not, Lynch had always been sure, bear a lot of scrutiny, either.)

Lynch had been good for DuBois's and wonderful for Geraldine, he flattered himself. But now he had enough money to give him the time to hide out until he could change his appearance again. To re-Leslie himself to his passport photograph, and travel to sign the necessary signature that would release his real money in Luxembourg and finally choose his future.

Though he had never really believed Geraldine was going to cure his loneliness, she was a sweet person who had needed him. He would try hard not to hurt her when he left and would never even contemplate using her to get him through customs, though smugglers and criminals insist that it is always easier to pass muster as an "ordinary couple."

He needed a different kind of a woman to extricate him. A willing woman to use and dump when he was over the border, wherever that border turned out to be.

Vanda, for example.

She'd be just fine. She could cope with dumping. He bet she hadn't minded at all two years ago. "Que sera," she'd probably said, smiling at the next guy through the fake sadness.

PAGING LYNCH MADISON

Yes. Vanda was tough. He could even warn her it was coming. "OK," Vanda would smile wantonly, in his easy fantasy. "Just make love to me a couple more times and I'll fix you some lunch and go pack my things."

Geraldine took his hand. "You OK?" she frowned.

He smiled at her, relenting. All right, Geraldine. Not at the interval. It was too cruel for her. She didn't deserve it. Later, then.

The very second the curtain-calls began, by which time Lynch had re-planned Geraldine's last night with him, with a longing lingering glance at the back of Bud's kind head, Laurence Miller whispered something to Geraldine and they slipped out instantly.

It was, Laurence said, taking her arm to move her swiftly along to his legitimately parked car, best if they get a move on. It was getting a bit late for Ronnie Scott's if they wanted to be able to see as well as hear when they got there.

The classy wholehearted jazz that was made at the club that night was the only sound in his head as he drove Geraldine home, nodding at whatever she said; at her flat, in the clean careful living-room, on the floor, on the lilac quilted bed-spread and finally there, the clarinet he had just been entranced by, played an extra rhythm section to him while they made love, music patterns and shapes more exciting to him than her sweet breasts in his hands as he kissed her goodnight, and, though she wasn't aware of it, kissed her goodbye.

PAGING LYNCH MADISON

"That's the best birthday I ever had," she said, stroking his face, "won't you stay tonight after all? I wish you would."

Tempting. Very tempting.

"I wish I could, Gerry. You know I'm flying off tomorrow to Berlin from Gatwick. I have to have some sleep. And if you're near me ----" he said in a rehearsed way.

Back in his car, he wound down all the windows and opened the sun-roof to let out the enticing, expensive perfume, the better to facilitate the forgetting of Geraldine.

Lucky Geraldine, after a dignified tear or two, would be handed back to her father, who would find a better man to replace Lynch at DuBois and with Geraldine. Then she could go forward to the proper and appropriate lifetime marriage that belonged to her.

But he was concentrating on something else. Trying to reconstruct that jazz phrasing. Off-beat, on-beat, dangerously close to the wind, nearly not getting back to the theme on time, always there and only noticeable, sometimes, by not being noticeable. Brilliant. He might tootle about a bit when he got ---ah yes, home.

He hoped Geraldine wouldn't think to phone him tonight as she sometimes did to say something naughty and cute in his weary ear. He wouldn't be at the flat the DuBois's had given him. It had been cleared out and cleaned out. He had had a room in a

PAGING LYNCH MADISON

small hotel near Paddington since two days ago. His cases were tightly packed with only everything he had bought for himself. In the perfectly clean flat he had left a lot of expensive new and nearly new very lovely things he'd never use again. DuBois things. He'd packed them nicely in appreciation. Poor Geraldine.

That tune was driving him crazy. Bit late to be playing music in a hotel though. Shame. Perhaps if he just blew very softly. He wet his lip as if in preparation, thinking through the bits he could remember. No he wouldn't. It might cause some attention he didn't need.

He parked the BMW in the service road by the hotel, turning off the lights and humming, shutting his eyes for a moment to revel in the solitude and peace he would have for thirty-six hours. Sorry, Geraldine. More lying. The flight wasn't really until Monday. And it wasn't to Berlin. And not from Gatwick. And he wasn't coming back.

In the back of the car, covering his clarinet-case from the idle window-smasher, was the cool style of trench-coat you have to buy to go with the life-style he had been living lately. The type you possess to put in cars and take out of cars and that never get worn but are neatly hung up by all kinds of flunkeys.

But when he leaned awkwardly over his front seat to reach for it, though he refused to believe it for a moment, he did to his back what he had done to his back before.

****

PAGING LYNCH MADISON

If you will now turn back to the page it was on, you will be able to remind yourself of the appearance of a successful back-specialist's waiting room in Harley Street, though this is a different one, it is incredibly like it, as are the elaborately ruched drapes of the nineteen eighties and the bright and lithe mistress or receptionist, not to mention those impossible chairs.

But it is Laurence Miller leaning against this other wall, hair already growing longer but only long enough for Leslie, not Lynch. (The all-important ponytail would have to wait.) It is Laurence Miller who wears this expensive conventional suit so well.

Laurence Miller is reading, surely, the same Punch magazine or one very similar - certainly as full of good cartoons about lemmings, penguins and song-titles - Laurence Miller is not the sort to ask for an instant cure. He's a realist in a hurry and will be demanding the fifty-fifty operation privately and fast.

Two days have gone since his real flight on Monday went without him. Geraldine would already be upset that he hadn't contacted her days ago from 'Berlin.' It might be kind to ring her tonight - keep her happy for another couple of weeks. No. Maybe that wasn't so kind. Cut and run.

This back business must never happen again. It was holding him up. He was unable to use his legally earned ticket to the bank in Luxembourg, and surely, though it is impossible to remember degrees

PAGING LYNCH MADISON

of pain, this time it was much worse. If it happened a third time, he might begin to feel it was some kind of message, an omen, and maybe even think of giving up.

The money in Luxembourg will always safely wait for him but he keeps seeing himself drift off past it on the tide. So he is in some desperate hurry to straighten up his rather less skinny body and climb whatever fascinating ladders are being let down by the fairy-godmothers these days.

Laurence Miller finds, when it is finally his turn with the specialist, why his appointment had been nearly an hour behind schedule as the man seems to require not just the history of his back but a life history too.

Answering the way he thought would most easily lead to an agreement to operate, Laurence and Lynch lied with care and good taste.

But medical men are a pain greater than a backache to a man with secrets. This specialist raised his eyebrows high when Lynch said that he hadn't consulted any other specialist before and began writing a short novel on a large piece of paper as this didn't tally with Laurence's earlier story. Spotting the folly, Laurence coughed. "Of course that's not quite true. I just haven't been to a specialist whose opinion I really respect ---"

Whew, all smoothed over, short novel crossed out, and the extra flattery oils a few wheels. Better than that, the man stops writing his damn notes and allows Lynch to remove his very best quality silk shirt and groan himself ready for examination.

PAGING LYNCH MADISON

(There is, despite the cold winds of this November, nothing else to take off - whoever heard of a hero in a vest.)

The specialist is thorough. Stripped, in the end, and stared at, cross questioned again and prodded, Lynch finally dresses himself, with great difficulty, giving permission to be watched closely while he did so. As a finale, Lynch re-knots Laurence's college tie and with as much aplomb as the pain allows, carries his jacket over to the other side of the large desk from where he was being observed.

"Hmm," said the specialist, putting out his hands to help him on with the jacket, coming from behind his desk, pulling up a seat so as to sit next to Lynch, a young forward-thinking medic, au fait with the new guidelines, the eighties feel of not separating oneself from one's patients.

"Hmm, you have a problem there," he said. Pausing. Holding onto his advantage.

"But you can operate. I'm willing to take the chance," Lynch said, jawline steadied for the knife.

"Operate?" The specialist looked around as if seeking a dictionary to check on the meaning of such a word. "I'm not that kind of a man, Mr Madison. Modern times, modern ways."

Lynch groaned to himself. Perhaps this fellow's grandfather would come out of retirement and perform the operation in his kitchen.

PAGING LYNCH MADISON

"You say your back just 'suddenly' cleared by itself last time. I find that hard to believe unless we take it that your trouble may be hysterical. That is to say, caused by some inner and mental conflict. Perhaps some career stress or some personal relationship? Are you a very anxious person? It all matters, Mr Miller."

Hysterical? Silence.

"You have told me nothing at all yet of your personal circumstances."

Silence.

"There are, Mr. Miller, many alternative methods these days that show excellent results ----"

"Such as ---" Lynch had already given this over-cautious and reluctant butcher up as a bad job and was wishing he wasn't so in pain that he couldn't just get up and walk out. He would have to stay and listen as politely as he could.

"Such as acupuncture, certain methods of relaxation, physiotherapy and hypnosis, of course."

Of course. Lynch felt in his pocket. His little address book was there.

"I could recommend colleagues in any branch of those skills if you thought you might have faith in them."

Silence.

PAGING LYNCH MADISON

"I'm afraid that I would insist that you tried them before I could dream of operating. I'm not turning away business, Mr Madison, I simply don't believe you are a suitable case for surgery which carries with it, in this case, the normal dangers of any operation plus a seventy-five per cent risk of failure."

"Seventy-five? I had been told fifty-fifty."

"But this is a second time, Mr Miller. A sign that all is not well with the spine. Perhaps you'd allow me to book you for a full scan ---"

"I'll have to think about all this," Lynch said, thinking that he really would have to think about all this. "I'll ring and tell you what I've decided."

All the rest was cautious flannel and their eyes stopped meeting as their interest in each other waned. Lynch was helped up and out of the room with a sincere enough hand-shake and he was on his way to telephone Stan-the-miracle before the specialist had finished writing 'dead loss' at the bottom of his record.

As only Millie Lambert could see him right away and Lynch had remembered the warnings about her from that long-ago conversation with Vanda, Laurence Miller agreed to wait for 'Mr Stan' at three o'clock this afternoon, held down the telephone and sighed carefully as even sighing hurt.

He killed some of the time grieving over his pain in Selfridges, choosing, without buying, new clothes and other things that might return him to impersonating Leslie Merrett who would be travelling to Luxembourg. Still too early. He took

PAGING LYNCH MADISON

the escalator to the casual section for other clothes he might buy for when he had Lynch Madison's money bulging in his wallet again.

He killed a bit more time gratefully leaning on a high ledge at the type of sandwich-bar he had previously hated because there were no seats.

He nearly killed himself killing more time by challenging himself to limp very slowly through the shopping crowds of windy November, all the way to Stan's, no hurry. Tense with the effort, tenser still from the cold.

He forced himself to admit some things. Had he made his back 'go' in order to bring him to Stan's where Vanda might be? Was that 'hysterical' enough? He was certainly as hysterically desperate to see her as he had been to leave her.

Another thing to admit. Ever since he'd left the flat early on that Friday morning, after he had behaved so disgustingly to her, for over two years he had been automatically checking all female faces in case they were Vanda's.

Was it crazy or just self-protective that he never worried for a moment about running into Jan who surely must come to London sometimes? As for Jo, or old friends from Crossbridge, or anyone else he had ever known, or even poor Geraldine - he never gave them a thought.

He could write a script for his first re-sighting of Vanda, but how could he deliver the words with the sincerity they needed and still have her be there when he'd finished.

PAGING LYNCH MADISON

"Vanda," he could say. "Don't come too close to me. I am not all I seem."

"What - whatever can you mean?" Vanda would say, a pretty frown on her pretty face, coming at least three paces nearer to him, so that now they would be centre-stage and the tension held.

"I've been living a terrible lie ---" he would say. Vanda gasps and holds pretty hand to pretty mouth. "But I can lie no longer."

Wrong. He could soon take his doctorate in lying. Lynch had become - had had to become - an alpha plus of prevarication, a doyen of dissembling. A record-smashing motivated lying confabulator of trust-destroying talent.

He watched the crowds hurrying into the light and warmth of Marks and Spencer and followed them in. Look, there goes B. Carfax hurrying past him up the escalator to buy a last-minute present not noticing his quarry of so long ago. Customers are de-gloving and unscarfing themselves as they go, to feel the benefit later, busy normal people who hadn't run away, contented mentally-healthy people thinking nicely ahead for Christmas and ticking their secret if predictable lists as they went.

People without pain or fears, he sighed to himself, unable in his own pain to notice the sitters in the burdening wheelchairs, their even more burdened minders, the polystyrene neck collars, missing limbs, white sticks, hearing-aids, leg-braces, disfiguring birthmarks, grey glue-sniffers' pallor of

PAGING LYNCH MADISON

coming death, the damaged, the strange and the loony of the average day in Oxford Street.

He had become quite odd himself, he realised for the first time in four worried years.

At first, it had been relatively easy to disappear and continue giving nothing in return for nothing. Easy to become grossly selfish, his only fear that he might be discovered, dragged back and never have the courage to bugger off again.

Because except for the feeling he had had for Charlotte in flashes, he had been unaware what love or friendship felt like.

The Amorettis had been the first to damage that safe screen he had. They took the place of the family he should have been born to. He had felt loyalty and responsibility towards them. He would love to go to see them again, tell them how much they had meant to him. Bud and Chi, too. He'd felt affectionate interest in them - it had hurt seeing Chi and denying he knew her.

Then Vanda.

But Vanda.

She wouldn't go away. A sort of obsession.

Any look-alike back of head, chin, grin or hair-style, any sound-alike laughter, any over-full shoulder-bag made him yearn and grieve. In short, Lynch was no longer happy to be alone.

PAGING LYNCH MADISON

Well, good. He was growing up a little late, that's all. Now he needed someone, just like the rest of us.

Fine. That should take him rushing back to Crossbridge, to gather Jan up in his arms --- no. Lovely if it had worked out like that but it wasn't Jan he had grown up for. It was Vanda.

Maybe we believe he deserves at least the humiliation of facing himself in the role of having performed the gross misdemeanour of abandoning a life, abandoning quite a few people, simply to fancy another woman. That would seem to make him human, ordinary, mortal, normal.

We know that he is. But will he ever acknowledge it.

The passion, the lust for even one sighting of Vanda could be rationalised neatly; he needed a little more time to be past any regrets about the fascinating singer and could more easily handle moving on, if, after a few quick, and hopefully, disappointing glimpses of her, he had the opportunity to see her in the dull perspective of everyday life. He had, after all, only seen her at Amoretti's twice and beneath him once.

Any bimbo would suffice and be less trouble than Vanda for this little holiday trip to Luxembourg, return ticket, luxury hotel and dumping expenses paid, a goodbye wave all he'd have to cope with.

Vanda. How could London be so crowded with people and none of them be her, his silly mind

PAGING LYNCH MADISON

said to him all the same. How like the rest of us he is. Except that he carried our fantasies into reality.

Lynch was all in; almost at the end of his mobility. He stopped and leaned exhausted against a parking meter not sure he could go on, grimly nodding thanks-I'm-OK to the one man who stopped to ask him if he was all right. (This may be fiction but truly there is always someone, even in Oxford Street, who will stop and care.)

Nearly there. Two roads to the left and up the alley past the antiquarian bookshop that was sadly too grand to browse in.

In his belief that Stan had some sort of power to cure him, and with it some sort of power over him in general, there was a definite frisson that Stan might lead him to Vanda again, but also the terror that he might see through this Laurence Miller, question him under hypnosis and get him somehow 'sent back' to Jan.

Few people could be expected to understand Lynch's crazy and individual view of desertion. Was it easier to understand desperate men in the forces deserting their country than husbands deserting their wives? In war, when death seemed the only alternative, some chose life and hopped it – a cowardly act, they say. Now you've thought about it, is it so cowardly?

Desertion from marriage was also a disgrace, but he had chosen it rather than divorce to give Jan some pride. He'd prefer, for their sake, that it was never questioned that he had loved Jan and Charlotte. Waking from his cycling-coma and knowing how

PAGING LYNCH MADISON

wrong he was for them, he had done the decent thing and kindly deserted, leaving Jan's dignity intact, he thought.

His case rests. For now.

Round and round and round, these thoughts. He'd had them a hundred times until they became neater than they were, more plausible than they were, very nearly watertight. So, round and round and back to the end. He was never going home.

If his spine ever clicked back in again or whatever it had done before, he would sit down with an A4 narrow feint margin pad of 200 sheets, a black Pentel and not leave his seat until he had sorted out his future.

If Stan asked him outright if he was Lynch Madison, he would deny it blank-faced, as he had denied himself to Chi, and pass on, grimly hanging on to his sub-conscious which he had trained to jump only for Laurence Miller with Laurence Miller's lifestyle.

And if when he was unconscious he proved to be indiscreet, he would, if questioned, just act dumb hoping Stan's silence was obligatory by some hypnotist's version of the Hippocratic oath.

Goodbye England, he'd write at the top of the list. He hated the cold and the dark winter at four o'clock. Hated all the Laurence Millers who kept quiet in railway carriages and didn't laugh out loud anywhere. He'd been meaning to try somewhere else for a long while; somewhere that he could be Lynch out loud.

PAGING LYNCH MADISON

As the lift cage bumped and jerked him up to the fifth floor he went through countries alphabetically, swearing he'd go to the one that he had got to when the lift stopped but stuck on 'F', as it shuddered to stillness, he could only think of 'Finland' and wasn't that colder and darker than London.

"Cars," Stan sympathised contemptuously, still in the same track-suit, his hair surely even more yellow than it had been, "don't seem to be designed with real people in mind. There is never anywhere sensible to put a coat. No wonder you put your back out reaching for it. Have you had any trouble before? No?"

His face hadn't seemed to change but Laurence Miller kept a tight hold on his implacability.

"My success rate, Mr Miller? I don't really know. Now what course of treatment had you contemplated?"

Lynch booked himself in for the most expensive and exclusive course of sessions available and insisted on giving Stan a cheque in advance immediately. One debt repaid.

Going to the gents unblocked his brain a bit. 'F' for South of France, of course. And 'G' - of course. 'G' for Guyana. Bud's family owned half of Guyana. They would find him a job, a hut on the water - Guyana was on the sea, wasn't it? Bud was always talking about how easy the fishing was when he was a boy. Bud would find him some nice white-sanded

PAGING LYNCH MADISON

beach ---- He'd phone Bud. He could even go to see him. Explain himself. Tell all. Bud would listen. Bud would help. Maybe Lynch could persuade him to go with him, taking Chi back to his family in Guyana as a bride - clear the air --- Then, they'd send for Vanda. Clear as a video, he saw their two white bungalows built a friendly amount apart on those steady sands, children running free and welcome in the sun -----

Was he going crazy? Was living a lie really too much of a strain for his head?

Nonetheless a fog was lifting; he didn't need dumping-women and solitude. He needed something normal; a bunch of people he didn't have to lie to. Or not much, anyway.

This year he had been able to think clearly about his unique situation. He had proved the unfashionable theory that the only way to stop worrying about money was to have lots of it. He had appreciated that he was freer than almost anyone in the world. He had concluded glumly that freedom doesn't eliminate problems, it just breeds problems of a different strain.

He could be, do, go, sure enough. Lately, though, it had come to him that he was being eaten up with the need to be, go and do with Vanda. For however little time it lasted.

Lynch had hardly spoken to anyone in the last few months without privately interviewing them in his head for project suitability. But as his requirements centred on a fiercely individual independence, tempered, emphatically, by total

PAGING LYNCH MADISON

obedience to his whim, it was hard even to find candidates worthy to sit his examination, let alone pass it.

Vanda. He always pictured her singing, recklessly showing and giving everything of herself as she sang.

Just briefly, twice actually, his body had reminded him of her. Once before, not very seriously, he had considered finding her. Certainly if her manner had been genuine, she had shown an instant and healthy adoring preference for him. But her possessiveness, so noticeably much stronger even than Geraldine's quiet expectancies, was a killer. And maybe her mythical relentless sunniness would pall as well - everyone likes a little rain to water the flowers.

He had run his hands under the tap for a long time. Reluctant to go back to Stan.

Nerves.

After another tiny unsatisfactory trickle and another wash of the Lady Macbeths, he was over to the mirror to check that he was still Laurence Miller, mature yuppy, as he had been to Geraldine so successfully.

Today he was decidedly Laurence Miller, wealthy executive, hobbies, the theatre, chess, gliding. His family were in high-class international art, lived in Jersey for tax purposes and bombed around Europe a lot in boats.

PAGING LYNCH MADISON

Geraldine had been innocently pleased with the sound of it all; the art bit even more than the yacht. Always asking his opinion on anything the faintest bit decorative; her flat riddled, now, with his erratic tastes.

A nice girl. The sort of nice girl who reminds you of a very carefully furnished guest room. Well-designed, everything matching, clean and warm but usually empty.

Gird yourself Laurence Miller. Lynch's back is killing him. He opened the door and walked hopefully, painfully back into Stan's ashram.

"What do they call you?" Stan said, serious again in a matching new chair opposite to him.

Lynch went cold. "I told you. Laurence."

"I mean never 'Larry?'" Stan said quietly. "No? Right, Laurence. You look very worried. Is something worrying you?"

"Well this is all jolly strange, really," Lynch improvised. "I mean I'm not really the hypnotism type, if you know what I mean. But frankly, how I feel, I'll try anything. But, you know - frankly I'm a bit sceptical. And what happens if I 'come round' as you put it and my back's completely better? I mean, I won't need the whole course then, will I?"

"That's a healthy attitude," Stan said, smoothly not answering. "Just leave everything to me."

PAGING LYNCH MADISON

And much as before, when he woke he was dying of thirst, (though able, as Laurence Miller, to accept two glasses of juice,) and worse than before, he was this time in noticeably more pain than when he had come in.

"How do you feel?" Stan asked, watching his face as he moved awkwardly to the door.

"Bloody awful," Lynch said, doing a stoicism suitable to his imaginery high-status rather well.

Stan came all the way down with him to put him in the cab they had called for. (Paying customers, Lynch had noticed, in the last year, get these extras as of right.)

They found little to say to each other and were both relieved when the cab pulled up and the driver shouted "Miller?"

Stan opened the door and handed him in. "See you same time on Wednesday, Mr Miller," he said. The cab door was slammed shut but didn't quite slam enough to fasten it fully. So Stan opened it a little again for a second try and smiled at Lynch's knees. "Vanda doesn't work for me anymore, by the way. But you're right. Bud will know where she is, Mr Madison."

Slam.

PAGING LYNCH MADISON
CHAPTER FIVE

"I hope you're not in a hurry, guv," the cabby said, when Lynch finally came out of shock and owned up that his destination was the Fontainbleau Hotel in Sussex Gardens.

"Know what I mean, if you look on the map it's a dead straight line, no problem, but what with the bleeding one- ways and 'specially tonight, soddin' Irish, there's the protest - you read about it? Yeah. Bleedin' Irish. You're not Irish are yer?   Soddin' Irish. Roads blocked, diversions, all that. I should've turned off me light and gone 'ome but I never learn. Let's see now. We can go-------"

"Bayswater? Holland Park?"

"Yeah, yeah, I can do you that. Right round in a big square but yeah -"

"No, I mean, skip Sussex Gardens. Make it Holland Park. Commonwealth Institute."

"Bleedin' women," he muttered, failing to hesitate for a procrastinating young woman with a pram. "Bleedin' bikers," he shouted, pulling out blindly in front of a motor-bike courier who swerved and two-fingered him. "Bleedin' diplosods," he screamed out of his window, sweetly cutting up a flag-flying bonnet.

PAGING LYNCH MADISON

It was quiet, waiting on the one mercifully hard high-backed African bench in the tiny lobby, watching the worried, "I've-only-been-here-two-days" security guard try any number of extensions, run a worried finger down a lot of lists and then give it up and volunteer to go up in the lift himself and see if anyone there knew where Bud and Chi were to be found.

"They've left," he said, when the lift door opened again and he got out, not so hot or worried or desperate once he had found that it wasn't his fault that they couldn't be found.

"People come and go here a lot, they tell me," he confided, smiling. "Maybe they all go back where they came from. If you will wait, a person who worked with your friend is due back and they say he knows where one of them works now."

The non-meeting of nations strolled endlessly out through the lobby, cases in hand saying 'night' to the guard and sighing as they took the exit to real life.

The machine coffee the guard brought him in embarrassment at his long wait was a dull not very hot gift and Lynch was stiffening with the ache of himself.

Meanwhile even the security guard's kindness was vanishing in his desire to get home when a few more ticks of the over-loud clock and Bud's friend arrived back late and in a very obvious hurry.

PAGING LYNCH MADISON

He was a very stout, very dark, very black muffled-up man crossing the hall at great speed for the lift when the guard called out for him to stop and answer Lynch's questions.

Quickly, he turned and answered them from a distance and without interest, looking longingly at the lift doors, but mercifully with the full information Lynch had waited for.

"You'll have to use the stairs, sir," the guard called. We're turning the lifts off now."

Lynch watched the fat man draw a breath, turn the other way and saw with envy how he two-at-a-timed up the steps in furious haste, thanked the guard and stiffly, agonisingly, bluffed his own body outside to hail another cab.

Hardly more than just conscious from the pain, now, Lynch got out and paid outside the amazing shop in Lisle Street with the Chinese calligraphy brushes and stopped to marvel at them first before girding himself for the steps up the side of the grubby music-shop next door. The neat neon announced itself as the Star Singers' Agency (Personal Management Guaranteed) and the carpet was expensive and at the top of the stairs, the office was smart and very white.

"Chi is usually right," Bud said, quietly pleased, putting a lot of affection into a very short hand-shake. "She insisted it was you in the theatre even with those silly glasses. Don't go anywhere. I will come out again to you after I have seen this --- gentleman here." He held Lynch's hand just a warm moment longer. "Please wait."

PAGING LYNCH MADISON

He turned to the gold-spurred riding boots with the gold toe-caps with the extravagantly decorated motorbike jacket and the gorgonian hairdo to apologize politely for keeping him waiting.

Boots, who apparently spoke crude taboo fluently as his first language, indicated in his native obscenity that he'd been kept waiting for far too long by this particularly Asian person and it had better not happen again or painful atrocities might occur.

Lynch, in facial retaliation, indicated to Bud that he was willing to mash the bastard but Bud smiled maturely and ushered Boots into his office as if he, like me, was welcomed with exemplary affection. "Half an hour?" Bud said over his shoulder before he closed the door. "If you are not here - please be here."

Lynch checked himself. That was some brotherly love he was feeling, wasn't it? Or was he going queer? Or was the emotion he felt nothing more than a loosening of the brain-box at the thought of another wait, the pain just about unbearable and no more painkillers on him.

Posters of good Lord, Boots, were everywhere. Posters of equally gross looking guys and girls, all with lunatic hairdressers. One of stunning Chinese sisters. All of them signed to Chi and Bud. All of them printed 'Star Singers Agency, Great Britain.' No Vanda, though. No posters of Vanda. Had they signed her that night? Had she proved to be just a flash in the throat?

PAGING LYNCH MADISON

Deep carpet, clever lighting, good design. An abandoned telephone system set for automatic night answering. And hey. Behind the desk a coffee-machine. Turned off but not as long ago as at the Commonwealth Institute from the feel of the jug. He could only see a dirty plastic cup but was too much in pain to worry and filled it with the bitter hottish liquid, drank it and took another one back to the window.

Outside in the street, the Chinese herbalists and grocery shops and the art shops and the restaurants were busy with early evening customers, hurrying before the theatre or unwinding with relief after their work.

Cabbage stalks, orange peel, leaflets, rubbish shiny from the rain in the gutters, cars parking gratefully in the muck, a child crying loud enough to be heard up here in the office, contented moggies strolling through this Ritz for cats.

You couldn't lose yourself in Soho, Lynch reflected. It was somehow very obviously intimate. Beautiful young Chinese everywhere, their ugly old mothers and fathers indistinguishable from their grandparents.

Bud, his busy little steps enharmonic with the spur-jangling ahead of him, seemed barely able to part with Boots at the door. Boots called out one final, you could only guess, affectionate vulgarity as he left and Bud waved a warm wave down the stairs.

"My first world tour, he is," Bud said, smugly, turning to Lynch as Boots' spurs echoed down the staircase, "it takes a lot of fixing."

PAGING LYNCH MADISON

"So will I," Lynch said, out of love already and waiting sulkily for Bud's full attention to return to him. "My back. I've no bloody pills."

Here it came. Bud looked at him very straight, very clearly. "We will have a lot to talk about, I presume," Bud said, raising his eyebrows and the telephone handset at the same time. "First, you need medicine. Tablets? Tell me their name. Again?"

Into the phone Bud told someone to buy them at once, to bring the car round also at once and finally, at once, to book a table for two at eight at Claridges.

"Two? What about Chi?"

"Later."

Then Bud sat opposite Lynch, behind the reception desk, making himself separate, completely still, absolutely silent. It was quite intentionally unfriendly, the unspoken rule seeming to be that the distance must remain unbroken until the telephone rang.

Unable to keep still, unable to move, annoyed and bored with all the waiting, Lynch's eyes closed and his head jerked forward.

When the message came that missions were accomplished, Bud woke him and handed him the tablets. Grabbing and swallowing down two with addictive haste, Lynch now let Bud help him down

PAGING LYNCH MADISON

the steps which seemed to have been banked steeper than ever and into the warm waiting car.

Lynch winced with the fear of being fussed too much when both the driver and Bud brought him a back-support from the boot which they jogged and teased with until he agreed that it helped, whether it did or not.

If things got worse, the driver said, there was also a wheelchair at the back hard by the tool box, torch, lap-robe, bottle-opener, half set of golf-clubs and world atlas.

Silence again until the car was driving smoothly in the heavy traffic of New Bond Street, by which time Lynch was drugged enough, to think about something other than how to sit, when the faint discomfort which was all that was left, became nearly a pleasure and he sighed a bit and settled down.

Bud pulled up the glass divider and sat sideways to look at Lynch again.

"Better? Good. We need privacy. This is why I have chosen Claridges. The phones are behind thick doors. I may need privacy to make our future arrangements."

Bud always spoke flatly - a linguistic problem, presumably - but this voice had been especially smoothed with a trowel.

"Thanks for making all the arrangements,'" Lynch said, getting expansive as the pain wore off, "but why such cloak and dagger?"

PAGING LYNCH MADISON

"A man with two lives must have secret," he said, coldly.

"You sound like a fortune cookie," Lynch laughed, but there was no response at all.

At the hotel, Bud sent the driver off, giving him a return time and walked straight into one of the telephone boxes which he was quite right about - very thick doors - how had he known that?

Though he stood closely outside, Lynch could hear not a whisper of the three calls Bud made. What part of Bud's blameless life had led him to need these secrecy skills?

Bud scurried in front of him to the restaurant entrance. The head waiter agreed to everything, calling him familiarly by his name a dozen times as Bud informed him exactly where they would be in the lounge when their table was ready and that it couldn't be too soon.

After a glass of Perrier, two slices of lemon, three chunks of immaculate ice, a third pill and the outrageous bill lying quietly between them, Lynch was soon euphoric with relief.

With a handful of cashew nuts at the halfway to being thrown neatly into the mouth position, Lynch considered the way to begin to explain himself. Would he be forced to explain how bitterly he had regretted leaving Bud and Chi and Vanda and the Amorettis and the best part of his life so far. Did he have to confess how he had used Geraldine like a rag to soak up his regret?

PAGING LYNCH MADISON

Before he could work out a plausible formula, (something to establish his sympathy first, "my back can't even be operated on, whatever shall I do?" Then swiftly in with the "by the way, do you ever see Vanda?") their table was obediently ready.

Thanks to the pills, he could ease out of this one seat with reasonable dignity and sit comfortably in the next banquette they were allowed to hide in.

"So."

When you have kept anything secret for long enough, there is an understandable reluctance ever to share it at all and in this case, a heavy penalty lay over the telling. Solitary confinement, in fact. So. Lynch had to speak yet he must be careful to put himself in the best light possible. But Bud spoke before he could begin.

"It makes me very sad," Bud said. "It makes me sad that it is so difficult for you to begin to tell me. All the time that I know you, that we play music together, I think you are the person that I see and really you are somebody else. I do not like that."

A courteous way of saying that when you find some so-called friend has been lying all the time you've known them, you begin to hate them.

Lynch must now open in his own defence in the most gentle and persuasive way and still his lips are stuck together.

Saved for a moment by the grand arrival of the melba toast, the two men kept still whilst the

PAGING LYNCH MADISON

young waiter who had perceived that they were too impotent to spread their own napkins shook out the pink starched squares and lowered them into deferential place.

A little more time won by the sound effects of the fragile papery toast crunching and snapping under the hardness of the over-cooled butter, and more as iced water was poured for them from the pitcher. Still silent as the hot rolls and garlic mushrooms were served.

"Enjoy your meal, sirs," the waiter improvised, the latest thing in British restaurantese, the language having failed to provide us with a 'bon appetite' of our own.

Pushing the tines of his fork viciously down into the gills of the second hot redolent mushroom, Lynch rose in the witness box and spoke.

"I walked out on my wife and child. On all my family. On everyone I'd ever known. I deliberately disappeared, three and a half years ago. I used to be a man called Leslie Merrett."

Bud continued to eat very carefully and slowly through the whole of his plate of pungent fungus while Lynch's forkful and its brothers congealed, forgotten, as he drew out from his overcrowded conscience every dreadful bloodstained piece of evidence against himself. Once started, no longer anxious to give himself the finest defence, he was abruptly more concerned to clean out the dirtiest corners and have every single axe-stroke taken into consideration. Charlotte. Christmas. Dawn. Jo. Even Geraldine. The debt he

PAGING LYNCH MADISON

owed the Amorettis. Their band. Everything. Except what he had done to Vanda.

Waiters came and went. Crockery rang, cutlery chimed, glasses filled and emptied and still he talked.

Bud abruptly leaned nastily across the table.

"What you have done is obscene and unforgiveable," he said."

Even said so calmly, imperturbably, it hurt. Bud continued poking out any bits of Lynch's dignity still preserved and stamping on them excessively hard.

"In the four further years, did you say, that your wife must wait before she is free again, your child and she will grow to hate you more every day."

"I know what I've done, Bud."

"Your wife and your daughter must be pointed to in the streets every day like freaks in a circus. Your wife wakes up every morning hoping that today she will be told that you are dead and she will be glad."

"I know, I know."

"How can you know and do nothing?"

"Because Leslie Merrett died ten years ago," Lynch shouted, covering the extra loudness he hadn't intended with a cough and lowering his voice. "I suddenly walked out on myself, Bud. But it was

PAGING LYNCH MADISON

anything but a crazy instant. I thought it over so long until I felt sick like I'd been over-eating. You must have seen quite a bit of divorce, haven't you? Your family? Never? Well, your friends? Yes? So did I. And I don't think that's terribly pleasant or friendly or easy. Death's the best because it's final and everyone can weep and start again. But I didn't know how to fake my own death."

"What you did is worse. What you did will --- well, heaven will know what it will do."

"I know."

Lynch pushed away his rightly pink rack of lamb, too tired to fight with it, the mint sauce piquant with Sundays at home, friends arriving, friends not arriving, Jan worried either way, Charlotte's eyes shining with laughter, Leslie Merrett certainly sitting at the table seemingly alive and chewing a perfectly baked potato but already vacant, silent, absent.

"You may need psychiatric help. I don't want to go travelling with a crazy man," Bud said.

"I'm not crazy. I've made a crazy choice, that's all. Travelling? What travelling?"

"Totally crazy. I don't know how long Chi and I will be together but if I decide to leave her I'll certainly ---"

"Shit, Bud." Lynch was holding down his fury with both hands. "If I have to I'll go back to being on my own. It's always been like that for me. I never had normal friendships till the Amorettis and you and Chi, not even Jan at our best times.

PAGING LYNCH MADISON

"Anyway," Lynch suddenly spotted the raw edge of a chink of a counter-attack and went for it. "Both you and Chi have walked out on your own families." Game and set.

Bud put the nine peas round his two carrots until it was a perfect circle. "Our families know where we are and their lives go on uninterrupted - by agony," he said in a frozen voice.

"Oh balls. You know what? You and Chi might turn out to be just too prissy for me. You and Chi - you're probably not so special. I'll find other - -- I don't expect you to lower yourself to the level of some bastard like me, some crazy - who's messed up a few lives around him including his ----- "

Bud nodded gravely, as if happier now that Lynch was losing control. He spent time concentrating on the sole that had been skilfully filleted for him and filleted it fussily a little more, taking irritating little mouthfuls and chewing them thoroughly.

"Jan might be OK with someone who loves her, Bud, that's what I thought. I never did. Love her, I mean. And nobody ever loved me."

Bud ate quietly on until a last small piece of roe had been examined, found fit, placed in the waiting mouth, masticated and the cutlery laid to rest.

A little time for Lynch to be able to bear what he had just said.

A little more to recover from the intense pain.

PAGING LYNCH MADISON

"Leslie Merrett was never loved?" Bud said.

Lynch shook his head. Negative.

"Lynch Madison is different," Bud announced, wiping the sides of his mouth with the pink napkin very very carefully. Even through Lynch's boiling empathetic emotions, he registered a warning to himself that a lot of things that Bud did could drive him wild.

"Lynch Madison is loved." Bud said, looking extra Asian, giving nothing more, excusing himself off to the telephone again and left Lynch for a great length of time, enough for him to conquer the overwhelming need to cry into the pink napkin, enough to feel miraculously cut-down-from-the-gallows yet still fearfully looking behind him for the posse and the vigilantes. Bud was gone a long time.

"I had to make three calls," Bud said. "First the police tell me that what you have done is not a criminal matter - of course I did not give your name."

"I know that. Why didn't you ask me? What is this? And what travelling were you talking about? You must realise that nobody - nobody tells me what to do or where to go. That's the point."

Bud gave him an "is it really" look and Lynch almost suspected that Bud was enjoying the impotence of his anger but was too angry to spit that out.

PAGING LYNCH MADISON

Bud made him wait while he called for another coffee, wait whilst he drank it, wait until he had signed the credit slip.

"Another call was to Chi," he said briefly. "Don't forget you also walked out on us two years ago. She was very upset. And I was. Very."

Was Vanda? Ask. Ask.

"She couldn't sleep after she saw you in the theatre. Now, the reason you left us - this you still have not given. But of course we know."

Vanda's writhing lusting body lay in full view on the bed in front of their eyes as they stared at each other.

Was the third call to Vanda? Ask now. Mention Vanda now.

Too late. Bud was standing. "The car is waiting," he said briefly, "and so is Chi. We need, she said to me, to sit and talk with you. I have told her a little and she has agreed that you may come now to our home."

Out on Brook Street, in the drizzle, hurrying to catch his Inter-City bus on his way back to Crossbridge from the American Embassy where he'd been doing quite an interesting visa check, B. Carfax stood back to let a small oriental person and a tall thin man enter the big limo door that was being held open for them by a Claridges doorman and sighed, once again, at the inequality of life.

PAGING LYNCH MADISON

Inside the car, Lynch was sighing too, uneasy, worried at being so vulnerable again, his secrets finally exposed. It was done. Now he must face whatever songs and dances lay ahead. Whatever travelling Bud meant, he was just too tired to ask.

When they got to the flat, Bud made no attempt to unlock the door, indicating that Lynch should ring the bell.

A set-up.

Vanda opened the door.

"Lynch, Lynch."

Lynch's hands flicked through his file-o-feel as she flung herself at him. She felt lovely. Lovelier than all the other bodies he had felt legitimately, illicitly, or lately. None of Dawn's flatness. None of Jo's wide ribcage, none of Geraldine's angles. None of Geraldine's admirable dignity and restraint, either.

"You shouldn't have gone off like that," Vanda whispered sweetly, on tiptoe, opening his jacket, running her hands round his middle, kissing his chin and his face so far as she could reach, giving his body no time to switch into neuter.

"I thought Bud and Chi would never forgive you. But for me - there was nothing to forgive," she said. "Darling," she said.

Knickers on a moose-head she was going to be hard to hide in his baggage and bloody impossible to unload when it was time to.

PAGING LYNCH MADISON

He reached down and kissed her self-consciously on the cheek then with real emotion again, seeing Chi over her shoulder, unable to feel enough regret, helpless, his face shamefully wet, speechless.

Bud watched Lynch greet Chi, watched him not know what to say or do with either her or Vanda or himself. Bud was watching all of them fail to form anything more than an awkward miserable clump and it seemed to cheer him up.

Chi, who had stood back for a moment to consider Lynch with serious reflection, also embraced him shyly, but without speaking went away again, returning with the familiar pot of jasmine tea in a cane-handled pot and the handleless cups that went with it, putting it round the places at the table on white mats, with her familiar stillness and dignity. Too much for Lynch.

He left the table, went over to the slatted blind at the big window and pulled the cord to the open position.

London, who had been following Lynch for a long time knowing that he would, in the end, make some silly move, stared in, suspicious but dispassionate.

The kind of tears that don't wet the face travelled from one place to another inside him giving the worst sort of pain as he blew his nose and stared back at the plain-clothes lamp-post.

Lynch Madison, human being, had been found out.

PAGING LYNCH MADISON

If he had now to tell his story, must he include all the details of all his secrets? Even his padlocked, real final reason for leaving Jan the way he did? No. No. And the fear that pushed him to do the same, but not the same, to these, his first friends?

To keep private those details only, he must submit, if that was what they chose to do to him, to any amount of punishment from Chi's rubber truncheon, from Bud's stretching rack, from Vanda grimly removing his shoes, socks and toenails.

But his other secrets? Were they really so precious? His belief that he had been swapped at birth with the real Lynch Madison? His stash in Luxembourg? His false passport? His wild foggy plans for the far future? To unlock those vaults, there would be no need for dripping taps or sleep deprivation.

These things would take their natural places at this most extraordinary meeting, listed on its strange agenda, presumably.

These three strangers seemed to have voted themselves the core of the secret society Lynch had waited four years to hunt and gather with.

Why them? An internationally unstable bunch of rebellious foreigners, none of whom had been wanted at home, till they'd left. None of whom had anything, except music, in common. All of them about to plight some dreadful sort of troth, (whatever a troth was) and by doing so, they would each lose the complete freedom that had been so hard won by each in their determined individual ways.

PAGING LYNCH MADISON

He looked back at the table. They looked absorbed, drinking tea, nibbling almonds. Neither waiting for him, nor lost without him. A good lesson. To themselves they were each as important as he thought himself. Of course. He had invented Lynch Madison and they had invented themselves too.

Bang the slats of the blind blindingly back over London's raised eyebrows and craning neck.

And as he turned Lynch knew his back had righted itself again. He pivoted. Punched the air. Bent and stretched. Yeah. Wow.

A wave of excitement that nearly sunk him floated him back to the table where the conspirators took in his re-appearance without comment.

"My back's back again," he glowed, "Whatever we do, Stan had better be in on it. I went to Stan. He did it again. He said --"

Disconcerted by the strangeness of the waiting silence, Lynch stopped.

Then as if unable ever to stop again, he sketched out those pieces of the last nearly-four years he wanted them to see, sometimes filling in background, more often leaving an outline to explain, right down to his present occupancy of the Fontainbleau's worst room.

He stood back to give them the full effect.

PAGING LYNCH MADISON

Quite a dark picture; their own appearance in it constituting the highlights and lively part of the composition.

Sensational, in its way.

The questions started slowly, then picked up momentum, Lynch passionate now to spill as many beans as he could afford, Vanda and Chi anxious to soften his beans into an understandable stew, wanting to know a thousand intimate things ---

Bud stopped them quite sharply and refused to let Lynch continue.

"Enough," he said. "Now we speak only of the future," he said blandly.

Bud was speaking not vaguely poetically but seriously literally; their pasts were now to be utterly private, no peeking.

Childish, naive, unworkable but the relief of tension in the room was massive. Only Lynch couldn't sit still and irritatingly paced and fussed and picked up objects and put them down and paced and paced until Chi, of all people, became irritated enough by it to shout stop.

No more tonight or they might burst some part of the new bright balloon they were carrying together.

Bud and Chi pulled out the sofa-bed, handed them sheets, pillows, duvet, towels and embracing them swiftly were gone, the door shutting loud and definite behind them.

PAGING LYNCH MADISON

Lynch felt that the wide bed was childishly leering and winking at them.

"We don't have to use that," he said nodding at it, hands in his pocket, feeling a fool, looking at his watch. Scarcely ten o'clock and the whole night ahead.

"Don't be crazy," Vanda said, lying flat on the bed, taking off her shoes and wiggling her clean small feet in his direction for his attention. "Leslie Merrett and Laurence Miller are completely dead?" she said, her eyes shining with the excitement of her new knowledge of him.

Lynch shrugged, no intention of discussing that part of his life with her, but sitting next to her glumly.

Miraculously, he had been restored to Vanda's side. She was the chosen accomplice he had searched for. She must and would always understand his every blink, his tiniest nuance.

"I never," he said, luxuriously literate, masterfully mysterioso, "turn to the last page of a book I'm reading, to see how it comes out."

Wonderfully put. Lynch supposed it was largely because Vanda could understand these convoluted things that he said without a lot of silly linking conversation that he had been so attracted to her.

"What do you mean?" she said frowning.

PAGING LYNCH MADISON

Lynch sometimes hated women. He hitched himself over, lay beside her and closed his eyes. Vanda must wait a minute while he dealt with the over-full filing basket that had suddenly been pushed into his head.

He had often dwelt on that last-minute phone-call he had made to Jan to come and join him at the Red Lion, (though he had actually been calling from a garage one mile, they told him, from the bus-station.)

Jan's fault, not taking his last offer. It had sometimes comforted him that he had given her that one last chance and as usual she had let it go by.

He remembered how he had bought a tuna and cucumber sandwich and a drink at the garage, eaten and drunk half, put the rest in the saddle bag and cycled on.

He hadn't planned on that bicycle giving him a shove over the last hurdle.

Coming round from the accident, exceedingly wet from the rain and sticky from the half of the drink that seemed to be everywhere on him, the fact of having absolutely nothing inside his head had been most refreshing for the while that it had lasted, he remembered that clearly.

And that tiny short memory loss, too, had been an unlooked-for ally. He could easily fake and plead 'amnesia' whenever the scent got too close.

PAGING LYNCH MADISON

There had still been choices in that December. For quite a few weeks he felt he still had the choice of going back.

Anyone would have understood that from the natural progression of the good Leslie's accident, there might well have been a very easily understood brief loss of memory, which could have been followed by a remarkable recovery.

Till his neck was reasonably mobile again, when the cuts and bruises were healing, at that stage he could have made mincemeat of his past in a much more understandable way.

He could have made a second wonderful telephone call ("Hallo, darling, it's Leslie) and made them happy again. He could have removed Jan's burden the easy way. He could have explained in what ways he was unhappy and why he'd gone off on his bike and Jan, rather than be without him for ever, would have agreed to almost anything.

There would have been a tear-jerking reunion they would never forget.

That's how it could have been.

But bad Lynch Madison had loaded his guns and was on the run. Bad Lynch knew where the detonators were in the libraries and with a bit of research had collected enough additional weapons from the missing persons' books and memory disorder section to make him too powerful to fear any posse the good Leslie could rustle up.

PAGING LYNCH MADISON

It forced a tight silence and a sort of anxiety tic on him for days, while he worked out his schemes and took the courage to carry them out.

The books taught him one inconvenient thing. He seemed to need an accomplice. Successful dematerialisations happened more successfully with someone you could trust, the case histories told him. Someone you could trust, quite literally, with your life.

Inside the good Leslie's head, clusters and groups of memory and knowledge kept flying in, happily refiling themselves inside his head; his life as a child, his schools, stolen kisses in cinemas, Sunday walks. Blameless life in Crossbridge and the Rotary life he led. Professional safety in his father-in-law's willing shelter. The return to the clarinet, the lessons, the total inability to share one small scrap of anything deep with Jan. No accomplice there.

Charlotte, he reasoned, wouldn't remember him in a year or so and quick, quick, think of the future before pictures of little girls playing with bubble-bath and little girls singing at school concerts and little girls in shorts laughed in trees.

Jan would one day be grateful for this. An ordinary divorce might have been arranged but he felt that that opened too many doors to their friends and families to see his best kept secret. Nobody, least of all Jan, had known how bored and miserable he had been with his life to date and this grand strange disappearance, he was sure, would save her the hurt of ever knowing. It would even give a sort of mystique to her that had been one of the things she had, for his true taste, lacked.

PAGING LYNCH MADISON

Hm.

You will have noted that Leslie Merrett, Laurence Miller and Lynch Madison were bright, if varingly selfish men, so it is hard to understand how they could pretend that this wildly inaccurate theory and warped philosophy of life was enough to clear the account with any normal conscience. Perhaps after all the accident had caused more brain disturbance than has been recorded and allowed for. They had maybe crushed and cubed his logic along with his weakened neck and his shattered bike.

So, heavenly accountants, charge the pain of 'never-knowing-why' direct to Jan Merrett, her of the sudden insomnia and depression until she has paid off. Till the passing of the years fix her, as with superglue, whole but a little cracked.

"Lynch do you mind if I say something?"

Just a minute, Vanda. One last thought.

Lynch had just remembered that the first hazy picture that his returning memory had brought him had been the pyjama-smelling Leslie-ish pyjamas beneath the pillow he had left in the home he had left.

At the time he had felt surging joy. He felt great freedom and even now, thinking about it again, the heart beat fast. He knew he would never be forced to own a pair of pyjamas again. Lynch Madison was a man who would never think of wearing them. Women - or would it only be Vanda, now, would like that.

PAGING LYNCH MADISON

"What, Vanda?" Lynch turned just his face towards her.

At last. Vanda, standing for offended womanhood, will face him with his inhumanity towards her and we can all sleep a little easier in our beds. Good. This is where Lynch gets some of what is coming to him.

"Lynch?"

Lynch is prepared for it and sits up a little higher prepared to take it and defend his position the best he can.

"Um?"

"It has to be discussed," Vanda said, leaning up on her elbow to face where he lay relaxed if cautious. True. Lynch hoped it wouldn't hurt for too long and braced himself.

"What you did was admirable, in a way," she said, full one hundred per cent smile in place.

Lynch, the much admired rapist, waited wisely for more from the sweet lips of his victim before committing himself.

"I don't think Bud and Chi appreciate what courage it must have taken. Just to walk out."

Oh, that.

"Never to go back, never to explain. I mean most people would have justified themselves. Written a thousand letters of explanation, held a

PAGING LYNCH MADISON

zillion post-mortems. It takes style, panache to just say enough is enough and phhttt!"

Bizarre as the situation was, lying still, next to this crazy disciple, Lynch couldn't help wanting any amount more of this healing balm rubbed on his aching conscience. So he waited again.

"I mean, like to actually do it. Jeez, like who hasn't wanted to, sometime or other. It's sort of exciting. Even if you do it again and leave, er, again - you really make me feel as if, well, exciting things could happen any time, do you know what I mean? I mean, I feel really excited right now."

Lynch looked at her. He knew what feeling really excited was, yes. He sighed.

Handling a woman was so easy. And it was so difficult. This particular woman happened to be the current woman he wanted to get excited for; and they were conveniently in situ on a bed for heaven's sake. She was free and absolutely willing, he was free too - given his freedom by her consent.

But did he really want a triumph quite so easy? It was a matter of self-respect. It was also a matter of self-preservation. In the last two years, when he hadn't been around, someone as compliant as Vanda must have creased a hundred sheets.

A shame if he had to lose Bud and Chi along with her but even that might have to be faced. Was it all right these days to ask the woman of your fantasies for some certificate of sexual harmlessness?

PAGING LYNCH MADISON

"Will you understand, Vanda. I can't stay here tonight," Lynch said, swinging his weary legs on to the floor. "We need some thinking time. Right?"

More than crazy. He'd been waiting, longing for her for two years and there she was sitting up in front of him, a hooked plaice, half-embarrassed with obvious disappointment, frowningly trying to understand what she might have done wrong.

"You're right," she said, brightening. "I feel inhibited here too. Every little squeak. Yes, of course I understand. The Amoretti's have given me Annetta's room. Did you know she's married? Come there with me."

"I think, Vanda, if you're wise, you'll let me go tonight. We've had a strangely back-to-front courtship. I'd sort of like to start again." Whichever way he said it, Lynch knew it sounded phoney but there you are, it was real and Vanda bought it.

So there he was: packing again. Packing up. That's what freedom seemed to be about since he'd had it. Packing up, moving out, moving on, hurting people, leaving people, lacunae healing up behind him.

"Yes," said Vanda gravely. "OK," she said, pulling the duvet high over her shoulders in one swift movement. "You go. If I don't see you again - "

Was she blowing him a kiss, a raspberry, snuffling, crying, cursing him? He didn't stay to find out.

PAGING LYNCH MADISON

But when he stepped out into the drizzle of his so-called hotel in Sussex Gardens in the morning, Vanda was waiting outside for him in a dull grey 2CV with a bright idea.

PAGING LYNCH MADISON
CHAPTER SIX

"Use the bathplug when you shampoo your hair each time, can't you?" Lynch said, picking woven sludgy spiderwebs of dark curly hair one at a time from the bath-drain with a large unwound paperclip.

"Jeez, Lynch, do me a favour, I'd quite like the bathroom to myself," Vanda said, in her second-best French knickers, leg up on the towel-rail, filing a snagged toenail, "fuss with that some other time, why don't you?"

"I'm fussing because I presume you don't particularly want half a bath of scummy water left here when you get up in the morning. Someone has to clear it. All you have to do is at least be grateful. The bloody thing's completely blocked and the hair that's blocking it isn't mine."

"We're living together, Lynch. You have to put up with these things. We both do," she said, standing on both tiny feet now, waiting for him to notice her provoking half-bareness and forgive her everything.

"No Vanda, we aren't living together," Lynch said, as the paperclip broke upwards into his hand, swearing ferociously, though it had only scratched him very slightly. "I've only moved in here

PAGING LYNCH MADISON

temporarily while I think things over. I'm grateful but that's all."

He walked out. He returned with a second paperclip, he unbent that one and furiously finishing the laborious clearing of the matted hair, waited until the water swirled successfully, gurglingly down.

He ran the water to clear the scum, wiped round with cleanser, sprayed it away, wiped it dry and left it shiny with cleanliness and shut the door annoyingly quietly behind him.

At the beginning it had seemed to them that whilst they had been parted, their fantasies had been similar.

Prince Lynch would return and kiss the sleeping Princess Vanda awake.

Where the prince and princess had been sleeping in the interim would be no part of the fairytale.

Then they would go somewhere warm, make love most of the time and make music their life. ("Not you, darling," Vanda laughed in her throat. "You'll starve." But Lynch had been prepared to overlook such talk at the time.)

But in reality there were new choices to make. He had quite fallen in love with being Lynch Madison. It was the best person he'd ever been. But lamentably weakly, the Lynch part of him needed this peculiar Vanda to complement him and she was becoming increasingly hard to balance in his new account system.

PAGING LYNCH MADISON

On the sunny side, it was good sharing his fears and hopes openly again and it had been good having someone to laugh with.

On the shady side, Lynch had been freer when he could spend time in his own way, keeping his own counsel, taking his aura to bed with him. There was no-one to please but Lynch - and certainly no one else's blocked drains to clean.

He heard the toilet flush, heard the tap run and run, Vanda humming as she cleaned her teeth, the soft sounds of the bathroom and the faintly enervating erotic whiff of the body-cream she used almost everywhere, all this leaked out to him.

On yet a third side, it had been quite good, too, to have someone care for him so much.

Nevertheless, he must stay firm in his resolve to be separate.

"No-one," Lynch said, firm as can be, a few minutes later, over at Vanda's side of the rather narrow double-bed where she sat, "ever belongs to anyone."

"Of course not, querido," Vanda murmured diplomatically, as her mind was, in any case, sensuously somewhere else, the room filled with the scent of herself and the roses she treated them to every Friday, the moonlight friendly on their warm limbs, "you're right."

But she knows and we know that only men believe that.

PAGING LYNCH MADISON

"I'm happy to be here with you, Vanda," he said, a little later, when their breathing was normal again, and he had been able to remember what he had wanted to be saying , "but ------"

'But', as ever, being a lever and a wedge and a scaffold and an axe and an escape route and a hiding-place and an impediment to justice.

"-- but I can't stay here sponging off the Amorettis any longer."

He meant he needed his own space and not Vanda's.

Vanda understood what he was trying to say perfectly well and so do we. So it seems important to stop for a moment here to marvel at the hugely imaginative leap from the five grunts of our ancestral caveman that meant I'm hungry, I'm frightened, I'm in pain, I'm happy, I'm in love, to the miserable and lengthy conversations of the modern human being.

"You're right, querido. Where shall we go?" the very up-to-date and tri-lingual Vanda says, turning into the circle of his now rather unwilling arms.

"Nor, for that matter, can I bear to sponge off you, Vanda - be quiet. I'm taking everything from all of you. Bud, Chi, you. That isn't what I came back for. I've let the rope go slack lately. I have to make my own money and not do this ridiculous errand running for Bud in exchange for pocket-money then coming home, lying to the Amorettis and sleeping in your bed."

PAGING LYNCH MADISON

"I'm making plenty of money, you know that, querido," Vanda muttered. "But if you want we'll look for a really grand apartment and you can find a real job. You buy the business paper. You know? Like New Musical Express is for me and my singing? The paper for architects. Everywhere all the time they build houses."

She stopped and looked up at him. "Am I as special to you, querido, as you are to me? I mean, like, are we special? I mean, like Bud and Chi? You know? Will we, will we ever make it?"

Lynch turned out the light and whispered back little reassuring sentences, little inaccuracies, little nips and tweaks.

These conversations in the dark are endlessly fascinating and absorbing at the time if painful in retrospect. They are at their best within the warm few hours that follow good friendly love-making and are best attempted by script-writers, poets and other experienced liars. They should only be taken seriously for very short periods of time. If the symptoms persist, most lovers consult a reputable travel-agent.

However, there is a limit to how many times even a disappearing man like Lynch can vanish overnight.

So he stayed in Vanda's bed, holding her lightly till she was asleep, stroking her dark tangled hair, whilst he kept his head to design a new system of hair-proof sewer-pipes he would need to finance his next amazing escape-route from Vanda.

PAGING LYNCH MADISON

***

When the fax came beeping and jangling cheerfully out of the birth-canal, foetally curved, vulnerable to the first hand that reached for it, Lynch was in Bud's office alone.

Bud had taken a shot at the foreign circuit for Vanda now that Boots had been such a success for them. "The Two Doves" weren't much to fly by but all Vanda's flimsy fame was in that one nest, so it wasn't surprising or even upsetting when Berlin and Las Vegas said no to Vanda.

Six weeks later, Acapulco had said no thanks as well, but not so nicely. New York had said yes but only as a support, which made it not worthwhile, Chi was sure of it. Chi then made an obvious and sensible suggestion of her own.

It worked of course.

Rio de Janeiro, the clubs and hotels around the Copocabana, Ipanema circuit had fallen for Vanda's video in a big way.

It hadn't been all that surprising. How often did a talented Brazilian girl want to come home? How often did such a girl have a Guyanian agent?

The Brazilians weren't so keen that they wanted her for the carnival weeks, of course, but

PAGING LYNCH MADISON

nearly as good: she was to sign a contract for the frantically busy weeks following the carnivals when the sated stranded tourists without a mind of their own started to clamour for further entertainment from the hotels, as soon as the last strains of the samba died in the streets.

Alone in the office, Lynch read the fax with a jolt of last-piece-of-the-jigsaw pleasure, and even kissed the shiny paper meaningfully. His plans had been laid for a while now, the tunnel was nearly dug. This fax represented Lynch's last-ditch shovelful before the light.

Through the whole unchallenging busy day at Star Singers he kept it folded in his back-pocket; his treasure-island map, his refusenik's permit, his prisoner's pardon.

"I have," Lynch said to his dear soon-to-be-betrayed friends whom he had summoned to their favourite and most privileged table at Amoretti's that night, "something to annouce which needs, hey, Elisabetta," he called, "ask your Papa what's the best wine in the house."

He was high with excitement, crazed with secrets, wagons roll.

"You just want to know about my wines or you want to buy?" Signor Amoretti smiled at them, the white cloth round his arm, the corkscrew in one hand, a bottle in the other just in case.

"We have good news, Signor Amoretti, we have a celebration. Bring the family and bring the

PAGING LYNCH MADISON

glasses, please," Lynch said, fuzzy with deceitfulness.

Whilst several Amorettis were sent for the glasses and the ice-bucket, Chi smiled shyly up at Lynch.

"How did you know about the baby," she said, luminous with happiness. "Bud, I suppose. Yes? Even though I asked him not to say, it's so early." Chi awarded Bud a huge loving look.

Vanda shrieked.

"I'm about ready for a baby myself, right now," Vanda said disarmingly, hugging her. "God, I'm jealous. It must feel wonderful."

"It feels wonderful," Chi nodded.

In the fluster with the glasses and the cork and the bucket and the bonhomie, Bud stayed quiet and apart from them in his best Guyanese restraint-jacket.

"I didn't tell Lynch about the baby, Chi," Bud said softly, after the Amorettis had cleared their own glasses and gone back to work, leaving Chi wet around the eyes with happiness for the child that they were toasting in anticipation.

"So," said Bud. "You must have other news that you wanted us here to celebrate?"

"Yes. But now, adding your good news, what we have," Lynch said, unable to look at Bud directly and talking fast to keep his up-dating ideas and his

PAGING LYNCH MADISON

nerve to put it over at its peak, "is what amounts to a double, triple or mass celebration."

He had their attention.

"In my pocket I have a magic piece of paper which will change all our lives." He stood and held it high, feet above little Chi, short Bud, small Vanda.

"Abra-" he taunted them, "cadabra! Want to see what it says? Come and get it."

Signor Amoretti looked up in surprise as chairs scraped back and cries of despairing laughter came from their table.

"Basta!" he called good-temperedly. "My other customers, per favore!"

Lynch finally spread the fax out on the table and watched their heads in silence as they leaned over one another to read.

Vanda screamed "Never!" and rushed out of the café and back into the side door, the door banging loudly behind her.

"Guyana's quite near Brazil, isn't it?" Chi said, putting her hands to the site of her baby, maybe unconsciously.

"The office tomorrow, ten-fifteen, bring Vanda," Bud said, standing, looking at Chi, waiting till she stood too. The cafe door closed softly behind them.

PAGING LYNCH MADISON

"Signora Amoretti!" Lynch called, sitting at the table again, alone now. "Bring a glass for yourself," he said, holding up the second still half-full bottle.

Signora Amoretti listened to him for a while and later it was her who crossly let Lynch into another tiny room half full of boxes of stock and handed him a sleeping-bag and a pillow for the fold-up bed inside, when Lynch came back down into the cafe later that night to complain that he couldn't budge Vanda's door.

"Why? Because at last Vanda is clever. She doesn't want you in there tonight," the Signora said uncompromisingly, "and she's right. My daughters, first they get married, then they unlock the door."

If only Vanda were as uncomplicated as the Amoretti girls.

Vanda certainly wasn't there, when he pushed open the unlocked door in the morning on her unmade bed, clothes tried and discarded, her two suitcases (he checked) still dustily up there, her waste-bin full of torn paper. Torn - ah. Torn details of flats available. Some ringed in red.

Despite his anger, his depression and his frame feeling a little unwise from last night's drinking he simply couldn't take, and the Amoretti's too short bed, his mind was working well and he had done several of the most urgent of his new arrangements before getting through Soho's new day's vegetable debris in Lisle Street, up the stairs to Star Singers' around eleven-thirty.

PAGING LYNCH MADISON

Surprisingly Bud didn't comment on his lateness; surprisingly, Chi looked very down; surprisingly, Vanda was there, cheerful enough, getting up to greet him with a kiss, back to some list she was making, humming that happy humming with one shoe half-off that seemed immensely erotic to Lynch.

"Not feeling so good, Chi?" Lynch said, with the absurdly patronising tone reserved by the male for the pregnant.

"We have talked a long time through the night and this morning," Chi said. "The Brazilian tour is like a miracle for all of us."

Lynch saw the other two Magi nod their venerable heads in some sort of agreement of this magical promise, only the insistent C-sharp compulsorily played by a large lorry backing into a narrow entrance and its inevitable chorus of left-hand-down-a-bit from the matey, filling up the awed silence that followed.

When you said this fax would change all our lives, you were quite right," Bud said. "But this is especially the right solution for you."

"For all of us," Chi said.

"Going home was a no-no for me," Vanda said. "I couldn't handle it. But I see now that this one chance is the best one for me. I can go back to my family without needing them. If things go well, they'll even come running to me. I mean, like, I'll be my own person. But I won't go unless you too go and I just know it will sort your life out too, over there."

PAGING LYNCH MADISON

"Of course, Lynch," Chi said. "Brazil is such a good place for you to be. In South America people just disappear, they say."

Chi answered the phone as they sat on, and soon answered it again.

Chi lifted the phone off the hook and hesitating now, she raised her eyebrows at them, dispensed four coffees for them, fiddled with her white plastic spoon, wiped the splashed drops from an invoice with the side of her little fist.

"Guyana is very near Rio de Janeiro," Chi began awkwardly.

"Two and a half thousand miles, I think, from my home to Rio. Two thousand at least," Bud's voice was tight.

"Your parents are very old," Chi said.

"They are not old at all, Chi. They ----"

"It is time for us to go to them now we have reason to be married. However far. But really it is only opportunity, on this tour we are being quite near, nearer than London. You know it is the right thing."

"I love the way you say 'Lon-don'," Vanda smiled. "Gee. Getting married and having a baby. In a hundred years' time that'll still be all most women want, won't it?"

"Maybe."

PAGING LYNCH MADISON

Bud looked glum even for Bud, but there was in his face some glow that Lynch could recognize as 'future.'

"Maybe," Bud started again, "I could persuade my parents that Yannick, my next brother, must run the plantation. I will say I am never coming home again. I will say that I loved them but that I love you more. That my home will be with you."

The female Magi were weeping into their Kleenex. Bud was sold, gift-wrapped and in the delivery van.

"Jeez, it's just the opposite for me, Bud," Vanda said, still sniffing a bit. "Me, I never wanted to go home. I wanted to go where the breeze blew me, right? Then lately I just wanted to stay where Lynch was, right? But hey if Brazil will be good for Lynch and all of us, let's go, right?"

"You two are so crazy in love," Chi said to Vanda without looking up, "you could marry out there too and have children --"

"Right," Vanda breathed.

Enough burglar alarms were going off in Lynch's system to give him a headache.

All he had foreseen was the Varig plane lifting off, taking them 'ahead' of him to Brazil. He would wave to them with his hands and run away on his feet in the opposite direction.

PAGING LYNCH MADISON

Wading through this love and devotion crap was slowing him down.

He and Bud ought to excuse themselves to the gents, escape through the staff exit and travel on with the first available willing women who stumbled into their path.

Lynch winked at Bud, trying to convey all that macho stuff in the gesture, but Bud was lost to him, gazing at Chi with love.

"Chi is right, too, of course," Bud said.

Lynch was extra dismayed. A woman must never ever be told that she may be right.

"It is time. Maybe time for us all."

His group had, it seemed, finished with the sentimental clap-trap of familial loyalties and the depressing end of all life's freedom.

At least they were certainly noses-blown and alert for the practical. Lynch could tell that by the way they were all sitting straighter, now, and looking ---to him.

Yes, of course. How long was it since he'd spoken? A week?

"Great," he smiled. "Terrific."

Two good words that meant no harm.

"Make all the arrangements you want."

PAGING LYNCH MADISON

He put up with Vanda flying to him, hugging him, kissing him. Why not?

"But first," he said, "I have a practical matter to see to that can't wait. "I have to do something before I go to Brazil."

"See Jan?"

"There is -- a man I have to reach."

"Back home?"

Lynch shook his head in the absolute silence they held for him.

"You can understand that I never want to live on anyone again." They all nodded.

"So. I've enough for a ticket to -- where I need to go and if you'll stand me a long-term ticket to Brazil and leave it here with the Amorettis, I'll pick it up and come out the first day I can, when --- everything's settled and pay you back for everything. When – when everything's settled."

"What everything? ----"

"I have to see this man."

Lynch could see the money piled high in front of his eyes and felt a bit giddy and sick keeping the glint of it from them.

"I'll come with you wherever it is, whatever it is. You're in trouble I will help you, querido," Vanda said. "Whilst Bud is in Guyana with Chi -"

PAGING LYNCH MADISON

"No, Vanda."

A heavy impasse. A heavy anger.

"No, Vanda, you have to go ahead to Brazil," Bud tutted, to Lynch's relief. "We need somewhere to live. I need somewhere I can call you. You need to try to be friendly again with your family. It's a chance for all of us."

"Let me come with you, querido?" Vanda said softly.

"No, Vanda."

"How long before ---"

"I don't know, Vanda."

"But if you have to ---- look, I will wait at Amoretti's for you to come back, querido."

"No, Vanda."

And no matter how many times Lynch tried to recall the end of that conversation, the details fuzzed out just there.

He remembered most of their last days together before all three of them saw her off at the airport: who could forget such a parting.

He remembered the lightening lift of responsibility that flew from him as her plane rose.

PAGING LYNCH MADISON

He remembered his inability to leave Heathrow after he had said goodbye to Bud and Chi six days later until after the 'last call' for the flight to Guyana had come and gone some while before and he remembered the foolish tears of regret he had had to hold grimly back.

And he remembered that no-one, no-one in the world now knew what he was up to, where he was going, and what was to become of him.

PAGING LYNCH MADISON
CHAPTER SEVEN

Over there, look, in the queue for tickets. Leslie Merrett, isn't it, posing as himself again.

Nice light-weight suit, very executive; good quality brief-case; but rather cheap and rather obviously new baggage, a bit of a giveaway.

With an Independent under his arm, (though Leslie used to read the Guardian) and hair brushed into a Leslie-Merrett-who's-been-so-busy-he-hasn't-had-time-for-a-barber style.

Yes, well observed, as the hair is not yet noticeably long; not in any way discernibly Lynch's style.

And he is quite patiently next in line for his ticket after the blonde woman with the legs.

Perhaps Victoria is always like this so early in the morning. There's certainly a dreadful racket here, trains revving, trains shunting, mail-vans shifting, parcels thrown and landing, loading, hooters, sirens, calling, shouting, running, doors swinging open, doors clanging shut. And there is a hint of worrying lateness in the air, as if no-one has left quite enough time to get their ticket, to get the right seat, to get to their destination.

Ssh. Quiet and listen for a moment.

PAGING LYNCH MADISON

First-class to where? Damn it there's such a noise it's hard to hear what's going on. But wherever it is that Leslie Merrett is asking for, it is obvious that he is on the run again. Look at that. He's using a credit card and signing the real Leslie Merrett.

That is a surprise.

What? You could be right. Maybe he's going home. Is Crossbridge on the Victoria Line? Haven't a clue. To be honest, if he were going home, it would seem a shame in a way. It is really none of our business, but didn't you think that Vanda was sort of good for him?

Just a minute. He can't be going home. Look, it says 'Europe' everywhere over there and it's the International Rail Centre sign he's buying his ticket under. Watch, but keep quiet and out of sight.

Tucking the ticket into a pocket of the new wallet he'd had to buy since returning Geraldine's, Lynch smiled to himself again, thinking of the endless talking with Bud and Chi and Vanda before they left.

But about leaving from Victoria, and about travelling this way, at least, they had been right.

So much more impersonal here than an airport; certainly less security and red-tape, as they had all agreed.

Their avalanche of unasked-for advice had seemed objective enough. Nobody pressurised him for details. They scarcely seemed to want to know

PAGING LYNCH MADISON

anything, except whether it was within England or not.

They said avoid airports, that's all.

They said train and channel crossings seemed less formal to them.

They had started by suggesting he travel as Lynch and change to Leslie when he got near to --- wherever his money was.

He agreed with them. Of course.

It is the height of summer, they had said, you're just about young and fit enough to look right with a back-pack, they had said, even if you can't get the student discount, your whole style is right, they had said, for a hot day in jeans or shorts with a 'How To Travel On The Cheap' guidebook in one hand and a beefburger dribbling on to your tee-shirt from the other.

Whatever it is you have to do is your own business, they had nodded wisely. Please just come as soon as you can to Brazil, we'll be waiting, they had said.

A salutary experience, being discussed; taking counsel again; trying not to mind the whiff of subjugation that often came with the kind perfume of solicitude. Siamese twins he had always had trouble parting one from another.

Despite their blatant interference which he deplored, going over it in his head, there was a funny fond feeling about it too.

PAGING LYNCH MADISON

Hot in his suit and worrying a little that it made him conspicuous, maybe they were right, damn it, maybe it was wrong to become Leslie Merrett so soon. He felt uneasy, unsure. He walked away towards the platform that the signpost pointed him to. He might as well board now. Only twenty-seven minutes to go.

Mints. He'd get some mints.

He changed direction abruptly, his sharp-edged briefcase knocking down a little girl running away from her family.

Releasing all his baggage on to the platform, he knelt at once to pick her up and comfort her held-in fear. He wiped at her grazed little knee with a quick tissue and made little sorry and soothing noises, unexpected gulps coming to his throat at the little-girl wriggle of her. Older than Charlotte? Younger? Taller? Lighter?

The mother had arrived, alternately telling the little girl off for running away, thanking Lynch and trying to kiss and plaster the little knee as the child, now safe, could cry at her leisure.

"Daddy and I were nearly at the front of the queue for a taxi home, miss," the mother said. "Now we'll just have to wait again. Thanks - well, thanks."

Lynch watched them go back to the taxi-rank where the father stood, stolid but as brown with suntan as they were, waiting anxiously for them, luggage and a little plastic case and a small doll piled

PAGING LYNCH MADISON

on a railway trolley all marked clearly with the name of Carfax.

On the train, back-packers and back-packs everywhere. Great-looking girls everywhere, in groups, in pairs with dull-eyed boys and men, gangs of fellows, strange mixtures.

The Lynch in him wanted to come out and play in the teeming corridors, but Leslie Merrett politely and patiently fought his way to his first class compartment, spread himself out with the only other occupants in the carriage, a businessman already working on some file and an elderly woman, holding a plastic bag very close to her.

The end of August. No families travelling. They were all going the other way with the Carfaxes, returning home ready to buy bigger sensible shiny new shoes and soft grey pullovers with the sleeves turned back a lot for the new school term. European paradise, this time of year.

Watching the corridor, as he adjusted himself to the rhythm of the train, Lynch noticed couples everywhere very together and very excited just being on a train. Trains did that to him too. Shame about the company in the carriage.

He checked out a concept. He would never see Vanda again. Yes, he did mind. Very much. He shifted and stared miserably out of the window.

On the way, on the way, on the way. The smoother movements of these new trains still lurched over tracks in a versified way which read poetry to you if your ears would hear it.

PAGING LYNCH MADISON

On the way, on the way, on the way. The blue and purple seating swayed and danced through the couple of hours of boredom and snoozing first-class between Victoria and Dover, though there were the false intervals created by trips to the toilet, a leisurely walk down the corridors, where you stooped to wake or nudge crouching passengers who had to stand and breathe in, a stumble past the cells where they locked up the dangerous bikes and parcels, Lifting your briefcase high above your head like something in a spy movie as you inched through crowded carriages some still filled with curling foggy smoke even after the prolonged lung cancer education in every school and on every poster. Through finally to the buffet.

There, the furious man who was forced to dispense food but was under no obligation to speak or smile, sourly took money and gave grudging change for the poor stock of sandwiches and chocolate biscuits which soon emptied, followed by the disappearance of the cokes, the Seven Ups and finally, the beer, no fill-ups along the route, good heavens no.

On the way on the democratic jet-foil without a first-class to hide in, Lynch smiled at this jumped-up boat with its pretensions to air-line grandeur, fielding only the comic GCSE French accents of the stewards and a feeble attempt at duty-free.

On the way again though it was after mid-day before the train left Ostend and not a thing to eat on the Belgian train unless you bought it at the station.

PAGING LYNCH MADISON

Yet again on the way from Brussels in another less hungry train, and on the way, on the way, on the way to Luxembourg.

On the way to the unworthy heady beautiful power of having money again.

Ah, that's where it was, was it.

After the comparisons of the signatures at the bank he could be sure that it would be the last time he would ever sign for Leslie Merrett - he must practise to make sure he remembered how it went - maybe they would ask a few casual difficult questions. He had thought that out: he would pleasantly answer everything, even if asked in English, only in his poor hesitant French. The flap of the dictionary and the slowness would cover any awkwardness and they would quickly tire of him.

One additional trouble was beginning to brew. He'd been on the trains and boats and trains for, what time is it, just after four on this beautiful summer afternoon? Say, around nine hours, then, and an hour to go, and what had he found? That being alone again was - great.

Stressless, calming, deeply serene and enriching. Time to look around. Time to answer the nagging internal private lines of questioning. Time to plan and consolidate.

Money too, of the large sort he was on his way to collect, might be a lovely sensation after its absence. Or it might be corrupting. Having money and not having Vanda might be the best combination of his life. Or the worst. Having no money and

PAGING LYNCH MADISON

plenty of women might be good, too. Or having ------ Lynch found his seat again and slept on and off thinking and not thinking, complacent and frantic, defeated and high.

***

Staring from the window as the train pulled slowly, slowly into Luxembourg Station, Lynch decided that the Luxembourg grass, trees and shrubs, the Luxembourg vistas and villas, and the Luxembourg railway sidings had all been purchased very economically at Universal Backgrounds.

And he had seen this video over and over again in his head.

He had chosen the Cravat Hotel for its uniquely central position, and had pictured himself confirming his booking at the desk, strolling in the sunshine until he found the type of shop where tomorrow he would buy the next set of clothes for his life ahead.

Lynch Madison again? Or was it time to try out the never used Leon Matthews, the ex-tennis professional and Wimbledon coach with the torn ligament and the large pension.

He'd decide later. Fine. Drop off his baggage at the hotel, book a table for dinner somewhere fancy that the hotel would recommend and go window shopping.

Later, showered and presentable in his Leslie Merrett evening apparel, whether he'd picked anyone

PAGING LYNCH MADISON

up to share it with or not, he would savour the most expensive, lavish self-indulgent leisurely meal he could get, and follow this up with a serious evening's touring to say hallo and goodbye to Luxembourg night-life, as he would never be back.

In the morning, the bank, the main feature of his video.

Then the fiddly bits; distributing the excess baggage of that other life: he'd certainly leave the new suit, the last tie of his life and the empty briefcase hanging neatly in whichever toilet he changed in, then off with the wind blowing through his lengthening hair-cut to enLynch or enLeon himself.

Some travellers who had boarded with him at Victoria had come this far with him all the way to this last-stage to Luxembourg and tiny phantom friendships were building.

So he moved off down the train carefully, anxious, now, to shake them off.

Alone was, after all, what he wanted, what he kept running to, wasn't it?

Two flavours of pain to choose from today. The fancy creamy pain of being lumbered, after all he had run from, with someone hard to shake off, or the plain pain of endless loneliness. Umm. He should maybe take the plain one and don't bother to wrap it.

PAGING LYNCH MADISON

Stepping out before the train had stopped properly he ran with the platform into the hot sun that 'abroad' ought to have.

He was hot and hungry and was looking for something.

Very soon now he would run out of turnings: after he had collected the money, some decisions were called for.

As possibilities flooded through and filtered out, he knew he must settle some debts before he bought his quick quiet one-way ticket to somewhere for himself.

He must send Bud, Chi and Vanda an enormous goodbye cheque to share out and a great big something for the Amorettis. Quick, quick, stop thinking about any of them.

Great out. Sweet warm air like loving. He shrugged out of his jacket and knelt to tuck it across his case.

"Boo," said Vanda.

Christ. That's what he had been looking for.

***

Frustratingly, it's very early morning before we catch sight of them again.

PAGING LYNCH MADISON

Lynch was pushing the heavy doors shut on the skunk and its family of little ones as they tried again and again to storm his house. He tried to call out 'help me, help me' but no words would come. He ran to collect his clarinet but it was under seven torn up telephone directories and the glass cut his fingers. The blood from his hands was paint. Green paint. Hot. He was so hot.

"Want to play a game, Lynch?"

A real voice or a dream voice.

"When I was in Brazil, I saw this really stupid TV movie, about two people –"

Hot. It was so hot.

"It's still dark, for heaven's sake, Vanda, I'm trying to sleep. It feels like - whew, I'm so hot. Open a window will you?"

"Do you know what the time is? Do you know what today is?" Vanda shook him again. "It's been the greatest day and a half of my life. I love it here. I love this hotel. I can't remember staying in such a big room, except in Brazil. It's like a conference hall." She walked to the end and swished the heavy brocade curtains cruelly back.

"It's glorious. Fantastic morning. Seven, er, let's have a look. Forty after. Look at that. Will you look, Lynch. It's terrific weather. That's one thing I hated in England, the cold. I wonder if Luxembourg's always hot? The porter said, didn't he, that it's a wonderful view over that valley thing, when the mist clears. What's it called? Lynch? What did

PAGING LYNCH MADISON

that fellow call that ravine? Couldn't you just spare one more day before you go off? All righty, sleep if you want to. I'll just uncover you a bit as you're terribly, terribly hot. There you go. Tell you what. I'll just play this game on my own, you join in when you wake up.

"Are you listening, Lynch? Wow! I love these new clothes? Did you always dress like that when you were married? Classy."

Lynch shut the door quietly and took his time. Coming out from the en suite he could see that Vanda was suppressing her impatience waiting for her turn.

Whilst she showered and sang, he dressed himself, high from her affection, sleek with pleasure, stage-frightened with purpose, wondering why he was so sure that he could cope with leaving Vanda this time better than coping with staying with her.

He finished fussing with the new clothes, put all the pins and cardboard in the bin and faced himself in the mirror. Not quite Leslie Merrett - too fulfilled for that - but quite a near-enough approximation. He knocked on the door. "Come and see this."

He turned on his left foot and posed, the poser of posers.

"What do you think?"

"You look edible, Lynch," Vanda said, stepping out of a cotton cover-up and into his reach.

PAGING LYNCH MADISON

To a man who likes women, there is no more beautiful thing than a slightly damp one, straight from her shower, newly brushed and shiny, so Lynch held this rare one closely, breathing her in, apathetic with content, for a minute or a decade, smoothing up and down the dividing line of her torso from hair to rounded bum.

"Order yourself breakfast in bed, if you like," Lynch said softly. "Take your time. Enjoy this room you like so much. Get my money's worth," he mumbled into her hair, never wanting to leave her, wanting to be gone. He was talking when there was nothing to be said.

"What's the rush, Lynch, why can't you stay and ---"

"I just can't." He moved away, smoothing the very minimum documents he must have neatly back into the suspiciously shiny briefcase, moving it near the door, putting only his clarinet case and the new set of Lynch clothes (he had decided to be Lynch tomorrow after all) they'd bought yesterday in the new back-pack he'd bought too. He was extra especially ready to go and yet couldn't leave.

"I'm starved," Vanda said, not dressing, but going to the phone to order. "You must be too. Shall I just order coffee for you?"

"No. After I've done a few things I'll stop at that place we went to yesterday for coffee and your chocolate croissants - stop worrying, OK. Now 11.30 at the station. Bring my case there. It's not heavy. It's practically empty. OK. Be prompt.

PAGING LYNCH MADISON

"That place in the square, do you mean? Where we went? I know, I know, at the station at 11.30. I know. You've told me and told me."

"Listen, Vanda. It makes me feel better to go over it and over it. Station 11.30. Wait for me at least until 12.30. Sit in the buffet ---"

"Look you've forgotten your things. Toothpaste, soap, deodorant---"

"For Christ's sake, Vanda, I'll buy everything new. So -- you'll be dead on time. Eleven-thirty and not a moment earlier or later?"

"Yessir."

"In fact, just in case I finish later than I expect, you'll be too conspicuous if you're there too long so ---"

"I'll die of boredom this morning. Look, maybe I'll go shopping and if I'm not there, you wait for me."

"No, Vanda. Take a book. Buy a magazine. Write a letter."

"Who to? You're with me." Vanda stroked his face and gazed lovingly at him. She was the last person he would ever allow so close, he reminded himself.

"And keep a low profile there; don't start getting noticed."

PAGING LYNCH MADISON

"Me? I wasn't thinking of singing. I'll just sit nice and quiet. In my bikini."

Lynch was checking his French again. "I can't laugh until eleven-thirty," he frowned, half sad to think he'd be laughing on his own. Sick to think he left Jan because there weren't enough feelings and was leaving Vanda because there were too many.

"'Zut! Elle aurait du me le dire - j'ai completement oublie mon passeport. Qu'est-ce que je - je -'oh damn it, pass me that piece of yellow paper - yes, of course – 'qu'est-ce que je vais faire?'"

"What are you practising? What's that about a passport?" Vanda called, starting to dress right in front of him so he could kill himself watching her.

"Telling someone I've forgotten --- something. It's difficult to explain. "Elle aurait du me le dire - j'ai completement oublie mon passeport. Er, vais faire, vais faire, why can't I remember that?"

What a fuss you're making," Vanda said quietly, persuasively. "Who is this fellow you have to meet so secretly? I don't get all the mystery. Why don't we just walk there together. I'll wait outside if you really want me to, for heaven's sake. Then - Brazil. I came a long way just to tell you you're going to love it there. I mean, like, you aren't robbing the bank, are you?"

Banque. She was getting close.

"Don't blame me you came from Brazil. It's crazy what you did."

PAGING LYNCH MADISON

"But nice?"

"Nice. Don't give up with your family - try again."

"That's rich after what you did. At least I'm not in hiding all the time. Trying again with those pigs isn't easy --"

"Look, Vanda, I told you yesterday. I knew you weren't listening to me, you were making such a business of -- your face was so full of creme patissiere that you couldn't --look, I only came to Luxembourg to see this fellow. It's a long story I'll tell you later. I don't want to hang about a moment longer. So I want to know exactly where you are while I'm --- busy. So -- so that afterwards I can come straight and get you ---

"Then I'll stay here at the hotel - no hassle."

"OK, OK, OK," Lynch said, readjusting everything in his head, though he'd been sure at the time that he had to get her out of the hotel and everything paid up for some reason. What was it, what was it? No. Maybe it would be less complicated. She'd stay and stay at the hotel until they chucked her out of the room at the noon deadline and he'd be long gone and she wouldn't have anywhere at all to look for him.

"Pay the hotel bill with this," he said, handing her everything of the last of the scraped up money except what he was keeping back for his own Last Breakfast.

"Show me on the map where you're going."

PAGING LYNCH MADISON

Lynch thought quickly. "It's tricky to tell you. Well - look, here. I'm going around here, the man said. Straight up Rue Chimay into the Place d'Armes -- where we were, you remember? There. Those chocolate croissants were the best I ever tasted. Then -- well, he'll tell me." He folded the map quickly, casually, added that to the still almost empty briefcase.

Briskly, briskly. He started to throw the bits and pieces of his life with Vanda in the bin, hesitating for a moment.

"Vanda, could you chuck this stuff and these large things and the shaver and stuff in the suitcase and just dump it on another landing."

"The bellhop would like that shaver, wouldn't he? I could use that case, Lynch, it's a shame to ----"

"Dump it, Vanda, OK. If we just left it here it would be very strange and I don't want --- Leslie Merrett remembered in Luxembourg, OK?"

"OK."

"You'll do it?"

"I'll do it."

She spotted something sticking out of the bin and walked over to it crashing the briefcase to the floor. "Look," she said, picking it out of the bin. "I'm really mad at you. You've thrown away that first

PAGING LYNCH MADISON

cassette I made you. Me singing just for you. It's the first thing I ever gave you, Lynch."

"Yeah, sorry, so it is," Lynch said, putting it in his pocket, relieved she hadn't noticed the torn-up creased written-on leaflet about Stan's College that was really the first thing she had given him and which had given him a real wrench to chuck.

She handed him the briefcase. "Hey, Lynch, that case is empty. I'll bring it for you."

"No, I want that, Vanda. It -- makes me look more like Leslie Merrett. He always carried one like this."

"OK, OK."

"A last kiss." Lynch held up her chin and gently sampled little places all over her lovely face.

"For now," she said. "Lynch, if anything goes wrong, where ----"

"I told you, pay the bill, see you back here. Eleven-trente or possibly trente-et-un. Eleven-thirty, that is. Au revoir."

"Lynch?"

"Um?"

Vanda smiled. "Roulades. The chocolate ones. Not croissants. They call them roulades."

Lynch closed the door and held it shut. Had she understood his French? De rien. She would

PAGING LYNCH MADISON

never see him again. And one thing she'd never be able to bring herself even to look at would be roulades, he was sure of it.

Not so hot out as it had looked from upstairs and the view of the valley wasn't quite edible through the early-morning mist yet, he smiled to himself, remembering her and her nonsense fondly like an old friend he used to know.

But with the clumsy half-empty backpack hefted in one hand and the empty briefcase in the other, he stayed leaning over the gap for a few moments, letting the beauty seep in as if it were eye-drops that might have to last for days. A couple of young tourists eyed him and gave each other a "what-a-local-toff" that he recognized with pride. Leslie Merrett had never attracted open attention like that, except on stage. So he had really shed Leslie now and was only dressing up as him for one purpose.

Elle aurait du me le dire. J'ai completement oublie mon passeport. Qu'est ce que je vais faire. Great.

Lynch Madison whistled "Sur le pont d'Avignon" quietly but not quite to himself, hoping it was known in Luxembourg and trusting that it gave the right impression of casual cosmopolitanism.

The world-wide car-rental place was right where it should have been according to the map, was open nice and early and the girl on the desk was full of smiles like the adverts.

"Mais certainement" a friendly white Volkswagen Golf would be made ready and filled

PAGING LYNCH MADISON

with l'essence by Jean-Claude and "but of course" he could drop it at any one of their many offices that was best for this valued tourist.

He had worked out what to do with the car long ago. With no way they could ever trace him. He planned to leave the car somewhere safe with the full amount for the hire on board and a little extra for the trouble. Then a discreet phone call to alert them. He was a deserter, not a car-thief.

"Oui. See Europe while you can, monsieur, it is all around you, and is very beautiful," she said, waiting for him to sign the forms. Lovely eyes she had.

Shame about her ankles, though, he noticed as she walked away with his forms signed with the name of the first teacher he had ever liked.

"Voila, je suis Jean-Claude."

"Bien," he said, cheered by having a car again, pleased with the newness of the Golf, throwing the keys up and catching them in a pleased sort of way.

When he was on his own, he loosened the screws inside the boot where the spare wheel went - great: plenty of room for the briefcase later - and left them loose. He left the backpack there in the - what was the word in French? He asked Jean-Claude. Oh there's a coincidence. Coffre: the boot of a car was the same word as a safe deposit.

He slammed down the lid hard and was about to find reverse gear and take the Golf for a spin

PAGING LYNCH MADISON

nowhere much before parking it outside the banque, when he had a better idea.

"Mais certainement," agreed Ankles. "Lock it, monsieur and collect it when you are ready, oui, certes."

Still too early for the banque. It didn't, after all, open till nine. He had been sure he had seen eight-thirty on the plate as he passed it yesterday with Vanda. An unimportant mistake. No point in hanging about. A short walk to breakfast at the Place d'Armes - by accident he had told Vanda one truth about this morning.

Vanda. Yes, it hurt. It pinched. He shivered as he walked. He'd get used to it.

Warmer now in the sheltered sun as he sat waiting for his cafe au lait and the hot - yes go on, say it - roulades, sipping the glass of tepid water and germs that was brought to him, he surveyed the Place d'Armes unexcitedly. Too early for the tourists, who wouldn't be able to get a seat by eleven. A shame that this touristy square of restaurants, strangely unknown for its superior patisserie, hadn't tried even limply to be more like the Champs Elysee of Luxembourg, but had settled lazily long ago for an effect more like an open-air airport terminal.

At L'Academie, he had barely started to enjoy himself before a man at the next table, any age between thirty and fifty, scraped his metal chair round towards Lynch. "Bonjour, monsieur."

"Bonjour," Lynch frowned, wishing he had bought a French paper to hide himself behind.

PAGING LYNCH MADISON

"Ah, bon. English?"

From one word? It would be harder at the bank. Banque.

"You like Luxembourg?"

"Je suis en Luxembourg seulement depuis er - demain, pardon, depuis hier."

"I can speak English, monsieur. I was educated at an international school. You find it is a strange country, Luxembourg?"

Waiting for no more small-talk, in a great rush, the man with the wide-open eyes took out his long-held theories and explained them in stiff but good English.

"I feel," he concluded, "that poor little Luxembourg has been drugged - dragged - yes - from its obscurity by the European Parliament but it is unready to admit it as the years of the nineties will soon begin. As I said on RTL, a radio station here -- "

Ah. Halfway through his coffee, Lynch, who had been nodding and saying mais oui when he could wedge it in, realised the man was just delivering a well-rehearsed speech and that he had been glad of a new foreign audience to share it with. No need either to attend to it or answer. Fine. He would need his energy later. Relax, relax, he thought, making himself tense just thinking about it.

PAGING LYNCH MADISON

Quite a bit of time to kill before the bank opened and surely sitting with this garrulous native must be some sort of a good cover, as they call it in the spy films. Better, anyway, than coming directly from the Cravat and perhaps being noticed and traceable.

"Luxembourg is not small only, but small of the mind," the man went on. "She intends to stay in that way ready to revert to insularity" (he looked with triumph at Lynch who nodded his appreciation of the grownupness of the words. "When the Communaut Europenne leave here and make their house in Bruxelles ---"

The man made a blowing up and finishing of Luxembourg with his lips and his hand. Lynch spent a long nod and yawned in a polite and secret way. He wondered how the Belgian had conveyed that gesture on the radio.

Vanda was right and she wasn't right. After all, why make such a secret about the money. It was his both legally and honestly. Jan and Charlotte had been provided far more lavishly than any divorce lawyer would have advised and she had her family to spoil her too.

Vanda, through all of the bad times they'd shared in London when she had often kept him from hunger without question, had never struck him as the kind to spend his every penny when she knew how very much he had.

Nonetheless, though he intended to pay her back at least triplefold, he still didn't want her to

PAGING LYNCH MADISON

know how and where he had his money hidden, or just how much he was really worth.

He didn't want her to know anything much about him - especially that the independence this quite vast amount would give him was nearer to the freedom he had envisaged in the first place.

How was he to know that it would be so long before he had finally arrived in Luxembourg to collect it?

It seemed to him now, that freedom without money was a contradiction in terms.

So he had had, in the end, to risk this one-off complete appearance as Leslie Merrett, asking for Leslie Merrett's money.

Without doubt, the chanciest thing he'd had to do since actually leaving Crossbridge. It had the nasty brown ring of finality built in. Lesley Merrett's last gasp.

But when he had visualised all the dangers of Luxembourg, he hadn't expected to have the burden of Vanda to cope with. How had she found him? Even in bed she had refused him the answer to that secret, whatever else she had so willingly given to him.

This last day and a half with her had been an unexpected bounty to treasure and pick over in the cascades of bad times he knew would soon bucket over his head.

PAGING LYNCH MADISON

But wouldn't the bad times be more easily cushioned by the money, this time.

The down-the-middle truth was that he had comprehensively tried life with money and without it, and whilst this had educated his priorities, he still couldn't bear to be so near to his own earned and sacrificed money after all these years and not now claim it.

"Dat geht?" this one called. "Gehd et?" that one called and his own personal internationally educated Luxemberger waved a hand to tell the passing natives that he was fine without stopping his flow of talk with Lynch for a moment. He accepted another coffee and a croissant from Lynch, smoothly on to politics and corruption, now. "--- not just here but also in your country, no?" Lynch just kept on nodding, trying to copy the Gallic shrug that meant 'what can you expect of politicians.'

The time, the time. Patience.

He could see the foolishness of being ostentatiously the first to rush in as the door of the bank opened. He would use the last of the useless Luxembourg play-money and take his time choosing some fresh-cream Belgian chocolates he'd seen in every street - they would be his first indulgent luxury. No. Too touristy to carry into the bank and he needed all the room he had in his empty briefcase.

He thought again. Of course. He could savour buying an especially relevant postcard to send to Bud and Chi and then he'd post it. Soon, he'd follow up with three cheques; one for them, one for Vanda, one for the Amorettis. He'd send them from

PAGING LYNCH MADISON

- three anonymous places. He would keep writing to them (though never with any address) telling them all his news.

If you have been able to travel this far to follow the making of Lynch Madison, you will be alert to the fact that this is, of course, the very first communication he has been able to send to anyone in four years. Think of that in terms of your own life. Never to say happy birthday, wish you were here, good luck, what a pity, bon voyage. (Card shops everywhere would close down.) Who could stand such isolation. This man's restraint has to be admired.

Time for Leslie Merrett to look at the watch theatrically and say "Mon Dieu! Il est tard. Je dois partir."

Time for "au revoir, monsieur." (Time for the graduate of English to bid him "cheerio, monsieur.") Time to pay the addition, choose the longed-for postcard, hesitate and reject an affectionate card for Vanda. Then window-shop a little, dragging the time out, straight along Avenue Monterey to the Banque Internationale ... Luxembourg.

Time for the long-awaited visit to his money.

PAGING LYNCH MADISON
CHAPTER EIGHT

Inside la bangue it was cool, almost cold, marbled and sad as a sonnet. The image-makers, back from a VIP tour of the States, (have a nice day), had tried to bring life to the lifeless by exhibiting their employees at their work along a long counter to make them seem as accessible and jolly as check-out staff at the supermarket.

No special security desk, dammit, so he'd need to ask in the phrase he had learned.

He knew the word, anyway. Coffres. Boots. He smiled to himself. God, he was nervous. Coffres. Like coffins and just as final. Was it des coffres? Les coffres? Je cherche, je veux voir, je ---

"Monsieur? Puis-je vous aider?"

"Bonjour, monsieur. "Des - les coffres ----"

"Yes, monsieur. You wish to open a safe-deposit? I will call Monsieur ----"

"Non, non," Lynch said, wishing he'd listened more closely through his years at the Crossbridge grammar school to the past tense of the verb I've-already-got-one.

Lynch tried terribly hard making at least eight mistakes. "Je desirais retirer quelques chose de mon

PAGING LYNCH MADISON

coffre - voila… - la recette pour mon coffre - numero - ici, le numero - je suis presse a prendra longtemps?"

Lynch heard his voice shaking a bit - and felt his hands shake too. He put them casually into his smart trouser pockets.

"We speak English here, Monsieur. No, we will not keep you waiting. I will call Monsieur Richaud and you may go with him to the box immediatement."

"Ah, bon," said the rather tiny Monsieur Richaud, summoned as if from bed, smoothing his hair, adjusting his tie. "La recette, monsieur? Bon. Et le passeport?"

Not so bon. Leslie Merrett now takes on the role of a man furious with his secretary and bangs his forehead in despair.

"Zut!"

It had gone. The whole phrase. Vanished. Elle, elle --what was it. Elle ---

"Elle aurait du me le dire. J'ai completement oublie mon passeport. Que'est ce que je - je - je vais faire?"

Monsiuer Richaud's face, which had been issued with no spare expressions and who had not yet saved up to buy any, blandly assured Lynch that it was nothing and that if he would sign here and here and here and make three signatures for them to compare with la recette --- the passeport could be overlooked but next time, please ---- a moment.

PAGING LYNCH MADISON

Happy enough for the pair of them and with plenty of expressions to spare, Lynch and Monsieur Richaud went down in the lift while Leslie told him in the little lift, in execrable French, that it seemed cold inside the bank, maybe because it was very warm today, was it not, that Luxembourg must be the most beautiful place in the world, was it not, and that on the whole he preferred Luxembourg roulades to anything they made in La Belle France, is it not so.

Monsieur Richaud considered all these matters unworthy of his consideration and within fifteen minutes was shaking hands expressionlessly with a happy man whose briefcase was stuffed full with his own dollars. A man standing, within moments, gulping in the air of freedom in beautiful Luxembourg in the sudden warmth of the street outside the bank. A man nameless for a while.

Standing there, in the doorway of the bank, lingeringly, the nameless one considered the situation. He looked down at his extremely rich right hand and smiled. And he was early. It had taken a lot less time than he'd even hoped. A breathing space.

He pictured Vanda innocently waiting, watching her watch, watching the time go so slowly. When he didn't turn up, she'd go on waiting, biting her lip, she wouldn't know where else to go. Then perhaps she'd go to the square - tears in her eyes if a roulade should pass by ---- he'd be miles off in his hire-car.

Drop the car off, hovercraft to Dover, say mid-afternoon. Fifty-four minutes past the hour

PAGING LYNCH MADISON

Dover to Victoria, just under two hours journey - allowing time for problems, hold-ups, seven o'clock in London and he could be anybody he chose.

Painful though it would be to ditch Lynch, when he settled somewhere else, he would have to start again. He could be Lionel, perhaps. Or Lloyd. Lloyd or Lionel Merryweather. It was easier, he had found, to make something of a characterful name.

Still standing. A flash of light. A leaping of excitement. No need to go back to England at all. Head his hired car in quite another direction. It was money that made a difference. Enough to replace everything he'd ever owned. Enough to buy himself into a really lucrative occupation, enterprise or even - yes, yes, yes, something much less selfish, much more worthwhile.

He'd buy himself a prestigious place in some charity - then cross and re-cross the world administering it.

He saw a new dam. He felt his pinged-up tension go as Lionel or LLoyd Merryweather cut the tape to open it. He heard the roar of the water and sound of applause. He saw vaccination clinics, heard music being made where there had been silence, saw schools in the jungle ---

Saw Vanda.

"I know it's wicked," Vanda said, taking her heavy shoulder-case off her shoulders and putting it right in the way of the people walking in and out of the bank. "But I followed you from the square. That man you were talking to, does he know your wife?

PAGING LYNCH MADISON

Is he blackmailing you? Look, I'm worried, Lynch, you can trust me, for Chrissake."

Lynch stayed silent, bewildered, furious.

"I didn't like him. After you'd gone and I was hanging about, he kept looking at me. You know. Looking?"

Lynch knew the looks she got.

"He was your contact? I guessed so. But he looked friendly as you were leaving. Did you have to pay him off? Is your problem over?"

Relieved at having the story misinterpreted so brilliantly for him, Lynch shook his head in silent, fake admiration for her powers of deduction.

"Then I looked at the time and it was still so early that I knew you must have other complications. I lost you for a while then --- well, I was so surprised when you went in the bank. Travellers cheques, I guess. The bastard must have asked for more than you promised to call him off, yes?" she said, looking back.

"Come on, Lynch, open up, will you?"

Lynch clutched the briefcase harder and swung it slightly behind his knees. But it was worse than that. She didn't mean his case. She meant his mind.

Lynch tried to think up a good bunch of new lies, tried to think out his next move, whilst not betraying his panic or his discomfiture.

PAGING LYNCH MADISON

He was out of ideas for a moment. Maybe he'd have to unload her, openly, finally and brutally.

"So you have to meet him again, right?"

Lynch nodded, still unsure how to get out of this one.

"Don't worry. I've got enough to get me back to Brazil and to stand you a ticket to London. But only if you hurry up and get out there to Rio, Lynch. I've told you and I've told you but you can't believe how beautiful it is out there. The mountains and the coast and the dancing and the weather and the people. You'll love it so much."

In a second she had taken the briefcase from his hand and was hefting it. "Hey, Lynch. It's heavy now. But you haven't been anywhere. Let me see."

Lynch snatched the case back from her and held it tighter. The combination lock and alarmed catch didn't seem quite so secure as it had done earlier.

"Hasn't anyone ever told you the truth about yourself," Lynch said tightly. "You're too possessive. You are trying to get too close to me. I don't like that. Most men don't. I didn't ask you here to Luxembourg. You keep turning up and bothering me. I didn't even ask you to my bed in the first place - you're just getting what you deserve pushing yourself on me."

"I love you Lynch."

PAGING LYNCH MADISON

"Crap," Lynch said. "You're just following me like a lost dog with nowhere else to go. And I'm not looking for a pet."

Great. They were still standing on the steps of the bank, she was crying noisily and noticeably and now she was clutching at him piteously.

He began to walk away fast, Vanda hesitating then ludicrously pacing along behind him.

"But you haven't heard why I followed you, Lynch. Look at this, will you. It's such a surprise, Lynch."

"If you're pregnant it's your own fault. Whatever else it is, your surprises don't interest me."

Vanda let out only a tiny sound, wiped at her face and kept on pacing.

"When are you going to change out of those awful clothes? Where's your Lynch stuff?" she said, snufflingly.

He looked down at his Leslie Merrett outfit. She was right. He was behaving like Lynch in the wrong set of garments. Not clever.

"In the ----" he started to tell her. "Christ, woman, will you go away."

He was killing her but there was no other way.

PAGING LYNCH MADISON

"I know you too well, Lynch," Vanda said, wiping her face with one hand and still trying to hold him with the other.

"You're only trying to get rid of me for my sake, aren't you? You think I'll mind not being able to be married to you for years. Well I will mind but I'll do it for you, querido. And honestly, I think even more of you for the way you're trying to protect me. But I want to ----"

"Jesus, you're really crazy, Vanda," Lynch said, stopping dead, giving every appearance of having simply given in, an idea formed and settling.

"Totally up the wall and round the twist."

Vanda was smiling, complimented by this.

"And maybe that's what Lynch Madison needs," Lynch said. "A crazy woman."

"Querido," Vanda smiled, victory in her face, unaware of being set up, targeted, both barrels of Lynch's cunning aimed at her soft centre.

Lynch Madison might need a crazy woman but Lionel or Lloyd Merryweather would need no one at all.

"OK," he said, magnanimously, "you show me your surprise and I'll show you mine." He was quite confident of his inability to be surprised and anxious to get her trivialities over with.

"It's partly why I followed you, Lynch. OK I really wanted to know what you were doing but look,

PAGING LYNCH MADISON

this fax came from Bud the second you left the hotel."

Plenty of time to find out how Bud knew what hotel they were at and what country they were in when he tortured her later with burning matches under her toenails.

He tore the sheets of paper she was tantalising him with out of her waving hand with fury rather than interest.

"It was addressed to you," she admitted, but with, it has to be admitted, love in her face. "You can't help reading someone else's fax, Lynch," she said, not in any way apologetically. "Read it."

Really quite surprising and interesting.

It said that Bud, initally given a warmer reception by his family than he'd expected, had turned them to ice when he announced that he wasn't stopping and that Chi was a little bit Japanese and a little bit not Muslim and also more than a little pregnant.

Under the weight of all this, his father's initial insistence on his immediate return had sunk. Quietly making sure that Bud understood that he had fairly renounced his birthright by so doing, his father had dismissed him, then had him summoned back, for some second thought, and almost shyly asked what he would like as a parting wedding gift.

Bud was given a batch of family documents to study to help him make this stunning choice.

PAGING LYNCH MADISON

He picked out a massive derelict ruin - a fazenda, a farm with a bit of a history –a no-hoper - he said that he was sure he could 'turn it around', (this property being a drop in the whopping great swamp of a trading coup throughout Brazil that the family had brought off) and asked politely for that and nothing else.

Bud's father was deliriously happy to get off so lightly, and immediately, therefore, pressed upon him not a bad chunk of conscience-money. Then turning to his less difficult son, Yannick, the reliable quiet resourceful betrothed one next in line, told him that if he failed to persuade Bud to reconsider returning to the family, he would be crowned newly anointed heir.

The brother failed to persuade Bud to reconsider.

There followed a surprising summons for Chi to be brought before them, a little defrosted hugging from Bud's family, the handing over of the deeds, The Big Goodbye, and the closing of the door.

So, as Bud put it, he had found a way to leave Guyana reasonably at peace with his family, a way to marry Chi, a way to live in Rio and run something of his own, a way to make the money he had been given grow and be repaid in some good and useful way and he would make his music too.

Great. Though not now of any consequence to Lynch.

Here it came. The Big Sale. Bud now wished to inform his two dearest friends that he not only

PAGING LYNCH MADISON

invited them to the quiet wedding they would have but had also seen the way to run their lives as well.

"Vanda will be reconciled with her family, as I have," he wrote. "Lynch will find this a good country to lose himself in, and of course he must resume his true career. Beginning with the renovation and re-designing of this ruined building to a Health Farm like they have in England - but half of it to be run for the poor people of Brazil, sent, maybe, by their doctors.

Lynch has carte blanche to do it whichever way he likes, Bud and Chi, Bud adds, will love to bring up our family in Brazil's wonderfully rich culture and climate near their dearest friends.

They would now fly to Rio de Janeiro to see exactly what Bud had picked out of the lucky dip, staying at the apartment that Vanda had chosen and leased.

"Hope things went well for you in Luxembourg. Return with Vanda to London soonest to collect tickets that await you. Advise arrival at Rio soonest. You will be witnesses at our wedding - in Rio soonest. The rains were late in Guyana and it has poured all the time we were here. They say Rio is summer all the year around. Life will be wonderful. Bud."

"There are a lot of beaches around Rio, aren't there?" Lynch said, marking time.

"Four thousand, five hundred and seventy-nine miles of coast, we learned in school. Oh, that's

PAGING LYNCH MADISON

maybe only the Atlantic. I can't remember. The number sticks in my mind."

The very European slow towniness of Luxembourg drifting drearily past his eyes bored him, weighed him down.

What did she say, four thousand miles of coast? Christ. To live on the beach all the year round. To be an architect again. To build something great. To live with friends. To live with Vanda.

"We will play 'The Two Doves' everywhere together, querido, and after the shows, we will make love and sleep late and after a shower we will come every day for a lunch barbecue on the white sands by the warm waters of the Copocabana beach ----"

"Wasn't it you who said I wouldn't be able to take the heat at noon on the beaches?"

"How can I tell if you'll be too hot," Vanda said impatiently. "I'm Carioca. Together on the beach we will forget anyone else is there but us ----"

"And didn't you say it was mobbed down there on those big beaches and that's why it's so easy for thieves?"

"How can I remember what I told you," Vanda said, tossing her hair, more Brazilian by the moment.

"There are twenty-three beaches in Rio. We'll choose us a quiet one, OK? And when they meet the English architect, my family will love you

PAGING LYNCH MADISON

and they will take you to their heart and you will build estates for them and --"

Lynch was really surprised. "You've seen them? Your family want to meet me?"

"How do I know?" Vanda shrugged impatiently, not concerned with 'accurate' when she was talking 'symbolic.'

"Plenty of time for that. Maybe they will want to love me again. If not - so I don't need them, do I, querido," she said, holding her head up proudly.

"Lynch, you are finished here, right? You are finished with Luxembourg, aren't you?"

Finished.

"Then let's go," she said softly, placatingly.

There were a lot of tempting options here. Many of the things he wanted seemed to be in or going to Brazil. Like a bad chess-player he seemed he had been splashing his King around contemptuous of those powerful little pawns.

He could see some moves ahead but wasn't good enough to know which ones would win him the game.

Ah, he recognized where they had walked themselves to. The hire-car place was two, three roads down on the right and then first left.

PAGING LYNCH MADISON

"Wait here, Vanda and don't move," Lynch said, with a degree of firmness that he hoped she would register and honour.

He took off his jacket and tie as he went, opened the top buttons of his shirt, rolled up the sleeves, walking quicker and quicker as if that would make him free, as if that way the decisons would come easier.

Should he come back for Vanda or not? Yes, he ought to treat her like nobody else because she was like nobody else.

She had followed him to his flat in the first place, she had followed him to Luxembourg, she had followed him to the bank, she had taken even his prolonged exits as mere intermissions.

He would explain his life plan to her, adult to adult, kiss her goodbye the nice way, wave her off to Brazil and think of her sometimes.

He tried thinking of her as he lifted the platform where the spare-wheel went, put the briefcase there locking it firmly, shoving the lid down far harder than it needed to close it as if that would keep the money safer and keep Vanda shut out too then shut the boot and checked it was locked too.

He frowned. He was still thinking about her and there was a funny unfamiliar feeling. He tried to recall what it was. Not regret. Not anger. Not relief.

He got in the car and looked up. Great. The Golf had a wind-back roof and it was a beautiful day.

PAGING LYNCH MADISON

Looking up at the blue square of complete freedom, he could so easily picture Vanda's long dark tangly hair whipping over her face until she tied it up in that glossy bun, half-singing because they were together on some sort of journey - wherever they might be going.

"Shit," he said, remembering now what the funny feeling was.

No good sitting there hitting the wheel with the heels of his hands.

"Come on. Get in," he said tersely, pulling up where she had stood exactly where he had left her.

"Can you open the trunk, please?" she said. "Jeez that wheel takes up all the space. What's it there for?"

Lynch shrugged and jammed her big shoulder-case in. "You'll have to take your bag into the car," he said slamming down the lid, scared to look at her for fear of his funny feelings still dragging him about.

He started to drive out of Luxembourg without even glancing at her. Into the increasingly dismal silence Vanda spoke very quietly.

"Which sign-posts am I looking for?" she said, the model passenger, going where the wind blew her.

PAGING LYNCH MADISON

"Belgium," he said, tonelessly. "It's all right when you're on the road, it's getting out of town centres that's so hard."

As soon as the words were out of his mouth, Lynch Madison had caught a faint unwanted whiff of Leslie Merrett starting out on a long trip.

Leslie Merrett had always insisted on hiring a car for at least some of the family holiday, excited at whichever one he was given, so long as it was some different make of car which had the indicator, let alone the steering wheel and the brake, on the wrong side, nowhere to put the over-large unfoldable maps and the sense that you had to make your own new routine on your own unknown route. Some seed of Lynch already there that he hadn't ever interpreted.

"I've been wondering if I ought to smoke, you know," Lynch said confidentially, unintentionally wiping the windows again instead of indicating his emergence from the slip-road. "I've never really sat down and thought out do I want to smoke or not. When I lived in Crossbridge it was the done-thing to worry about lung cancer. But ---"

"And now lung cancer is OK?" Vanda said, staring at him until he was forced to look at her when a clear enough space came in the traffic.

"No, that isn't what I mean. I mean I was taking smoking as an example - I mean -----"

"You're weird," she said.

Lynch stopped at a garage and parked away from the pumps - no need for Texaco juice yet. Just

PAGING LYNCH MADISON

fill up with drink cans, a Billy Joel cassette he had had long ago, and, of course, some Raider chocolate bars without which no European trip can be made.

He bought a map, remembering to discuss the route to Geneva at length with the owner of the garage, so that he could be easily remembered Swiss-bound in his last wearing of Leslie Merrett's suit.

"I'm feeling pretty free now," he said, embarrassingly anxious to explain himself when he was back in the car.

"Yeah?" Vanda closed her eyes and put her head back.

"So I have to be honest with myself about absolutely everything."

"Yeah."

He was in terrific danger of spilling out his feelings right there. Silence for a while would be a good idea. "Leave me to think a while," he said, clamming up, speeding up.

"Just in case I'm being followed, and I never forget that I might be, I've headed for Switzerland first, see what I'm up to?" he said to Vanda, after doubling back on himself an hour later, back and under the road they'd come on to return to the route through Belgium to Calais.

"Yeah."

"We'll stop for lunch the very first large service station we come to and ----" He looked at

PAGING LYNCH MADISON

Vanda. She had been uncharacteristically docile, silent, obedient, asking none of the difficult questions he had been trying to anticipate.

"When we're there, I'll get into my real clothes and ---"

He tailed off, unsure of himself.

"You're really weird, do you know that?" Vanda said, sitting up, tearing the top off a Raider, sliding one of the thick bars out and holding it prior to biting.

"Are you still on about the smoking thing? I was only ----"

"Like, weird. I mean why all this stuff with the bank? You went to the bank for the same reason everyone goes. To get out wads of money. We all know that's what you came to Luxembourg for. Like, what else do people go to Luxembourg for, for Chrissake? Why not just say 'look I don't want you around. I'm collecting all my dough and I don't want you to know my business.' I wouldn't mind. I mean, I don't care about your money, Lynch.

"Bud and Chi and me we were larking about. Like, we wondered how long you'd have to save up to get as much as we could make our families ladle out to us. Look, we've all got enough. We don't need any of yours. It's yours legally, isn't it? And with the secret meeting hours later and that crap. Like what were you trying to do? Unload me I guess. Well OK. But do it nice, can't you?

PAGING LYNCH MADISON

"I mean like half the world says one thing and does another. Things don't always get to be completely straight up and down. People have lovers here and lovers there or a guy can want to run, sure. Well OK. But at least do it honest."

She stuck her teeth down into the sticky bulk of the biscuit as if she had finished talking to him then continued, mouth-full and furious.

"I mean, why doesn't anyone ever say something to you? Stand up to you? I mean, why didn't you ever write to whatasername - Jean? Jan? - if you were too lousy to do it to her face. You could have said 'look, it didn't work, I want my own life. The key to the safe is under the second best cutlery, have a good life.' Why weren't you just straight with her? Jeez. To be your kid! Whatever did Charlotte say to the kids in school? And --jeez, Lynch."

The car started to shoot through the traffic at an enormous speed. It rudely pushed in and overtook thoughtlessly and got hooted and gestured at.

"Yup," Vanda said. "Got it. Nobody can ask you any real questions - especially about Jan and the kid, right? We all play let's-pretend. And nobody, but nobody is allowed to point out that Lynch is a shit."

The car weaved and ducked and skidded some more before simply going dangerously too fast for quite a few horrific miles.

When the car had finished its tantrum and returned to its polite path amongst the other vehicles,

PAGING LYNCH MADISON

Vanda removed her hand from the roof grip and Lynch let his shoulders down a few inches.

There was silence until just before two o'clock. The Golf squealed into a large, busy service station and angrily put up with a not very convenient space right over by the lorry park. Its driver got out, leaned in to pull open the boot-latch before slamming the door, reached in the boot for his clothes bag and slammed that too.

Lynch didn't look back to see what Vanda would do. In the busy toilets he changed in a cubicle, squashed the smart suit into the bag, and decided that he would just leave the whole thing in the restaurant after he'd eaten and let it take its own chances.

He washed in a very leisurely way, a little calmer, brushed his hair back - not long enough for the ponytail yet.

In the unattractive cafeteria, Lynch picked up a smeared tray, filled it with unattractive food and paid the bored man at the till. Sitting at the only spare place at a table near the window for a little light in the gloom, he shoved the bag firmly into the corner and ate, no question in his head of where's poor dear Vanda.

Who was standing hesitating between hunger and anger, tensely between decisions in front of the ladies' mirror a comb unused in her hand.

Lynch finished the smoothed-out sheets of the weeks-old Telegraph he had used in the bottom of the bag hundreds of years ago - before Luxembourg.

PAGING LYNCH MADISON

He filled in a few of the more obvious crossword clues, and, less violently angry now he'd eaten, stared blankly out of the window that looked out over the children's play-patch, hating his present impotence, trapped between decisions himself.

It had been unbearably painful having to listen to Vanda annihilate Leslie Merrett and his pathetically transparent plotting. Brain-damaging to think of his dear friends killing themselves laughing at him.

Dressed in his Lynch clothes now, he told himself that Lynch was wiser and more tricky, more ruthless and quite unfeeling.

It wouldn't faze Lynch a bit coldly to hand Vanda a substantial amount of money for services rendered (he'd make sure it was given in some way that would hurt a bit,) add a little honeyed talk about 'just one of those things', a bit of ambiguous eye-contact and let her hit the road out of his life.

(They say in Brazil it's summer all year around. Four thousand and what miles of coastline. Barbecues. Twenty-three beaches. Playing The Two Doves over and over on the big hotels circuit with Vanda. Building health hydros and a nursery for Chi's new baby.)

Buy a globe and spin it: weren't there a million choices just like that.

Look at the time. He must be on the road. Hurry.

PAGING LYNCH MADISON

Hurry? What for? Who for? Never mind. Hurry.

Where the sod was she?

Lynch was ready, now, he congratulated himself, to give the appearance of dealing quite kindly with Vanda's unacceptable interference. He got up and stretched and made for the door, leaving the angry Leslie Merrett and the Leslie Merrett clothes behind.

Ah there she was. And not alone. Two wild-haired boys with clean brown faces were jostling for her attention - she was giving them plenty of it. They looked stricken.

He hesitated, watching her across the large space. At a table behind a bank of plants they were settling down, taking food they had chosen off the trays, clinking down the cutlery, scraping back the chairs, making a party of it.

The boys sat while she still stood, digging in that huge bag she always carried, for a pencil and paper which she gave to one of the boys. Now she was sitting, ripping the cellophane from and holding the first of two large triangular sandwichs in both hands, elbows on the table, talking too much to eat, shining, glistening, entertaining the two backpackers who had presumably paid for her meal.

Now she was digging again. What was it this time? Quite small. Maybe it was that photograph of herself in a wildly erotic fancy-dress. They certainly seemed extra fascinated at the something she was showing them.

PAGING LYNCH MADISON

Vanda was an easy pick-up, he should warn them. Just a singing tart. She'd picked him up in a cafe, hadn't she? And followed him home and loved what he had done to her when she got there. Let her follow those two sex-crazed adolescents home and see what she got.

And she was being quite remarkably childish. She was looking right through him. He was sure she had seen him and was playing being ridiculously animated with the spotty perverts.

He tried to out-guess her. Could be she would ask him to give the two boys a lift to Calais, figuring he'd be unable to fight with her with them in the car.

Bad luck. He'd give her the money right in front of the boys to further embarrass her. And give her just a cheerio and strand her. The lesson had been learned. Enough Vanda. He watched her for just a painful moment longer then walked out.

At the car he leaned over to get the maps, then immediately wound the roof open. Her damned perfume -----

After checking some distances, he drove to the pumps at the filling station and stood by them, nozzle in hand, thinking.

Where was he going? How much petrol would the car hold so that he didn't have to stop again before he got there. He wanted very badly to be alone for a long while.

PAGING LYNCH MADISON

The pain and the muddle was coming back. He tried to think positive and helpfully brutal thoughts. Vanda: sexy, exciting but tiresome. Dumping time.

In Brazil she'd take up her family life again, Bud and Chi and she would get together now and then to discuss old times. The hole would close over. Life should be easy for Vanda out there where she belonged.

He was sure she'd make it in the clubs and any family will bury any number of hatchets for a star. (Would his? He shut that door quickly before anything could get in.)

Lynch had been, (he floundered around for the truth of the matter) passionately befriended at last but was too vulnerable to stick around, that was it.

He reached for a map, turned the pages, trying to excite himself, trying to feel wildly liberated, unconstrained, 'carte blanche' I think you call it. Not lonely. God, no.

Yes. Draw a line through France into Switzerland into Italy, down the Adriatic coast - or all the way through Yugoslavia to Greece. Plenty of beaches on Greece and strangers easily taken to, according to Homer, though his poor eyesight made such a judgement suspect.

With a full tank and an empty passenger seat, Lynch adjusted the wing-mirrors, checked the light-bulbs, re-arranged the now nicely folded maps, cleaned the windscreen, filled the windscreen washer, took the water-can back, revved the engine

PAGING LYNCH MADISON

slowly, revved up again and kicking himself for hanging about like that for Vanda to come screaming out "wait for me, wait for me" and the happy ending, drove thoughtfully and foolishly back to a space nearer to the main buildings.

He was reconciled, he was sure he was, to travelling on without Vanda now.

But he had to ----- He slammed out of the car and back to the cafeteria to drag her out. Screaming, if necessary. Sort things out. She had asked for honesty. She'd get it together with the big goodbye.

She was not, however, in the cafeteria. Nor were the baby-faced guys with the back-packs.

Back to the car. Hanging about. Hanging about. Getting angrier.

Fifteen more minutes and Lynch knew he couldn't stand himself waiting for nothing any longer.

Lynch drove off alone up the road to Strasbourg, burned up by the way she had chosen to leave yet half-pleased that she had been as outrageous as that. No conscience required. Nothing but the blue and white of the imagined Greek coast in his head ----

Until he thought to pull over and check that the ----

He pulled up the boot-catch, loosened the screws and lifted the part of the floor where the spare wheel usually went. Where the briefcase had been.

PAGING LYNCH MADISON

Just Bud's fax and a note. A note from Vanda. "Your money's gone with me to Rio, querido. Your money will be more useful in Rio. Come and get it. Your ticket's waiting at Heathrow." Then a number. "Ring this anytime. Even better, ring it from Rio airport. Come soon. Love and kisses."

The sodding, buggering bitch. The sodding, buggering bitch. The bitch. The bitch.

Off the motorway and round and back on it. Back just once more to the cafeteria. Not there of course. Non. Personne. Une fille avec deux ---? It is so busy, monsieur -----

He checked his wallet. All he had left in the world again. He felt hot, tight, nauseous. He was having a stroke. He'd die. Be buried unknown in an unmarked grave to the music of Sacha Distel at a service station on the outskirts of Luxembourg.

Or he could fight on. With a tank of petrol, he could still get to Greece and start again. Or - hang on, get to Calais. He could just about pay a pedestrian's fare to England, he would think. And get there before that sodding buggering bitch left for Brazil with his money. If the two guys didn't steal it from her.

He checked. Yes. Inside his overnight bag, the clarinet case was still inside. (How kind of you to leave me that.) He didn't seem to be angry. He just seemed to be dead.

Which was a coincidence because the car was dead too. Nothing. Not a cough or a groan.

PAGING LYNCH MADISON

"Il ne marche pas," he screamed down the phone at the hire company, though they were being very gentil. They were tres sorry. But they were tres busy. Despite the advertisments, they could only supply another car that did marche when they had one. They believed it would be tres quick, monsieur. Two, three hours maximum.

Two, three hours? He left the car unlocked and the keys in it, picked out his case and walked away to where several intercontinental lorry-drivers were filling up with diesel.

After a fews nons he got a cough-choking nod of the head from a particularly fat driver and mounted with him into the smoke-filled cab, while Fat-Man's teeenage spot-encrusted mate or son moved, without comment, into the back of the lorry.

"Calais?" the driver said, once.

Lynch nodded. And not another thing said by anyone to anyone, just the radio on, irritatingly just too quiet to catch anything but its foreignness.

For a while, just the rustle and drop of cigarette packet after packet, sweet wrappings, chocolate bar papers and biscuit boxes, on the floor in heaps around the driver's feet which still found their way to the pedals. Monotonous monotony.

The lorry was still.

"Merci, monsieur," Lynch said, waking suddenly, feeling dreadful, stiffly getting out and looking in desperation for a toilet. Good of the bloke

PAGING LYNCH MADISON

not to drop him outside the port, but straight up to the door for tickets. Very good-natured of him.

Lynch put his case down between his feet and reached into his back-pocket for his wallet to give the fellow something so he could buy himself a kilo or two more cholestrol. The least Lynch could do.

But the driver drove off fast with a tiny nod, chewing on something, the spotty boy once more beside him. Did he just eat and say nothing endlessly? Surely the first signs of indisoluble unhappiness. Lynch felt guilty: he could have spoken to him, maybe helped him by listening. Would that have solved his weight problem? Helped him to live longer? Should people interfere with each other out of human kindness?

The wallet had been in his back pocket, surely. Lynch tried everywhere else he might have put it. Then he took everything out of everywhere twice more.

Sodding buggering thieving fat lorry drivers.

As he stood at the urinal, the water spouting angrily from him, he felt that he had come out of a lonely long dark tunnel to find himself walking towards the next deep dark pit crawling with plague.

Are you still standing there with your hands on your hips canting coldly through your prejudices? Slit-eyed-certain that Lesley Merrett made a rod for his own back and it serves him right if things are constantly going wrong for him. Why, he should never have left home in the first place, you're saying? Have you learned nothing?

PAGING LYNCH MADISON

Any fool can stay in the half-light of safe tolerance with a life that isn't fulfilling, drinking enough drink to prevent the chinks of emptiness filtering in, hiding in dark glasses from the low voltage of life's expectations. It is right, it must be, to run like mad after the dazzling lights of happiness.

Isn't there a shift of sympathy in you lately for the runners and the hiders? If it ain't broke, don't fix it, they say. Sure. But on the other hand, if il ne marche pas, get out and get on. What's so absolutely upright about half-living somewhere, giving not-much to someone who needs all of you, only to say, however nobly, to a friend you think will understand and admire you for the sentiment, "but that isn't where my heart lies." At least it can be seen that throughout, Lynch has had disappointment and worry, no one to share it with, no one to blame. And despite the overwhelming weariness in him at the endless troubles, he seems willing enough to pay these exorbitant rents in part-payment for the gaping rents he left. Don't you just warm to Lynch in his troubles?

And that's another stupid place to leave a wallet, Lynch thought furiously, watching the unbuttoned pocket of the jeans at the next sink to his bulging with money and credit cards. He would have to reach out about - about a foot. Lean over, drag the wallet away and run. Run where? Run into the first shop, band his growing hair back, put a jacket on. And his sun-glasses. Out into the crowd, sit quietly, read a paper till the fuss died down.

PAGING LYNCH MADISON

Lynch had been washing his hands and watching the fellow's bum for too long. He became aware of the inviting smile.

Lynch shook his hands quickly and disappeared with that quickening change from despair that positive action always brings. Plenty to do. First, look for Vanda. She had only been trying to rattle him. She'd be here at the hoverport, he was sure. It would be best not to scream at her. Sweet-talk. Anything. Get the case back, make the goodbye very final and forget her.

The bastard lorry-driver hadn't made bad time whilst he had slept; he could have been delayed at the French border, as lorries often are. Though what difference the time made now, he wasn't sure.

His mind began to swim clear. Of course. The time-difference. Offices were still open in England. Phone-calls to be made. He was penniless - or should that be francless. Just a reverse-call to Bud's office would sort everything out for him. Then wait here at miserable Calais till il marche.

On reverse charges they wouldn't let him leave a message on Bud's answer-machine. Stuck without even the price of a coffee.

He laughed out loud.

Five minutes later, in the warmth of the hoverport concourse, Lynch stood playing "Annie's Song" with a poignancy all too sincere, the empty clarinet case ready for the chink and clink of the thrown coin and the occasional folded note.

PAGING LYNCH MADISON

Money that would be no use to the traveller once home, he rationalised, forcing the shamefulness of begging from his head. "Somewhere over the Rainbow" brought in the money from the kids. "Lullaby of Birdland" the oldies, but Piaf tunes proved to be the best and he could stop after a bit of that and buy himself plenty to eat and drink and a bit left over for those he was attracting to himself now. A different sort of groupie from those he was used to with the band; buskers gets drunks and loners and the damned.

Standing at the phone again, with coins in his hand this time, he wondered if this was the best money anyone ever earned. Money to survive on, work only to eat. Maybe it was how things were supposed to have been and went wrong the moment the first over-enterprising caveman had 'a little something over' at the time of the new moon.

The telephone answering machine on the desk at Bud's was asking him to leave a short message. He couldn't think what to say. (Vanda's a thief. Tell her to keep the money. I'll make my way without it.) He thought again. Maybe, yes maybe when they were all discussing him, laughing at him, Bud or Chi might have suggested the idea of pilfering the case from him.

Maybe they told Vanda it would be good insurance against him failing to show up in Rio. Balls to that. He could sing for all his suppers. Nobody would ever ever tell him how to live again. He left no message.

But back at the concourse, whatever he played, Piaf or even Mozart, business had tailed off.

PAGING LYNCH MADISON

People were looking but not throwing money. (He swore never ever again to pass unheeded the hat of the crummiest violinist in Oxford Street, the sax case of the worst 'Take Five' on the underground.) Then the boat-load boarded, the place emptied, the sweepers appeared. A hiatus.

Lips aching, reed a little cracked but useable, he put his clarinet back in the case, put the half-handful of coins in his pocket and went to the phone to leave Bud a conciliatory message - asking for his money back, in short. On the machine he would coolly demand that the money should be left for him - where. On the machine he would compose himself and make sure he sounded unemotional, impartial, glacial. Hell, the answer-machine had been switched off. Just Brr Brr and nothing else.

The only other people in the world he could phone were the Amorettis. No. He couldn't do it. He shouldn't. He mustn't.

"Hallo, Signor Amoretti? It's me. It's Lynch here. Lynch Madison. I'm in France, Signor. Yes, France. Somebody has stolen all my money -------"

Several choruses of "Blue Moon" (you'll play anything if you're thirsty) netted Lynch two coffees, a dry croissant and a sit down amongst several transcontinental no-hopers.

Heart-pounding at the phone, exactly an hour later, just as Signor Amoretti had promised, he learned that money was on its way to shelter him from the storms. Several other 'arrangements' had been made. But Lynch must do everything Signor Amoretti told him and he must come directly to the

PAGING LYNCH MADISON

cafe on his return and stay with them until he had somewhere to live. Signor Amoretti absolutely trusted him to do this, yes?

Yes.

Lynch wept. In short, like the rest of us, he was most easily destroyed and seduced by kindness: fierce independence is carelessly shattered in the shortest puff of sweet friendship.

The Amoretti's, without any responsibility to him, were once again sheltering him from the storm.

PAGING LYNCH MADISON

CHAPTER NINE

Rio de Janeiro - the late show - Vanda in a spotlight that failed to cheapen her or her silver sheath.

From the wings, Bud, Chi and the baby watched Vanda sing with her recording guitarist as he played Mario's 'Two Doves' just that little bit more up-tempo - they liked it like that in Brazil.

Still good, though.

There was rapturous applause, of course. Two Doves was Vanda's most requested number since it had first come into the South American charts at the bottom and then risen to the top.

An encore? Of course, Chi whispered over Baby Lee's sleeping head. Even if she did two encores, there was still time for Vanda to change and they'd go en famille, as they thought of themselves, to pick Lynch up from the airport.

Really? Lynch Madison coming out to Rio? Why on earth would he need the whole bunch of them to meet him? There must be some long story behind that.

Yes, of course there is.

PAGING LYNCH MADISON

In the long and busy months the three of them had lived in Brazil - no, four of them since little Lee was born five months ago in November - Bud and Chi had had to have great patience with Vanda, whose moods had vacillated wildly with Lynch's phone-calls or, more often, their absence.

Vanda had been quick to get a key made for the case and had held her hand to her mouth in wonder that such a small case could hold such a fortune.

No doubt about it, she had smiled to Bud and Chi. Lynch would follow in a day or two. No-one would just abandon that amount of money. Once Lynch arrived in Rio she just knew she could make him stay.

At first Lynch was just bitter; crazy to get his money back, but too proud to come and get it. He had bullied Vanda just to send it to a box number, never revealing where he was, what he was doing, just saying he couldn't cope without cash. Not nice calls. Down to business. Unfriendly. Then one days a different call.

Lynch sounded, suddenly, very relaxed. It was fine with him. He didn't want the money. They could give it away. Lynch needed nothing from them. Lynch especially didn't need Vanda. He wasn't coming. He couldn't ever live in South America. This was goodbye.

Vanda wouldn't sing that night or all that week. Vanda wouldn't eat. Vanda wouldn't get up in the morning because Vanda couldn't see the point of living.

PAGING LYNCH MADISON

"Where shall I send this letter to Lynch?" Vanda said, her lip quivering, the letter in her shaking hand.

The letter said she'd burned Lynch's money and would forget him before the smoke cleared.

Chi took the letter from her, promised that she would address it to the Amorettis for her, tore it up and went to Bud, her own lip quivering a little.

Bud frowned a lot and went silent for a day or two then he and Chi began to interfere quite a little and started the long secret process of negotiations to get Vanda's Brazilian family back.

But the Vasconceloses proved very obdurate. The family remained unresponsive to her re-appearance in Brazil and unmoved by her overtures of friendship.

With the exception of just one of her cousins, she had said glumly. Aha, Chi and Bud shone and winked at each other.

"You must come to the discoteca tonight," her one friendly cousin Carlos Antonio, had said, shaking his head when he had listened attentively to her sad love story through her sniffing and sobbing. "I will meet you after your show and take you there. There I have many friends. You will not be lonely."

Crying and protesting that no one would ever be her friend again, Vanda nevertheless was ready in a sleek white dress when he came to pick her up and

PAGING LYNCH MADISON

with eyes shining and legs twinkling she had danced till the morning.

By the following week, this step-cousin, the kind quiet Carlos Antonio who had grown up with half her step-family, had fallen for her in a wonderfully Brazilian way, sending presents, romantic letters, begging meetings, staring at her from one of the front tables of every show and scarcely speaking to her at all.

On the other hand, beautiful Osvaldo Oliveira, newly in from Sao Paulo for six months, took no such cissy other with any such Carlos Antonio niceties but after dancing once with Vanda, took her to the bar, bought her a drink, asked her to go to bed with him, preferably now, and was amazed and rather cross that she said no.

Vanda remained somewhat aloof from either of these approaches. Or to quote from her own trembling lips and proud chin, there was left for her, in life "nothing but my music."

This meant Vanda now made time for some singing lessons which even the teacher admitted she needed only for refinement, and sang herself silly at almost too many gigs for her own good.

Her two suitors persisted in their own ways - Carlos Antonio never missed any of her performances and the flowers kept coming.

Osvaldo Oliveira just told her what she was missing by refusing him, quite unemotionally by telephone daily, not even pretending to be interested in her singing career or her emotional state.

PAGING LYNCH MADISON

And quite incidentally, at this time, she had become quite startlingly quickly a Latin American sensation.

Right from her initial popularity at the second-best gigs their agency conquered first, to the slightly more up-market places they landed through the best of the media time - in May, the cultural saturation month - she had arrived fortuitously at the top clubs and hotels just when the long-awaited moment arrived for Brazilian music and singers to hit the top of the charts in Europe too.

The Brazilian papers had pronounced her a singing 'find' often enough for her to be really 'found' and now they had begun praising her as an all-round entertainer and she and her fees were really on their way to the stars. Recording contracts had to be sifted just to be managed.

If you are the type of person who never believes anything until you have tangible proof, for confirmation of her stardom just look over there.

Who's that? Her family. The Baptista Vasconceloses. In strength. Mounds of them. The Baptista Vasconceloses who went nowhere en masse unless it was the right place to be seen in.

Here they come from behind their barricades in platoons, clamouring for tickets, claiming kinship, ready to forgive - ready to forgivingly exploit her for all that she might be worth. Whether this would be a temporary or a permanent rebonding would depend on the extent of her success and the measure of her

PAGING LYNCH MADISON

gratitude. And maybe, like everyone else, they would grow to like her too.

In the warmth of their flattering attention, her understandable coldness to them was overlooked and was thus melted. Family bridge repairs were under way.

As a first gesture of reconciliation, after the third-night party thrown for Vanda and Bud and Chi by the uncle who had been worst to her when she was down, the Baptista Vasconcelos family recoiled in horror from Carlos Antonio's comic but tragic description of the squalor in which their precious family star was living with her Asian servants.

After apologies had been extended to an amused Bud and Chi, the family phoned to tell them that a large (understated, it was vast) apartment overlooking Copacabana Beach would be put aside for the use of them all use until further notice.

Bud and Chi had to overcome their scruples about this and then Vanda's but well before the winter, better known to you as the summer, they had moved into the lovely apartment, only a few things to buy ready for the baby.

With space around them now, and a telephone of their own, there was time to worry about the dilapidation of Bud's farmhouse property - this broken-down 'fazenda 'in the mountains of Petr¢polis, less than an hour away from the fancy apartment.

PAGING LYNCH MADISON

Bud, the health freak convert, (Chi's influence) was to spread healthy living to the poor and the very rich of Brazil.

Time to take endless trips there, with a machete first, to hack a path, with a dismissive surveyor, then with another surveyor who didn't tell him to forget it. And a special quiet trip with a snake-expert from Sao Paulo to gauge what precautionary measures to take before any further trips.

That quietly and effectively done, time to start talking the Brazilian equivalent of 'outline planning permission' and the Brazilian equivalent of 'preservation orders' and the Brazilian and globe-wide equivalent of 'red-tape' tied so tightly it will one day stop the world from turning.

It took months and multiple fees for Brazilian lawyers specialising in land development and property development; specialists in leisure and sports matters; specialists in getting things done. Brazilian men in the know. (Everything, they found, came back to being 'in' with the Baptista Vasconceloses.)

Time to bring the new baby girl home from its very short stay at the maternidade, time to get to know her and call her Lee (though her name like those of her parents was more complicated than that on the certificate), time to begin the Star Sing Agency again just to cover their living expenses.

Chi was still keen to run her own agency; to have something of her own. And baby notwithstanding, the agency proved to be a cinch from the start. Rio was such a centre for music

PAGING LYNCH MADISON

festivals and concerts and entertainments, everyone needed singers anyway.

For Vanda, doors had flown open as easily as the slightest sound from her talented throat - maybe extra easily because she was local-girl-made-good. Baptista-Vasconcelos-girl-made-good, even better.

And from Vanda's success, it seemed everyone wanted to be represented by Chi. This way Chi had control of fine substitutes she could suggest for the tricky and quite unexpected problem of keeping Vanda's gigs and tours down to a well-judged number, keeping time free for rehearsal, recordings and videos, keeping Vanda from voice-strain and keeping them all from freaking out with the pressures everyone's success was bringing.

Meanwhile, Carlos Antonio was persisting with the sighing looks and the ever present thoughtful presents and Osvaldo with the ever-active unwanted hands under the restaurant table.

(The meaningless conquesting impatience of Osvaldo was the more difficult of the two to resist, of course, which is why most women are stuck with unkind, selfish and demanding men.)

Osvaldo Oliveira was from a very poor family in Sao Paulo who had once done a life-saving favour for Vanda's step-father. This made the two families lifelong 'compadrazgo' - sort of blood brothers - sort of South American Mafia, Bud and Chi whispered to one another, when Vanda explained all this to them.

PAGING LYNCH MADISON

So that's the reason Osvaldo Oliveira was promoted over the head even of grumbling Baptista Vasconcelos boys.

Osvaldo was now at the crucial "I'm a busy man and thousands of women are waiting for me so make up your mind" stage of his heavy groping, when luck gave him a little opening no Osvaldo would desist from pushing wider.

Reliable steady Carlos Antonio had been sent off by the Baptista Vasconceloses to 'release' the staff at all their Manaus branches and to put his mind to rehiring a less successfully buccaneering management team at these not-so mysteriously unprofitable sites.

But busy though this made him, (and unflatteringly soon after he got there,) Carlos Antonio had forsaken Vanda and fallen in love for good.

No more presents and sweetness and adoration from him for Vanda. He brought his Elisete, his poor but beautiful Manaus girl back with him to Rio to meet the family, and all Vanda heard from him now was Elisete, Elisete, Elisete and the sweet sighing of the wedding plans.

Never mind she had always laughed at Carlos Antonio. That really hurt.

When this was followed by quite a few more restless weeks without reply to her letter to Lynch, when her frantic enquiries after him to the Amorettis and then to Stan came to nothing but sympathy, when one particularly bad week the notes she encouraged

PAGING LYNCH MADISON

the audience to send to her dressing-room during her show proved to be almost exclusively on the subject of her body and not her songs, when a particularly hard-up music critic decided to use his column as toilet-paper with which to wipe her out, Vanda was ready to let her tears trickle silently back over her ears onto the frilly pillow under the full weight of the skilful triumphant Osvaldo.

They queued up to warn her off. All the young Baptista Vasconceloses, her cousin Carlos Antonio in particular, and even his Elisete, had the cheek to mix in. More interferingly still, Chi and then Bud in sorrow and in detail. Did they think she didn't know that Osvaldo Olieira was no good?

Pause here to consider and agree that no-good men are, short-term, inspirationally good companions.

Utterly guiltless, professionally selfish bad-men like Osvaldo know what a trip to the moon should be, never mind the searing burnt-out debris from the subsequent descent to earth.

Sensibly reserving a goodbye-date in her diary by which she would attempt to leave Osvaldo before he could leave her, Vanda locked her finer feelings in a safe place and came out fighting; glittering with enough imitation tat to dazzle anyone - except real friends and other human-beings.

Vanda moved out of the home her family had provided, and into Osvaldo's graceless apartemento.

PAGING LYNCH MADISON

Vanda turned up to her gigs, was never late for a recording but never stayed a second anywhere to face questioning or advice.

Vanda lost weight, lost her, in any case, understandably tenuous credibility with the family, lost her concentration and lost the natural sympathy of both Bud and Chi, (though Lee still thrilled to her Tia Vanda.)

Nonetheless, Vanda, had she lowered herself to tell her, would have declared that Osvaldo was giving her the support she needed right then, and in her spotlight, his extravagent bills paid without question, even Osvaldo glowed a little, held back from the worst edges of the violent tempers he was prone to.

The natural sell-by date for such a cynical liaison had come and just slightly gone; the faint spot of mildew could be seen, a sour whiff could be smelt - the flap of the letter-box put the lid on it.

A letter and a cutting arrived from Stan.

Leon Matthews, stage designer, had been unable to leave the stage where he lay immobilised after sudden agonising pain. The lighting director had agreed to go and collect this 'Stan' person so that he could hypnotise the design chappie in situ. At least the dress rehearsal might then be able to go on.

It was a sensational recovery right in front of an actress who appeared too distraught at Leon Matthew's pain not to be something special to him, to the waiting technicians and cast of dozens and it

PAGING LYNCH MADISON

proved to be marvellous publicity for the show, and for Stan of course.

No doubt that Leon Matthews was Lynch. No doubt that that publicity was the last thing that Lynch wanted.

Stan thought Vanda would like to know.

Almost immediately, the Lynch messages to Bud had started again.

You could tell he'd had some sort of a scare after the public hypnotising though Bud wouldn't give Vanda any details of anything Lynch said at all.

"What sort of trouble is he in?"   No answer.

"Did he ask about me?" No answer.

That's what Bud thought of singers who slept around.

But something big was up for sure. Lynch wrote the most strange and unlynchlike letter. Maybe he'd try Brazil and see, he said.

Vanda got to see the letter of course. (Easy. Chi had left it where it could be found on purpose. That's what she thought about singers who slept around out of loneliness.)

Before Lynch's firmly stated date of arrival clattered out on the fax, the wicked singer had read this stolen letter ten or fifteen times.

PAGING LYNCH MADISON

Immediately she had even heard him mentioned, she had, in a commendably virtuous way, given Osvaldo his first 'I've got a headache,' treatment with a view to telling him goodbye. Maybe it was the headache that gave him ideas, but he responded by hitting her head quite often against the wall before he punched her across the eyes and slammed the door as he went out.

It was then that she began to realise that she had a bit of a problem.

She stayed in for a couple of days to let the swelling round her eyes go down, (but not so much that Chi didn't notice it).

On the third day, after spending the night diplomatically silent under Osvaldo's full weight, as he let her know what he would do to her if she refused him again, Vanda knew she was in deep trouble.

The next morning, Vanda walked miserably down to the dirty sand at Copacabana, with a towel tied around the gap between the two halves of her bikini, (it was safer than carrying it in this thieves' beach) looking for the exact spot where she had always gone as a child when she needed to think.

Sure that she had found it, she smoothed the towel and lay down with the seventy-two people who had also chosen to lie right there, near a sad looking lifeguard at his posto (another wise safety measure) and let the tear-filled surfing waves cry for her.

PAGING LYNCH MADISON

(Hands up all those who nearly made a mess of their lives for lousy reasons and regretted every second of it. What? All of you?)

Bad enough that Vanda has been grossly unwise with someone as obvious as crudely tempting Osvaldo that she never even bothered to lie to herself about; and worse still that while she was guiltily doing that, Leon Matthews had invented himself and found himself an actress. Did the two circumstances cancel out like plus and minus?

Ice-boxes slung over their shoulders, the drink sellers stepped patiently over Vanda and all of them, dodging the volley-balls and the surf boards, the endless futebol, the tottering toddlers running away from their mulattas, the excited teenagers running as slowly as they could from their pursuant boyfriends,

Vanda refused kites, coconuts and skewered shrimps, dismissed hats and corn-on-cob, and tried to ignore coca-cola twice from a drum-beating Carioca who was volubly annoyed by her disinterest.

She needed at least three plans of campaign. The first to off-load Osvaldo, preferably amicably and quietly; at the very least without being beaten like an omelette; the second to keep Lynch from ever hearing about Osvaldo; the third to get Lynch to marry her and never disappear again.

So hard to concentrate when the sun was so hot and the noises around her so happy, and the waves were so huge and the children. Were there children anywhere to compare with these beautiful -
---

PAGING LYNCH MADISON

Never mind plans two and three. She jumped up, tied her towel round her waist again, anxious to be back to put simple, foolproof, Osvaldo-vanishing plan one into immediate operation.

***

"But exactly what did you say to Osvaldo?" asked Chi, on the floor of Vanda's old room in the apartment, helping Lee build a castle of brightly coloured tubs of reducing sizes as Vanda unpacked her cases.

"I said 'Osvaldo! Osvaldo querido! I used all the most poetic Portuguese I could think of, Chi. And I know a lot. I called him, well, you know? And 'Osvaldo!' I kept saying. He likes that. And having his greasy hair, you know, there? At the back of his neck? You know how they love having that stroked."

"Then what?"

"Then I told him how I longed to live in his precious Sao Paulo - he thinks it's heaven there with the smog and the traffic. He thinks Rio is too hot, too airless, too many beaches, too small-town, not enough night-life for him. I don't know why he believed what I was saying suddenly. Always I am arguing and saying how Rio is better."

PAGING LYNCH MADISON

"All fall down," Chi said into Lee's wonderful laughter as she toppled the tubs again. "Again? Watch, sweetheart. One, two ----"

"'Osvaldo! Osvaldo!' I said, like in a film, you know? 'When shall we be married, querido, I want to have a house full of babies' ---- an hour later, he found an excuse for a big fight about nothing, made me pack my bag and threw me out."

Vanda shrieked with laughter, Lee laughing with her in training for womanhood.

Chi smiled and frowned. "Good. Good idea. So you are free of him. He's finished here, you say?"

"Back in Sao Paulo. He told my step-father he wanted to be near to his family - he hates them, Chi. He's ashamed of them. Anyway, so my step-father was very disappointed. He had big ideas for Osvaldo. Anyway, he gave him some crummy place to look after out there."

Chi waited quietly.

"I'm free of him, but --- like, it's true, Chi, I do want to get married and have babies," Vanda cried miserably, folding a bra three times one way, three times another, then throwing in on to the pile for washing.

Even Lee seemed to be waiting for her to get to the point.

"Maybe Lynch isn't Lynch any more. He's my only hope. I could never love anybody else. It

PAGING LYNCH MADISON

has been awful without him," Vanda said in a tiny little voice.

Neither Chi nor Lee commented at this point on fidelity or on chastity, or on the unusually defiant gutsy manner in which poor dear Vanda had compensated for this awfulness.

"I'm real scared," Vanda said, head down, tears dripping on to one of the Indian rugs Bud loved so much, "will you come with me to meet him when he comes."

"Of course. We all come to meet him with you if you like," Chi had said, smiling and playing don't-see-you-yes-I-do to make Lee chuckle. Chi who cut through nonsense and fears as if they were jello.

"You will?" Vanda said, glad of the excuse to hide her own eyes for the baby's game.

See? That's why they going en masse to the airport. That's what Bud and Chi and Lee were doing backstage during the time that Vanda was completing the last notes of a Billie Holliday number she sometimes used as an encore.

PAGING LYNCH MADISON

CHAPTER TEN

Vanda was singing her scared little heart out tonight at this Rio top-spot and the audience knew it.

The sun-bronzed seen-it-all, heard-it-all locals, cousins and friends as well as the easily pleased tourists rose everywhere to their sandals shouting 'local equivalent of Bravo' and 'local equivalent of More,' clapping with the enthusiasm of dolphin starving for fish.

After they'd had a short row with the management, who didn't care how compassionate Vanda's seven-day leave was, who didn't want Carmelinda das Neves as her substitute however encouraging her debut had been, who didn't want anyone but Vanda and were very sulky about it, they shrugged it off and walked back in the calm of the evening.

There, Vanda watched Chi give Lee a middle-of-the-night drink and a clean-up, smiled at how settled and serene the baby was again, then carried Lee's neat small canvas carry-cot between them, putting her down gently by the table where Bud waited for them in the late-late coffee-shop for a snack and a talk through of a rough plan of action.

By the time Bud had come back with some early morning papers - the reviews of Vanda's show were standard, flattering and professionally

PAGING LYNCH MADISON

unhelpful - it was time to dawdle down to the airport with the baby quiet in the same cot, now safety-strapped, at the very back of the Range Rover.

They drove through the now quiet streets that even an hour ago would have been paisley with night-time noise. From Copacabana Beach to the constantly busy area of the Aeroporto do Galeao Vanda quietly sang her show-songs, too nervous to talk, but too nervous to be silent.

And once just inside the airport, the disappointment of an hour's delay and the prolonged inactivity and boredom only airports can bring you without apology. (Something to do with the sheer miracle of flight allows that.)

Vanda nervously tried to make them go home and leave her, relieved when they wouldn't. But time crept on and more delays were announced.

Bud finally agreed they would take Vanda to the arrivals place then return to the car so that they needn't wake the baby and wait for her there.

Vanda took her place behind the barrier where many sleepy but determinedly wakeful people waited for the London flight. She was hot, worried and tired but still so high from the show she had just given you could feel the glow from a distance.

Vanda, (her, with the bounce and the tiny white skirt and the big smile) was soon starring as the main attraction of this airport arrivals show, till the boards finally showed that the plane had landed, that baggage was being cleared, that the passageiros were in the customs hall. Somehow everyone in the queue

PAGING LYNCH MADISON

nearby had told the story of who they were waiting for without her giving a thing away about herself. So, naturally, it was now everyone's business who such a girl as this would be waiting so long to meet.

You are perhaps also patiently waiting along with the queue to see how Leslie Merrett, the man with the easy aliases, will turn up. Who he'll be portraying.

Good. As they say in British pantomimes, here he comes.

Lynch Madison.

Of course, Lynch Madison.

Lynch Madison's pony-tail is neatly in place but it's rather short so he hasn't, you could guess, been Lynch for long. And he's very pale (but then every Englishman coming to Brazil looks like that) unshaven and lean to bony now. Somebody hasn't been looking after him. Will Vanda be pleased or sorry to see the state he's in without her? He's frowning. (A long journey to be cramped up with long legs or something else?) He is looking straight ahead. (Not expecting anyone to meet him?) He's travelling suspiciously light. (His bags lost in transit, maybe?)

The reason for all these mysteries are easily cleared. In the excitement of all their arrangements, nobody had replied to Lynch's fax and he is preparing himself for rejection.

He's had a lot of it lately. He proudly fidgets along catching nobody's eye - he is alone with his

PAGING LYNCH MADISON

light backpack and no duty-free, shut-in behind the many other cumbersome heavily laden trolleys of people who belong places, people whose eyes yearn for other eyes they know. Lynch Madison is inching along the Brazilian concourse with anxious impatience.

His journey had consisted of a tiresome seat-mate, lousy food, a film he didn't want to see but was too stressed to turn off and face his thoughts. He was pushing off a dozen second thoughts about coming out here.

All this had oiled the 5,750 miles of resentment into a kind of fury. If he ever finds Vanda, maybe he should greet her with a threat, a demand for his money and a cutting coldness.

She would hand over the money in return only for Lynch's promise of no further action. Then Lynch would have a quiet first-class air-trip alone again in another direction. The unfinished business of nine months ago.

Aching for Vanda's longed-for face and absolutely sure she wouldn't be there, Lynch's fist clenched ready to attack his disappointment in the best way possible.

At the same second Vanda spotted him, dreading him being on the plane, dreading him not being on the plane, so nervous of meeting him again and of his reaction to her that she had run to kiss him hungrily, holding him too closely for him even to look at her.

PAGING LYNCH MADISON

    Confused and disarmed, not even hugging her back as she pulled him along in a decided direction, he was aware of the usual airport-familiar line of friends and relations standing behind the barrier with her, waiting for the other people on his flight, all of them waving her goodbye. Did she know so many people in Brazil?

    The line shuffled in mutual disappointment at her unshaven crumpled stringy choice. Lynch supposed the men were muttering that he must be really rich to get a bird like that and that the women assumed he was great in bed.

    He found himself speechless, almost shoved towards an exit, Vanda's slim arm awkwardly round his still unresponsive body guiding him unwillingly to Bud's car where, bemused, he was not coldly rejected but hugged and kissed and welcomed and introduced to the sleeping baby whose name, Lee, they smiled, was derived from the same root as Leslie.

    Rigid with unfamiliarity, Lynch clung to the hand-hold in the back of the uncomfortable vehicle whose movement made him nauseous, while Vanda, holding his hand when she could and laughing into his eyes when the lights were bright enough for him to notice, became more and more Brazilian as she pointed here and there to his corpse giving historical, geographical, political, anthropological lectures the whole stretch of the surprising streets to Rio de Janeiro.

    Having run out of amazement, Lynch suddenly took her hand and like a pianist too long from the keyboard tentatively picked out a tune.

PAGING LYNCH MADISON

He had found middle C, all right. In the light of the next advertising hoarding, Vanda turned her full orchestra to him.

"Querido, how I missed you, querido," she murmured into his neck. Please forgive me for trying to ruin your life, taking your money, forgive me for Osvaldo, she didn't murmur at all.

"Vanda," Lynch said, swallowing hard. Sorry about the cruel silence, about the actress, and all the other things I have done that I have no intention of you knowing, he didn't even mention.

Bud saw that they were locked together like Velcro in his mirror and smiled at Chi. "I know where we'll go," he said and swung and swung the Range Rover round in the road, and took the turning he'd just passed on the other side of the road.

"Not tonight, Bud. Lynch has just travelled for - how many hours was it?" Chi said, smiling round at Lynch.

"However many," Lynch shrugged, the gaping lull between the free newspapers in London and the bad journey and the dropped landing-cards and the hard questioning at Rio now rosier in the glow of Vanda.

Bud went on driving up the wide avenues off the coast road, into narrow ones and up and on up the winding mountain roads.

"I suppose someone's going to tell me where we're going," Lynch said, after a little quiet while.

PAGING LYNCH MADISON

"North," Vanda said.

Up and up, European style houses and chalets scattered on the hillsides.

Suddenly turning into a hidden driveway, bumpy now, the ground wild and uncared for: the roadway rough, pitted, gravelly.

Bud stopped and got out, unpadlocked the big gates and drove up to the house, turning towards it and turning his lights full up.

They all stared at the fazenda. Lynch didn't ask a single question.

"Do you know what this is?" Vanda said.

"The wing over there is the wrong style and ruins the whole facade," Lynch said. "And from here I'd say those balconies should be roped off - one touch and they'd fall on you. What was this? An ancestral home turned into a farm but it didn't work?" he guessed, turning to Vanda. "It's the same in England. Nobody can afford the up-keep. Pity. Do they have a 'National Trust' over here?"

"The fazenda," Bud said, as if it were the beginning of a lecture, "was indeed once the home of some Guyanian ambassador for an extremely short while a very long time ago - a gift from my family to him for reasons I still don't know. But fearing corruption, and I shouldn't be surprised, Guyana supplied him with a more modest residence which he was told to move into or leave the service. But since then ---

PAGING LYNCH MADISON

"Come," he said, taking a torch out. "We'll walk round it once."

"Now? Why?"

"You'll see."

Chi and Vanda and the baby stayed where they were while Bud and Lynch strode on.

"I have been waiting every day for you to come back to us," Bud said quietly, after a few silent steps, coughing his tiny cough that meant that that brief conversation was over for now and could be discussed by arrangement another time.

"It wasn't until a few years later," Bud said, resuming his place at the lectern, "going through his papers that my father decided to do anything about this place. It wasn't important to him; it was part of a very big deal indeed. My brother tells me that my father sent a manager in to run it as a fazenda - a sort of model-farm. Anyway, the manager kept the budget that was meant for the rebuilding, and after letter and letter of complaint about him from anonymous letter-writers, one day he was gone without notice and - you can see how quickly after that things went wrong. But look at the setting, Lynch. Only the summer palace has a better one. I wish it was light so you could see."

Through the archway and round the back, Bud stopped to move the torch slowly over the acres ahead for Lynch to gasp at.

PAGING LYNCH MADISON

"In the morning, Vanda will start to show Rio to you. We want you to treat however many weeks you want as holiday before – well, let's not rush. You are maybe overwhelmed to be back." This wasn't a question.

"But I had to show you the fazenda tonight. This is yours, Lynch. All of it. Well, that is to say we made a legal agreement and we --- invested some of your money for you in a quarter share of this place and of course you will get a quarter share of all the profits. The money Vanda took from you was only to make sure you came here - and it will be delivered to you at once."

"Less 'the investment'?"

"Less the investment."

Lynch put his hand out for the torch and shone it behind him to the rear of the building, up high, down low, over the fields and back to the building, and shook his head trying to understand.

"I get quarter of all the debts you incur? Quarter of all the troubles. And all of the initial responsibility."

"It is going to be your triumph if you want it to be," Bud sighed, shining the torch ahead of them and walking confidently on through the dark.

Lynch stumbled along behind him hating the way he could hear himself grumble, but feeling honour bound to do so, nonetheless. "You might just as well have thrown my money down the drain. The place may be crap, Bud."

PAGING LYNCH MADISON

"But we will make a health-farm like nothing ----"

"Yes. Or we can run a circus here," Lynch said. "That would complete it. A circus. Rio must have dozens of health farms already, hasn't it?"

"Of course, I know. But they are spas in the spa towns and they are - ordinary. But you can build ---"

"I don't know anything about building health-farms - especially neglected tat like this. It may need almost demolishing, Bud. It isn't a little-bit-of-wall-papering-and-a-couple-of-shelves job. I'm out of date and out of practice and anyway I don't believe it will make money any more than it did before. The best places would be by the sea, I suppose? And this isn't by the sea, is it. Anyway I've come here to be free from --- look, Bud, I don't have to justify myself. You've asked me, I've said no. I'm not in any way interested. It's a bad idea. Not only for me. These places don't work."

"Right," Bud said, sweeping his torch again. "Look. I think something's wrong with the ground there. Over there. At least the pool cracked and had to be emptied. Yes, you're right. It's a ridiculous place and a huge challenge. That's what I thought. But you will love my ideas. Everything that is eaten will be grown or farmed in the grounds. I had the soil tested. It's perfect for cultivation, there and there.

"Everything will be organic and wholesome and good. Also we will build a hall and bring our

PAGING LYNCH MADISON

music here. The most popular stars will be brought here for the concerts and of course they'll stay here and at first, for publicity, we will let them stay so long as they sing for their supper and later --- it will be wildly expensive.

"The main aim is health through excellence. There will be excellent value for money and everything of the best. The rich will fight to get a place here.

"And from these profits, we will decide a proportion for charity and build clinics and schools and centres run on the same lines for the poor of Brazil.

"Tomorrow when you start your journeys through Brazil you will understand why. You are going to build this place, Lynch. Just the way you think it will work best. No interference. The first time you ever do what you were born to do, yes?"

"Never." Lynch took the torch from Bud and swept it over and over. "Can you imagine how long we'd need to hire earth movers for and --- and heavens knows what for the swampy land - if that's why the pool cracked. So there would have to be new groundwork for any new pool area, and we'll need to re-landscape all that land - how much land is there? Look at it.

"Let alone remodelling this brilliantly unusual custom-made building itself, there's other things to consider. I saw something in an architectural magazine - hey what was that - yes, I know. It's very specialised. Not to mention expensive, special equipment and special insurances

PAGING LYNCH MADISON

and --. All our money would be gone and the thing still not up and running."

"Money isn't any problem now, Lynch," Bud said. "This I will explain later."

"Your money may not be any problem," Lynch shouted. "But you've taken mine."

"Borrowed some of it, Lynch. Don't shout. It is an investment. We'll talk about it in the morning. If you like I will get Vanda's bank to write you a cheque for every penny back tomorrow. If you decide that's what you want. But wait. And you'll see. Can't you just visualise the opportunity I'm giving you?"

"It's not an opportunity. It's financial suicide. That's gone native out there," Lynch said, indicating the wildness ahead. "That isn't just foliage. Heaven knows what rats and -- and nasties are out there."

"Yes. It's been totally neglected for many years. In fact that was partly why it closed down. Running about out there, a child was bitten by a snake, the serum took too long to come from Sao Paulo and that was it. It was the publicity about it that finished the fazenda off for good. It's been closed like this for decades."

"Snakes?" Lynch looked round.

"Brazil's running alive with them," Bud said. "That's why the world's best serum-farm is in Sao Paulo. It's where there is the most need. I'm thinking maybe we should give some of the profits for a

PAGING LYNCH MADISON

snake-farm here so that the serum will be right here in Rio, too. Snakes! Look!"

Suddenly jerking the torch round, whilst Lynch tried not to jump into Bud's little arms. "There, did you see it go? Must have been fifteen feet long - longer. "Look, there's six more over there. Quick - "

Making a quiet laugh which for someone like Bud passes for wild hysteria, Bud ran back towards the girls, the spot of light running ahead of him and Lynch trying not to throw up behind him.

Back at the Range Rover Bud told and re-told this rare joke to Chi and to Vanda who overlooked it kindly in their anxiety to hear from Lynch.

"Are you going to do it?" Vanda said, taking Lynch's hand again.

"No," Lynch said, the touch of her reminding him of something so illusive he couldn't bear the thought that it might stop.

"Bud's offered me my money back and I'm going to take it and invest it in something worthwhile," he said, trying not to let Vanda disperse his sulkiness, wondering why he had travelled so far to be pushed around again, trying not to hear and appreciate the tender interest in him that Bud and Chi were showing and feeling Vanda's warm knee near to him and knowing perfectly well why he was back.

"Let's go home," Bud said, turning in the gravel, throwing Lynch and Vanda even closer. "We'll talk in the morning."

PAGING LYNCH MADISON

To lovers, there is magic in the word 'morning' in that it comes so deliciously slowly after the words 'dark', 'night', and 'bed.'

All of them knew that there would have to be many days and nights of explanations, fighting, shouting, compromise. They all knew that there were storms and volcanos to come, planning and failure to bear. All this covered by 'talking in the morning'. But for now, it would be dawn any minute and was well past the time human-beings stop worrying long enough to look for a place to lie down.

The future would be all the better if it would hold its breath and wait for the morning.

Now, back at the apartment, Chi carried the baby, still sleeping, in the carry-cot and put her down in the corner of their room, tactfully leaving Lee's little room for Lynch should he need it.

Bud gave them a generous and ambiguous pile of bed-linen and towels to decide from, an ice-cold pitcher of water, and a good night, firmly closing the door as they had so long ago in London.

Three steps to the door of Vanda's room and the door clicked shut, their two bodies holding it closed (and us outside curious but discreet.)

***

PAGING LYNCH MADISON

And when the morning came it was Brazilian.

"So hot," he said, "When does it cool off here?"

"It's always summer in Brazil, we say," she said, her ambassadorial role unfinished. "Brazil is perhaps the most surprising and varying country in the world. You'll see. I want to show you everything. We'll start in Sao Paulo - you'll find it is always colder than here, querido," she said, trying not to think of any particular residents of that city. "And the best way to enjoy ourselves is not to fuss too much. Not to make too many arrangements. We don't have to book on the Ponte Area flights - there are so many a day. So - we can take all the time we want," she said, the tourist lecture over, caressing him again, half incredulous that he was not imaginary any more.

"But so hot."

"Brazil's into air-conditioning these days. I'm talking rich Brazil, of course. The one in the apartment will be repaired by the time we get back from our vacation," she apologized. "You'll love July and August. Your sort of weather. English weather. Warm but comfortable, usually. You'll think it's warm but real Cariocas wear sweaters," she laughed."

"Oh no - it isn't July for two months," he moaned. "And I'm so hot."

"Mmm," she said. "Get dressed and let's go see Brazil."

PAGING LYNCH MADISON
CHAPTER ELEVEN

Back from 'seeing Brazil', Lynch is unpacking at some speed and Lynch is thinking. And he is frowning as he folds and stacks and discards.

Unpacking the second he hits base is Lynch's way of creating order. We all have our own ways of doing this. (Vanda's, of course, is to continue living from her suitcase until it has naturally emptied in usage.)

Lynch is troubled. His life is a mess. Usual reason. Women.

There's a puzzle here. Leslie Merrett had for years been a faithful loyal husband, as we saw. Exemplary behaviour a feature of his personality. Growing your hair long and changing your clothes doesn't change any of that.

So where did this love-em-and-leave-em Lynch emerge from? Was it, after all, that blow to the head on the fall from the bike? Or the free fresh wind in the hair in the dash from the safety of Crossbridge?

Is Lynch Madison, in fact, not Leslie Merrett at all?

We have observed that Leslie Merrett certainly spent his married years in sensual dullness,

PAGING LYNCH MADISON

feeling nothing much, though he tries and tries to remember the love he must surely have felt for his parents, for Jan at the beginning – but the only thing that comes back with a surge of unbearable love is thinking of how he saw Charlotte when she was born.

Since becoming Lynch Madison he has had five years of random coupling, sometimes politely, sometimes absentmindedly, always selfishly.

And now suddenly love. Love for Vanda. Long-time, long-lasting, want-to-talk-about-it, want-to-think-about-it, never-touch-another-woman, kill-anyone-who-hurts-her, terrified-it-won't-last, his-last-chance-his-best-chance, love in all its naked and shame-making exclusivity and greediness.

This same wild travelling-man, this same want-to-see-the-world-and-then-go-on-somewhere-else-man, had nonetheless and all of a sudden been strangely restless and inattentive through most of the wonders of Sao Paulo, impatient only to be done with them.

"You know what," he kept starting to say, " I think we should ----" but Vanda had the need to give him Brazil, her biggest present to him yet and she wasn't listening.

Vanda rushed him first to the place she and Queen Victoria marvelled over and loved the best in Brazil. (After the beaches, anyway.)

But Queen Victoria never had Vanda shoving her ruthlessly into a helicopter for the big treat of flying over the very rim of the amazing Iguassu Falls in awed delight. (Lynch marvelled all right, whilst

PAGING LYNCH MADISON

gripping the arms of his seat and checking for sick-bags.)

Vanda had him on boats, up mountains, and round exposed bends on the railroad that would make any self-respecting thrill-ride-designer blanch.

Vanda had him trying not to notice the suddenly exposed poverty that yearned towards him round every bend as she enthused him down to where the gold-mines were.

Shortly afterwards, she was all animation, interpreting for him earnestly in the high street farmacia, begging for a miraculous cream - anything strange from the rain-forests considered - for the swollen and spectacular bites his legs puffed up with.

It was through that night, scratching half his skin off and hardly sleeping that he decided to give up on Brazil for a while. Definitely giving up the Amazon, for now, where surely the bites would be bigger. Even giving up the flight to Brasilia - the one architectural wonder of the trip he had himself insisted on. Not now. No. Things to do.

"In the morning," he woke her to say, moving so she wouldn't touch his painfully swollen legs, "if I can still walk enough to get to the airport, we are going back to Rio. I will see your Brazil another time when I'm not stratching and I'm more in the mood."

He let her moan and plead with him, listening only vaguely. Then he stopped for a moment and explained himself thoroughly, so that he could get to sleep untroubled and leave her to worry: a male-skill handed on from the hunter-gatherer era.

PAGING LYNCH MADISON

"I want to walk and walk over that farm, fazenda, really long and carefully without any of you to influence me. I want to do it without anyone knowing that is what I am doing. I want to -- make a great deal of enquiries. I want to think about problems none of you are aware of and wouldn't think of. If I do this thing it will be from strength and it will be my project - not theirs or yours."

Vanda's silence was so long he thought she was sleeping again and turned over.

"I understand," she said. "It's good. But, the place is padlocked and wired up," Vanda muttered. "You can't get in to it without them. Sucks."

"I've thought of a way round that already," Lynch said smugly, still scratching wildly.

Restless for another few minutes, Lynch gave some thought to the hot-spring spas they had seen here in Sao Paulo. Maybe they should, on one hand, scratch, scratch, on the other hand, scratch, scratch, a better idea, scratch, another idea, scratch. He only finally fell asleep when he had admitted to himself that he was crazily excited about building the bloody thing.

***

"And," he said, on the shuttle-flight back to Rio the next morning, smothered in cream that had greatly calmed the itching, "after my days of un-interrupted thinking, when we announce that we are officially back, as soon as I have announced whether

PAGING LYNCH MADISON

or not Rio gets its world-class hydro, you are going to have to take me to meet your family. I think we're going to need a bit of Brazilian 'pull' for this project."

And this brings us back to where Lynch is unpacking his things, frowning and highly troubled after his researches and his decisions.

And Vanda is also frowning, a couple of miles away as she sits in yet another dressing room, this one located under the stage, thinking about those few sentences of his.

She is thinking about their last few secret days in Rio but she is thinking most about the dangerous and difficult days ahead in which she is to present Lynch to her dear Brazilian family. A family who had firmly stated principles of killing married men who lust after the Baptista Vasconcelos girls.

"It was a great vacation," Vanda lied, the second time she was asked, too busy in her head to listen the first time.

She got up and peeled her head-band carefully backwards, critically examining her eye make-up. "I couldn't bear it when he was out of my sight," she smiled truthfully, avoiding the travelogue, and sticking with the truth. "Jesus, Chi, I feel so good with Lynch, you know? When I sing tonight they'll think I've been to master-class at La Scala Opera House."

She la-la'd up and down a contralto arpeggio then pursed up her lips and put on the lipstick she hated and only wore on stage.

PAGING LYNCH MADISON

Chi moved Vanda's suitcase again to get to the other side of the hanging space. "Chi? What's eating you, Chi?"

Chi stood carefully still looking directly at her. "We are still very angry with both of you. Bud especially. But you know how Bud is: he won't show it to you when he comes back here tonight. But he has been furious all day. I too am angry."

Vanda turned to look at Chi, standing quietly to one side of the door, her tiny arms folded neatly as usual, her face gentle and sweet as usual.

"It is unprofessional behaviour, Vanda. Carmelinda das Neves hasn't got your voice or your personality but she was here when she was needed. The hotel had to spend much money billing you 'back tonight' and you weren't back. Juscelino Costa went crazy. He kept banging down your contract with his hotel group and spitting and I think he ended up threatening to break both your legs."

Vanda made a very foreign noise and a very international gesture.

"I don't know why I was so hot to come back to Brazil," Vanda said, turning back to her lipstick. "Brazilian men always want to break your legs, take your money or kill you," she frowned, fear for Lynch leaking through just for a moment again. "So - we were one day late. So."

"I lied for you last night. I hate to do that thing. I told Juscelino your flight was delayed too late for the performance. Now you must tell him that too."

PAGING LYNCH MADISON

"I will tell Senhor Costa that when I am with Lynch, time doesn't matter. I will tell Senhor Costa that I was here last night but couldn't be bothered to sing in his stinking hotel.

"And anyways, I'm here now," Vanda said dismissively. "I'm real sorry it upset you, though, OK?"

"Vanda, if Carmelinda had gone on again tonight, you would have been blacklisted. You know better than we do how Brazil's a small place when it comes to gossip. Here," Chi held out the tight bright bolero unsmilingly.

"Chi, Lynch is so wonderful to be with. You just don't think about anyone else. He's so ---- I mean, like, we were in Sao Paulo and he comes out of the bathroom and he's someone else, you know? There I was sleeping with Lombardi Malino. An Italian plumbing engineer, right? Can you imagine?"

Chi bent to hook Vanda's tight waistband at the back and frowned. "You mean even here in Brazil he still does this dressing up as someone else? That's peculiar, Vanda. He still doesn't feel safe?"

"No. That's not it. I'm sure it isn't that. You know, it's become, like, a game? Don't make faces, Chi. He's really good at it. He should be on Broadway. When we did the helicopter flight over the falls he was Lord Moore from the UK and an ex test-pilot. You should have seen him. It's all very simple what he does but – he's so wonderful."

Chi looked less than delighted.

244

PAGING LYNCH MADISON

"Lynch just can't seem to stay himself for long," Chi said, "I wonder if that is something to worry about?"

She caught Vanda's anxious eye in the mirror and they both looked down, unable to tackle it right now.

Chi put Vanda's wrap on a hanger and turned Vanda round and round. "You look special. Very special," she smiled.

"Of course. I'm in love. I wish you'd let Lynch play his clarinet for me on stage again. He wants to so bad. Maybe just 'Two Doves'? When he's practised a bit?"

"I'll ask Bud," Chi said, anxious to put that argument off till later, at least till after Vanda had sung her heart out. "Good luck," Chi said, kissing Vanda. "I'm going home. Don't fight too hard with Bud when he comes. You're in the wrong. Bow your head and it's quickly over."

"Japanese claptrap, Chi. I will sweet-talk him, instead."

"Latin-American bullshit, Vanda," Chi laughed and was gone.

Vanda filed a nail, stood up, put her hands on her hips and looked carefully at herself in the mirror. Great.

Letting her stagey expression fade she sat again, pudding-dull. So much to worry about. But it was fun seeing Lynch be funny and brilliant as a

PAGING LYNCH MADISON

Brazilian financier with such severe pharyngitis that Vanda was obliged to speak for him in the front office of the security firm they went to, wasn't it?

A little time and patience and the security firm had unwittingly revealed that the inexpensive and dopey system (even proudly named on the board outside the fence) Bud had put in, simply to keep the casual wanderer from the property (and from the snakes) could be put out of action with one cut of the cable and its cutting would set off no central alarm.

Pausing only to leave a false address for a leaflet and quotation for his own fazenda, they were quickly striding down the road to buy the necessary cable-cutter.

Then Lynch and all his other selves had dismissed her and seen her only in the evening. She had been sure who he was only in the night when she checked him out in the wide-enough bed at the small motel he booked them into.

Nothing normal about Lynch. But was she so normal either to love a man she knew was strange. A man who had run out on his entire former life.

And still an hour to go to curtain-call. No way she'd go and see the French illusionist up on stage at the moment, though the applause was wild for him. She'd sit and think and think till she'd worked her own private illusionist out.

***

PAGING LYNCH MADISON

There now followed a series of escalating fights. The small 'back late from their vacation' fight with Bud was mere iron filings to the fight about Lynch's secret investigations into the fazenda when he confessed them, never mind the steel bars of the prolonged fight about Lynch's 'stolen' money.

Lynch never even looked like winning that one. He was to get not one sniff of his francs-turned-cruzeiros that Vanda, Bud and Chi continued to insist that she had merely 'borrowed' from him until he either started on the work or, if that's what it came to, it would be handed to him at the airport on the day he was ready to leave Brazil for good.

"Under the new regime here in Brazil, the money is frozen anyway, it's the best for you," they explained ten times to him, force feeding him newspaper articles and the English language programmes on television.

At this stymied stage, Bud and Chi constantly restrained Vanda from any more questions and nagging though anxious to remind Lynch that time was going on. Impatiently, Bud assured him that Lynch wasn't the only architect in Brazil ----

That didn't help. Lynch just continued his theme. They had gone about things wrongly. He would never again live under orders: he would do nothing he was told to do. He would do nothing he hadn't chosen to do himself. Nothing. Lynch would do only what he wanted when he wanted.

This was no surprise to his friends; they had expected at least as much resistance as this.

PAGING LYNCH MADISON

But they were surprised (and wisely quiet about it) by three things: firstly, that he stayed so close to home; secondly that he was becoming so docilely dependent on them, and thirdly, and most unexpectedly, his affection for Lee.

"I'd quite like to get a clarinet tutor for a while," Lynch said, Vanda beside him, pushing Lee in the buggy down to the park while Chi saw a client.

"Sure," Vanda said. "Nice for you. While you're building it'll help you relax. And maybe Bud'll let you play for me again."

"You know I'm building nothing until I get some -- answers to some questions. I mean I'd like to get really good at playing and maybe earn my whole living as a musician."

"You're no great musician, Lynch, you're an architect, and you haven't done a useful thing since you got here," Vanda said, finally frustrated enough to be blunt.

"Never mind a tutor," she said. "You ought to get to work. Have a bit of self-respect. You've done nothing since you came here. And so far as music is concerned you're OK to play something you know well - but - a musician, no, no."

Lynch turned and strode back the way they had come and went missing - they thought he had gone for good. Vanda was hysterical then contrite then furious.

PAGING LYNCH MADISON

He was back in a few days, his thinness more defined, his frown-lines sharp on his forehead. Up and out every morning by six, back covered in dust, shoulders aching from a hod, back sore from the digging, he'd become a casual labourer down by the docks, learning about Brazilian building and Brazilian builders from the inside, no reasons given, no reasons required.

His friends were appalled but oddly, coldly, Lynch also went on. His lovemaking with Vanda continued, (though mostly half-awake at dawn without much enthusiasm) his non-attendance at her gigs excused by his early mornings.

"Just don't ask me when I'm starting one more time," he said so quietly it sunk in. "I'm waiting -- for something. You want this health hydro so badly, do it yourself. As a reluctant major shareholder I have earned nothing but the right to be free to do what I like. I've come to Brazil to be myself."

"You came to Brazil to hide, amigo," Vanda whispered, half-scared for him to hear but unable not to say it.

***

It was the best time of the day. All of them occupied in the front room of the apartment, Lynch showered and relaxed after his obstinately held job, reading a magazine and marking passages in it, Lee ready for bed smiling up at Bud as he helped her with

PAGING LYNCH MADISON

her favourite large jig-saw of a small girl her size on a huge elephant, calling to Lynch to help her too, Chi doing her accounts, plenty of time to spare before the gig tonight.

"I see you read that architect's paper and I think it is almost a shame you have such a gift, Lynch," Vanda said softly into the prevailing pleasantness.

Heads shot up. Everyone but Lee watched Vanda's hands arranging spray orchids with some fluffy greenery, clearing the wasted bits of stem and leaves from the floor, wiping the secateurs with a tissue, head to one side, fingers adjusting and lifting, while she crashed into Lynch with her words.

"You were a really fine architect and what did you do with that talent? What did you do with your ambition? You married the Boss's daughter. You built offices for money. A prostitute with bricks. I say what you say to me, yes? You never had the chance to do something so good on your own - you dream that one day it will be - what did you tell me - a funeral - no, a memorial to you after you're gone. You told me that once. This fazenda is that chance and you are still arguing and holding us all back from the new start we all want. Why?"

Lynch put the New York Times architectural supplement down on the inlaid table, pushed himself up and towards the door.

"If you had listened, Vanda, you will have remembered that I also told you -- some other things. My only money in the world has been completely tied up without my permission. If I succeed, you get

PAGING LYNCH MADISON

rich," Lynch said, stopping some sentences as he looked at Lee playing before him. "But I'm not too sure I get anything much." When Lee wailed because suddenly nobody was playing with her, Chi quickly stooped to pick her up and remove her from the room with the puzzle and a big frown across her face.

"I've got a quarter of nothing but a dream. And it isn't even my dream. It's yours."

"You know why you're so angry?" Bud frowned, speaking as quietly as ever. "You're angry because you're not doing it. And maybe you're angry because you have left unfinished business behind you. Until you rid yourself of the anger you will be useless to us and to yourself."

"I'm -----"

"It happens that we all have money, Lynch, all of us. We don't need your investment at all. If you would only read about Brazil. You haven't learned a thing since you got here. The land is worth a fortune even if the fazenda never gets built.

"You still don't seem to understand the economics of a place like this where there is so much intense poverty and intense wealth. This health-farm is something good for Rio and maybe good for the Rio poor who will come to work there, let alone the ones who come for the treatments and in the meantime it will be good for all of us to work together for the good of the people."

"The good of the people?" Lynch said intensely. "Why don't I rebuild some of those slums,

PAGING LYNCH MADISON

those hovels, those favelas, you call them. That would be for the good of the people."

"Where would they live while you tear down the only home they have? While you build? Many of them would die in that time. A million schemes have been proposed for the favelas, Lynch. Be realistic. You aren't angry about the Brazilian poor. You're angry that you haven't succeeded in isolating yourself no matter how hard you run."

This was true enough to hurt.

Also, members of the jury, it must be conceded that however grandly Lynch's shareholding had been granted to him, the truth of it was that his money had been confiscated. His resentment was atural.

"What will you lose if you try to build this thing," Bud said, trying the civilised way out again in his calm neat way.

"See how it goes for a few weeks, that's what I suggest. We leave it all to you, Lynch. What do you think? I can begin the publicity - it's what I'm best at and I have some wonderful ideas for this because I believe in it. Chi will continue to run the agency as much as she can with Lee on her hands, because that is what she loves to do and when the place is built we will need our own agency so it will be filled with stars, and Vanda will do her gigs because that is what she loves to do - with some other musician for Two Doves and you ----"

"I'll do what I like," Lynch said, though his interest in the project was hitting him hard now.

PAGING LYNCH MADISON

"You'll have to give me time," he kept saying. This was a cunning weapon he fashioned that could be used to hold things up till he could give in.

Maybe they had disrupted his whole life quite selfishly just to be their cheap architect and designer. He'd left all that behind to be a musician and traveller, hadn't he? (Which reminded him he hadn't practised his clarinet in weeks. He'd do it right away. On Thursday.)

But the weather was so good and the country so beautiful and Vanda so happy to be with him, and Bud and Chi such good companions and the new people he was reluctantly meeting so cosmopolitan and too busy to be nosey and the food and the living so -----

Suddenly, tired to cutting off all his fingers to spite his hands, Lynch made a deal with himself. He was living free, he was living wonderfully, Brazil had other great advantages like being huge and international enough to get lost in and if he made Bud's dead fazenda live again, it would be his huge debt to Bud and Chi paid off.

If he did it remarkably well, he thought, pencil in hand, happy for the first time since - so long ago - if he did it extraordinarily well, as he had always believed he could, he could feel proud of something. (The last time being, being, um, yes, so long ago he couldn't remember.)

As a newly successful architect, one happy customer would lead to good recommendations, like with the Amorettis - he dare not think of them or how

PAGING LYNCH MADISON

he had used them or how he regretted never being able to --- enough. What was he thinking. Oh yes.

One good building would lead to others and important Brazilians would be proud to pay any amount for the fine touch of Lynch Madison's creation. So - voila…, or however they say that in Portuguese, Lynch Madison, clarinet case under his arm, would be on the road again with a first class ticket to freedom in his pocket.

"How do you say Leisure Farm?" he asked. "Does that sound good in Portuguese?" Lynch asked, just a couple of rare spare hot nights later, free of gigs as they sat out on the wide esplanada that fronted the apartment, sipping their sharp-limed caipirinhas that Vanda was so fond of.

"Fazenda de Lazer" Vanda said in an actressy voice. "Why do you ask?"

"Just wondered if that would be a good simple easily remembered name if we ever open the place."

Chi looked at Bud and smiled. Vanda didn't dare look at anyone. This was the first time Lynch had even mentioned the place himself.

"I don't know why people fuss so much about a name," Bud said, straight-faced. "I mean people are people whatever they're called, aren't they ---- Leslie?"

But a day or two after this, he turned up unexpectedly at the hotel Vanda was singing in and

PAGING LYNCH MADISON

insisted on treating them to a meal in the rooftop restaurant whether they wanted it or not after the gig.

"I'm starting on the Fazenda de Lazer in the morning, he said mildly, conversationally, eating an olive and taking another. "Brazil isn't like anywhere else I've ever been. This may, after all, be a very exciting project for me. For us."

He looked down at the menu. "Good heavens. You don't come to Rio de Janeiro for canard a l'orange and champignons. Waiter? Garcao? Se faz favor! "My friends and I would like some real Brazilian food."

PAGING LYNCH MADISON
CHAPTER TWELVE

As soon as he made the first tentative markings and sketches of the first vague outline of the projected hydro, his tension had lifted for the first time since - since he had arrived in the sun on to the platform in Luxembourg. Or was it -- since he had left Crossbridge.

On the top right corner was that little cherub again, that he had always used as his motif. But it had Lee's face, now.

As soon as they saw that he had made those first tentative markings, Bud and Lynch and Vanda, too, had breathed easy.

Silly, because of course it didn't go easy. But at least it was going.

"As you have been so good and not nagged me to show you any of this before," Lynch said, shading his eyes from the sunshine as he looked up into Vanda's eyes, "you may now see my toy-town elevation of the front of this projected goldmine if you like," he said, not more than a week after he had started.

He picked up a band from the concave centre of an Amazonian feathered body ornament and pulled his long hair through it with relief. Now for

PAGING LYNCH MADISON

some audience reaction. Syncophantic adulation, at the very least.

"So long as you realise," he added cautiously, "that it may not end up anything like this."

Lynch drew the stiff paper out of the folder, feeling as if he were undressing for the first time for a new woman.

He tried not to be observed, seemingly unconcerned, casually engaged, whilst thirstily drinking in Vanda's first sight of it. (Yes, very like undressing for a new woman.)

The room they stood in was the small bedroom baby Lee had been cribbed, cleaned and powdered in. For Lynch's purposes, Lee had been made to abandon this light bright nursery with the frieze of ballet dancers

Lynch had been upset to move her but Lee slept just as well in Bud and Chi's room, they assured him. And she would forgive him, Lynch promised, when he compensated by building her a nursery to dream about to dream in.

Vanda had revelled in surprising him with the small draughtsman's board and a large noisy but effective fan for this still not air-conditioned room. Fussing about the appointment of this make-shift study until Lynch shoed her out impatiently, she had creditably stayed away from Lynch during the day, leaving a silence for him in which to crouch over papers and pencils and rules until the spaces began to obey him.

PAGING LYNCH MADISON

That is, usually she stayed away. Today, her own hair back to match Lynch's in a bandeau from her aerobics class which made her look like the ballet dancers on the wall, Vanda looked and looked at the drawing silently.

Rigid, waiting for her reaction, only wanting to hear praise, but tensed for the kicks, Lynch fussed mentally over a difficult finger-change in the new clarinet piece his clarinet tutor had given him, seeing in his head, in the right or possibly in the wrong order, the buttons and holes to cover and uncover.

"Oh Lynch. Lynch," Vanda had tears in her eyes. She hugged and kissed him. "It's tremendous," she said.

Lynch relaxed. It had been what he wanted to hear. He was ready to work till he dropped.

"But ---"

Lynch froze. 'But' is blight to the creative spirit.

"But, see, I don't understand plans and all so I can't tell whether it's good or terrible, but don't you think it would be a more attractive package if you - look, give me a piece of paper. Yeah. Like -- here and here sort of over there so that - see? It would save wasting the space there and here, too? Querido, if you want the chamber municipal to pass the plans, you have to grab them, isn't that right, Lynch, querido?"

PAGING LYNCH MADISON

Lynch never showed her another thing, after that. Just worked for days to avoid taking her suggestions.

Having given in and put them into secret and frustratingly excellent action, better and better ideas of his own for the health farm gushed from his pen tips as he reluctantly peeled himself from Vanda in the mornings. His enthusiastic concentration improved and his stamina grew with every pound of much-needed weight gained at Vanda's own health farm of loving care.

Lynch blossomed as he worked. He kept saying yes when Vanda asked him if he were happy. He kept saying nothing when Vanda asked any single question about the future. He did however, keep asking to meet her family. That she wouldn't discuss at all.

"I don't want to get friendly with them," Lynch said. "I only want to lean on them a little, and I know you go along with that. What's the problem?"

Vanda would only shrug.

"Lately," Lynch said, walking hand-in-hand with her down to Copacabana's beach for a five o'clock swim after Lynch had read a story to Lee, "we seem to be able to disagree and stay in tune."

"Mm," she smiled vaguely, every day further from knowing how she would bear it when Lynch had had enough and moved on.

Vanda and Lynch walked down these mosaic pavements near the beach most days after he had

PAGING LYNCH MADISON

worked, playing in the warm water when they reached the raft, swimming back, walking back, still dripping a little, stopping for an ice-cold glass of chopp at any of the chopparias, sharing a huge slice of pizza, talking, laughing whilst they showered, made love, showered again and went off for a gig or a club, sometimes a danceteria or Vanda's friend Josefa's karaoke club if they were in the mood.

"When I was married it was never like this," Lynch complained on the way back, trying to steer a pattern through the patterns beneath his feet, running his middle finger lightly down her spine and back up again so she could barely walk on for thinking of him.

Never like this when he was married? Jan was a nervy, miserable wife and mother in a cold climate with a cold husband. Hard to expect Jan to find a warm beach in the winter, near to the far-inland town of Cross-bridge; harder still to expect Jan, daughter of the respectable Graygroves, to turn out to be a young, wild, beautiful carefree Brazilian singer.

"If you marry me," Vanda said, unwisely, on this same way back, her still-tingling spine a foolish accomplice, "things could always be like this."

"Marriage doesn't work for everyone," Lynch said, leaving not even the inch left on the ledge Vanda was clinging to for her comfort. "You know that."

Vanda, bleeding from her fall from the narrow precarious ledge she had guessed would not hold her, made a Brazilian sound that meant nothing-

PAGING LYNCH MADISON

is-as-disgusting-as-a-man-who-wants-something-and-is-prepared-to-give-nothing but it was lost on Lynch who spoke so little Portuguese yet.

"And when," he said yet again, as if one thing did not obviate the other, "are you going to arrange for your Baptista Vasconceloses to meet me? You keep saying if anyone does, your family know the right people and that they are supreme at knowing how things get done in this country."

It would serve Lynch right, Vanda smiled to herself, if she did take him to the family. Right.

"I'm nowhere near ready to start sending the plans in yet, but well before I do," Lynch frowned, using his fingers now only to scratch his ear in thought, "I'm going to need as much inside information as I can get. In fact, I really need some Brazilian pull quite soon."

Vanda considered the situation, considered her pride.

"Yes, querido, I guess it isn't any more corrupt to use the Baptista Vasconceloses here than the way you used the Graygrove family in England for inside information," Vanda said, holding her breath for the fury this would inevitably bring on her head.

"Yes," Lynch said, walking on mildly, steering a wiggly path through the mosaics at his feet.

Right, bastardo.

PAGING LYNCH MADISON

"Family?" she would announce. "I would like you to introduce Lynch Madison, meu amigo, meu amante," she would say, holding his arm and smiling as she introduced him to the insanely protective Baptista Vasconceloses. Cousins, aunts, uncles, nephews would rise to their tiny feet and clap his shoulder, kiss his cheeks, grip his hand tightly.

Her step-father, Gilberto Nelson Baptista Vasconcelos would take him aside and listen carefully to whatever lies Lynch chose to make up to get the help with the inside workings of the Brazilian councils and the insider information necessary to facilitate its easy passage towards the lucrative seal of approval.

The Baptista Vasconceloses would beckon smilingly to Vanda to come and join them now that the too-hard-for-her-to-understand difficult masculine business conversation was over.

And Vanda would then, in neat quiet Portuguese, turn to Gilberto and inform him that Lynch was not a Catholic, that he was a married bastardo who had run away from his loving family to sleep with her twice a day, that Lynch wished only to use her to get to the Baptista Vasconceloses influence and possibly money, and finally that Lynch kept her almost a prisoner yet had refused to marry her even if he were ever free.

Then she'd stand back a little so the blood didn't get on her dress.

"You really want to meet my family?" she smiled. "OK," she said. "You got it. I'll call them tomorrow."

PAGING LYNCH MADISON

Lynch decided he'd hire a Brazilian Beetle for the proposed trip to the family as he said he found it embarrassing to seem so dependent on Vanda's family transport.

Vanda shrieked with laughter at his sudden attack, she said, of integrity, and although he had blown up about that for a while, he didn't mention the Beetle again.

She had already gone out and bought him some real genuine gorgeous 'South Zone' Brazilian clothes (the kind you put a sack over if you're walking in the Rio streets if you don't want them pinched from your back) when a letter came back from Ponta de Vista, the Baptista Vasconcelos home.

"Oh, querido, such a pity. They don't want us to visit with them right now because my step-father's taking his new wife on a trip back to the Argentine where she came from. We'll go one day. It's wonderful, I love it, but it isn't Brazil. And the people - the Argentinos can sit two, three hours over one cup of expresso to discuss how wasting time is, like, bad. Don't worry. We'll go see Brazil anyway, a little up there in the mountains. Go see my home, my Ponta de Vista and save the big family meeting for another time. You'll see my step-father soon, anyway, because is coming to my opening at the Yacht Club and says he expects to meet with you then. OK?"

Lynch wasn't happy. He really did need to know about the ways of Brazilian planners, but much

PAGING LYNCH MADISON

more than that, (and how could he tell Vanda) he wanted to see Vanda in the frame of her family portrait: just wanted to see her amongst her own people.

Still, Carmelinda das Neves had sprayed her throat ready to substitute for Vanda for two days, his drawings were at a standstill, the bags were packed, so though he was heavily disappointed, maybe he would learn a little.

Vanda suggested they take a different route from their usual one through Petr¢polis to the hotel fazenda and to go down by the Santos Dumont place - "Never mind your Wright brothers," she bragged. "Santos was the first man to fly, believe me. Crazy not to see everything, Lynch."

Lynch grunted and tutted at a slow lorry on the bends in front of them.

"It's less than an hour to Petr¢polis, you know that, and then on to Teres¢polis and the rest of the journey's not so long," Vanda said, navigating, although traffic being traffic all over the world, it proved to take a little longer than not so long, and they had a bit of a row, after he'd missed Santos Dumont - on purpose, Vanda sulked. Then they were travelling around the area of the Friar's nose in Teres¢polis.

Lynch was getting absolutely cheesed off with Vanda praising the mountains of Brazil one after another like she'd personally had them built.

Vanda had said very tightly that there was heaps of time and what was the big rush and led him

PAGING LYNCH MADISON

down and up and around to see things she found in her infuriatingly full guide-book as well as the things she half-remembered. She read to him sometimes correct, sometimes wildly inaccurate but enthusiastically fascinating snippets of historical reasons to explain why she was so passionately keen for him to stop here, and here and especially here.

Lynch muttered that that he had heard enough about Dom Pedro now, thank you, and anyway he'd seen the Crown Jewels in London and that was quite enough jewellery to last him a lifetime and he didn't really need to see the Count of Novo Friburgo or his gardens.

The travelogue stopped for a bit but when they came to the Sitting Dog rock, Vanda just couldn't resist pointing it out, then each gorgeous estate, each spectacular ranch, each odd-shaped gigantic mountain peak and its glorious local name.

Suddenly, Lynch tired of being sulky. He began to cheer up and ask some questions. (It is, haven't you ever noticed, you miseries of the world, less tiring to be cheerful.)

"It is very beautiful up here in the mountains," he said, driving more slowly and letting his eyes drink from the pools of brilliance.

He was rewarded instantly, of course, by Vanda's easy sunshine and an all-singing journey on the last tiny bit after fondue and clear German wine at an unexpected Swiss chalet-inn in the hills.

"You thought the other parks were terrific. Get this one," Vanda said, pointing. "That's Sao

PAGING LYNCH MADISON

Clemente park. Some park, huh? I'll bet you don't even want to know who designed the gardens, right? That country club is something, I'll bet. Now - it's straight up that hill there, and second right, third left. On up. It's right at the top. OK? See, up yonder?"

"Christ," Lynch said, stalling the car at the entrance to Ponto de Vista - the Baptista Vasconcelos estate sign - in shock.

Rather more than living up to its named promise of a 'Viewpoint', ahead of Ponto de Vista to the right, was land of the utmost beauty winding up to nothing but one of the most extravagent facades he had ever seen, outside of design books.

"Who designed that?" Lynch said quietly.

"Meu padrasto; my step-father," Vanda smiled, pleased to have impressed him at last.

Ponto de Vista was arrowed on and on up through an avenue of fat silky eucalyptus-trees that Lynch was sure were rare and mysteriously curative and had been transplanted expensively, maybe illegally, straight from the rain-forest. The lawns and the flower beds had been dry-cleaned this very morning and the wide bamboo seats were nicely spaced around the marble seating areas and barbeque pavilions. Boats on trailers were parked in a matching garage to the one with the Mercedes, the Cadillacs and the limo-stretch. And on up past the Monza Classics and the Santanas.

"What are you thinking?" Vanda smiled at Lynch, into the silence.

PAGING LYNCH MADISON

Dollars. Diamonds. Gold. Easy living. Way to go. Cushy number. Fall on your feet. Family fortunes. Brazilian pull, all right. Morals and principles, let alone his sometime integrity, goodbye. Sponge off this lot to your grave. He felt Vanda beside him stroke his leg. 'Vanda Raimunda Neocita Baptista Vasconcelos, heiress. Will you take Lynch Madison, this shiftless alias, to be your lawful wedded bigamist so long as ye both shall get away with it.'

"Big place," Lynch said briefly, pulling his greed on to the floor and kicking it as near to death as he could. Hard not to speculate, though. "How - how close are you to your family?"

"They'd like me to be close and I play along with them but --" she shrugged. "My step-father's been my stepfather since I was three and wants to pretend he's my real father. But -- I just never trusted that he loves me. Like he dropped me for so long, you know? He didn't want me to be a singer and gave me a hard time about it. Then when I make it big and I'm not starving any more he walks in and gives me an apartment and a car and wants to, like, own me again."

Lynch drove steadily on up and up, marvelling at the colours, at the space.

"He's the uncrowned but everyone knows it 'godfather' of the Baptista Vasconcelos," Vanda said. "His power always frightened me. I think it still does.

PAGING LYNCH MADISON

"And Ponto de Vista is kind of his headquarters, he runs most of the Baptista Vasconcelos enterprises from here.

"What enterprises? Annetta Amoretti told me your family had cars, was it, garages? Yes because -" he flushed, hesitated. "Yes, of course I remembered it was cars ----"

"Cars and who knows what else," Vanda said lightly.

"I don't guess he and his brothers and sisters are wanted for murder or anything but a bit of violence wouldn't be beyond any of them, any amount of funny dealing, a lot of fingers in pies, a sniff of corruption, a great deal of what you call 'pull' and plenty of trouble wouldn't surprise me. I just don't guess they are a thousand percent straight. He adopted me legally but - gee, I hate being a Baptista Vasconcelos.

"I mean, they say he set fire to a real smelly favela - you know? the pits? the slop bowls of the world? they call them slums in England, right? - the favela was near here; that's the point. It was too close to Ponta de Vista.

"The papers said Gilberto Nelson Baptista Vasconcelos was so upset by the cries of the homeless, that he gave all the money necessary to rebuild it. But he sure as hell had it built it a lot further away from his own property when he did it."

"Still ----" Lynch said, frowning.

PAGING LYNCH MADISON

"Then he, like, threw in a free school for the little ones, and sensationally, he gave the kids a hot meal every day - I mean, like, wow, because in all the favelas, the kids are dying of hunger."

"So, he did all those good things, then. I can't see ----"

"And he built a clinico, the best in miles. Even he left a big space for everyone to play futebol. I mean space. You know, Lynch, which one of them ever grew up with a space? Shrewd move, huh? That way he gets to own a lot of people, you know? So, he's got his own little army right around the corner. He's like their Pope or something. Since those days, the people there will do anything for him, of course. I mean, like, anything."

"Like what?"

"Like proteçåo? Like persuasion when it's needed? Like blackmail, like drug-running? Like murder? Who knows? My step-brothers used to admit a lot of things he did smelled funny but they seemed to have stopped criticising since ---" Vanda stopped herself.

"At last! We're here! So? What do you think of the Baptista Vasconcelos palace?" she said, pointing to the place where he should stop, right here, a tiny distance back from the steep steps up to the broad beautiful mansion.

Lynch hesitated. He had caught himself almost nagging Vanda lately to come here. Not just Brazilian pull he wanted at all. It worried him that

PAGING LYNCH MADISON

he was becoming obsessed with Vanda and everything he could learn about her.

Soon he would be asking to see the school where she first sang her nursery rhymes and hanging about wet-eyed around the exact spot of the car-crash that had changed her life.

Annetta had told him the story of how in one big bang she lost her whole family so long ago, in her tragic and most artful raconteur's way, but Vanda's horse's-mouth account of it had been bland to the point of boredom - from having told it too often? From unexpressed sorrow? He glanced briefly at her. No. No sign of all that. Enthusiastic life sparkled in her right down to her tonsils.

When he had been obsessed with seeing her again in London he had kept in his mind a strict rider that she only seemed exotic because she was a Brazilian amongst the British. But even here amongst her own she was exotic and different and brilliantly candid.

Lynch took her small head in his hands and drew it towards him, kissing her with little fragile kisses as if making her better from some damage, kissing her softly and then gently again.

"You like the house that much?" she teased him, but her eyes were already in a naughty nightie with the lights dimmed and 'Feelings' playing on the CD.

"Show me round," he said, stroking her hair, stroking it, neither of them moving, neither of them breathing.

PAGING LYNCH MADISON

"It's lovely," Vanda said softly.

"What?"

"Being quiet with you."

(Wait patiently, please. No fidgeting. Can't you remember? Don't you agree? Aren't those tranquil moments some of the most powerfully moving? Don't hurry Lynch on, please, in your anxiety to see what happens next. There's some loving going on, here. He's had to wait a long time for that.)

When they did climb the steps, Lynch was surprised from the first that the staff didn't know Senhorita Baptista Vasconcelos and Senhorita Baptista Vasconcelos didn't know them and didn't appear to want to.

Lynch was disappointed, a bit. He had sort of expected some kind of old B-film family retainers who'd call her 'missy' and tell him loving stories about her teddy bear. Laugh about the old days when she was oh so frightened of the dark.

Idalia and Flavio had certainly been told to expect her. They were efficient, courteous, proud and formal - but distantly, coolly attentive, nothing more. These two weren't at all a good sample, so far as he could see, of Vanda's down-trodden 'owned' people of the favela.

Lynch's eye and thumb were still mentally sizing up the splendid proportions of the hallway and staircase, and the mean proportions of the light

PAGING LYNCH MADISON

fittings, when he admitted to being both thirsty and starving and after some exhausting Portuguese, some menu was chosen without his help.

Aside from the usual useful bits, the downstairs guest toilet contained more interesting objects than some museums he had been to.

The small breakfast room where they waited for their food, was overwhelmed by bamboo in such profusion that Lynch felt like asking for a machete to hack his way to the table.

"Doesn't this room remind you of the simple lovely way you designed Amorettis?" Vanda beamed, proving that no amount of kissing and holding hands can make any two people anywhere in any way understand one another.

Vanda barely thanked Idalia for the freshly prepared salads and the ubiquitous caiparinha even Lynch had begun to like, though this one was more swamped with rum than usual. Lynch found himself being overly obsequious to Idalia for every little favour in compensation.

The hot and spicy dish when it came was rich, voluptuous, plentiful, and, as Lynch put it, wonderful to eat, hot as hell and heap it on please but don't, don't, please don't ask what on earth, apart from the obvious coconut, cashew and chicken, was in the beastly thing.

The tour of the house was agonising - Vanda kept wanting to know what he thought of it every second. He finally requested a solo wander and went on alone.

PAGING LYNCH MADISON

Generally, the house itself was as elaborate as the outside, fabulously spacious but quite unexciting, traditional and European. He had expected to learn something 'Brazilian' from it and felt a grave disappointment at its absence. So he amused himself by imagining Vanda in every room, changing her clothes and size and age at his own whim.

"Quite nice," he said, meeting her down in the jungle-room again. "Let's go."

"You'll like it better when it's full of people," she said, frowning, equally disappointed that the house itself hadn't managed to impress him. "When it's full it's ----"

"Not so empty," Lynch said, wanting to be out of the place so he could think about it. "Come on."

Idalia herself looked more pleased now that they were going and closed the door behind them almost before their feet had left the door jamb.

"OK, querido. The rest of Brazil is waiting for you," Vanda said waiting for him to unlock her car-door and looking back at the house. "Where do you want to go now?"

Lynch sighed. "I'd like to see a nice Brazilian hotel or motel, I think."

"OK, querido." She picked up her guidebook. "But first, west a little of Nova Friburgo is a charming --- hey, Lynch, don't. Don't throw my book out of the window."

273

PAGING LYNCH MADISON
CHAPTER THIRTEEN

The door opened. Gilberto had arrived as promised.

Nudged by Vanda from their back-row table, Lynch had watched Gilberto Nelson Baptista Vasconcelos come very quietly into the Yacht Club considering the big party of family (or minders) he had with him. He nudged her back and nodded watching carefully. The grovelling of the formerly icy maitre d' was shameful.

Vanda had stood up at once, gone over to be kissed on every cheek the many times Brazilians find necessary and then done her gracious introduction bit, leaving Gilberto and Lynch together on the pretext of having immediately to change before her late-show appearance.

After a few short questions about the Hotel Fazenda and its progress, and a few scaled down, skeletal enquiries about how Lynch was going about things, Gilberto was on his feet with his hand outstretched.

"For a good and honest friend of my dearest daughter, Vanda, I will do much," he said, folding his short bulky arms over his short square frame, somehow managing to convey with every ounce of his body what much he might do, on the other hand, if anyone were to harm his dearest daughter, Vanda.

PAGING LYNCH MADISON

"Enjoy the show," he said, sitting down, Lynch forgotten.

And that had been that. Lynch had been very disappointed by the briefness of the audience he had been granted, but maybe something more than that had happened after all.

After the fazenda plans had been sighed over, modified, reconsidered, torn up, restarted, details redrawn and redrawn in agonies of excitement and tension until they smelt and tasted right and had been gloried over by them all, they were finally sent in to the authorities tentatively by a very nervous Lynch. When outline planning permission had been, praise to the heavens, granted, without qualification (and with a pencilled handwritten note in Portuguese that Vanda said was the equivalent of 'well done') Lynch was happy but puzzled and suspicious that it had all been too easy.

Bud, almost moved to smiles by Lynch's success, waited patiently for Lynch to offer him a copy of the plans for his files.

The moment he had them, good PR that he was, he secretly put the plans in for the international architectural award for the restoration of old buildings. After its controversial short-listing, which news Bud discreetly kept from Lynch, there was a delayed silence and then Lynch received the invitation for the winner's award-winning ceremony.

Bud and Chi and Vanda were beside themselves with delight, planning celebrations of such dimensions that they even considered letting

PAGING LYNCH MADISON

Lynch play the Two Doves - somewhere quiet and unimportant.

Until.

Until the significance of the success sunk in.

Until they saw that the good news, which had been plastered all over every architects' magazine in the Americas, had been chewed over and spread into a finely-written but insensitive piece by one of the most widely read Brazilian journalists. The prestigious O Globo article justified the giving of a prize for this new type of luxury leisure building which pledged itself to very reasonable prices for the treatments at this hitherto only-for-the-rich concept. Not a slum clearance but a mind change of what was needed for the poor. 'How wonderful in this land of violence, rush and stress ---" the article went on and on.

But in the Jornal do Brasil, though there was brief praise for Lynch's original ideas, much comment on the baby motif and a remark or two about the beauty of the planned building, the article concentrated on pouring scorn on the whole concept of any sort of leisure-park at all being contemplated before tackling the quite desperate need of decent housing for the horribly unhoused of Rio de Janeiro.

And this paper added, in the manner of this type of newspaper all over the world, plenty of mindless jeering innuendo about the so-called modesty (or is there something suspect we don't know?) of this English architect, Lynch Madison, who refused to be interviewed or photographed.

PAGING LYNCH MADISON

Only a try-on, of course, but bullseye this time.

South America is full of such people. People hiding out from who knows what. And South America is inevitably, therefore, full of associations and investigators keen to smell out the rats from the sewers, either for reasons of justice or profit.

And journalists are hungry, too.

The name Lynch Madison went down on some casual and some not-so-casual lists. The sniffers and the pokers sniff and poke disinterestedly and daily for names that re-appear. All Lynch had to do was to stay low after this unwanted publicity and let his brief glow fade.

So with the award framed proudly by Vanda and hung behind the door on the wall of his office by Lynch, Lynch took a deep breath and began to supervise the actualisation of the rebuilding of the fazenda using the businesslike straightforward English methods he had taught himself doing those flats in London.

What he had learned on the sites as a labourer also proved more valuable than he could ever have imagined for the small difficulties, for the management minutiae, for understanding the way things worked.

But now he was no longer a labourer, nor was he only an architectural designer. He had become the gaffer, the boss, the capataz, the chefe, and it took only a day or two to confirm what he had dreaded: that this was Brazil and he'd better try to think like a

PAGING LYNCH MADISON

Brazilian or end up earning his money down in the new Rio shopping precinct playing 'Girl from Ipanema' with an upturned cap to catch the cruzeiros.

Brazil. Take notes here, if you'd like to be a builder in one of the most temperate, beautiful, opportunity-rich, enigmatic places in the world.

Labour in Brazil, Senhor, Senhora, is pathetically and sadly cheap, all too readily available, exploitable, highly skilled and good-natured beyond expectation. There are probably no craftsmen more able. But there prove to be a lot of buts, here.

The Brazilian workman appears to be activated only by his own inspiration and individual enthusiasm.

However precisely the order in which tasks are to be done are charted, however pressing are the deadlines and the priority rush-jobs, whatever promises are extracted and, with exquisite Brazilian politeness, agreed to, all of this is a waste of the sweet warm balmy breath of air out there by the still-standing heaps of brick and timber.

If you have ever had so much as a shed put up in Santos, you will be nodding your wiser head with the memory of the frustration you suffered. Imagine, then, the complicated processes of renewing a crumbling wreck into a smart spa of a kind the labourers had never heard about, were not capable of reading about and simply could not imagine.

278

PAGING LYNCH MADISON

The instructions Lynch gave to the good man he chose to be his foreman and this wise craftsman's interpretation of them, never dovetailed as neatly as the joints the carpintieros sawed very slowly, quite divinely, one at a time, observed closely by many of the other spellbound workers, between siestas (sonecas, they are called here in Rio.)

Also, of course, there were the strikes. The long, silent Brazilian construction workers' strikes.

(Another useful note for the would-be builder: the Brazilian strike is similar to any other except that it seems longer and appears characteristically to be about nothing very acrimonious at all.)

Did the stress of all this force Lynch to abandon the project? Not at all. On site from early to late, he noticed nothing else that went on around him.

It was great, Vanda said understandingly to Bud and Chi, to see him totally involved like that and in any case, since Chi had landed the first really big recording contract for Vanda, their days were too full to notice his absence.

As days and weeks came and went, his three friends noticed for themselves how Lynch had stopped agitating himself over the mail in the morning, saw that he had cancelled the British papers he used to order, smiled when he gained more than a little weight, lost his hunted look.

PAGING LYNCH MADISON

And they thought him quite ridiculously pleased when Carlos Antonio's wedding invitation came for Vanda and included him by name.

"Great," he said, kissing round the rim of Vanda's cool left ear, "there's a lot I'd like to talk to your step-father about before my first visit from these inspectors of the municipal chambers. Inspetors? Cambria -----"

"Just stick to English, querido," Vanda laughed, stroking his eyebrows smooth and shifting her head a little from the sharp corner of the bed-side cupboard. "Your words are horroroso."

Vanda sighed, letting herself drift. The trouble was that with only a few numbers still to be recorded for her first compact disc, it was all too exciting to spare the energy it would need to take revenge for Lynch's indifference to her own yearnings for marriage.

She must candidly explain the truth to him. Soon this 'thing they had going' would be over, she could see that for herself. After the building of the fazenda, whether Lynch decided to stay in Brazil or not he would leave her, she was sure. But it would now be necessary to warn him of the perils a little.

"If you want to come to the wedding of Carlos Antonio, it's fine with me. But if they find out you do these things with me," she said, "when they find out you are a married man and that, anyway, you are not even a Catholic -- they will have you beaten, maybe killed, Lynch. This isn't London. This isn't some ordinary family. The Baptista Vasconceloses protect their women any way they can. I mean, if I

PAGING LYNCH MADISON

were them, it would be the easiest thing if you fell off one of the scaffolds at the fazenda. Just 'Jeez what a shame' and two lines in the local paper, querido."

Lynch Madison, threatened with a very real and possible sounding death, wasn't nearly as heroic as some of you might have liked. He had dryness of the throat, pumping of the heart, popping of the eyeballs and a sudden desire to collect airplane schedules.

But by the morning he had decided that the occasion of the wedding would just be another part for him to play. Lynch Madison, lapsed Catholic, willing to learn; Lynch Madison, bachelor, here to plight his troth to Vanda once the building was finished.

Vanda wished the last part hadn't made him laugh out loud when he said it, but she tossed her head, like any wild Brazilian singer would and nodded and agreed. Poor Vanda would now have to be at the wedding and watch him play the only role she wanted him to play for real.

The building went on and the strikes went on and it was during one such lull that Lynch, the frustrated music-man, who wasn't regarded as much of a musician by musicians and proved it by being too lazy to practise, and by being too unknowing to know he needed practise, tripped over a rich musical idea.

In a rehearsal studio waiting for Bud and Chi to turn up to a session, on this rare day-off from his fazenda in Petrópolis, Lynch twisted his clarinet

PAGING LYNCH MADISON

together, as he rather fancied hearing himself play near the adjacent mikes, woofers and tweeters.

Softly tonguing an exercise he'd mastered rather well, from out-of-the-air, where all the magic of the world hangs around waiting for discovery, came a sweet poignant song, born ripe and mature and fruity, from the right side of all the hills.

Thinking 'Red Roses' to it, he found he had invented a complete gutsy soft-backed samba and played it over and over.

Vanda, waiting with him impatiently, put down her poetry book and really listened to him now, humming along with him, repeating some phrases, ya-ya-ing to it and singing only the few words that Lynch muttered had been in his head before the tune.

Bud and Chi came startled into the middle of this and instantly recognized its originality.

They left Lynch's simple honest tone for the bass (that anyone could play) and Vanda's melody above it vague and sad as if she were kicking her heels in a quiet room waiting for someone to call who never called - they left well alone and only asked for a few more of those natural-sounding sentences. Brilliant.

It seemed to be ready so they recorded it roughly in the time they had left at the end of the studio session.

Sensation. Lynch puffed up from it. Vanda proud of it. Bud and Chi amazed by it. Even the technicians loved it.

PAGING LYNCH MADISON

For a frantic little while there was nothing in all their busy minds except 'Red Roses' and its arrangement, its backing, its rehearsing.

Then came the fear of its failure and the over-and-over-again-until-it-was-right final recording at the only really good studios Bud trusted.

At the club, they tried it out as an encore number.

From then on, wherever, whenever they played it after that, it was necessary to keep a set of tall vases for the long-stemmed red roses that arrived at every venue after every performance of that number.

Red Roses overtook The Two Doves and everything else in South America, Central America, soon North America and, oh my, Europe took it up and the money came rolling in.

Vanda was a hot property. All the media attention was hers, of course. But oh-stupid-man-of-many-names, why credit Lynch Madison with Red Roses?

If Lynch had made himself a vest with concentric circles on it and handed a bow and arrow to the pokers and scratchers he couldn't have made himself any easier a target.

He was also handily on show at the weekly gigs at all the best hotels on Avenida Atlantica and all the swankiest clubs that throng Rio de Janeiro adoring Vanda singing his love song.

PAGING LYNCH MADISON

Lynch Madison has only himself to blame. He did it. He was the one who insisted on being the only clarinettist to play the accompaniment of Red Roses (though anyone could do it) or he wanted his tune back. Very able people are immensely stubborn in trivial ways, sometimes. This way he became, for the second time, easily visible. His own fault.

So one of those hungry journalists who had put him on hold, raised a happy lucrative eyebrow, and together with a photographer he owed a favour, earned an honest enough living exposing him, not much caring whether Lynch Madison turned out to be a mass murderer in hiding or a genuinely shy wimp.

"Who is Lynch Madison?" he wrote for a fair fee, "Publicity-shy prize-winning architect of Rio's first subsidised world-class Leisure Centre and Health Hydro crazily intended, if we can believe it, for the poor, turns hit song-writer of 'Red Roses.'

"What's his secret? He certainly tried to buy the negatives of this exclusive photograph from us with a lot of those prize-winning cruzeiros of his."

"Lynch Madison in the limelight again," he wrote later in the week. "Publicity-shy song-writer and prize-winning English architect seen sharing the stage with the star everyone calls Vanda. Is that all he shares? Vanda, Brazil's number one singer, didn't make it from out of nowhere. We can now reveal that Vanda, Brazil's number one singer, has some family behind her. Her full name is Vanda Raimunda Neocita Baptista Vasconcelos. Yes, that family."

PAGING LYNCH MADISON

"Vanda and her English songwriter hit the number one spot," the hard-up journalist wrote and faxed before rushing off down to Sao Paulo after a big drug story.

That was the trouble: the word 'English.' Anything English is 'big news' in Brazil. It got to the press agencies and it was a quiet week - you know how it is.

The music papers were pleased with all this in their quiet week; useful to have something with a new slant in the big spreading Brazilian music scene; until they tried to contact him and found out that, sure enough, he was unavailable and elusive. That was a challenge they couldn't resist.

The dangers of this publicity grew silently day by day while Lynch, unaware of the ferment, enthusiastically shopped with Vanda for the right outfits for them both to wear at the wedding.

"Did you know that your step-father owns the spa-water bottling plant at Sao Paulo?" Lynch enthused, their cases filled with gifts and their new clothes, speeding thankfully past the beauties and the sights of the journey through the mountains that Vanda had made him stop at before on the way to the house.

"Gilberto owns everything," Vanda said gloomily, watching three horsemen race through the valley beneath them and remembering that she was missing the outdoor life she had given up for the stuffy world of clubs and studios and Lynch.

PAGING LYNCH MADISON

"I'm going to ask him if there is some way we can pump spa-water to one of the pools at the fazenda, as well as serving only that for drinking," Lynch sparkled, pleased at the way the building was going, pleased with Vanda, pleased with the fact that his song was out there for her, pleased with the thought of the power of the Baptista Vasconceloses he would be able to exert once he had soothed and charmed them. "That'll go with Chi's whole concept, won't it?"

"Hey, look at that, will you? "

Ahead of them, a procession of frilly white awnings began. Some up and proud, some half up, some still pretending to be just poles on the ground and the tops furled like while lilies not yet ready to blossom.

Men and boys everywhere were running, carrying, fetching, building. The awnings were going to cover a vast area and ahead of them a wide deep platform was being built with small cabins behind.

"I'd forgotten how the Baptista Vasconceloses throw a party," Vanda laughed. "It'll be, like, Carnaval tomorrow. All our family wedding parties are like this," she said, laughing into his face as he drew up outside the steep steps to the mansion.

She swung her legs out of the car and leaned into him. "My stepfather is dying to make one for me. But --- what did you say? Marriage doesn't work, yes, querido?

PAGING LYNCH MADISON

"I think maybe you don't say that to Gilberto or to our Carlos Antonio, querido. He's one happy bridegroom. Let the valet park the wheels, querido. Oi, Carlos Antonio!" she shouted upwards, running herself up the steps after her words, Lynch behind her. "Como vai isso? Onde esta sue noiva? Where's your bride? Elisete? You remember Lynch? Come and meet the family."

"You remember Lynch Madison," Vanda said again, this time to her step-father, holding out her hand to him, like a toastmaster, when he arrived inside the marbled hallway. "At the club? Yes. A presento, Senhor Gilberto Nelson Baptista Vasconcelos, meu padrasto.

"Nao. Nao. Padrasto? Papai, papai, you call me, Vanda Raimunda Neocita," he frowned at her.

Gilberto, a solidly chunky, golden-skinned, moustached man who though he had kept his hair dark with dye wasn't vain enough to touch up his eyebrows and moustache to match, held himself like a man who could carry a tune, charge a bull and change his mind.

Carlos Antonio stood aside while Gilberto welcomed Lynch in fervent and lengthy Portuguese until Vanda explained that this stranger, though an architect who was enthralled and interested in the beauty of Ponto de Vista, spoke only English. Whereupon Gilberto did the honours again in even lengthier but passable English and with much proprietary pride in his house.

"You have come to us at a great moment," Gilberto smiled. "The house is full of our family who

PAGING LYNCH MADISON

arrive here for the wedding of our dear Carlos Antonio and Elisete, and the adega - adega, Vanda? Yes - the cellar is full of the best of our Brazilian wines and French champagne. You are from Londres, senhor? And you are a good friend to my daughter or she would not have brought you to us. Good. First, you will want to meet the young people. Then come to me and we will talk about the making of this house; it will interest you. Carlos Antonio? You will find Senhor Lynch a bed in your room and Vanda must share with her cousins, yes? Your old room is still full of young Baptista Vasconceloses, querida," he said to Vanda, squeezing her hand and answering some cry from a room to the right. "Desculpe," he apologized, hurrying off in that direction.

"It is good to see you again, and to meet your friend," Carlos Antonio said formally to Vanda, taking Vanda's case and walking the long walk to the staircase with them. "You will love Elisete when you meet her. I hope we can be all together good friends."

He turned politely to Lynch and smiled. "My room is full, Senhor, but come with me. My father's cousins are coming to stay here from Sao Paulo, so your friend," he said turning to Vanda carefully, "can share with our cousin Osvaldo Oliveira."

Despite the beauty of Elisete's wedding gown and head-dress (paid for, she said candidly, by the Baptista Vasconceloses) despite her careful dancing and clear happiness, Elisete had the look of a girl who had she not run into such luck as the protected and well-to-do Carlos Antonio, would have been

PAGING LYNCH MADISON

ready to slip into her house-apron and clean the place a little.

Elisete had the look of a girl who had expected that life would have been like her mother's. While the feijoada completa cooked, she would have hurried to the porao underneath the house to make cakes of soap from pig-fat, feed the baby then get down to the piece-work the factories would bring her to do.

But Elisete would not, now, as a Baptista Vasconcelos, be expected ever to work. She would have many children, if the good Lord saw fit, and she and they could, as Vanda translated from Gilberto's tearful speech, expect the same protection, the same respect and the same *tranquilidade* that the rest of the family and the *compadrazgo* give.

"*Compadrazgo!*" shouted everyone, glasses raising here and there. Several other men now stood and clapped this sentiment, all bowing to each other and sitting down again to allow Gilberto to continue.

"What's *compadrazgo,* I know you told me before?" Lynch whispered.

"It's Spanish, really, from my stepfather's new wife's side. It's like, you scratch my back; like, kind of brotherhood of rich powerful families who are maybe in-laws or maybe god-parents; it's kind of a Brazilian mafia," Vanda whispered very very quietly. "Only, if things go wrong for any member of the group, much more violent."

Lynch nodded slowly. He met Vanda's eyes squarely.

PAGING LYNCH MADISON

"It's, for me, querido, another reason I went to the States and then came to England. It's medieval. The women stay home and they don't even mind the kids. They have nurse-maids from the favelas dying to do everything, falling over themselves to be perfect just so as they can live in luxury while they're doing it. Now Carlos Antonio is her protector, Elisete won't lift a finger. Suits her. And that's the life they think I'm on the road to," she said, "and if anyone hurts me in what they see as the process ----- ssh. ssh," she said, nudging and shushing Lynch's hardening eyes, as Gilberto reached the come-raise-your-glasses, champagne-and-toasting part of his speech.

Lynch had received her message of danger and it took him no time at all to work out how to play the new part that would render him safe - for now. In fact, his real fear moved him to heights of acting ability almost beyond his capacities.

Leslie Merrett had never played anyone so neatly as he played this new Lynch Madison, English Catholic, the openly besotted, ardent but obedient, unattached and hopeful suitor of Vanda Raimunda Neocita Baptista Vasconcelos.

It didn't please Vanda Raimunda Neocita Baptista Vasconcelos to see Lynch sit up and beg so easily. In fact it drove Vanda Raimunda Neocita Baptista Vasconcelos crazy.

It drove the hitherto hard-faced Osvaldo Oliveira a little crazy too, watching Lynch's adoration of Vanda.

PAGING LYNCH MADISON

Temporarily discarding the perspiring bridesmaid Osvaldo would be concentrating on later, when the samba started to get wild up there on the dance-boards in front of the tables and the awnings, Osvaldo stepped in, courteously but firmly extracting Vanda from Lynch's side.

The dance floor was Osvaldo's natural habitat and there the elegant precision of his feet could sometimes win points his ugly disposition would lose him.

"Como vai isso?" Osvaldo said politely to her, adding the three worst names you can call a Brazilian girl.

"Bem," she thanked him, adding a little comment on something she remembered that no lady would make in any language.

They were, despite this, already drawing a little applause to themselves for their dancing. Lynch, who had been watching them with polite envy, was now approached by her step-father and two of his chums who led him to their table. Vanda bit her lip. Lynch over there so far from her help. Lynch over there when she needed help herself.

(She shouldn't have come to the wedding, you're saying? She shouldn't have been so vindictive. She should have erred on the side of caution. Given Lynch time. Well of course. But was that in keeping with Vanda's temperament?)

"Ele , muito fraco, teu amigo," Osvaldo said, swerving and weaving.

PAGING LYNCH MADISON

"He isn't in the least boring," Vanda smiled politely.

"Muito fraco," Osvaldo repeated. "Very very boring. I will get my little brother Jaime in a minute; he's in the first grade now and will enjoy the boring one's company. Then little Jaime will fight him while I take you to bed. You are longing to go with me, don't say you aren't."

"You are disgusting, Osvaldo."

"In bed I will give you the baby you asked for. The boring one will never know. It will be good for you and will be an aperitivo for me before my bridesmaid and I find somewhere quiet."

Vanda tried to move away but found she was held more tightly than she had even feared. Danger. She tried to appear relaxed, frightened and furious but very very careful.

"I have good news, Vanda. When I saw you yesterday I knew that I must marry you. So. After tomorrow I must leave. My poor little business needs me back in Sao Paulo. But in four weeks I will come and find you in Rio. You still sing at the same hotel they say. I read about you even in the Sao Paulo papers. We will announce our betrothal. And in half a year, we will be married."

Vanda tried just once more to pull neatly away, to find Lynch, to run and run with him wherever he went. But Osvaldo was very strong and his eyes told her how much real danger she was in. She danced on, even smiling at an uncle as he danced past with an older cousin.

PAGING LYNCH MADISON

"Um," Osvaldo smiled. "When your padrasto hears the news of our wedding, he will at last give me the agency I have been asking him for in Sao Paulo. Like that," he said flicking his fingers but never losing the beat, "the agency will be mine and soon I will be able to settle down with plenty of money - just like Carlos Antonio.

"Yes. You will be a good marriage for me. I will at last be one of the Baptista Vasconceloses. We all know that you, Vanda, are not Virgem Santissima, so no decent man would marry you anyway. You will not mind when I am home and when I am not home. I will please myself what I do and who I do it with and you, Vanda Raimunda Neocita Baptista Vasconcelos, you can do what you like as well, within reason. My reason. I could, if I had to, tell your boring one much more about you than there is to tell if you like or you can just lose him nicely, goodbye Lynch, no harm done. You understand?"

Osvaldo shrugged. "You know how to get rid of a man," he said bending her to hurt her and making it look like part of the dance. "You thought you got rid of me, eh, Vanda?"

The music stopped. The cheering escalated. Vanda and Osvaldo were being toasted from every table. "Outra! Outra!" The party was coming to life. But Osvaldo's grip held.

"At your hotel in four weeks, Vanda. There we will make arrangements for our marriage festivities. Perhaps we will make it the week after Carnaval?"

PAGING LYNCH MADISON

"Stupid one." Vanda said softly, "Lynch and I -- we are already secretly engaged. Look, he is speaking to my stepfather now. I was, of course, heartbroken when you left ----" she added quickly, sensing his temper, sensing his total implacability.

"If you were so heartbroken, then you will want to come back to me," Osvaldo said coldly, making her look at him. "You will tell your padrasto you have changed your mind. You will tell him it is always me that you have loved. You will tell him this, Vanda."

"Bastardo," Vanda said fiercely. "When I tell my step-father you are trying to marry me so you can have plenty of his money ----- "

"Then, Vanda, I tell Senhor Gilberto that I have found out that the boring one is married, that he is not a Catholic and has not told you this and is playing about with the honour of a Baptista Vasconcelos."

They danced on inspirationally, Osvaldo cheered and excited by her fear and her fierce but impotent resistance.

"I will write to you," he said pleasantly, as if off to the mountains and planning a postcard.

"The letters will tell you what you must do. And if you make trouble, I will have the boring one taken care of," Osvaldo said and walked quickly off the dancing boards into the crowds and out of sight.

PAGING LYNCH MADISON

Vanda stood still, staring at Lynch's doomed back as he continued to be grilled by Gilberto and his friends.

Cousins and step-brothers and old friends now hurried on the floor to be seen dancing with the popular but suddenly frozen Vanda, coming back to whisper to each other that she wasn't 'vivo' like she used to be. That she had scarcely said a word to them. That she had become too 'esnobe' for them now that she had condescended to return as a great singer.

But Vanda stayed very quiet and withdrawn like that even in the car going home, even when Lynch was imitating how he had passed himself off as a 'good prospect' to Gilberto. Even when Lynch was holding her, even when he was animated about the spa-water triumph, even when she lay hiding herself round him, even when he puzzled over her sadness and her sudden hot quiet tears, even when he slept.

Three days later the letters started coming from Sao Paulo.

PAGING LYNCH MADISON

CHAPTER FOURTEEN

The broad stocky foreman, him with the fascinatingly uneven moustache and teeth to match, him with the so-many-children-it-keep-me-away-from-the-women, Pedro Dias, by name, was sorely unimpressed by the recent absences of Lynch, known to them all as 'o capataz.'

Unaware, mind you, of the sudden songwriting fame of o capataz, (though he hummed Red Roses as he threatened the men and shovelled himself) he was second to nobody, certainly not Lynch, in his zeal to create the greatest Hotel Fazenda the world had ever seen - whatever was its mysterious purpose.

His men said he was a little crazy; his men said he was always like this over the building of the smallest shed; his men said having so many children had done something bad to his brain; his men said very rude things about him but they loved him.

Pedro was a hitherto unprized though consummate craftsman. Now that he had been elected foreman of a prize-winning building it was a matter of daily bragging and bravado. So with 'o capataz' out of the way for whatever disgraceful reason, although it was annoying, it meant that Pedro Dias could take the opportunity to do things the Brazilian way.

PAGING LYNCH MADISON

Though throughout Pedro had approved of most of what o capataz had proposed, he had steadfastly stuck to his own ideas of order and purpose. Given even the few fingers of a free hand that Lynch's song-writing busyness had given him, Pedro had, magically, made all strikes and even the long sonecas vanish with heaven knows what dreadful stroke of his Brazilian wand.

Lynch returned from the days of recording his one-off glory of a song, returned from the days of Carlos Antonio's wedding to find that the top-floor, penthouse, elaborate, luxury units that had been designed for the management and the staff quarters had been elaborated even further and were ready to be furnished and moved into at once.

Open-mouthed at the insubordination, dazzled by the speed he hadn't himself been able to evoke from the trabalhadors previously, Lynch inspected the excellent building, the neat adjustments Pedro Dias had made without him and nodded seriously as Pedro explained to him that in Brazil, you make the staff happy first, then the clientele. The custom of the country.

And, Pedro added, quickly and pseudo-confidently, though actually terrified of a refusal, with the permission of o capataz, Pedro's wife, Josefina, a gifted cook whom he had hitherto kept firmly at home, would be permitted to take charge of the kitchens and make every patient well just by the smell of the cooking.

You could imagine with every word he spoke, and see in the reflection in his eyes, the large Senhora Dias and her big big string bag stuffed with

PAGING LYNCH MADISON

the surplus goodies of this generously laden kitchen, walking it home to fill the grateful stomachs of his previously empty-bellied children.

Back at the apartment, at a quick committee meeting over hot rolls and sweet mango juice, Lee demanded that Lynch must brush and brush her growing hair. Brush in hand, he toiled at the job smiling at her whilst frowning and arguing with the grown-ups.

After some manoeuvring by them all, and after discussion at a good clean depth of friendship, it was more or less democratically decided that the huge whole top floor would not only be instantly fitted out for management and staff but, to put the place on the equality footing they had long ago agreed on, it would be home for them as well.

Lynch would specify in writing how this would best be achieved, Vanda would contact the Baptista Vasconceloses for know-how on the back-door way to get instant and cheap delivery of everything for their new home in return for which, on the first day it was possible, this Baptista Vasconcelos apartment would be handed unsullied back to them with thanks and complimentary tickets for any treatments at any time.

Bud, whose fussiness suited such things, would see all plans to fruition in his neat way.

Then Chi, the most tactful and patient of them all, was chosen unanimously to do that most tricky of tricks - the hiring -the moment the curtains were hung. Agreeing happily, Chi shyly now produced an incomplete but desperately clever and attractive

PAGING LYNCH MADISON

training programme she had started to write so that the fazenda, which they had agreed would quite simply be called, Fazenda de Lazer (leisure farm) would have just one voice for fitness, health and beauty. "And peace," she added.

"We will try out the scheme on ourselves first and then the staff," Chi said. "For the mistakes that I must have made and then ---" Chi stopped and listened for a moment. "Listen, Lee, do you hear? Yes, the letters have come. Go pick them up for Mama, please."

Vanda hurried after Lee. Anyone even vaguely attentive would have noticed what a fuss Vanda had been making lately about being right there when the mail came. First it was Lynch and now Vanda. Bud and Chi glanced up at once and raised an interested eyebrow at each other.

Chi had noticed Vanda's tension about the mail before and alerted Bud who then reported many more incidents. So they had been less pleased than suspicious when all of a sudden Vanda took an uncharacteristic interest in the new word-processor in Bud's new office on the top-floor though earlier she had almost passed out when she heard that they had thrown out the old typewriters.

Vanda stayed up later than she should have done after her late-late shows to learn enough to work it by herself - she was particularly anxious to learn how to erase a document for good, Bud confided.

And one early morning, Chi watched Vanda carry two crisp envelopes to her car; you could see,

PAGING LYNCH MADISON

she said to Bud later, that they were, in their way, bombs. Just the way Vanda carried them, watching them all the time, putting them tenderly into the passenger seat. Vanda, quite obviously, had nothing else on her mind than delivering those two letters, anxious that the timing devices didn't tick off too soon.

"Should I have followed her?" she said to Bud, as they sat watching Vanda wild with some of her old spirit again, singing her kidneys out at the Golf Club, later the same night. "Should I tell Lynch?"

Bud looked over at Lynch, handling 'Red Roses' as he'd been shown, almost as if he knew how to play a clarinet, his eyes lit with love for Vanda, or for himself or maybe even for the music.

"We are their friends, not their nursemaids," Bud said quietly. "When these bombs you say she's sent go off, we will heal the sick, yes?"

So Chi and Bud bided their time and noticed everything whilst Lynch built with and chivvied the trabalhadors, and Vanda sang and pretended not to worry.

Though Lynch ate with Vanda, slept with Vanda, he still didn't notice her jumpiness, her fear, her contemplative scheming, her knocker-watching, remaining sweetly unaware, ah almost like a husband then, digging in the sweet skin of his avocado and dreaming, in his wonderful one thing at a time way, of a completed perfected Fazenda de Lazer.

It was time to hire and train the staff.

PAGING LYNCH MADISON

Chi girded herself for the task, writing and rewriting the advertisements for the professionals over and over, hanging over Vanda's translations into Portuguese, worrying at her for the exact and precise words, then insisting on an English version as well.

"You must watch me a little, because I will do the choosing with prejudice, maybe," Chi smiled, meaning that she would be inclined to favour the indigenous Japanese, of course.

But in the event, the long list of names chosen for the professional skilled side of the staffing - the initial interview sort-out, that is, was the jumble you might expect in such a place as Rio de Janeiro. The gifted rich mix of hybrid nations. The gifted rich scheming mix poverty brings.

That completed, there came further problems.

"However will we attract the rest of the staff," Chi worried late at night to Bud, "I can't work it out. They say that most of them can't read the advertisements." Bud promised to think that out and that she should give him a little time and not worry about it herself.

Meanwhile, the slow Brazilian mail took its time getting the first letter to Osvaldo in Sao Paulo.

Osvaldo was flattered and soothed by the longing Vanda expressed for him and nicely proud of the fear he felt he had aroused in her. Yes, he wrote. I will wait a little longer for you to sort out your boring one, your half-wit, but not too long.

PAGING LYNCH MADISON

Vanda shone that night with the time she had gained to save Lynch and write more letters.

Than the British mail, there is no finer but you need to have the address right for speed.

As he no longer worked from the address Vanda had known, it was no-one's fault that the airways took so much longer than usual to get the second letter to Stan.

If you have been attending nicely, you will remember that Cyril Graygrove was not only Leslie Merrett's senior partner but also his father-in-law.

You will also remember that he was conscientious about keeping up to date with all the international building regulations and trends and that he was a bright, domineering sort of cove.

So you won't be surprised that he had read about Fazenda de Lazer in Rio de Janeiro. He had even half-registered the baby motif and smiled, thinking of Charlotte, but none of it, why should it, had rung any alarms.

But when the anonymous letter arrived from London that morning with the newspaper cuttings, he had got up from the table without eating his breakfast, alarming Lily even more by going straight off in the car without saying goodbye.

The prize winning architect. The baby motif. And now he looked very carefully at that exclusive photograph of Vanda with Lynch Madison ringed in the background ---- frankly, the letter was disturbing, but sort of inconclusive and circumstantial. Until ---

PAGING LYNCH MADISON

He could feel his blood pressure rising dangerously and stopped to have one of his tablets.

Back from taking a little drink of water, he picked up the cutting again and ---- he peered, he squinted. The phone rang and he picked it up automatically.

Cyril Graygrove put the phone down unanswered to run and get the most powerful of his magnifying glasses in his office.

***

"Yes," Jan Merrett said, unenthusiastically. "I suppose that is him, Mr Carfax. I think."

"Your father seems absolutely sure, Mrs Merrett. Are you sure, too."

"Yes, well ---- my father has thought he's spotted him before," she said blandly.

Cyril Graygrove stood up and unclipped his case to bring out three further copies of the newspaper-cutting and three glossy photographs.

"That's true, darling, but look." He handed it all to Carfax who stared at the highlighted blobs trying to remember the pictures he'd been given years ago. Hadn't Mrs Merrett's husband been a neat guy in a suit?

PAGING LYNCH MADISON

"Naturally your mother and I have indeed been checking people in crowds - such as at airports and sports events and rallies and celebrations - in the background, in the streets, that sort of thing," her father said positively. "Haven't we Lily?"

Lily Graygrove blew her nose.

"My family know me," Cyril said to Carfax. "Whatever I do I try to do thoroughly. I always expect attention to detail to pay off and it has," he said gravely, then waited as if expecting applause. "I think I'd have made a good detective," he said, brushing half a mote of dust off his cavalry twill and reminding Carfax he must take the trousers he'd been wearing since last autumn to the cleaners when he could find five minutes.

"But even I never expected a half-page spread in the nationals," Cyril said, as smugly as if he had organised it. "Quite honestly it didn't look that much like Leslie at first. But then I spotted that carrying case for the clarinet that's over his shoulder," he said. "Well it's a dead give-away."

Jan turned away. Her father had told that story twenty times to everyone who would listen, always concluding with that 'dead giveaway' bit.

Mr Carfax was being paid to be polite to her father and listen to him repeat himself. Off he went about the cartoon, now. She sometimes wondered if it had affected her father's marbles when Leslie left.

"He was crazy about his clarinet," Cyril Graygrove went on. "Well he played it most awfully well. But this was only the case for it. On the

PAGING LYNCH MADISON

pocket. See? There? He smacked Charlotte for doing that. Jan told us about it at the time because it was such a ridiculous story. I mean fancy the man minding. Charlotte was only a child then. And it was only one of those silly cartoon labels. Anyway, whatever Jan did, it wouldn't come off - it half tore off then stuck. Look you can see the long thin legs. So if that's his clarinet case, that's him."

Jan's mother wiped her eyes again.

"Clarinets often get sold, Mr Graygrove," Carfax said, routinely.

Cyril Graygrove shook his head. "No, no, it's everything together. The case and the article about this mysterious architect and the baby business. It just shows he still has Charlotte in his mind, that's one good thing. That's Leslie for sure."

"It's such a burden lifted," Jan's mother spoke softly, "I mean, knowing he's alive. But so thin. And maybe no money to get his hair cut. He must have been so ill. Fancy losing your memory like that. He must be frantic not knowing who he is --"

It had been her contention all along.

Cyril looked at his wife coolly, waiting for her to regain at least a modicum of composure in front of this employee.

"We'll find out the details when we're face to face with Leslie again," he said sternly to Lily. "I want you to re-open the case, Mr Carfax ---"

PAGING LYNCH MADISON

"We don't open and close cases, sir. We aren't policemen. You pay me another retainer and I'll have another go, if you like. Right? It's becoming quite interesting. Quite out of the usual."

Jan's father hesitantly decided to ignore this out-of-place enthusiastic vulgarity and mm'd a yes. "By this time Leslie will be glad to go to a psychiatrist, when we find him. We'll soon sort the whole thing out for you," her father said, smiling a little at his lip-chewing daughter. "He'll be back with us in every respect, my darling. And if you find him quickly, Carfax," Mr Graygrove said softly, "we can talk about you handling the security arrangements at the shopping precinct and industrial complex I've an interest in, if you'd like that."

Carfax's insides jumped up and down and threw caps in the air and made silly noises of joy.

"We can certainly talk about that, sir," he said. "Yes," he said, mentally closing the door of his damp little office and renting a whole floor at the Civic Centre, "perhaps I could look it over and start by sending you some preliminary costings -----"

"I mean, Daddy, have you looked at him?" Jan said, continuing to bite her lip and pointing at the man in the picture with the stubble and creases. "I mean he could be on drugs, the way he looks."

Her parents drew in a breath and looked at the pictures again fearfully.

"I don't want him back, really, do I Daddy. I sort of hoped he was dead."

PAGING LYNCH MADISON

Into the silent shock, then the explosions from her father and the tears from her mother, Carfax withdrew from his dreams of a new car, a holiday, a pleased wife on his lap and listened more carefully.

The plain and mild Jan Merrett, nee Graygrove, was trying not very eloquently to explain to her bemused parents how much she loved the not-long widowed Victor and to impress them with how well Charlotte got on with Victor's slightly younger daughter.

Once started, she didn't seem to be able to stop saying his name caressingly.

She was letting any numbers of cats out of any number of bags all at once, describing how wonderful it had been living secretly with - Victor - when she could. She enthused over their immediate and obvious harmony, how they were so openly dancing to the right happy strains of live music that even small-minded Crossbridge must surely hum along in favour of the tune.

Soon, in the light of Jan's unexpected emergence as a real person, Leslie's disappearance was beginning (at least by Jan's old friends) to be taken as some sort of fine cosmic planning, some wives here and there even sighing for the day it might happen to them.

"Victor's terribly good about it all. Victor's quite willing to wait it out at my place, bring his Amanda to live with us now until ----"

"Live with you?" Lily said faintly.

PAGING LYNCH MADISON

"Move in, mother," Jan said firmly. "There's no need to go mad looking for Leslie. I mean he may not want to be found and that's OK with me."

Lily clipped her bag open and shut. "Jan, think of him - looking everywhere for his lost family, desperate since his accident so long ago ---"

"We don't know that, mother. I think leave it. Carry on as we have been until the seven years is up, then Victor and I can marry," she said her eyes softening. "We'll pack up and take the three children to - Manchester or Cornwall or somewhere and start again. We've talked about it for so long ---"

"Three children?" her mother said faintly.

"I'm due in November, mother," Jan said firmly.

"Due?" her father said faintly, frowning at Carfax as if by doing so all this dirty-washing would escape his notice.

Carfax, on the other hand, saw his involvement with the Graygrove/Merrett disappearance melt like butter on a skillet. These valuable clients were going down the plughole like a last leak in the worst financial period he could remember. One glance at him and his tatty office and you would know that this man, this great detective had domestic troubles enough of his own at home.

"Do you know how boring you are?" Carfax's wife had screamed at him. "And look - look how you've let yourself go." He was still walking to the mirror to check what she was talking about when she

PAGING LYNCH MADISON

screamed on. It appeared that apart from being boring and scruffy, Carfax had also failed to have ambition or to move house when the time was right. All their friends had done the right things.

"You're supposed to be observant. How can you be the only one to notice that the area's crumbling round us? It's a dump," she screamed for the last time, tearing at the dirty piece of wallpaper that had nearly parted from the wall years ago, running out and slamming the door.

Three weeks after the row, the bare patch on the wall stared accusingly at him if he looked that way. But in those three weeks, Heather Carfax had been exceedingly busy. She handed him a diet sheet, the brochure of adult classes at a college ten miles away with crosses at selected classes they could join together and house agents' details of the house of her dreams.

Lovely secluded garden for the children, near a better school, near a better class of washing on the line. And the crazy vendors wanted to leave the almost-new carpets and curtains. An en-suite, a utility room --- she'd move on her own if he wouldn't co-operate, she had said. And to prove the point, she and the children had moved out to her sister's place till he agreed to the changes.

It had been a dreadful fortnight before she agreed to come home and then only to cold truce and him falsely enthusiastic and very depressed.

Jan Merrett must come to her senses and want her husband to be found - quickly, Graygrove had

PAGING LYNCH MADISON

said. Slowly would be better for Carfax's purposes, however.

"No, Mrs Merrett, you have the wrong attitude," Carfax braved. "You can't just leave raw ends like that. What effect would all this have on the good new life you envisage? And on your daughter, Charlotte? Umm?"

Cyril and Lily nodded approvingly.

"Clear the air properly and then you can start again."

But just for a moment, Carfax fantasised following Leslie Merrett's flight path so that he too, could disappear.

"I think we must act swiftly, sir" Carfax said, turning seriously to Cyril. "If your son-in-law is part of this touring group, we must check at once on their schedule and pounce now. It will be necessary physically to go to Rio, sir. Naturally I won't spend an hour more than I have to before I bring him back. If you can afford a cheap return flight for me, that is."

"Afford? For our daughter we'll afford anything necessary ----"

Danger over, for now. Nice trip, too. He'd book one of those 'see the country' trips before 'finding' Leslie Merrett. He'd never have the opportunity to go to South America any other way. And with the mortgage his wife planned to rope him with, even simple holidays were over for them. Did his wife honestly think that spending money

PAGING LYNCH MADISON

recklessly would make him more exciting? She hadn't been all that thrilling herself lately.

Rio de Janeiro. Lovely. He needed to get away from home and the tension mounting there and the frightening quietness of his answering machine. If successful, Mr Graygrove's cheque would buy them the deposit and if he then landed the security work for Graygrove's complex, he'd take in a couple of bright boys and a couple of youth opportunities ---- that could be his pension as well, if his wife would excuse him thinking of such boring matters. This dear, underground, bright-button of a missing person must be his finest, most competently handled job.

"Look, while you're here, in my office, I'll book up right away, get things started," he said lifting the phone, turning to 'travel agent' in his brown book. "Though it will mean putting all my other work aside for ---- hello?"

"What about me coming with you, Carfax?" Cyril mouthed.

"I think that might be unwise," Carfax whispered back desperately. "South America is very volatile as this time. Leave it to me. Don't you think, Mrs Graygrove? I can get in and out quicker on my own." Lily was nodding a very tiny little bit, her hand to her mouth, the photographs in her lap again.

A seat would be available the day after tomorrow though only the standard and wildly expensive fare at that short notice, of course. Carfax wrote down the prices from dictation and showed it to his client. Cyril nodded at once.

PAGING LYNCH MADISON

"Of course; time is of the essence," Carfax frowned, nodding. Carfax shook their hands, marvelling at the way rich people decide things.

"This will all be over in a few days," Carfax said, cheerfully, "I'll keep in touch by telephone and yes, give me your fax number, Mr Graygrove."

"One of you had better tell him I don't want him back, when you find him," Jan said, getting up and walking out of the door.

Jan's parents stared after her, white-hot painful tears in both their eyes at this daughterly ingratitude.

Cyril, humanly, gently, leaned over and wiped one glistening tear away from Lily's face.

Touching, very touching.

Carfax took out an expenses form and began to fill it in.

PAGING LYNCH MADISON
CHAPTER FIFTEEN

The hotel club was smoky and expensive and the clientele inattentive to the cabaret until the singer began to sing.

Carfax shook his head regretfully at the girl who wanted to 'escort' him for the evening, (Aids shaking his head more powerfully than any wife,) ordered a modest meal that would not outrage the Graygroves, sipped the Almaden wine that had just been recommended, and started to fall in love with Vanda.

And that went for most of the audience too. They had all stopped talking about themselves. There was much calling out of further favourite songs for her to sing. She seemed to give people their lost hopes back, she seemed to make them want to be noticed again, made them sure that they were being noticed; men nudging their women with Vanda's praises, marvelling at how she lit up the room, how great was her personality; the same wives they frowningly subdued in public if there was any danger that they were becoming too vivacious, too conspicuous.

"And now anyone want to have me as their ---pen-pal?" Great. So it was a regular game he'd seen her play last night. The same formula. Simply the routine of the show at this stage of the evening, as he had suspected. Carfax had had a note ready

PAGING LYNCH MADISON

since this morning. So he called one of the waiting waiters over to collect it.

The waiter uninterestedly added this neat brown envelope to the pile of notes written on drip mats, dish-of-the-day slips, business cards, envelopes, one American five-dollar bill and handed them up to Vanda as he passed under the stage, as did the others.

"I'm going to take five," Vanda said, waving the notes. "When I've read every one of these, I'll come back and ----see what I can do," she said provocatively, surely it couldn't be natural, that bright-schoolgirl-under-the-sequins.

"Let me leave you with Tiago Navarro Garcia --- music-man."

Tiago Navarro Garcia a small, dark-browed, intense band leader, waved his heart out making his band play the bland music-to-dance-to that they were paid to play before the evening hotted up to the samba. Nobody listened and not many danced. It was still eating time for most of them.

The club girls were sent to dance with all the unattached males (three smiles inclusive) and Carfax even refused that, not knowing how much it would cost him.

He was waiting, in any case, for an answer to his note. It really bugged him how predictable and manipulative most men were - sending notes to the singer. His was strictly business, of course. Did the others really feel she would read their scribbled offer

PAGING LYNCH MADISON

and jump at the chance to sleep with anyone who asked? The sheer effrontery of the male.

Tiago Navarro Garcia, unappreciated and cursorily applauded, saw his men off the stage then brought a high stool out from the wings before going off for his 'five'.

From the right of the stage a big spotlight waited just the right amount of breath-taking time for Vanda. Into the circle of light, into a circle of percussionist's frenzy, she ran on carrying a small basket and wearing, now, a theatrically neat straight long dress topped by a tiny high collared jacket with long sleeves.

Just made to take off, Carfax whined to himself, half sorry for Jan that Leslie Merrett's bird had turned out to be so predictably blatantly sexy.

"I've read them all," Vanda said, taking out the notes from the basket and settling herself very comfortably on the stool at the front of the stage in the spotlight.

"Naughty, naughty, some of you." She let the laughter begin. "First, I'd like to send this back," she said, holding out the five-dollar bill which the waiter took back to the table it came from.

"Tell me, sir. Do you usually get all that for five dollars?"

She got a good laugh and at least the fellow got his money back.

PAGING LYNCH MADISON

"And this," she said, waving the envelope. "Please don't ask me what's in it," she said, her whole face lighting so that you had to smile, like it or not. "But if I accepted it, I think I could buy this club and hire a singer to sing for me."

"Anyway, I wouldn't like to do that," she said, through the laughter, sincerity, or was it, dripping from her, "because I was born to sing." It got the applause it asked for, hammy as it was.

"Anyway, I've chosen something from the basket to sing," she said, "and to the rest of you, thank you for your notes." On cue, Joe was back to take away the basket and the stool.

"Ooh it's hot in here, Joe, isn't it? Or is it just me?"

Here it came, the dignified nod towards the other clubs down this street of clubs, the tiny gesture towards strip as she made the very most of easing off her jacket and giving it to Joe, though the dress under it was, Carfax was forced to note, perfectly ladylike.

She turned to the mike and seriously to us all. She would have made some great preacher. As it was, she was some woman.

"There were a lot of requests tonight but I've chosen something asked for by Brian Carfax - which are you, sir? Jeez, I hate the name Brian. Can I call you The Brain? You look like it would be appropriate. Who said professor, yes that's a good idea."

It got the easy laugh she'd played for.

PAGING LYNCH MADISON

"Now, Professor. I'm going to sing "Lover man, where can you be," she said smiling naughtily, letting it sink in. "Some man you're hoping to meet, sir?" The laughter rippled and grew.

Carfax had thought it pretty clever when he'd written it but was reduced to looking coolly masculine through the cat-calls and whistles he had brought on himself.

"Billie Holliday sang it her way," Vanda breathed into the microphone. And I sing it ----- like this."

It was forty minutes after her act before she came to his table, dressed very quietly, but noticed by everyone just the same.

"You really are a very good singer," Carfax said, getting to his feet and smiling politely.

"I know," Vanda said, turning to sign someone's menu, and still standing. "Thank you a lot," she said to someone else. "Do you have wheels, Professor? Oh sucks. Then I'll get a cab. Meet me here tomorrow around seven before I start getting ready for the early show and we'll talk."

She rambled out with a fast walk that told you where everything was. He was almost running along behind, fully aware of the glances and comments they were receiving, half-wishing the jealous imaginings might even turn out to be possible.

His image stopped and turned towards him in the big mirror in the foyer. He must lose more than

PAGING LYNCH MADISON

a few pounds, take up golf when he got back. Go to a gym even though the very idea of gym had disgusted him at grammar school. That's what guys his age did.

Her walk preceded him right to the front desk where she was stopped, mercifully, by the bell captain.

Carfax stayed back watching her nod and shake her head and take a bundle of letters and messages from him then moved up to speak to her.

"Miss Vanda. I need to speak to you tonight. May I take you for a drink."

"Never mind the Miss Vanda crap and never mind the drinking. I'm starved. I'm going to eat, professor. We'll talk tomorrow."

"I'll take you for a meal, then, I don't want to wait until tomorrow."

Vanda looked at him again then smiled. "OK. Let's eat. Your place or mine?" She smiled a full Vanda smile. It could straighten out a bend in the road.

"I'm – I don't know the --look, I'm only here to find out about Leslie Merrett. I'll certainly buy you a sandwich or whatever they eat here in Brazil but -----"

"Jeez, Professor. You haven't got a sense of humour at all. That must really hold you back."

PAGING LYNCH MADISON

"I'm not a comedian," Carfax said, suddenly on duty and proud of it. "I'm not even a singer on a high salary. I'm an investigator on a job and I just want --" He smiled suddenly. She was right. That's how he'd been lately. Too tired and bored to see any jokes, let alone make any.

"I'm staying at a dump, Miss Vanda. Where should we eat? There must be hundreds of places around here."

"Sure. Exactly where is the dump you're staying at, professor? Anyways, if it's so awful, why did you book in there?"

"I only came in two nights ago. It was hours later than expected. Nearly the morning. So I took a cab and he, the cab-driver said he knew somewhere. - I don't even know what the area is called - oh yes, Flamingo? Something like that."

"Flamengo."

"Maybe. I don't know what the motel is called---" he took the key out of his pocket and made a shrugging attempt at pronouncing it. "The cab-driver said it's very cheap and clean and I was tired and I said OK. I was trying to save money. A mistake. Still it's only for a day or two."

"Oh sucks," she said, looking at his key and chewing her lip.

Vanda went back to the desk, made a call, called for the manager, made a small disturbance, held a tiny conference right there on the marble

PAGING LYNCH MADISON

concourse, then smiling, turned round holding up another room key.

"Yours," she said. "Here on the sixth floor," she said. "On the house," she said. "A suite is all they have. You could bring a couple of friends."

Her eyes danced. She was waggling the key at him; flashing it; dangling it.

Though I am happily married, Vanda, my dear and though naturally as a responsible citizen I'm quite worried about sexually transmitted diseases, I'll make an exception for you. He wished he could carry it off.

"And look, this hotel's coffee-shop's open twenty-four hours a day. Will that do? I'm really hungry. OK. We'll eat here. Also on the house. Right?"

"If you're trying to bribe me in some way," Carfax said, looking at himself in the huge mirror as he hurried after her and sucking in his stomach as a temporary measure, then frowning as he read the unpayable 'coffee-shop' prices on the pages and pages of menu, felt the softness of the napkins, watched the candle being lit on the table, "I bribe very easy," he smiled, relaxing into the luxury and unbuttoning his jacket.

"Oh, you are a human being," Vanda smiled. "Great. This may be easier than it looked. Let's order. Then we'll talk. OK?"

PAGING LYNCH MADISON

"OK. This is a nice place. But of course I can't stay here. I'm sure it's not really 'on the house.' Someone has to pay."

"Sure, professor. Someone always pays." She called over a waiter, took a pen and a tear-off pad from her handbag and handed him a note, wrote something on the outside as well and waited until he had gone out of sight.

"A coded message for Leslie Merrett, I take it?"

She ignored him, looking all around her, smiling, waving to some tables. "This place may be professionally very interesting to you," she said. "You can see every kind of pick-up in the world happen here," she said, accepting a small vase of flowers for the table as a gesture from the management gracefully and throwing her jacket off over her chair.

She looked round happily at the busy yet intimate place. "It's that sort of a joint, I guess. You know? Men, women and goats."

Aside from the goats, who had perhaps already been successfully picked up and gone, she had described the place so accurately he awarded her the long vacant post as his brilliant assistant who worked for a pittance, at his side devotedly all hours, falling into his arms after dark. Having recently been elevated to professor without benefit of tiresome examination, he wondered what else he could get away with being elevated to as well.

PAGING LYNCH MADISON

To business. He frowned himself into duty. "And where is Mr Merrett tonight?"

"Por favor?" she called to a passing Brazilian, who smiled his white teeth at her and took out his notepad.

"Can we eat? I never have anything until after I've sung," she said, holding herself under her arched ribs as if there were a space she could fill with a shovel. "Do you mind - I'll ask for hot rolls and butter and gallons of coffee right now while you read, do you mind?" she said, giving Carfax a warm look and his menu a tweak over into the English half of the thick menu, too familiar with it herself to bother with the Portuguese.

"You want to get right down to business, professor?" she said, brushing a tiny crumb from her lip, after she'd helped him order and stirred her second coffee.

"Yes," he said, reluctantly. putting down his knife and getting out his tiny Sony recorder, setting the counter to zero.

She reached over the table and took the machine out of his hand. Opening it, she took out the little cassette, popped it into her full water-glass and stirred it all in one swift little movement, smiling.

Carfax sighed, took a second little cassette, fitted it in and held the machine on his lap.

"Sometimes I forget things," he said. "I just like to go over conversations later.

PAGING LYNCH MADISON

She pointed, still smiling, to her closed lips.

"OK, I give in," he said, but actually pressing the button that made it work on voice operation

She frowned and pointed again to her closed mouth.

"OK," he sighed, putting it back into his pocket, thinking with affection of his wife who couldn't set their three-year-old video recorder yet.

"'Lover Man where can he be'," Carfax tried to sing. "I don't know where Leslie Merrett was tonight. They tell me he usually plays the clarinet for you and takes you home. But he wasn't here last night or tonight, was he? But if I don't let you out of my sight, I've found Leslie Merrett, haven't I.?"

"Not exactly, professor; you're actually just a few days late. He's said goodbye for a while. When he gets back, I'll tell him you called. Your work must be so interesting. How long have you been in this business? "

"Look, am I going to be taken to meet him in a civilized manner or do I break in on you early in the morning in embarrassing circumstances," Carfax said carefully, trying not to think how she would look if he did.

The straight question was the first law of investigators. Go to the heart of the matter. He so hoped she would shrug and agree that they would go and get him right after they'd eaten, then they could settle back and enjoy the meal.

PAGING LYNCH MADISON

They'd argue the details then he would compromise, seemingly reluctantly, nodding on a stay of execution of just a few more days so that Vanda and Leslie could spend their last days together and he himself would hire a driver and see as much of Brazil as he could cover in the most luxurious way he could organize.

"Honest, he's really gone, professor. Sometimes I wonder if he comes unhinged when he disappears. You know, I ought to have been a private -- eye, do they call you?" she said. "I look great in a trenchcoat and the game's so easy. All you have to do is pretend you're them, don't you?"

Carfax sighed. Funny about his job. It was not much better than a sort of mucking out of human stables and everyone not only thought they wanted to do it but were sure they could do it brilliantly.

"It's hard to pretend to be Lynch though. All the time he disappears, saying nothing about where he's been when he's back. He seems to need that. He seems to need to be a mystery man. I don't know. Like, I really love the guy but he's a privacy freak, you see, and ----"

"I know all this. Go on," Carfax said, sliding his hand down to his pocket.

"Chrissake, professor, you activate that recorder, I quit. Thank you. How would you know what Lynch is really like?" Vanda said, smoothing the bits of her hair up that were falling, a waste of time as they fell again instantly in fronds around her face.

PAGING LYNCH MADISON

"His wife told me," he said wearily, wondering if he should leave her in charge of this 'easy' investigation and fake a disappearance himself.

"Oh sure. Yeah. But that was only once. He's disappeared on me lots of times."

What was she, bragging?

"I mean at first when I saw your note, I thought hell, now Lynch's number is up. I decided not to talk to you but then I thought, hell, Lynch has gone anyway maybe this guy will get him back for me."

Carfax sighed, and dug gloomily into his food wondering yet again why women couldn't wait to fall over themselves for bad unpredictable men.

"When I find him, I shall take him home to his wife, because that is where he belongs," Carfax lied, visualising the plainness of Jan's surroundings, hearing Jan's cold disdain for Leslie, ('I hoped he was dead') and hearing Vanda's 'I really love the guy' seem so honest and natural even in the surrounding opulence and lushness of this Rio de Janeiro hotspot.

He'd also seen a lot of divorces. Lousy marriages were the mainstay of his profession. None of them had been noble or pleasant or compassionate and he could whip up a little sympathy for Leslie's amazing way out. A kind of seven-year pilgrimage worshipping only yourself.

"Of course," Vanda said lighting up. "You know Lynch's family - Leslie's family, I mean. It's

PAGING LYNCH MADISON

funny to hear him called Leslie. He just isn't a 'Leslie' at all is he? Tell me about them. I think it's a shame he ran out on them but I've always hoped that they're dreadful. Are they?"

"Very nice people, Vanda. They have been made extremely unhappy by Leslie Merrett's cruelty and the sooner we can clear it all up, the sooner they can get on with their lives and he can do what he likes with his. And if you don't mind my saying so, you'll be better off if he does go back to them. It isn't normal behaviour to keep disappearing. You may be right that he needs psychiatric help."

"Yes," she said leaning towards him, as if pleased that he was showing some perspicacity at last. "That's exactly what I'll do when he gets back. I'll fix him up with a shrink. I think he just needs to settle down with someone he loves. Me, professor.

"If you were me, where would you look for him?" Vanda said seriously. "I mean you're the professional."

Carfax rubbed his hand over his tired eyes, whizzing through his past files now, looking for comfort. Last year there was that post-natal disappearance cleared up within the day, two football-fan stowaways, an Arab tug-of-love father letting him return with the children on the next plane. Reasonable people. Ordinary people. Where would he look for Leslie Merrett if he were Vanda? He didn't have a clue.

"Under your bed, maybe?"

PAGING LYNCH MADISON

Vanda threw back her head and laughed until everyone around had noticed.

"That's real good, you know?" she smiled, wiping the mascara from under her eyes.

"Look, don't get mad but of course I'm lying to you. Sure he ran out on me a few times but right now of course I know where he is. He's at home with us. But he is in terrible danger. You want to hear the whole story?"

Carfax thought lovingly of his last missing person case. A young girl shacked up with an unsuitable unstable older man. The girl had left her new address with half a dozen of her friends. She had been in when he called, had answered immediately to her own name and was only too glad to go back home. A very satisfactory client.

She had to be exaggerating about the danger. What could she mean? Carfax decided to be patient and hear her out. It was all just too tiring. Anyway, he'd found Leslie Merrett. Now for Cyril's new projects. Go home just as soon as he'd travelled around a little.

"I thought I'd send him to Argentina," she said, pouring and mixing thick olive oil into a tiny bit of red-wine vinegar, grinding black pepper in, agitating the lot and dipping her hot roll into it as if cholesterol had never been invented.

Carfax, beyond caution now, reached for the oil bottle and copied her, the corners of his mouth turned well down as he composed a mental fax to the

PAGING LYNCH MADISON

Graygroves.   JOB OVER.   FEE HONESTLY EARNED.

"Why Argentina, you're going to ask," Vanda said, cutting open another roll to dunk and chew whilst waiting for the ice-cold chopp and the tiragosto and the side orders of batatinha fritas and saladeiras she had ordered for them both, though after just half a hot roll and half a coffee Carfax had temporarily cancelled his mind in favour of a violent attack of indigestion that seemed to be his body's answer to anxiety.

Holding his ribs and waiting for the pain to go right through to his back, he concentrated hard on not belching out loud.

"I haven't got the papers on me, of course, they're - hey, are you all right?"

Carfax held his chest hard to stop the pain from killing him. "Papers?" he said, concentrating hard on his inside.

"See, Lynch is in terrible danger. Not that stupid stuff he thinks is so important about being found by his wife. I'm talking real danger, here."

"Real danger? Why?" The girl had flipped her lid. He'd listen, nod a lot then leave her, follow her home and apprehend Leslie. Then it was up to him to decide whether to go or stay.

"I was going crazy," she said. "So---"

PAGING LYNCH MADISON

Carfax wasn't wholly concentrating. Here came the heartburn. Too late and too embarrassing to cancel his unnecessary meal. He'd eat it.

"----in every paper I could lay my hands on, I clipped the articles about the disappearances in Argentina. You know? There are dozens and dozens of them all the time. If Lynch was just another one of those ---- if I could fix it so it looked like he was in Argentina --- I thought it was neat."

"Very neat," he said, one hand to his diaphragm, the other reaching for a paper napkin to wipe his forehead. She seemed to be waiting for something. "Go on," Carfax said, groaning out loud for a moment. Better. All better.

Carfax, cured, restored, picked up a second roll himself and sloshed it into the oil mix. "At last," he said, spotting their own waiter coming their way with the cold and the steaming platefuls. "They took their time."

"So," Vanda said, "that's how I figured I'd make out to his family and mine - and you - that he was gone, really gone. I mean, the way he comes and goes, everybody would be irritated with him but nobody would be surprised, right? He could send, maybe get some rigged communication sent, from Argentina to his home, and you could maybe show them this bunch of cuttings about Argentina all marked in red.

"Well, then they'd give up on him, wouldn't they? And feel real sorry for him too. And my family could count him out too. So if you could, like, arrange to 'discover' those papers ------"

PAGING LYNCH MADISON

"Maybe I wasn't concentrating. I don't get it. But life isn't like that," Carfax said through a large forkful of wonderfully greasy fried potato, "unfortunately."

Vanda frowned and played with her fork, annoyed.

"The world would say well he's definitely not in Argentina if he's leaving those very obvious clues, is he?"

Vanda had slowed down, disappointed for a second, but in a tiny time, her eyes brightened and she resumed her meal. Carfax had never seen a woman eat like her. Neat and dainty just like nice girls who behave themselves are taught to, but enthusiastic, appreciative, not pick, pick, like his wife and Jan Merrett, looking for slugs even when there wasn't a lettuce.

"Umm," she said.

"Umm?"

"Tricky," she said, but smiling.

"Yes, Vanda. And what's this danger you're talking about? And what has that to do with your family? What are you trying to tell me?"

Vanda wiped the corners of her mouth, took a drink of iced chopp, and breathing little faint fumes like light beer, put down her glass and stroked it up and down thoughtfully, tucked into her food again, savouring, enjoying, suddenly not enjoying,

PAGING LYNCH MADISON

suddenly scared enough, pulling out letters banded together from her pocketbook, finally pulling out her long-kept secrets.

Even Carfax stopped eating when she got deep into the real Osvaldo Oliveira story. And oh my, it got more exciting by the minute when she got to the power of the Baptista Vasconceloses. Was she right? She was telling it too starkly for the dangers to be imaginary; besides, this was the Brazil he had read about. Corruption, sex and violence, not luxury hydros and singing stars – who anyway all of a sudden turn out to be heiresses.

"Osvaldo plays dirty," she sniffed, getting out a photograph and weeping when she looked at it.

"That's him dancing with me at the wedding. He sent it to me. And that's him months ago when - it makes me shudder, the bastardo."

"He always wears that big medallion?" Carfax said, comparing pictures, looking for something to say.

"Yes," Vanda said low, "it's Brazil's patron saint. Nossa Senhora do Conceicao da Aparecida. Many people wear one but smaller. Him, Osvaldo, he has to have this big vulgar - well it suits him. Osvaldo gets what he wants, professor. It scares me to death.

"My family will take any revenge. Murder is nothing to them if family honour is in it. Not just them. You don't understand Brazil unless you understand this. Professor, did you realise it was me

PAGING LYNCH MADISON

that had that stuff sent to Lynch's wife's family? Through a contact of mine in London?"

Carfax felt ill.

"I figured Graygrove was, like, an unusual name and being an architect and Crossbridge isn't so big, is it? I want Lynch, sure, but I wanted him alive, so - how was I to know they'd send an eye? I mean, if he was my husband, I'd come and get him myself. I wouldn't be able to wait to see if he was OK. I mean that's natural, right?"

"Yeah, natural," Carfax said, holding a headache off with one hand.

"I thought her father would give Lynch's wife the money to come here and I'd meet her at the airport and I'd explain the whole thing, out in the open because Jeez, professor, he's got to go home. He'll be safer there than here, whatever silly bit of trouble he thinks he's in.

"Once he's gone, I'll be free of Osvaldo. See, I can only get free of Osvaldo if I lose Lynch ------ She was weeping those painful quiet sobs now and Carfax took her hand and patted at it like an overfull sandwich.

"Lady, eat up and go home. You've done a brave great thing shopping Leslie for his own good."

Vanda just cried harder.

"You've made my job simple," Carfax said, hoping it was true. "You show me where you live with him and -- look, don't cry. I'll take him home

332

PAGING LYNCH MADISON

out of danger. OK? You'll get over him and you'll make his family very happy," he said, knowing as he spoke that the right way to make everyone positively ecstatic was if he could get some death warrant forged for Leslie Merrett which would make Osvaldo's threats invalid, would make Jan free and free Lynch Madison to live in peace with Vanda after which the bastard could fend for himself.

"I will never be happy without him." She sniffed and stopped. "I'm only interested in making Lynch happy," she said dramatically. "And myself," she added, likeably, humanly.

In the silence, Carfax made inroads on the tira-gosto while there was still time.

"Professor, I've been thinking. If you can find some way -do you think - look, the main thing you need to know is that whatever his family are paying you to find him, I'll pay you double to save him from Osvaldo and his paid murderers," Vanda said, miming to the boy they needed more coffee.

Carfax felt ill again. Was it the meal. Or the deal.

"I mean, to put it on the line, after you find him, you conveniently lose both of us permanently. Yeah?"

Carfax had much to consider. He had been prepared just two seconds ago to do just that free of charge. But the consideration of double the crazy fee he was already charging the Graygroves would be very very nice. He rolled the feel of double around his mind.

PAGING LYNCH MADISON

He stopped dreaming abruptly. He was going soft. She was not to be trusted. She may have some money, if her family were indeed close enough to open their safes to her, but maybe she was just the poor working-class branch of this fancy family with the fancy name.

Vanda certainly doesn't appear to have a property complex for him to run like the Graygroves. She more than probably didn't have a bean. Or a scruple. She was bluffing him, using her well-filled dress to take his attention off what was up her sleeve. What about his future, his pension?

"What you are proposing isn't ethical, and you know it. I have accepted a retainer to find ----"

"Sucks, professor. We're talking double to find him then a retainer for your silence into your dotage. I mean, like, be practical."

He'd have nothing but the best. At home and abroad. He'd take Heather everywhere with him and teach her to reject everything but the best. She would love all that crap with the kind of people who loved it too. They'd go alone, sending the big kids off to that adventure camp they'd been pleading for, the little one to Heather's mother, for whom they would buy a spacious ground floor flat with a huge garden near the beach.   All this, of course, whilst their own new house was being done over by the interior decorators -----

"Do you think you could sell Lynch's family the idea about Argentina? I mean, it's quite good isn't it?" Vanda said. "That would hold water wouldn't

PAGING LYNCH MADISON

it? Then they can all forget him without too much conscience - they'd have somebody to blame, a grand memorial service -" He waited for her to stop crying.

"To help you Vanda, try putting yourself in his wife's shoes - Mrs Merrett and her child, Charlotte, standing by the window and waiting for him every day of their lives," Carfax lied. "It is my duty -------"

"Every man has his price, is the only sober thing my father ever taught me. You have the rent to pay, right, professor? A mortgage? Um. I'll pay that off for you then pay you all the rest I've offered. Just save him for me, that's all you have to do."

The fact. Leslie Merrett had surfaced again. The problem. Now he was found, to which woman should he be returned? The other question. Was there any way that both their fees could decently be earned?

"Um. Wait a moment. First I need to speak to him alone and in detail, Vanda. He doesn't know about Osvaldo? Nothing? Look if I tell him, he may be relieved. It may be a good excuse for him. Forgive me, but how do you know he hasn't got tired of you. Maybe he's had enough adventure and is really quite desperately anxious now to go back to where he belongs."

"Lynch doesn't belong there. He belongs with me. As soon as we met, we knew that. As soon as you meet him you'll understand too. He can't live without me although I think he often wants to try, you know?"

PAGING LYNCH MADISON

Carfax looked at her and sighed his cynicism. Vanda laughed.

"Sure he keeps wanting out, that's like, that's his problem. He runs off when you get too close. That's Lynch. But I know he loves me. But he comes back to me, doesn't he? It was he who first gave me the idea about Argentina. Once I followed him and all the time I just knew he knew it ----"

No need to urge her. Vanda was dying to tell him the story of how she had followed him for the rest of the day, how direct he had been, as if trying not to lose her. She would swear he knew she was there. No doubling back, no covering his tracks, no checking behind himself, nothing in the least bit tricky or subtle. He did everything openly, slowly and carefully, chopping, changing, changing his clothes -----

"Changing into what?"

"You don't know how different the guy looked by the time he'd done himself over and went to get the ticket for the bus."

"Bus."

"The bus to Sao Paulo. I had to stop him there. Just in case he had found out about Osvaldo - Osvaldo lives in Sao Paulo - and was planning to take him out on his own. He wasn't even all that surprised to see me. That's how I knew he knew I'd followed him.

"But he didn't know about Osvaldo?

PAGING LYNCH MADISON

"Not at all. I heard him ask for Sao Paulo and the falls - you know the falls?"

Carfax let down his tired eyebrows and reached for his much-folded map. Sao Paulo. The Iguassu falls. Argentina. A good easy unremarkable route for any tourist. Just in case he had to fall back on it, it was actually a good enough plan.

"So will you do it. professor? You will do all right out of it. The mortgage, double the money, a retainer and a wedding invitation - don't hold your breath on that, though," she smiled. I just know Lynch will wait for the whole damn seven years."

Carfax gazed at her with fascination as she precision-cut a huge juicy mango in the Brazilian way, not fazed by the stickiness on her hands or troubled by the etiquette of the thing as she carved out a superb square of it and offered it to him on the end of her knife.

For one last lustful moment, before pulling himself back to business, he pictured her offering him other intimate lush treats and wondered how real men knew the right things to say and do which will steer a friendly woman into bed.

"Your ideas are crazy and far too vague for me," Carfax said sternly. "You are not only trying to bribe me to lie to Leslie's family but how do I know you're not just -- some little schemer?"

"I am," she laughed. "That's what I am. Yeah. Some little schemer." She loved it. It was the best thing she'd heard in years, you could tell from the laughter.

PAGING LYNCH MADISON

Look, I'm tired," she said, getting up suddenly as her watch bleeped a bleep. "You'll have to sleep on it, right? I'll charge the room with the meal, OK?"

"I invited you, I'll pay," Carfax said automatically, thinking of other things.

"Oh heavens, Professor. One thing I'm not short of is money. You enjoy your stay here, hear? We'll talk tomorrow and make the arrangements. I declare tomorrow a vacation. There's a lot to see in Rio, you know, whilst you're here? Come to the show at the club again tomorrow night, if you like and we'll go from there."

Fax two to the Graygroves. DO YOU WISH TO TREBLE THE FEE?

Carfax tried to ground himself, keep reality in his head. "It seems to me you are very interfering. I must pay for the meal, of course. Then obviously I must speak to Leslie Merrett myself and hear from him how things stand. In any case, what I have been commissioned to do is to return him to his family, and that should keep him safe even if it is sad for you ----"

Vanda's eyes cooled to defrost. Her voice matched.

"Sad? OK, it's your bag, professor. I'm not taking you to him, that's for sure. Find him yourself. And you're right," she blazed. "I was very interfering," she blazed. I sent to the dump for your valise. It might be in your room here by now. Maybe

PAGING LYNCH MADISON

you'll be here tomorrow night. Maybe you won't. If I speak to Lynch, I'll keep the bad news of your visit to myself."

She got up, paused at the desk to say something for a small moment, turned back and pointed to him and had almost run away. He really couldn't move that fast to follow her.

When he had consulted the menu and counted it all up, he took out his wallet and cursed himself for his independence. Reluctantly gauging how many of Graygrove's cruzeiros he'd have to lay out for this meal, he called the waiter and asked for his check.

"It's charged to your room, Senhor," the waiter said, waking brightly to the thrill of Carfax's relieved over-tipping, suddenly feeling the urge to escort Carfax personally to the door, even pressing the button for the lift for him, begging him to come back again rapidamente.

"Somebody has to pay," Carfax whistled, looking in awe at the palatial decor and the king-size bed in the emperor-size room and the swimming-pool size bath with jacuzzi, of course, and all the trimmings and another big jacuzzi out there by the sound of it - hey, that's the real life ocean itself making that sea-sized noise you could hear. He swished open the large door and leaned over the breath-taking secluded balcony that was larger and better furnished than his front-room.

"And I hope it isn't me," he breathed, tearing off his clothes.

PAGING LYNCH MADISON
CHAPTER SIXTEEN

Carfax's principles started to ache just a little when he came down in the morning and saw the views he was being allowed from the terrace of this dream-location. They ached a little more when he noted the deference he was being given as he was shown to the best table in the place the second he showed his room-card; they ached just once more then evaporated into simple gluttony as he goggled at the lush buffet, Aladdin's cave itself, continuing on and on, wonder on wonder, round at least a couple of terrace bends.

An hour later, nearly sick from the amount of breakfast he was obliged to eat (on the grounds that this bounty might never come his way again) Carfax sat still, nursing his stomach while they removed his detritus, hands round his third coffee, a strange perfumed coffee that was never served very hot but was almost painfully perfect, nibbling little salty biscuits he hadn't liked at first but was getting a taste for.

He was out of his league in every way and he knew it. But when he did find the time to look up from his food, he had found it fascinating observing the other guests, because they seemed, on the whole, not the usual international tourists you would expect at such a place. Americans, mostly, of course, but something somewhere here in Rio was a puzzle to him.

PAGING LYNCH MADISON

His holiday experiences had hardly been of this standard, of course, but even allowing for the fact that these guests were likely to be old wealthy, and certainly spoiled by familiarity with good living, they still seemed nervy, quiet and mostly in a hurry for guests in one of the most beautiful settings in the world, as the hotel brochure he'd picked up on the way in to breakfast put it.

It seemed to him that Rio was alive with secrets, with mysteries, with intrigue. An investigator could be really busy busy in a place like this.

He looked, now, less than idly at the other leaflets he'd picked up at the same time; flights every half hour to Sao Paulo; overnight tourist buses direct to Sao Paulo; how to do the falls; helicopters over the waters. Vanda's idea wasn't such a bad one. As yet, he certainly had no better schemes of his own.

He could do with researching the routines of the control they must have on the borders of Argentina. Hell, Carfax really wanted to see the Ig - the what was it - the Ig - those falls anyway, so one excuse was as good as the other.

Sighing, he pushed his coffee-cup away and cleared a tiny space. He was behaving in a very amateurish way, and he knew it. He was also acting 'spoilt' and corrupt after such a small contact with temptation. Good thing he hadn't often been tested before. It was depressing to find that all it took was two bright eyes and some red carpet.

PAGING LYNCH MADISON

He cleared his throat. He took out his small notebook and cheap pen and made a reluctant checklist. He was here to work for the Graygroves.

Dazzling, that view out there. The mountains in the distance hurt your eyes and the sea below - and Christ on a pedestal, arms out, just asking you why on earth you didn't try harder.

Heather would love it here; the scenery and the warmth and the beach, if not the hotel or the food. He smiled, picturing her slim little body and the way she would, even here, have cut up her one piece of toast into a thousand pieces. If he were honest, he would have to admit that he hadn't thought about her at all since he got here - well only in the kingsize in a vaguely married sort of way.

She was all right, Heather. She didn't have much to her, so far as personality went, and she dressed as if she would prefer to go unnoticed, but in a way that meant she could fit in anywhere, Heather could. And she'd make things 'right' wherever she went.

She would have seen straight through this business with Vanda offering him money to hide Leslie Merrett. Dishonest and therefore wrong. And she would have no hesitation or excuses regarding Leslie Merrett's selfishness. Just after greener grass, she would say dismissively. Or more money, perhaps.

Money will corrupt anyone, she'd always say, straight out, like that, without a second thought. She'd be horrified her own husband could sit there

PAGING LYNCH MADISON

even contemplating it, no matter how easy the opportunities were.

Honesty is very nice, Carfax mused, circling his pen round and round the boob-like doodles that he always drew when he was thinking. But he had worked long and honestly for so very little.

He needed a list of things to do.

One, he wrote, SEND POSTCARDS HOME.

Two. FIND LESLIE MERRETT.

He had certainly cherchez-ed the femme already. He'd meet Leslie Merrett within a day or two, he was sure. By which time, he could get some spadework in.

For a start he could ring the customs office at the Argentina border right away, say he was looking for a missing person, give a false name, see how they reacted. Yes, at once - he should have done that last night, curse it. They were supposed to be super-inefficient out here, according to the newspaper stories. Obstructive and bloody-minded, if the documentaries were to be believed. It was important to penetrate as many of their procedures as he could.

Tall and thin, Vanda had said, or long and slender as Jan had put it.

Just looking casually around at the men it occurred to him that it would be a bit too easy to pick out such a man in Brazil and wondered whether they were any nearer that shape in Argentina.

PAGING LYNCH MADISON

Tall thinness eliminated most of the men of Europe and South America. Even if this beanpole master of disguise managed to lie low for years, how long could a woman who looked like Vanda expect to remain incognito anywhere? Was Argentina a good place for them to hide out?

Christ, look what he was doing. Going along with Vanda's madness. What was he thinking about poncing around in this luxury play-ground.

He scraped back his chair angry with himself and excited about the real possibilities, now, of ordinary success. He would stick to routine investigations and get his man. Graygrove would reward him honestly for a difficult job well done and he would have more security than he ever had before. There would be content in that.

She thought Carfax could easily be bought and kept here whilst Leslie Merrett got away. She was probably moving him right now. She thought all it took to call Carfax off would be a tempting night or so here at the hotel and club.

The bent detective: tied up and sold to a tarty singer for a jacuzzi ensuite. He'd check out now. Disappear himself. Let them guess where he was tonight, not walk into their cosy little web.

"Por favor, Senhor, your car is here for you." The head-waiter stopped him in the sudden dark cool of the empty dining-room behind the terrace as Carfax made for the door ready to do some real work at last. "The driver said to wait until you had

PAGING LYNCH MADISON

finished your breakfast. I hope everything was satisfactory, Senhor."

"It's not for me, the car," Carfax said, frowning." There is no car ordered for me."

"A million apologies, Senhor." The head-waiter flicked his fingers and explained a great deal to the boy who had come over to bring him this message.

Carfax went to the desk to learn the Brazilian art of telephoning, bought the necessary telephone tokens, then settled himself in a telephone booth, arranging and re-arranging the heap of grooved fichas into different patterns as he waited for the first of the list of calls to come through to him. No answer. Try the next.

"A million apologies, Senhor," the head-waiter said again at the door of the booth. The car is for you, Senhor. The gentleman there at the door will explain to you, por favor, Senhor."

Carfax walked across the slippery cool floor, down the three steps, past the huge vases of somambaias, past the over-the-top displays of wild orguideas, past the thickly-staffed reception desks to the swing-doors where a small Asian waited by the gleaming side of a huge dark-windowed limo or hearse, the door welcomingly open.

"Professor Brian Carfax? Miss Vanda arranged the car for you this morning. Please--?" The Asian indicated the nice comfortable seats inside.

PAGING LYNCH MADISON

Carfax, who had, in his time, been better than average at all the strength sports like shot-putting and javelin-throwing and weight-lifting, so long as they didn't ask him to run anywhere, judged that he could put this fellow under his arm and throw him off down the road but, with the courteous nod of a man expecting a lift and being pleased it was on time, he got into the car without comment.

Even before he had first opened his first office, when he was still working for British Business Investigations, he had dreamt of adventures like this with strange inexplicable women and quiet mysterious men in exotic places. Not debt-collection and missing teenagers.

Getting into the car without questions, his audibly pounding heart beat out a message to Heather that though this might be crazy, careless and dangerous, even if it led to ---whatever it led to, it wasn't ---- boring.

"Welcome to Rio de Janeiro," the driver said, pulling back the talking-glass between him and his guest in a friendly tone. Don't you find this one of the most beautiful cities in the world, professor?"

Carfax didn't bother with the explanations about the professorship Vanda had conferred upon him. Besides, he rather liked it. No-one had ever considered his brain before or even appeared to wonder if he had one. He wasn't the sort of person anyone thought about at all unless they were employing him at the time. As for Rio being the most beautiful city in the world, when had he been around the world enough to judge?

PAGING LYNCH MADISON

He gazed now out of the window to notice everything, especially which route his kidnapper was taking.

"Where are we going?" Carfax said, belatedly, trying not to sound like his children on a half-term holiday outing.

"Petr¢polis," he said. "Up in the mountains. To Fazenda de Lazer."

Carfax brought out a notebook and tried to write it down then flicked through the leaflets looking for clues. Yes, there was Petr¢polis, marked. It was miles away, wasn't it? Hard to tell on this little Rio leaflet.

"I've been thinking that we are all in competition for the same person, sir," the small Asian said, as Carfax's pulse decided not to stop after all but simply to conform to a faster pace.

"We all appreciate that you have a hard task to do, professor. Lynch's wife wants him brought back to her in England, Vanda wants to keep him for herself and thinks you are the person to help her do it, and if you ever catch up with Lynch, I'm sure he will try to buy you off somehow as well.

"When we first heard Lynch's story we were very indignant at what he had done to his family, of course," the little Asian said, puzzlingly. "But - you'd have to meet Lynch yourself to understand why we changed our minds. It is all very confusing for you so I thought you might like to stay somewhere quiet and comfortable for a while, so you

PAGING LYNCH MADISON

can spend some time with him and with us and think it out for yourself."

Quiet and comfortable. Carfax, who had deliberately muffled his own alarm bells in the hope of adventure, was now overcome by the bell going off and by memories of a relevant psychological technique he'd been taught on a course they sent him on, years ago.

If one can exaggerate the fear or the problem until it is comically unreal, the message went, then it can be handled. Right. Take the words and analyse them.

'Quiet and comfortable:' that meant solitary confinement, of course. And, for good measure, dripping taps, bright lights, manacles, toe-nails removed.

'Stay for a while:' a euphemism for years of isolation in a dank cellar.

Too bad. His enthusiasm for this careless rapturous adventure was still there. There hadn't been as many good fantasies in a lifetime as he had hoped. In fact, this was the first, if you didn't count Heather once agreeing to make love in a lay-by one suddenly passionate November night.

"And Leslie Merrett will really be there?" Carfax said, trying to breathe normally and wishing he didn't sound like sub James Bond.

"Sure. He's at Fazenda de Lazer."

PAGING LYNCH MADISON

Carfax tightened his lip and decided to ask no further questions. He wouldn't know a lie from the truth, anyway.

"It is not very far but I will take you first on a scenic tour of a few places en route. Life is too much of a hurry, is it not?"

Oh yeah. This was code for lie back and enjoy the scenery, feller: they need time at this unpronounceable place to set up traps.

"Chi and Lee are there, of course, and Vanda. We all want to sit and talk together."

He could have asked the next obvious questions. About Chi and Lee, and who this man was, himself. But Carfax wasn't sure that it mattered very much at the moment.

It was a simple matter. He had come to collect a deserter. These outlaws wanted to prevent him from doing this and were hiding him in some encampment. That was the measure of it.

What would be would be; he could sing a song about it.

For now, sitting in a traffic jam, he would divorce himself from it all, look out of the window and enjoy the admittedly glorious scenery. It was stunning. He kept wanting to ask what's this, what's that.

Nice if he could get out to see some more of Brazil before it was time to go home to Heather and

PAGING LYNCH MADISON

take up his own problems - as soon as he could after he had recovered from the torture and beatings.

"Vanda said you'd probably decide to go to Sao Paulo today on your own if I didn't stop you and she wanted to stop you because - well there are reasons.

"She also said you were a professional and might realise, on the other hand, once you had checked things out, how to find out about Argentinian routines without going there and she didn't want any names on Brazilian police files. Not hers, not Lynch's, not yours, either. Why? Once on you can never get off," he said softly. "That is so urgently true, professor, I'm afraid, that I came to collect you right away. To keep the files clear, it was necessary to stop you quickly. Calls are traced fast in this country. It has been found very necessary."

Carfax was hating himself more and more every minute. Some international wizard he was proving to be: he had been thinking petty British knavery, instead of stop-at-absolutely-nothing Brazilian.

"Vanda also said ----" the driver hesitated. "Forgive me, professor, but she is a candid person and believes that life is for living. She said you needed a bit of fun in your life and that we should pick you up at the hotel and ---" he shrugged.

What had Vanda gone on to say, exactly? Nothing he'd want to hear.

"Her hunch was that you wouldn't go to the show tonight in case it was some sort of trap, right?"

PAGING LYNCH MADISON

Carfax looked through his own thought processes. Snap.

Carfax sheepishly fingered the leaflets in his jacket, his check-list and his conscience. He was agonised at being out-guessed and diagnosed so easily - and by a – a – singer. He'd announce his retirement the second he got back from this God-forsaken place. He was too old and too fat and too unsuccessful to go on.

"As she says, the main point is, for the first time in his life, Lynch is very happy --"

"If Leslie Merrett - alias Lynch, alias lots of other names," Carfax said clearly, aiming to remind this little Asian that the Lynch they were all eulogizing wasn't the saint he might have represented himself as, "is so happy, why has he run away so often from Vanda? Why didn't he come to the show last night: I'm sure Vanda must have phoned and told him I had shown up?"

"Yes she did, but he was -------"

"Weakly hiding behind her instead of explaining himself to me?"

"He --- we can discuss that later when we're all together." He drove in silence for a while. "It really isn't far, if we just get through this traffic onto the main road - He pointed out with pride first this feature and that monument.

"The thing is you don't know this man Lynch," the driver suddenly said, (interrupting

PAGING LYNCH MADISON

himself as he raved about Rio's museums and botanical gardens to the west of Petr¢polis, emphatic that Carfax must not return to England without seeing this, that and the Emperor's picnic table,) "is that people love him. Everyone will tell you something different about him but nobody can forget him. He's the most unusual and a quite marvellous person. He's never had the chance to --- look, I'm sure they are all offering escalating amounts of money to find him, but honestly, if you really want to make a profit out of this case, professor, I'm the one you should negotiate with."

Carfax was busting. More fabulous sums being offered for this Lynch. And was this guy only a driver? Maybe he had a boss. And a boss's boss? Now a traffic cop was holding them up. (Maybe he, too, would lean into the car and say "doan you listen, hey senhor, I giva you even more cruzeiros fora this Leslie Merrett thana he will.")

He'd soon be home. He would apologize to the Graygroves, shaking his head sadly at having to report that Leslie Merrett had eluded him, take the Graygroves' kill-fee and never tell anyone he had ever even contemplated any of this funny money being showered upon him.

"You're wondering why I would offer you money not to find him, professor?" Bud said softly, as if Carfax was still capable of asking such decent questions. "I just want to buy him his freedom, which seems to mean so much to him that he dared to try to disappear and keeps trying to do it again.

"I want to look after him until he finds it is safe to stay with us - or stay somewhere, anywhere.

PAGING LYNCH MADISON

So long as he gets over the fear he seems to have of being 'owned.'

"I think I am very close with him. professor. And you will see the way he is with Lee - he is a good man, I know. I hope so. We think he loves Vanda and wants to stay with her but maybe she is - too much -"

Too much. Vanda would always be far far too much but Carfax felt sad he wouldn't have the chance to taste just an exciting little bit more of her. He knew they had had their last tete-a-tete. He coughed. A little adult business had to be conducted.

"Give me a moment to think," Carfax said, "I need to ---think."

Leslie Merrett aka Lynch. The lucky bugger had an amazing number of champions- even a man's natural enemies, his in-laws, wanted him back.

"Exactly what I said at the beginning, professor. You need time to think. Maybe you have seen enough for today. If the traffic is reasonable, we'll be at the fazenda in half an hour or so. By the way, do you like the water?"

Christ. Water. They would drown him with the shock force of fire-hoses. That was big over here in South America, wasn't it? What film was that in?

"We've the most marvellous natural lake in the grounds," the driver said enthusiastically.

What are lakes for? Only for dragging.

PAGING LYNCH MADISON

"The pool's warmer, of course," he said, drawing the glass- divider quietly, tactfully across.

Such a wonderful day, such beautiful air streaming past the windows and such an easy case turning into an impasse. Morally, of course, there was no problem. The Graygroves had literally 'retained' him so he was honour bound to make every effort to be on that plane at the very soonest, handcuffed to however reluctant a Leslie Merrett. Vanda had pleaded that she was what would make Leslie Merrett - or at least Lynch - happy. This guy here insisted he wanted his friend's freedom. Who ever was so altruistic? Was Jan? (Was Heather?) Didn't everyone just want something for themselves?

A man should be free to be and do what he liked. (Wouldn't Carfax like to be free himself, not to have to buy the right house in the right neighbourhood of a country where it always rained on school fete days and where the opposition government always had the answers to the problems of the world until they were elected.)

He would accept nobody's money. Waiting for his new toenails to grow in, waiting for the cigarette burns to fade, he would move in with Vanda, or if she refused him, he'd go into business with the first - any - of the amazing girls they were passing right now as they drove, girls who were incredibly just walking up and down the roads unescorted.

For now, he'd enjoy the '15 miles of Sao Sebastiao do Rio de Janeiro nestling between tall green mountains and deep green sea' like the leaflets said, and swim in the natural lake this guy was

PAGING LYNCH MADISON

driving to. It was hot and wow, he couldn't keep his eyes open. Late nights killed him. They always had.

"I don't want to have to do this," Vanda said, sliding out of her silver sheath and kicking it over the other side of Carfax's stretching-rack, where he lay helpless. She came towards him and smiled. "But I'll do anything to help Lynch Madison."

Carfax was still in half a dream as he woke, struggling with real fear now that he might truly be walking into some sort of, at the very least, threatening behaviour. And the car wasn't driving right.

Hey. That's what had woken him: sleeping policemen. Slowly slowly over the huge unfriendly bumps of a long winding driveway. They had turned in. What a place.

The sculpture of the small child holding a cornucopia of fruit spilled over the FAZENDA DE LAZER logo, and was echoed in fountains right down the driveway.

"What's the sign mean?"

"Ah, you're awake. Welcome, professor. It means Health Farm - farm of leisure, literally. Like the place? Lynch designed every inch. He is so talented."

These had to be the most perfect grounds he'd ever seen outside a cricket pitch. Mind you, look at the number of gardeners they were passing, intently working as they drove.

PAGING LYNCH MADISON

The sweeping driveway led forwards like a film set and yes, there was the lake. Lake? It was enormous and so beautiful with a fountain - he might just, for once, have met the right people. Unconventional people, right, but they seemed simply loaded with money, who cared how, and like all such people, they needed to have admiring crowds around them and who could wonder if the lost and wandering Leslie Merrett picked up with them.

He pictured Jan's tired slippers-and-green-veg personality. He pictured Vanda. This was surely a no-blame situation.

And Carfax himself was prepared to admire them too. He'd have himself a little holiday, enjoy everything they offered him and worry about Leslie Merrett when it seemed to be time to.

He frowned. He'd revert to the psychological techniques he'd learned, nonetheless, imagining the worst just for safety. Health farms; compulsory colonic irrigation, of course. And complete starvation. A health farm is a natural, a fiendishly clever guise for persuasion techniques.

"You've arrived," the small Asian said. "Here you put down your troubles. You're here for rest and recuperation, as the squaddies in your country say."

That was a very suspicious speech, Carfax registered. What does an Asian know about squaddies?

"But first come and meet everybody."

PAGING LYNCH MADISON

Everybody. "How many of you are there," Carfax frowned. He wasn't sure how it would help if he knew, there being only one of him.

"You make us sound like a gang," the small man laughed. "There's just Chi, and Lee and Vanda and did I say I'm called Bud by everyone but my father? And the staff, of course."

Vanda. His heart jumped about a bit. Bud and Chi and Lee. All silly nicknames. He'd wait to find out about them. He just wouldn't ask. It was all very neat Vanda being here with them. Vanda who had out-thought him, trussed him up, part-roasted him and then frozen him for later consumption, turned out to be cook-in-residence in these strange kitchens.

Just wait, Vanda of the long surname.

Some of 'the staff' - their uniform made them look more like servants, (bodyguards, thugs, frighteners,) - were coming out to greet their arrival with smiles and great deference.

So the small Asian was the gang-leader. Which made it strange that he had come to get Carfax himself. Strange that he did the driving himself.

What was that? The little bastard was taking his case out of the boot and handing it to a young boy. His case. But he'd left it at the --- who had packed it? Who had collected it?

"We had it packed for you while you were at breakfast," the Asian smiled, seeing his surprise.

PAGING LYNCH MADISON

Carfax groaned aloud at his own carelessness.

Inside the cool marble lobby, the driver asked the smiling black girl for "cinquenta, por favor," at the desk where they handed him a key with the baby logo holding a 50 in her hand.

"You see his size?" said the small driver nodding at Carfax to two men in white track-suits. They walked round him and nodded.

"Go with them," he said, smiling at Carfax. "They will bring refreshments to you and in two hours, they will bring you to my rooms for some surprises."

Cell fifty? What sort of people were in the others? Why would they need his size? Did thumb-screws have sizes? Refreshments? Ah yes that would be bread and water. And surprises? You bet. And even more surprising that he was standing by listening to this crap. He must have gone soft.

"I don't know who you are," he said, speaking clearly for hidden microphones, "nor do I understand what all this is about but it's certainly all ridiculous. Please return my case to me immediately. If anything is missing I shall have to --- I would thank you now to contact Mr Merrett and bring him to me as you obviously know exactly where he is."

"Sure we do," the driver said, astonishingly.

"Tell him I am on my way to apprehend him and we will get straight on the next flight to England where I am commissioned to return him to his family,

PAGING LYNCH MADISON

after which their arrangements are their own affair. Nothing can stop me," he said, wishing he could feel the nice heaviness of his gun instead of just the straps of his empty gun holster, knowing he sounded priggish, like Biggles on a mission.

He was sure that when they found his gun in the hotel drawer, he'd bet they hadn't packed it under his new underwear like he did.

The small man looked astonished. "Of course," he said. "Though should you find you like it here and would like to protract your stay, that would be most pleasing to us. Of course you want to get home. But for now, professor, I have to go out. I will try to make what arrangements I can for you to carry out your commission." He bowed slightly and left Carfax gasping.

Aha. So they did complete brainwashing here, too. God, of course. That's what had happened to Lynch - Leslie. He'd run away briefly, as any man could, run into this mob and now he no longer had a will of his own.

This wasn't the real world. This was South America. People disappeared here like nowhere else. He looked behind him. Up the driveway, the gardeners still slogged on. Not gardeners at all, of course. Lynch himself was probably rooting about down there as happy with his hoe as could be after the mind-conditioning programme they'd put him on.

If Carfax wasn't ever-vigilant, he'd be wheeling his barrow contentedly down to join him later in the day.

PAGING LYNCH MADISON

Drugged, at the very least, by unreality, Carfax allowed himself to be shown into room fifty and gasped with horror.

Worse, almost, than the hotel. Palatial. Aesthetic. Air-conditioned. Unutterably luxurious. A view right to the Sugar Loaf, was it? Some mountain, anyway. Outside, past what must surely be synthetic grass, past the plastic palm trees, were pools, jacuzzis, tennis courts, stables.

And that silver gleam. Yes, the lake, distantly.

Inside, everything. Including an unlocked cupboard with iced soft drinks, a full bottle of old old brandy, wine he'd never heard of and not a price list in sight. (His idea of luxury in any strange room latterly had been a kettle and a tea-bag.)

A knock on his door. There has been a mistake, Senhor. Your tiny garret attic unfurnished hot little cupboard, number two thousand and fifty is ready for you now. Come this way.

Or it might be his case, now that it had been thoroughly searched. He opened the door to receive a white hooded bathrobe, a white track-suit, white shorts, white tee-shirt, white trainers. All sizes correct. White towels and a small white bag of exotic toiletries. The danger signs were everywhere. Maybe not torture and brainwashing as he'd joked with himself, but with such big money being staked out to him, with such vast perks there had to be a vast catch.

PAGING LYNCH MADISON

He was just about to take a savoured swallow of the brandy when one sensible idea came to him. There is no such thing as a free drink.

This bottle was quite likely to be, joking apart, heavily adulterated with drugs. It was, in this most likely of countries for it, an evens-on possibility that Lynch was into drug-running with this tempting, attractive and obviously successful crew. No wonder expense could not be spared to keep Carfax silent.

And of course a singer on tour with her manager was a great cover. How did that tour list go? Rio, then maybe on to La Paz in Bolivia, then Bogota; easy peasy, as his children said when they were small. Would he ever see his darling children again in their grotty, unkempt, overlooked but safe little garden.

A shower and a think, a dusting of talc and clean teeth, the white track-suit felt light and comfortable.

He turned to his bag for the schedule he had looked at so long ago with the dear uncomplicated Graygroves in lovely boring England.

Still no bag, of course. "The porter will ------ " the small man had said - ah, but the porter hadn't yet. The gun, of course, would be gone. Grams of the drug-of-the-moment worth millions was at this very moment being crammed into every orifice of the bag. Then nothing but courtesy until they'd waved him goodbye - an anonymous call to the policia when he arrived in the departure lounge. Easy peasy. The policia only needed incriminating evidence once and it would be the Brazilian equivalent of curtains.

PAGING LYNCH MADISON

South American jails? He'd be better off as one of those zombie gardeners.

He quietly opened the door - no guard- paced back quietly down the corridors, down the stairs as he hoped to avoid calling attention to himself by not buzzing for the lift.

At the ground floor, hidden from view in a small alcove where the scent of wonderful white fragrant flowers he didn't know the name of wafted, he watched the hallway in which the reception area was set.

It looked authentic enough. Just as if there were really a health farm in action. Notices about exercise classes in and out of the water, brisk walks, cycling parties, aromatherapy, beauty treatments, a lecture on drug abuse tonight: well that was a clever cover-up, of course.

Certainly that tall thin man in the white track-suit to match his own, this man who was walking sideways and as though he had pebbles in his shoes, held up only by his strong brown supporting hand on his buttock looked remarkably like a patient.

"Any word?" he was saying quietly to the tiny oriental girl near the door.

"The plane's landed," she said. "He should be here in a couple of hours. Can you last?"

"A couple of hours? No," he said, beginning to crab away.

"No more drugs," she called.

PAGING LYNCH MADISON

Carfax's eyebrows shot up. Evidence.

Mind you, she might mean, at a health-farm, no more pain-killers. Still, it would be nice, if he could, whilst here, scoop some vast narcotics ring. It would make him an international reputation. Nothing boring about that. And the rewards they would heap upon him would be more legal, more spendable, than the sudden cache of hush money he had seemed to call down upon himself over the last couple of days.

The thin man didn't reply to her as he put one painful step in front of the other to go out into the gardens. The tiny girl followed after him slowly, sympathetically. "Bud's back. He's out there. If you going to lie on the grass again, I got a bit of time now. I bring that book for you both and we go through it - keep your mind off your poor back. OK Lynch?"

Bullseye.

Fax three to the Graygroves. TODAY, IN THE GARDENS OF A BRAZILIAN HEALTH_HYRDO, BRIAN CARFAX, PRIVATE INVESTIGATOR, USING IMMENSE INGENUITY, COMPLETED THIS MOST DIFFICULT AND DANGEROUS COMMISSION. LESLIE MERRETT APPREHENDED. HOME SOON.

(But there's no call for you to force your shoes back on your swollen feet just yet: the story's far from over.)

PAGING LYNCH MADISON

Right. Now Carfax would pull his licensed gun, drag Merrett's arm behind his back, face any comers, force him to go to the cars that were standing there, taking advantage of their surprise, demand to be driven to the airport at gunpoint if necessary - whammo.

The trouble was that his gun was in the bag he didn't have, passport ditto, tickets ditto, money ditto. What an amateur screw-up letting them take his bag from him like that.

The other trouble was that the bugger couldn't even walk.

What a state the chap was in. Carfax watched him sympathetically till he finally reached the small group on the grass and was helped to the ground where he lay helplessly.

He was not the bold hero he thought he had been trailing. Was the injury anything to do with why he hadn't returned home. Was he perhaps partially paralysed and maybe impotent and had reasoned that he shouldn't ever go back to Jan as damaged goods.

Rule six. Facts. Find out the facts and act accordingly.

Anyway, before taking the bloke unwillingly home and away from all this, should he wait for more evidence of real crime, staked out here at this peculiar set-up, taking fair advantage of the luxury himself whilst taking everything in. Or should he----

PAGING LYNCH MADISON

"Why are you hiding?" Vanda Raimunda Neocita Baptista Vasconcelos hissed at him.

Vanda, in a pink towel-turban and desperately short towelling robe to match, (pink for girls?) popped her head cheerily in and waited whilst he stood frozen to the alcove having his second heart-condition of the day.

"You must tell me sometime what you are doing playing hide-go-seek in this corner, professor. You sure take your job seriously," she said, taking his arm and marching with him to the gardens. "Come and meet Lynch. You'll like him," she said. "He's cool."

In an instant Carfax acknowledged to himself that up to now, he had actually detected nothing yet by himself. Nothing. He wondered what Lynch really knew. Vanda said that the Osvaldo story was completely unknown to him. Was that true? Had she had him cruelly incapacitated for his own sake to stop him disappearing yet again?

Carfax was dizzy with probabilities and possibilities, but one thing he was certain about. This was a great moment.

Carfax is about to be introduced to the long-looked-for disappearing Leslie Merrett of many aliases and no fixed abode.

Your ready-made prejudiced, pre-conceived notions of a shamed and humbled husband, almost pleased to be found, ready to go back and take the rap like a man, your sense of justice and the fitness of things may need more than a little adjusting.

PAGING LYNCH MADISON

Because there he is, lying grimly on the lawn groaning slightly in pain and completely helpless at the moment if you wish to kick him anywhere vulnerable now that he is down.

But it is obvious that Lynch is an immediately attractive person. That he is not only likeable but liked. That he is contented here despite his pain. That he is amongst friends.

His brow is at the moment, and without pretension, being caressed by the gentle tiny Chinese woman from the reception desk on one side of him, the kissable thighs of Vanda are next to his on the other side as she flings herself down on her front and she props herself on her elbows to talk to him and comfort him.

The concerned voice of the small gang-leader who is seated near his head, is urging him to 'take it easy and think of other things', long cold drinks are on their way across the lawn to the white wrought-iron table nearby, the whole thing a hymn to friendship and ease.

Carfax is only waiting to be invited to lie right next to the four of them and he will, (forget the brainwashing) volunteer to join the gang, volunteer to forget not only who they are but who he is himself.

He can't help thinking he should tell his own wife and the Graygroves not to wait up for him.

"Professor Brian-the-Brain Carfax," smiled Vanda. "I just love names, you know? Meet Lynch. I sometimes call him Lynch Mobb, don't I, querido?

PAGING LYNCH MADISON

This is Lynch. Lynch Madison. Leslie Merrett. Laurence Miller. Who else were you, Lynch?"

"Vanda says you're the detective Jan hired," Lynch said smiling a little. "Shit. I'm really sorry she ---I never thought Jan would do that," Lynch said, faintly. "And I'm really sorry you had to come all this way."

A really nice guy. Polite. Worried about Jan. See? He must have done it all under duress. This case was turning out very interesting indeed. Carfax must tune in very carefully.

"Fancy Jan coughing up all that money just to get me back after ignoring me like I wasn't there all the time I lived at home," Lynch said softly, alienating Carfax again.

"Your in-laws paid," Carfax said coldly, warning himself to be professional, to say nothing recriminatory, to make no judgements, to desist from castrating the arrogant bugger.

"Did they really? What's the time?" Lynch said, closing his eyes in pain, lying still in the uncomfortable twist he'd put himself in to look up at Carfax.

The triumvirate looked to their task: hastening to assure Lynch how quickly time would pass before the plane landed, how comfortable they would try to make him, how anxious they were for his pain to diminish.

"I would have thought," Carfax said, staring disapprovingly just slightly over all their heads,

PAGING LYNCH MADISON

trying to get Lynch to look at him again, "you might have asked just some little question about your daughter, to take one example, if not your wife.

"I mean, whatever is going on here, whatever future you have planned for yourself, whatever medical problem you might have at the moment, common humanity seems to dictate a little interest in your own child."

"She isn't his own child, of course," Bud said. "But you loved Charlotte, didn't you, Lynch? Lie still. There's no need to get upset."

Revelations. You should only have revelations on a full stomach and preferably on video. Then you could play them over and over until they are understood, fully absorbed, completely accounted-for, and neatly trimmed to fit as well as could be expected their new, uncomfortable place.

Silence, except for a little soothing humming from Chi.

"Are you going to talk to me," Carfax said, "or shall I ---He couldn't think of a single thing he could do if Merrett just continued to ignore him.

"Look, Mr Merrett," Carfax said very coldly, remembering that the rights and wrongs weren't his concern, except out of natural interest, "it's simple. You have to come home, sort things out and by all means come back here if that's what you want. It's your life. But Mrs Merrett is unable to sort her --- arrangements out until you do. I have to report meeting you which means she wouldn't be legally

PAGING LYNCH MADISON

free to marry and it all seems exceedingly unjust to me."

"She wants to marry?"

At last. Merrett was looking and speaking directly at Carfax, who felt instantly more useful. And the man did, to be fair, sound distraught but whether at the finality of this further revelation or with pain it was hard to tell.

Either way, Carfax was empty of any sympathy whatsoever for him. Carfax was up-to-here with them all and their smug selfishness and had lost interest in detection, in getting rich quick, in short-changing the Graygroves, even in seeing South America.

"She is living with and is pregnant by a man called Victor -- Victor someone. I can't look up his full name as you have stolen my case," Carfax said, not bothering with diplomacy. "So, yes, I suppose you could say she does want to marry."

"Oh no. Oh no. Not Victor, again." Lynch laughed painfully. (Only hurts when he laughs?) "Yes, I see. Yes, in the end I suppose that's what would happen. So Charlotte gets her father back after all."

Ah. Victor was Charlotte's real father and -- Carfax saw some of it and knew the rest would get explained to him in the end but he was waiting for the remorse. Where's the remorse? Did remorse go out of fashion whilst Carfax wasn't looking, like tie widths and patterns which he wore just slightly behind the trend.

PAGING LYNCH MADISON

Bud frowned at Carfax. "By the way, I'm sorry about the delay with your case. I will see it is delivered to your room at once. Can I have a drink brought out for you? Have you tried the native 'chopp?' Yes? I'll get some sent out."

A flunky was coming across the lawn.

The plane would be an hour early, he revealed.

You would have thought the Messiah was coming an hour early. The girl, Chi, clapped her pretty little hands together in pleasure, Bud beamed, Vanda squealed, Lynch looked up to the heavens in some sort of thanks.

Bud reached into his trousers for a huge bunch of keys, called across the lawn to someone and waved his keys at him.

"Don't send a driver," Vanda said, lifting the keys from Bud's hand, running towards the drive. "I'll go. Come with me, professor. We'll talk," she said, still running, down the driveway, past the drugged gardeners.

And what do you think Carfax was doing?

Foolishly lumbering after Vanda, that's what.

PAGING LYNCH MADISON
CHAPTER SEVENTEEN

"Whoops," Vanda made a 'naughty girl' face as she cut into the speeding traffic dangerously for the third time.

"Sorry, sweetheart, but we just, like, have this date with a jumbo." Carfax knew she was talking to the woman driver she'd just cut up, not to him.

"I couldn't bear to be late for Stan and by the way no good you doing that, sir, there's no brake on your side of the car," she smiled.

Carfax sighed, checked his watch, took his foot foolishly from the car-carpet he was flattening and waited to hear why this Stan couldn't be kept waiting. But she said nothing more.

"Who's Stan," Carfax said carefully. "You all seem -- what do I mean -- a bit anxious to please him. He's certainly getting some sort of VIP treatment."

"Yes," Vanda smiled. "For Lynch he certainly is a VIP."

Lynch again. How depressing.

"I used to work for Stan. It's ages since I've seen him. You may not like him; people often don't like him. I mean, even Lynch doesn't, you know, exactly like him."

PAGING LYNCH MADISON

"He was your manager? Or your agent? I just get the feeling he's got something over you all, the way you run about for him."

"You don't know anything about us, do you, professor? Some detective."

It was a joke, what she was saying, he thought. Sort of.

"Reach me a Kleenex, why don't you? Thanks. Look, I said I'd explain everything to you but I'm not sure what you need to know."

"Try everything."

"You think I'd tell you? It seems a long time ago. Anyway, when I was living in London I was out of money so I worked for Stan. Then, quite coincidentally, I met Lynch while I was handing out Stan's leaflets."

"Love at first sight?"

"I guess."

Carfax sighed. He could picture it. "What leaflets?"

"Stan's a hypno-therapist and when I met Lynch he was in agony, just like he is now, with back trouble for the very first time. He gets it on and off. It's dreadful when it happens."

"Ah. And when you met him he agreed to limp back to Stan with you and you cured him?"

PAGING LYNCH MADISON

"Hell, no. I couldn't hypnotise anyone."

She smiled at him, hypnotically.

"But this Stan cured him." Carfax didn't want to rush her, but this was all too slow for him. Soon they would be arriving at the airport and he still had no overall view and not a clue for a plan of action

"Right. Wasn't it wonderful that I was sort of 'sent' to bring Stan and Lynch together when the time was right?"

Carfax nodded a little. "Keep your eyes on the road, will you?" he raised his voice suddenly.

"Whoops," she said again. "Yeah. I was only pushing the leaflets for Stan, that's all. But that's how I met Lynch so now I look back on it, it was the best job I could have had in the world."

Two hearts entwined glowed through the air in her smug sentimentality.

"You worked for Stan in the day for---"

"Yeah, like, for money to eat, and I sang at Amorettis in the evenings. You know, Amorettis? Of course you do. While you were hunting Lynch down you'll have found out about Amorettis, all right."

Sure. Carfax the great detective knew Amorettis all right. (Amorettis?)

PAGING LYNCH MADISON

"The Amorettis gave me my first chance and that's how I got to know Lynch's friends, Bud and Chi, of course - jeez, everything good in my life came from working for Stan, when you think about it."

"Hold on, hold on," he said, trying not to look at the speedometer, "so Stan cured Leslie - Lynch's back. And now Lynch is in trouble again. But what do you need Stan for. Find a hypno-therapist in Brazil. It's a big country."

"You're not listening to the whole story. Anyway I don't know if such sophisticated stuff has reached Brazil yet. In some funny ways, it is very behind, though you wouldn't say that in front of too many Brazilians if you want to live.

"In any case a lot of water's gone down the fall since then. When Lynch was being Laurence Miller ---"

She turned to look at him for far too long in such heavy traffic, attracted by his intake of breath.

"Oh. Didn't you know about that? Oh well, another time, that's not important to me because we, Bud and Chi and me, had lost touch with him completely at that time. He went to ground, you know, for a couple of years? Anyway, then Stan cured him again and ever since, Lynch sort of believes he is the only one that can do it. He's sort of Lynch's guru - so of course he's ours, too."

Of course. "Is this Stan straight?"

"God, no," Vanda said. "But why did you ask?"

PAGING LYNCH MADISON

"It's easy. He sounds like an old-fashioned crook with a trendy new way to take money from fools."

"Oh that sort of 'straight,' like, honest, like the English mean. I guess he's completely straight in that way. It isn't crooked at all, hypno-therapy, do you know anything about it?"

"No. But I'm sceptical. I've got my feet on the ground."

"Right. Lynch was like that. Ask Lynch how he felt before he was cured. Anyway, Stan is almost rigidly poor-but-honest though he's real strange. I kept writing to Stan, explaining where I was and what I was doing because, when Lynch disappeared I knew he might one day put his back out again and have to contact Stan and I turned out to be right.

"When Stan wrote to me out here, every so often, I mean, like, he didn't have so many friends he could tell the truth to, he recently sent me this, like, big brag and his new address - it was some fancy place he took over there when things started looking up.

"He explained that the jet set who were too bored to do anything but be ill, had got to hear about hypno-therapy and he'd got himself a terrific connection and wow for a while back there he couldn't spend it fast enough.

"Stan's only agreed to come to us because of -- a little local difficulty. And it'll do as a sort of tax haven for him as it turns out. He'll work hard - that's

PAGING LYNCH MADISON

the way he is. And he thinks of me as being lucky. It's funny but wherever I am, things just seem to work out."

Carfax sighed, noticing the increase in the numbers of the red-plated yellow taxis, wishing he was in one beside a meek grateful Leslie Merrett, their suitcases side-by-side on the roof-rack clearly labelled with their English addresses.

"What does CUIDADO - TRABALHOS mean?" Carfax asked, beginning to read every sign in the hope that soon there would be one that said 'aeroporto' on the auto-estrada.

"Slow for roadworks," she said, foot hard down and racing.

"What I meant when I said, like, he'd had difficulties," Vanda went on conspiratorially, "Stan's gay as they come so Bud's arranged a boy-friend for him that we know is security plus and at least we know he's well over the legal age, for one thing, for heaven's sake. Otherwise, Stan'll get himself into big trouble here like he did - well, never mind."

"I still don't get it. If this Stan is such trouble, and money seems to be absolutely no object with your friends ---"

"Right," Vanda said ingenuously. It stopped Carfax for a moment. He must get back to that.

"Then why didn't you just buy this Stan a return ticket, let him cure your 'Lynch' and send him away again?"

PAGING LYNCH MADISON

"You simply don't understand our set-up. Let's say that so far as we know Stan is the only person in the world that can make Lynch well again. See, we are all pledged to Lynch's happiness for the rest of his life."

Carfax had gone cold. He had thought them all a little loveably crazy but this sounded like dangerous madness. More cultish. Definitely peculiar.

Vanda looked seriously at him, taking her eyes off the road for far too long for Carfax's liking. "We're like your Knights of the Table," she said. "All for one and one for all."

Carfax didn't even say she had her legends muddled - he just nodded and waited for her to talk on, like you do with mad people.

"Stan, you see, like Lynch, but in a different way, is gifted. He is a Great Healer."

"Ah, I see."

More nonsense. Carfax sighed. "And where's this great healer coming from?"

"London. He's --"

"London? Oh not Lourdes, then?"

A puzzled frown. "From London," she said again. Over her head. Never mind.

PAGING LYNCH MADISON

"It was my idea. It's going to be a great new life for Stan out here. And if we go to Argentina, he won't have so far to come if he need him."

Everyone's fantasy, that. That someone would ever care enough to hold your hand long and lovingly enough for you to take the difficult steps over the slippery terrain of life.

"It wasn't easy. I talked to Stan a lot before I wrote to him, and asked him to contact the Graygroves."

"Stan knew the Graygroves?"

"Jeez no. It's just an unusual name and an architect and all and a small town. He found them, no sweat. But honest, professor, he thought I was crazy. Like, making trouble for the man I loved? So I had to tell him a bit about Osvaldo and that made him mad enough to agree to do it. Then when Stan's own trouble hit the fan he rang me and I could tell he was, like asking to hide out here. And it was just then that Lynch's back went again. So Stan's here to sort Lynch out first then to talk things over with us, see how he can help us and we can help him. I never saw Brazil like this when I just lived here, but the way most people keep themselves to themselves here, South America could be the answer for a lot of people."

Driving like the last desperate contestant for the eligible prince, Vanda wove crazily on.

Carfax, feeling so far out of his depth that it was scarcely worth sticking his arms up and calling

PAGING LYNCH MADISON

'help', tried hard to stick rigidly to his effective if rusty investigative techniques.

"I understood you had come to Latin America only because you were being sponsored by a record company as touring musicians --"

"Jeez, so you did find something out, then, professor?"

Carfax let that pass and wished he still smoked. A few more miles with Vanda and he might begin again.

"You don't know how people here hate that 'Latin America' stuff. Sure, we came here for our music in a way but --- it's very difficult to explain. You know I'm brasileira? I'm Carioca. Now I'm back I know this is where I should be. Look at me carefully," she said, horrifically eyes off the road again, "yet a million times a day in England they asked me, 'are you Spanish?' Do I look Spanish?" She tossed her head contemptuously, looking like every Brit's idea of a native-born flamenco dancer as she did so.

"Spanish! So now I'm back I can be, like, myself, you know? And Bud's little bit of bad luck brought him here too - so it's all just worked out. Now, what else do you want to know about?"

"Vanda - just talk. Assume I know nothing."

A reasonable assumption.

"You know when Bud chose the fazenda it was such a crummy place ---

PAGING LYNCH MADISON

"Chose?"

"Yes. Gee I don't know where to start. Like, Bud's family are mega-loaded."

Carfax tried to re-adjust the little driver to being yet another heir, failed and tried to sit still and listen.

"He could have had anything from his family but he would only take something they wouldn't miss. Like me, I guess. So he chose the fazenda -I mean, you should have seen how it looked. Anyway, Chi and I thought he was crazy but look what he's done? It's like a magic place. You understand? Like, it's made Lynch so happy getting it together; and it brought me back to Brazil and to my family."

Her eyes were shining with familial love and devotion. Great family the Baptista Vasconceloses. A little light revenge and a soupcon of killing the only disadvantages of belonging to it.

"Bud only wanted to find a pad he could build into someplace that will help people, anyways. That's how he runs things. You know this country is full of violence. Oh come on, why are you smiling like that? It isn't just Osvaldo, you must know that. Well Stan, for example. He could maybe for the first time live here in peace. Stan would run a real good therapy department and he knows how to handle crazy patients and Chi's working on a programme –"

"Chi's an heiress too, right?"

PAGING LYNCH MADISON

"Hey, you know more than you let on, don't you? She's got this idea of sending out a team - maybe free, even, for the publicity, a team to the prisons - ncluding Stan especially - to humanise some of the violent prisoners - and that's not all. One day we will have grateful patients from all over the world, that's for sure. When we look back at the successes, we can say that our own lives will really have been worthwhile."

She beamed smugly and waited a moment as if to let the orchestral strings swell a little.

"Now Chi's had another good idea ----"

Carfax could have asked a thousand questions. It was getting more complex. Simply, for now, he asked who Chi was.

"She's Bud's wife, of course." She looked at him with great puzzlement but carried on. "Anyway the Japanese are crazy about their health so she advertised in the Japanese papers and they're actually beginning to turn up, here, and of course it spreads like wildfire. I can see some of them will end up living here, too. There's a big population of Japanese here. In Sao Paulo. You knew that, didn't you? Didn't you? We're on our way. We're going international. Isn't it amazing?"

As if to illustrate this, she executed an amazing figure of eight round a large lorry.

"So Bud's a Japanese from Sao Paulo, then," Carfax worked out, relieved that it was all neatening up. "And his family are in health-hydros?"

PAGING LYNCH MADISON

"Bud's Chinese. They're Chinese in Guyana," she said, almost beside herself at Carfax's ignorance.

"Bud's family own half of Guyana and a bit of Brazil, I guess. No. They know nothing about beauty farms - what you call health hydros - the idea is quite new here in Brazil except for the super-rich, and they are mostly down at the spa places. It's up in the mountains it was crying out for a place where the air is so good for ill people. And then Bud's trying to run it so really poor clients can be sent here by doctors, the fees subsidised by overcharging the rich, you know? The greatest thing was the way Bud made Lynch whole again by giving him this filthy, falling-down place and ---"

Could she be talking about the perfectly appointed, cared- for white mansion they had been in a half hour ago?

"Now it's up and running, we will really make it, you know, 'something.' Lynch is happy being part of that 'something' too. Me too - you know, like, help the world, right?"

Help the world, right?

Carfax closed his eyes. So Bud was a super-rich Chinese Guyanian. Chi was a Chinese, no, Japanese what, princess? Lee would probably turn out to be the king of some little-known throne or other.

What was he doing here with this super-rich bunch of health freaks, on the way to meet a pansy hypno-therapist whilst breathing in the heady

PAGING LYNCH MADISON

perfume of this sleazy singer - at least that seemed to be her job a few days ago. No. Yesterday. Lord, only yesterday.

Known facts. Twice two is four, oil is heavier than water and pop musicians are always on the brink of poverty. This singer and her gang were a little different, right? They could move fast about the country, right? Their publicity kept them from suspicion, right? Ideal for drug-running. That would explain all the easy money.

He tried to reconstruct the English newspaper report and the photograph: if only he hadn't amateurishly left that bag for them to tamper with - he'd like to see the picture again; read the story again; see if it all came straight; see if it all tallied.

An indigestible dilemma kept coming back to him like spring-onions.

Leslie Merrett was one person. Lynch Madison was quite positively another. If he did, in the end, deliver this Lynch he had found to the Graygroves, would he have done his job properly in any case?

Yes - and who else had Leslie been? Laurence someone, Vanda had said. Undoubtedly others. It raised all those damp questions about who a person really was. (Carfax had stopped asking himself such deep philosophical questions about the time he first learned to fit a new washer into a tap to impress his new wife.)

PAGING LYNCH MADISON

He sighed, anticipating the digging and the explanations and the complications and the doubts that would keep him lying awake hating himself and the interfering way he earned his daily boredom.

Drugs, though. The only firm ground he stood on. Despicable drugs. All of this would be easier, in a way, if any of them had anything in the slightest to do with drugs ---

Was it drug money that had built the health-farm? Did this deadly team perhaps first make whoever they could dependent on drugs in the night-clubs they controlled and then cleverly offer to 'dry them out' at the mansion?

Excellent idea. Money would be no object to a client as hooked as that. So, they would never go short of clients for either business and they'd never go short of funds 'for the poor,' oh yeah, and of course, how neat, as a guarantee into the future, they'd never go short of easily blackmailable former clients.

And Stan. Yes, that explained him. A good risk. An easy asset to afford as he too could easily be kept quiet with his 'little local difficulties.'

There was much good (if bent) business sense being shown here. Bud would bear talking to. Maybe the black sheep of a rich dynasty? And drugs would even explain Vanda; fabulous on a stage and off, always on a high, and driving, he closed his eyes in despair, like a lunatic.

PAGING LYNCH MADISON

At the next lights he grabbed her, forced her sleeve up her arm with an ungentle hand, looking for puncture marks.

"Stop it, you animal," she laughed. "I belong to Lynch," she said, good-naturedly, driving off fast enough to push him back into his seat.

"I wasn't --- I didn't---" Christ, he hadn't been called an animal since his clumsy groping schooldays, and her very golden tormentingly smooth right arm was unmarked, almost unveined and the damned small encounter had infuriatingly excited him.

"It's OK. Singers get used to it," she said. "Easy stereotypes like mothers-in-law and queers. I don't take it to heart. Listen, you and I have a lot to talk about. I love Lynch," she said, making it sound noble, not sentimental.

"When Stan's cured him I'd like all of us to sit down and work out a proper solution. I mean, like, that won't involve Lynch in going back to sort things out. I can see he should, but I'm scared of losing him, Brainbox. I've even thought of going back like two centuries and getting pregnant on purpose."

"That never solved anything," Carfax heard his voice say tightly.

Though maybe it did. When was he such an expert on hopeless love? He had wanted his women and certainly his wife, lustfully, for such pathetically short times. Who else did he know about? Certainly Jan Merrett was radiantly pregnant by, and still in

PAGING LYNCH MADISON

love with someone she'd loved and had a child by before her marriage.

That needed thinking about, too. Charlotte, the love-child, had been, everyone said so, brought up kindly by quiet Leslie Merrett, all the time knowing that she wasn't his child - not an easy thing to do - and now Jan seemed to have ungratefully picked up with the original child-abandoner - extenuating circumstances if ever a court heard them.

In all, a lot of long-term pain and maybe a previously unknown excuse or two there. On both sides. Three sides. Four sides.

Vanda sighed. "You know, professor? Maybe we should get Stan to say he can't cure Lynch without taking him back to England? Would that work? Then he'd be safe, wouldn't he?"

Vanda was crazy for the Lynch part of this man, however many times he tried to get away, whatever his blood-soaked past was, however chequered her future looked. She was crazy enough, caring enough to let him go. It was touching. And tiring. Carfax closed his eyes.

"Straighten up, straighten up," he heard himself scream as he woke, bracing his legs as tightly as he could. Good thing he had already started to let his past life flash before him.

She had nearly passed the turn-off marked for the Rio de Janeiro International Airport and was screaming past the wrong lanes into the right one several days too late at an angle of thirty-two and a

PAGING LYNCH MADISON

half degrees, he estimated roughly through the briefly opened slit of vision he allowed himself.

"Wow," she said. "You made it!"

Was she talking to him or herself?

Slowed now to a frustrating crawl in the roads near the airport itself, partly from the volume of traffic, partly from the re-building going on, he checked his pulse-rate with horror, quite glad to be alive to do so.

He would offer to drive back himself. No. He'd make sure she had plenty to drink then refuse to let her drive.

He must get straight into direct interrogation. What he was best at.

Leave her alone now, lull her, he told himself, as they inched forwards in the congealed mass of cars heading the same way. Even after the aircraft landed there would be clearance, baggage and custom time, too. Gotcha. He would encourage a relaxed Vanda to go on drinking and talking, filling in any gaps he couldn't reach now. This would be his big opportunity to clear the way for a quick end to all this and home to Heather.

On the whole journey he had been so absorbed in Vanda's wild driving and in her fragrant nearness he had let her off very lightly, softening her up, not querying the nonsense she was handing him about adoration and pregnancy, about Lynch's divine right to happiness.

PAGING LYNCH MADISON

Big money would be in it somewhere. The clothes Vanda was wearing today were very expensive. So was her jewellery. Not the singer's stuff she had on at the club. And, he checked, the designer bag thrown on the seat behind, not to mention hidden extras like her nails, her haircut, her whole -- Vanderishness.

He began to wind down the tension by asking desultory questions about her past to which he knew he would only get vague and veiled and probably invented answers. She tried to con him that though her family was so rich, when she was in London they left her to starve and made her find out how to live hand to mouth.

And now, she was making enough as a singer to tell them to stick the money they wanted to bribe her with and she'd only take enough to help Lynch and not a centavo more.

All this made her seem honest, less of a gold-digger - an understandable face-saver and he pretended to believe her.

He countered with inconsequentialities about his own life, although he could hardly remember how horribly inconsequential it had been, away here in fairyland.

He 'made conversation', leaving a nice soft cushion of questions to break the fall of the heavy stuff for later.

There is some excitement to the arriving and waiting around at airports that is unique. Every airport seems vivid with odd juxtapositions, odd

PAGING LYNCH MADISON

pairings, odd luggage, oddly over-emotional greetings or the odd lack of them. Filled with the tasty beginning and endings of stories all balled up together waiting for a patient unraveller.

Vanda was unreasonably put-out to see on the electronic board that far from the London flight coming in an hour early, it was an hour late.

Why was it such a catastrophe? She was behaving as though it was a tragedy. But of course. So many things could be hidden, changed, organised while he was neatly out of the way. First his suitcase and now look how easily they had got rid of him himself.

What other lies had he swallowed? Of course. The bad back. Carfax closed his eyes for a moment in pain from his thoughts. Leslie Merrett was probably not incapacitated at all. And now, Stan would turn out to be - oh how incredible - not on the plane of course. He felt a bit sick. They must be killing themselves laughing. He was as lousy a detective as his order book showed.

He must demand to be taken back to the Fazenda de whatever it was at once.

Then he remembered the way she drove - he didn't feel ready for the risks. Or had that been calculated too? In any case it was pointless worrying about what they were up to back at the ranch, so to speak.

Whatever it was, they'd have done it by now and, there again, this long stretch of time with Vanda should reveal plenty. They'd settle down somewhere

PAGING LYNCH MADISON

and soon he'd know the name of her first nursery teacher and what Lynch liked on his toast.

"Come on, let's eat. Will this airport place do? At least it's not busy, or do you know somewhere good nearby?

"The restaurant here is supposed to be very good for an airport, but I am into only health foods," she said primly, perhaps not remembering the piles of unhealthy food she had stashed away at the hotel with Carfax last night. She wouldn't, she said, eat a single bite in any place on the airport.

However, if he would wait while she -- wait, and she'd take him to a place just back aways round the cruzamento circular. "I'll be one second, right?"

***

He turned his head to watch her go through the door marked 'senhoras' but cursed himself, afterwards, for simultaneously dashing for the door marked 'senhors.'

When he came out, the concourse which had been so empty was now thronged with travellers, a few meeters and greeters, but most of them only carrying small cases, briefcases; the sound-system was apologizing in Portuguese and English that this flight from Sao Paulo had been so delayed and through it all there was no sign of Vanda.

He waited patiently at first then impatiently when she still didn't emerge, then furiously, realising he had been dumped, he strode angrily towards the car-park exit.

PAGING LYNCH MADISON

Half way there, he saw the bank of orange telephone hoods, like large ears, saw Vanda, phone to her own ear, and moved back into the shadows. Watch her carefully. Surveillance and more surveillance. All there is to his stupid job.

Vanda was using her hands and her shoulders into the phone as well as having much to say, not so much to listen to. She had an impressive pile of fichas and a little white piece of paper in her hand.

Though a fellow with some luggage was leaning insolently on the upright, waiting to use the phone after her, she took no notice of him and went on looking at the little piece of paper, dialling and speaking, then the paper again and dialling and speaking again, four or five different numbers, it looked like, and nodding at the phone-voices till her head might drop off.

Another phone became free and another but the fellow with the luggage stayed waiting at Vanda's phone. Well, Vanda was a great-looking girl. Somebody was understandably trying to pick her up. No. This someone had a lot to say to her, after the fourth call, sideways on and fast.

Now Carfax interested himself in the man, who had dark stubble and a crumpled travelled look. He was carrying a shabby hanging wardrobe with a much-mended strap over his shoulder, but a smart clean black briefcase. As he put this down, the light caught a necklet. Yes, it was a very big vulgar medallion indeed, so this was undoubtedly the dreadful Osvaldo in on the late flight from Sao Paulo.

PAGING LYNCH MADISON

Osvaldo checked his watch, checked the big clock, said one last thing to Vanda who put her head in her hands and he was two at a time up the escalator that said SAIDA - exit - and was gone.

Hey mister you've forgotten your --------

Vanda had the case in her hand in an instant. Ah. Now she would dash after him - hey mister - no, she went on staring at the telephone for a moment as if to recover herself and then she turned again to watch the up-escalator as if entranced before walking slowly away.

Quite right. She would take it straight to the desks for security purposes - she would take it to lost property.

Frowning, Vanda went purposefully on down to the car-park with it, not in any way seeming indecisive or even glancing guiltily behind her, though Carfax had given up even trying to shadow her quietly. She opened the boot of her car, took out, good heavens, a long screwdriver, undid some bolts, withdrew another similar black briefcase, swopped the cases, did up the bolts, walked back with it, went up the escalator where the coffee-coloured man had gone, spotted him on a stool at the bar right by the exit and gave him the case without even glancing at him. He called something after her and she stopped for a moment, shrugged and went on down, settling herself on a bench, like everyone else, to await the arrival of the Varig flight from London.

"Where the hell have you been?" Vanda said, mildly, when she spotted Carfax. "I've been looking everywhere for you," she said vaguely.

PAGING LYNCH MADISON

Did she think he was that stupid? Did she think, even if he hadn't seen her, that no-one had seen her deliver the goods.

And what were the goods. Silly question. The right size case. Unobtrusive but a case that size would hold enough uncut drugs to - in short, the risk would be outrageously worthwhile, if it came off.

But why would they choose such a stupid 'drop?' South American airports must be fuller of surveillance cameras watching for such dead-easy handovers than any in the world. He looked for the cameras. Yes. Not even hidden. There. And there. And there.

Was she a regular link carrier only handling the goods briefly in whatever country she happened to be in? She was a bit visible to use regularly, he would have thought, though that could be a double bluff. After all, who would think of using a girl like her whose appearance automatically drew attention?

His heart was unzipping with excitement. This was it. This could make him. If he could be just sure 'the gang' weren't in any rush to do whatever came next, just be sure that he could convince them that he was only concerned with the case of the piddling Leslie Merrett.

He might fake an illness or a breakdown at their convenient rest-home to give him the time he needed to win this game. He was sure he now possessed all the bits necessary to play but there were no pictures, no instructions and no rules in the box.

PAGING LYNCH MADISON

He was also coming to the infuriating conclusion that it would be very thick wool indeed he'd need for Vanda, for Lynch and for the eyes of Bud and Chi and the rest of them.

"Still want to eat?" he said.

Now Vanda argued that as Carfax had 'been gone so long,' she wouldn't leave the airport because of the fag of parking again and maybe they might be back late, she argued foolishly, like it would matter if her poofter ex-employer had to wait for a bit.

"Let's eat here, OK?" she said, the same girl who had been sure that the airport food would poison them.

But when they had been seated and had menus in their hands, she suddenly became aggressively restless and impatient. She didn't fancy anything except something that wasn't on the menu. After Carfax had eaten a large pizza too quickly, but not quickly enough to please Vanda, she didn't want to observe at the observation area, because it depressed her, she said, for an unspecified reason, to see people fly up and people fly back. She didn't want him to buy her a paper or a book, she didn't want anything in the shops, she didn't want to sit and she didn't much want to stand still either.

She was having an anxiety fit, that's what, and it served her right.

She was now doing twenty miles or so, pacing over to the boards to look at the flickering changing, or mostly unchanging information, tutting and frowning and walking back to a stand-up juice

PAGING LYNCH MADISON

bar, back to the best vantage point again, over to the stairs, back to the boards, until he wished she were his wife so that he could shout at her to sit down and stop fussing.

Never mind, let her, if it helped calm her, he thought sympathetically. He sighed, realising he was softened again on Vanda, heaven knew why. Yet if Vanda looked like the foot-aching fat-faced barrel-bodied woman over there sweeping the floor, no one would give a spit in the wind for her. An unfair world.

He was even ready to conjecture charitably that the naughty wicked gang might just be using Vanda as a reluctant, black-mailed victimised drug-courier - that would certainly explain her agitation with the man and the fear after the handover.

Despite himself, he couldn't help hoping Vanda was being used and was not the femme fatale she tried so hard to appear.

He put into his head, for police purposes, the details of the man. Medium coffee-coloured, young, stocky, moustauched, swarthy, unshaven - quite exactly like most of the people around, he noted, frowning. And the big medallion. Yes, well most of the luggage handlers were wearing smaller ones.

What did it say in that Guide to Brazil? One hundred and thirty million inhabitants and seventy percent of them under 30? From light coffee to deepest black. Maybe, but to Carfax, the typical Brazilian, so far as he had observed, looked just like the man by the telephone. Or at least, Brazil would be the right place to look for a man like that. Yes,

PAGING LYNCH MADISON

look. Two more walking past and another three over there. He wasn't going to be easy to describe to the airport police if he decided to go to them. There were probably no passenger lists on internal flights, either. More like going on a bus, they said.

So what was his next move supposed to be? Wait till the queer hypnotist loony flew in and then ask him to put Vanda in a trance? Sometimes he wished he had time to watch more TV. Heather said the TV investigators had a hundred percent success rate. At least.

He watched Vanda lean over the barrier, shoulders hunched, feet almost off the ground with tense yearning for Stan's arrival and as if my magic he knew what he must do.

He wedged himself in by the excited family next to her who were waiting for someone else, took her roughly by one slim arm and turned her towards him.

"What did you give Osvaldo in that case from your car?" he said.

Vanda's eyes went big, then she laughed. "Jeez professor. As a dick you really stink. I had to slow down all the way for you to keep up with me. Hey look, they're from London, Stan'll be right here."

"I want to know what was in the case. Drugs? It was, wasn't it? Look, I'd recognize him again. You're in big trouble here," he lied, holding her very tightly, hurting her on purpose in their last seconds alone as Stan advanced on them.

PAGING LYNCH MADISON

"It was money," she said. "Just money. Big money. But the bastardo's promised to ---"

"What money? Did you arrange to meet Osvaldo here?"

"Me, Arrange? Like I'd want to meet Osvaldo? Osvaldo's in and out of this airport several times a week. I was just unlucky to be here the same time. But he'd only write and phone his filthy threats anyway. I can't stand it any longer. So I was just paying him off. With money. He's got so much money now he won't need a job with my step-father."

"There's Stan. Stan! Stan! Over here!"

Carfax looked Stan over quickly. Christ, he hated them.

"Where did you get such a lot of money?" he said, anxiously clutching her arm. "And how did it just happen to be in the back of your car?"

"It's Lynch's. He thinks I burned it," she said, conversationally. "But I just knew it would come in handy sometime."

Carfax's mouth had fallen too far open to speak.

"I mean after all, I finally spent it to, like, save his life, didn't I?"

"Oh Stan you are so welcome, you don't know how welcome, " she said, shaking his hand over the barrier. "Come on around. Meet the professor."

PAGING LYNCH MADISON
CHAPTER EIGHTEEN

In the hot whitey spitting spray that bubbled up from the pipes below the water in the jacuzzi, Vanda made pleased little noises and stretched her arms to the shape of the rounded rim, just touching Carfax lightly with her wet fingers on his thick freckled shoulder.

"I always say a jacuzzi has got to be the sexiest thing they'll let you do in public," she laughed, throwing her head-banded head back in abandon, exposing her beautiful throat.

Carfax, who had been in this hot water so long that his fingers looked like over-boiled macaroni bows, explained curtly to his body that he was not, though he wished he were, alone here with Vanda, but bristly-leg to bristly-leg with Stan's new boy-friend, who only had eyes for Stan, who was the other side of the deep wide tub, and over there with him were Bud and Chi, serenely kicking their feet in friendly little circles towards each other.

"Have you ever, thought, Bud, that closing this place to everyone but us at night doesn't exactly go with your ideas of equality? Yeah?" Vanda feathered a splishy arc of water in front of her, screwing her face up against the drops.

"In Guyana," Bud said wisely, quietly, "we say something like 'it's my turn to play.'" Through

PAGING LYNCH MADISON

the laughter, he leaned out and turned the fierceness of the bubbling up, one final fraction higher.

Throughout the few days Carfax had spent at Fazenda de Lazer with this unlikely bunch of fugitives, he had known that he was happier than he had ever been.

Lying awake long enough to rationalise these positive feelings of happiness into sensible negative terms, he was aware that his reasoning was depressingly trivial: firstly, he had, for a few precious days, put down his heavy bag of worries, secondly, here he had no pressing responsibilities, and for the insubstantial rest of it, the parts of Rio he had seen were stunningly beautiful, the immediate environment of his everyday living was sinfully perfect, easy money eased his every little difficulty, and lastly, because most difficult to admit to, these people he was spending the time with were rich, untroubled, attentive, interested, interesting, kindly and fun.

Not much to be proud of, being sold so easily for so little.

He was, however, quite proud of the real fax he had composed and actually sent through to the Graygroves. In just two short paragraphs, it laid bare the brilliance of his exhaustive investigations so far, and the results he expected to follow his amazingly successful ploy that had led to a promise exacted from an uncovered 'source' which would lead him directly to a meeting with Leslie Merrett. 'If he is still alive,' he had added, classily, at the very last moment.

PAGING LYNCH MADISON

As the water gurgled and lunged hotly at him, he just wished he could send a fax to the Graygroves to tell them to go about their business without him or Leslie, and a second fax direct to Heather to bring herself and the children out here to live.

He pushed his wrinkled hand over his eyes. What was he talking about? Live in a land full of slums and Osvaldos and people with the crippling powers of the Baptista Vasconceloses.

When he had arrived back here from the airport with Stan and Vanda, Carfax saw Stan welcomed like money in the bank and taken off to Lynch's room before the bags had been unpacked from the car, before Carfax had time to get out and demand to go with him.

"If you don't mind, I must insist that I spend some time with Mr Merrett, now," he had said honestly, gravely to Bud.

"You know why I came to Brazil. All Mr Merrett has to do is fly to England with me. He can be back in a short while with nothing to fear and can start his life again out here with you all - if that's what he wants. He'll - you'll be free of all this stupid subterfuge --"

"Subterfuge?"

"Secret. Hiding. Er -- incognito."

"Ah, yes." Bud looked behind himself. "When Stan's made Lynch well, in a couple of days, maybe, we can talk again."

PAGING LYNCH MADISON

Though his eyes had turned cold, Bud still smiled politely.

"I meant now, if it is convenient," Carfax said, just as politely but with a busy look at his watch. He put his head in his hands with a quick cry of pain - an insurance policy for later.

"Are you all right?" Bud said, on cue.

"I don't feel too good. The altitude, I expect."

"Not unless Vanda drove you to the airport through Bolivia or Peru," Bud smiled. "Brazil doesn't have such problems. But I can send for some excellent pain-killers for you, if you like. No? I'm afraid you do not understand us, nor do you understand South America. You are bound to feel unwell, Professor Carfax. You gave yourself no time though I begged you to, you remember. As the Brazilians say, Brazil should be taken like a leisurely bath not a quick shower," Bud said complacently.

Carfax doubted it. In the leisurely historic times when people had time to make up crap like that there weren't any quick showers, only rainbutts.

"Speaking of which," Bud smiled, "I have booked a steam-bath for you and then a massage. Then you will want to shower and rest yourself and join Chi and Lee and myself. I want to introduce you to them both before we go. Later, you and Stan will come with us - "

"Where to? I will stay here. I want to speak to Leslie Merrett. Now."

PAGING LYNCH MADISON

"It will be a long wait, Professor Carfax. Lynch will be asleep. He will sleep long after his treatment, I remember. So. Then you will be our guest for dinner at the Palacio Dourado."

Bud seemed to be waiting for some reaction.

Carfax frowned. "Thank you but no."

"The bar there is the finest gig in Rio, and the restaurant -" Bud made the universal sign of excellence. "Vanda will sing in the bar after dinner - it will be ---"

"I've heard her sing. I want to be here. Unless Leslie Merrett will be well enough to come on later to the club?" Carfax said, hoping maybe that was what Bud was getting at.

"No, no. A Brazilian is playing the clarinet in Lynch's place for Vanda tonight, again. You have not heard him play yet, have you? But truly, Mr Carfax, you will not notice the difference. We will," he laughed suddenly, honestly. "The Brazilian plays, frankly, better than Lynch. For the Palacio Dourado, only the best ----"

"It wasn't the music I was worried about, sir. I intend to talk to Leslie Merrett immediately and I need time to do this - like your leisurely bath," he said, pleased with himself.

Bud frowned. "He's in too much pain to make sense, Mr Carfax."

Carfax thought quickly. "OK. Then I'll do what you suggested earlier and just take it easy.

PAGING LYNCH MADISON

Stick around here quietly. Potter around. Read some magazines. If Leslie does wake ----"

"No. Lynch will sleep at least until tomorrow morning. And anyway, Vanda wouldn't like you to miss her singing. She says you are very appreciative. It'll relax you."

"I'll stay here, all the same, thanks. I'm quite tired."

"You'll come with us, Professor Carfax."

"I see."

Carfax rubbed his hand experimentally over his head again, trying to look fragile. Christ, it was working. He was actually giving himself a headache.

His suitcase. Where was it? A bad move to ask for it, he could see that. Bud looked up and called.

"Claudia?"

What now?

Claudia appeared and stood so perfectly still waiting for orders with her small feet neatly placed, it reminded Carfax of end-of-term at his daughter's ballet class.

"Claudia will take you upstairs." Claudia, a tiny sculptured black, uniformed in sculptured white, smiled and waited for him to follow her.

PAGING LYNCH MADISON

"She will show you the treatment rooms and demonstrate the treatments for you to choose – whatever it is you would like to choose."

He'd bet. Other parts of Carfax began to ache.

"For the record and," Carfax said loudly, suddenly thinking of it again, "for the benefit of any bugging devices you have here, I would like it to be known that you are holding me here against my will."

"Claudia? Help Professor Carfax, will you?" Bud said, as if he hadn't spoken. "He has a bad headache." And he was gone.

Walking up the staircase after Claudia's tiny backside, Carfax was full of smiles. What the hell. He might as well accept that he was under a rather lush kind of arrest and enjoy it. In all his uninteresting career nothing had come even close to this near ideal excitement.

Claudia stopped off politely at his room, even opening the door for him, saying she would wait outside for him to change into his white robe and, as she put it "arrange oneself." A new phrase for taking a leak, cleaning the teeth and washing the bum, he supposed.

Surprisingly, the first thing he noticed in the room was his case. Poised neatly on the rack for it, wide open and empty.

But the pyjamas folded on the bed weren't his Marks and Spencer paisley. They were lush and

PAGING LYNCH MADISON

monogrammed with the F de L crest. Abruptly, he was absolutely bloody furious.

He flung open the wardrobe looking for more interference.

Everything from his case was neatly hung there - newly pressed, by the look of them, if you could call that interference. Everything else, folded and orderly in the cupboards and shelves. Everything?

He laughed out loud. His gun was in the bedside table - the one with the Bible, the one nearest the new pyjamas.

Still laughing, he 'arranged himself' good and proper, tied the cord of his white robe tightly under his sagging stomach, and pulled that offending bulge in as far as he could.

Then he opened the door and called out to Claudia that he was ready for whatever treatment she could show him.

***

Something had startled Lynch awake.

He jumped out of bed, ran to the windows and jerked the thick curtains open. Night.

Christ. He could jump and he could run. Stan. He remembered where he was. Remembered. Plans.

PAGING LYNCH MADISON

He checked the time. Lucky. He threw the exact things that he had planned before he slept into the small case, then wrapped the whole lot in a beach towel and waited, watching from the window, pulling on the new thin socks that had been left neatly folded into his new trainers.

Bored after a long period of watching, and still appreciative of the way his body moved again, he quickly, skilfully, mobilised the dangling laces of the second bent-up leg and smiled at himself in the mirror, making fists and squaring up at his reflection.

Ponytails were becoming very fashionable for men. Perhaps he should move on, change, experiment again. He didn't look too bad. Good living was already filling out his boniness a little though the recent pain had dulled his bright eyes a bit.

He'd do. He stretched and bent and sat again at the window, waiting, thinking.

Fazenda de Lazer had come up shiny and splendid. Better than he'd hoped. It would do a lot of people good to be there.

He heard the car on the driveway and watched very closely. Precious infuriatingly correct Bud - Lynch's father, brother, doppelganger and irritant; Chi, the angels' angel.

Here came Vanda. And the dick waiting at the doorway for them. Funny he hadn't gone to the hotel with them, though.

PAGING LYNCH MADISON

He had to smile at the way Carfax almost ran to help Vanda from the car. She was high, he knew, from the singing, from the adulation, not alcohol. Such a thing was beyond the uncreative Carfax so he handled her over-the-top gaiety as if he were just praying she'd hold the vomit till they got to a basin.

Lynch switched off the light, grabbed his carefully towel-enclosed bundle and rushed down from his room to be in time for their entrance.

"Voila!" he said, striking a heroic pose by the impressive front doors, under the little scroll of Lee in the plaster, "or whatever they say for Voila in Brazil."

"Lynch, querido!" Vanda threw herself at him, reaching up on tiptoe. "Querido, querido," with little tiny spaced kisses on his face, "why are you dressed? Why aren't you asleep?"

"I don't know why I'm not asleep, querida, " Lynch smiled down at her. "But I am and I'm dressed because you're coming for a midnight swim to celebrate with me before we go to bed. Yes, I'm fine, thank you Chi. The clarinet will be played by me for the rest of the week, you'll be enchanted to know. Did you like the bar at the Palacio? Did they listen to you there? Or just go on eating and clap politely?"

"That never happens to me, Lynch," Vanda said seriously for a moment. "To some, I know. You certainly," she smiled again. "Swim, querido? Terrific. Let's all go. Where's Stan?"

No answer, but all five heads worked out where he might be.

PAGING LYNCH MADISON

"Who's coming? The pool or the lake? Are you well enough? The lake will be nicer, won't it, at night?"

"I mean let's get out of here, Vanda, just you and me. Down to the beach. I feel so good. I need to exercise a little. Whichever beach you say."

"It's an hour to the beach, Lynch," Bud shrugged. "And it's very dangerous indeed down there at night. It's asking for trouble."

"Really, Lynch, it isn't even safe to walk about up here in the hills, let alone the beach," Chi frowned.

"You must have noticed, my dear friends, that I only let you tell me what to do when I'm immobile," Lynch said pleasantly, putting his arm through Vanda's.

"As you seem to be so much better, Mr Merrett," Carfax spoke up at last, "I would appreciate it if you would please arrange with me your immediate return to the UK and -----"

"In the morning. Come to my room in the morning, professor, and we'll go from there. OK? Tonight is mine, right?"

Nobody spoke.

"Look, Vanda, go up and change into your swimming gear and bring your things. I'll wait for you. OK?" He bent her to him in a kiss and whispered something long and intimate in her ear.

408

PAGING LYNCH MADISON

She stopped. Whispered back. He whispered again. She ran up the stairs and out of sight.

"OK," Lynch said, turning round from watching her and smiling at the disapproving line of grown-ups. "Can you give me some keys. I'll use one of the cars. We'll drive down to the beach and I'll take great care of her, I promise. Don't wait up. OK?"

"Mr Merrett," Carfax said, " I think ----"

"Are you sure Vanda isn't too tired?" Chi asked stiffly, as if reminding Lynch that if would have been nice to consult Vanda first. "She gave a terrific performance tonight. And besides you are only just better yourself and it seems foolish to go into danger for the sake of it."

"Sure. Everything's dangerous, Chi," Lynch said, not looking at her.

"Lynch. You need tonight badly?" Bud said, sympathetically.

"Please. Please," Lynch said again quieter, looking at Bud very seriously. They all coughed a little. "Keys please, Bud?" Lynch said, looking impatiently up the stairs for Vanda and barely able to stand still.

Carfax watched Lynch heft the keys and whistle the type of happy little tune a sexually lucky man whistles when his bird is getting ready for their date. Why, why, why were they all so obedient to

PAGING LYNCH MADISON

Lynch's whims? Oh hell. The morning would do, wouldn't it?

"Papa, I can't sleep," Lee called from the top of the stairs, rubbing her eyes helplessly with her knuckles.

It was Lynch who dashed up the stairs two at a time and held her close, took her to the little dining-room where fat clients drank their lemon juice and poured her some aguas gasificadas straight from the little fridge in there. He brought her out again to the reception area to sit on his lap while she drank it, teasing her, stroking and stroking the top of her head, watching her, Carfax thought, as if --- as if

Yes. Carfax had cracked it. As if he would never see her again.

The liar has planned yet another get-away and must be stopped.

Carfax said goodnight abruptly and went to his room but once up there did a bit of his own packing and planning, ready to run straight down the stairs when he heard the big hall doors shut behind them.

Listen. There they go. Ker-thunk.

The liar is, of course, as Carfax guessed, not taking Vanda either for a drive or a swim.

Lynch has his plans. He too, is 'high', tonight. He has done his homework: he already

PAGING LYNCH MADISON

knows somewhere private, comfortable enough and exciting to make love to her with his beautifully mobile body again. And it is a gloriously warm Cariocan night and he believes that sex is a fine way to finish a great evening and start a new life.

"You know we're being followed at a discreet distance, don't you?" Lynch said, not long after they had travelled down some of the mountain road from Petrop¢lis.

Vanda shivered. "Doesn't that make you nervous? Who is it?"

Lynch shrugged. "Watch this," he said, overtaking two, then three more lorries around blind bends and sweeping off the road in front of one more.

Amongst the winds and turns of the broad road down from the cool mountains were many long driveways. These belonged to the wealthy who preferred to live here, around Petrop¢lis, Teres¢polis, now that the glorious beaches of Rio were so 'spoiled'.

Vanilla flavour winning the Brazilian vote here as everywhere, freezer lorries packed with creamy white ice-cream for tomorrow roared past the driveway Lynch chose to duck into.

The dogs of the house, of course, went mad. Lynch is sweating, anxious to leave before the dogs draw attention to them. Hurry, hurry. There he goes. He sees through the shrubs that the car he thought was following had now passed serenely by.

"The professor?"

PAGING LYNCH MADISON

Lynch makes a face. "Sure. Probably. A real nothing," he said.

"He was OK," Vanda said.

They drew out into the traffic. Lynch had stopped checking his driving mirror. Lynch had relaxed. Lynch was humming 'Red Roses' and feeling very good.

"Not that I care, querido," a tremble in the voice saying that Vanda did care more than somewhat but Lynch wasn't listening. "I meant what I said, I'm, like, going to follow you anywhere but -- but where are you really going?"

Vanda's voice was tight. She seemed to be holding herself in somewhat, worried that she hadn't packed the right things, enough things, hadn't said, hadn't done, had left too many loose ends, had agreed too quickly, had burned a million boats without a raft in sight.

"Back where you were tonight, Vanda, I think. What's that beach I like next to Copacabana?"

"I was singing at Leme Beach"

"Yeah. Leme. Nice. The beach first. Then do you know a really expensive restaurant that will still be open around Leme? Yes? Great. Then we'll go there. Then ---"

"I hope I've brought enough money."

PAGING LYNCH MADISON

"Money? Didn't I tell you? We'll never have to worry about money again." He wouldn't say another word. Not one. Nothing.

Lynch doo-doo-doo-dooed through the second half of 'Red Roses' like a man with nothing on his mind, cars behind him on these lonely roads no longer of interest to him, Vanda's unaccustomed silence taken for serenity.

His happiness, however, has always been infectious. So Vanda, shrugging her shoulders and riding with the strange waves Lynch has always made since she found him, relaxes as he drives down and down into Leme.

Vanda calls him querido a thousand times and unambiguously demonstrates her impatience, telling him to please stop, kissing him quickly on his right ear.

He smiles a big smile at her and strokes her hand a little but still he cannot seem to make up his mind where to stop.

"Jeez, Lynch, I don't see why the view makes any difference, querido. We won't be looking at the scenery, right?"

"It must be just the right beach," Lynch said laughing. "It's my special last request."

"Jeez, there are twenty-three beaches around here, for Chrissake. Any one will do, right? It reminds me of when I was a *garontinah*" Vanda says, more and more Brazilian the longer they were on the

PAGING LYNCH MADISON

road. "Papai and mamae would argue like this where we should stop for a picnic. Here, Lynch, querido?"

"Not there. Half Brazil could see us in their headlights."

"I suppose. Hurry, querido. Here?"

"Vanda, there it says PRIVATE in every language ever so clearly, that's what *'particular'* means isn't it? Hey, what about that bit of beach with the huge rock - it'd be nice and private behind there."

"Here is perfect? Why here? Oh, OK." Vanda shrugged."

"Come on. I know the right places, right? Lynch went round to open her door. "Let's walk, Vanda Raimunda Neocita Baptista Vasconcelos," he said.

"Walk? I'm not getting out of here. Jeez, Lynch, in Rio, the first thing you learn is never never never walk on the beach at night," Vanda murmured, sitting still. Would you at least park the car under that light? For safety?"

Lynch moved the car, sighing, after which Vanda got out of the car very reluctantly and holding his hand extremely tight. "Mamae would have gone crazy if she'd been alive."

"Leslie Merrett would go crazy, too," Lynch said, laughing and beginning to run with her over the hard packed sands.

PAGING LYNCH MADISON

"Here, lie here. Stop worrying, Vanda. They say the whole of Rio is full of thieves and muggers?"

"Yes, querido, it really is."

"And especially the beach?"

"Yes, querido."

"Then we will put your jewellery and your case over there and let the thieves and the muggers take them. You – are all I need."

Hot night air, the mouth-watering fear of even benign discovery, the highly energising glorious freedom of bareness on a king-size mass of sand would make most lovemaking awesome but this turned out to be better than that.

Lynch was still murmuring smaller crisper words that meant I love you into her left ear when the first sound of breaking glass reached them. They stilled and pulled further into the shadows of the straw beach umbrella he had pulled down for a shelter, dry-mouthed through the continuing smashing of glass but then there was just a little running of feet and silence again.

"The beach must be littered with people like us," Lynch soothed her anguish, helping her dress and dressing himself clumsily, speedily.

"Querido, querido." It was all she had said for so long that he bent and kissed her mouth as she said it, all the better to taste the word.

PAGING LYNCH MADISON

Unable to move, they lay, each tiny wriggle, each slight caress, every gentle smoothing a thank you, oh don't thank me it was a pleasure.

But when they walked dazed and happy back along the piece of promenade to where they had parked in such a hurry, glass crunched under their feet in the shadows of darkness under the three smashed overhead lights and it was their car, the one they had borrowed from Bud, the one they had driven in so emotionally, whose windows were, every one, smashed, the tiny pieces of glass skittered everywhere inside and outside. The radio ripped out, the seats slashed, the tyres cut.

"O, O, O," Vanda kept saying fiercely as if it would keep her from thinking any further.

"I sodding wouldn't listen, would I?" Lynch said into the silence.

Vanda whimpered, wiping her eyes.

"Got one of those phone things?"

Vanda fiddled and nodded holding up and rejecting coins and fingering them in the almost dark, looking for the groove. "I have three fichas, I guess."

"Great. Let's get away from here. pronto. We'll phone and someone will come."

"Yeah, Lynch. Who you gonna phone?"

Lynch was quiet. "I'll phone Bud. Perhaps I was too quick leaving. Christ what a mess. Hey

PAGING LYNCH MADISON

listen, they didn't mug us yet, did they? We've got all our things. Come on, sweetheart. Walk."

"Jeez, it's like, you feel, you know? Aren't you really really scared?" Vanda said, her voice wobbling in her tense attempt not to seem as weak as she felt. "And it's so dark."

An instant strong concentrated beam of light made her scream a nearly silent scream, cover her eyes and reach for Lynch.

Osvaldo Oliveira carried the large torch in one hand leaving his best hand free for the thick bladed knife in the other.

He spoke softly but at great length to Vanda in Portuguese after which Vanda was screaming and pleading and cajoling with every Brazilian bone in her body but Osvaldo had stopped listening to fasten his attention on Lynch.

Lynch had seen this situation lots of times. You held the attacker's knife-hand up in the air whilst knocking the torch to the ground with the other. Or did you hold the torch-hand high and knock out the knife? And how did you force a man's arm up if he wouldn't let you? And how did you get them to stand still while you worked it all out? And without any light, who knows where the bloody knife would end up? On top of which Lynch had never used a knife on anything more vicious than a potato.

And you out there muttering that Lynch is a wimp, a fairy, is yellow to his manicured fingernails, should try being eighteen inches away from a sharp blade in the hand of an unknown foreigner. No of

PAGING LYNCH MADISON

course he didn't know it was Osvaldo - when Osvaldo was dancing with Vanda at the wedding, he wasn't wearing a scarf round his mouth and a big hat.

"Ele , muito fraco," Lynch heard the man say a dozen times, now holding Vanda's left arm behind her back until she wept with pain.

"I don't know what you're saying," Lynch suddenly screamed himself, rushing for Osvaldo forgetting which hand he should avoid, getting himself held tightly and the knife now conveniently at his throat.

Now fatally anxious, like all foreigners, to practise his English, Osvaldo explained that fraco meant weak, impotent, useless; explained that everyone knew it was estupido to go to the beach in the dark these days and a little mugging and murder of a foreigner down here wouldn't even raise an eyebrow; explained that Vanda's money having been already spent on a horse that wasn't as doped as it might have been, marriage to her was the only answer to his problems; explained that fear of him doing to Vanda what he was now going to do to Lynch would keep Vanda from confession to the Baptista Vasconceloses.

Syntax, grammar and vocabularly aside, Osvaldo was making himself horribly clear.

But as he screamed on at Vanda, who was frankly gibbering with fear and pinning her only last hopes on Portuguese rhetoric, as Lynch fought to get free, the light of Osvaldo's torch moved and was reflected back from his constantly worn medallion

PAGING LYNCH MADISON

depicting Nossa Senhora do Conceicao da Aparecida, Brazil's patron saint of goodness.

"Osvaldo?" a voice called out pleasantly from the puzzling darkness.

"Sim?" Osvaldo called, automatically turning to the voice.

And that's when Carfax took aim and shot him.

Osvaldo didn't go up on his toes clutching himself first like you see in the Westerns. He draggled like an abruptly un-stuffed scarecrow, horrifingly dead on his bending knees for weeks before he fell.

Carfax made just one sound in the silence that could have been anything between a cheer of triumph and a call of human despair.

"You heard what the man said," Carfax breathed very noisily. "This is a violent country. No one will look too closely at Osvaldo if we take his wallet," Carfax, who was wearing plastic gloves, handed it up to Lynch.

"Then we'll take his watch and his ring and we should definitely cut this off," he said, cutting off Osvaldo's medallion with one good swing of Osvaldo's own knife.

"He's right. It'll look like a mugging," Lynch said, dully, on automatic.

PAGING LYNCH MADISON

"Go, will you. Swop keys with me. Good. Now go get in the car I followed you in and get going. Back to your friends. Get married. Stay in Brazil, Lynch. They are your family. Don't leave again. Just go, will you?"

Lynch and Vanda stared woodenly at him, not speaking still, then bending to reach their strange bundles, Lynch tucking his clarinet more firmly into the centre of his.

"Go," Carfax said again. "Look, I never saw you. I never found you."

He watched them walk away clutched together, his eyes hot, somewhat towards the end of himself.

"I'll tell them—I'll say that the rumour is," he called to their disappearing backs, "that Leslie Merrett has gone to live in Argentina."

ENDS

Printed in Great Britain
by Amazon